SNOW BEAST

MARK L'ESTRANGE

SEVERED PRESS
HOBART TASMANIA

SNOW BEAST

Copyright © 2017 Mark L'estrange

WWW.SEVEREDPRESS.COM

ISBN: 978-1-925711-32-5

DEDICATION:

For Claire, Pebbles and Hayley.
Rosie, Joseph and Jasmine.
You may not all have met, but you all have a special place in your uncle's heart.

PROLOGUE

"Oh come on lazy-bones," Laura Connolly called back to her fiancé Simon Goddard, laughing to herself as she watched him slip and slide whilst trying to make purchase with his snow boots on the icy ground.

"This isn't funny you know!" Simon stopped trying to make progress and relaxed, satisfied that he was at least still standing having spent much of the day either falling over or sliding backwards. This trip was fast becoming his 'holiday from hell'. He had never been the most energetic of individuals, preferring the comfort of watching sport from his armchair rather than physically taking part. His idea of a holiday was booking into a luxurious hotel where he could be waited on hand and foot whilst soaking up the Mediterranean sun.

Instead he had allowed Laura to talk him into spending the week traipsing through the Cumbrian mountainside during one of the worst snowfalls in living history. Her argument had been that this would be a cheap holiday with minimum overheads and gorgeous scenery, thus allowing them to save more for their end of year break which they had planned to have in America.

The truth was that having forked out for all the gear they needed to rent, plus the parking for leaving their car back at the lodge, not to mention the petrol they had used to get them here from Kent, they could have saved more by booking a last minute all inclusive trip to the continent. But in fairness to Laura, their last three holidays had been beach ones, and he knew how crushingly bored she became if there was nothing else to do but spend hour after hour lying on a crowded beach.

Laura was definitely the more energetic of the two of them. Her work as a school-trip organiser meant that she was constantly on the go, travelling up and down the country inspecting potential sites for days out, weekend trips and full weeks away for the kiddies. Laura could certainly never be accused of not throwing herself into her work. She made a point of sampling every amenity and adventure on offer before making her recommendation. And if she was not entirely satisfied with the arrangements, regardless of how up to date their health and safety certificates were or how many points they had been awarded by official bodies, she refused point blank to endorse them.

Simon on the other hand was more the stay at home and take things easy kind of guy. His work in a bank, which he joined upon leaving sixth form, meant that he spent the majority of the day either behind his desk or in meetings. Even lunchtimes often found him eating a sandwich from behind his computer screen. So much so that it often amazed Laura that he was so skinny, considering he ate like a horse and never took any exercise. Laura often teased him about it, but in truth she was somewhat jealous, especially on take-away night when she would try to make her small thin-crust Hawaiian stretch, while Simon devoured his eighth slice of thick and meaty.

Besides her hectic working schedule, Laura also spent three evenings a week at the gym and was extremely careful with her food. Even so, she had always carried around an extra stone which no matter what she tried she could never shift. She was not fat; no one could ever accuse her of that. She was a comfortable size fourteen and even in just a knickers and bra ensemble she had no extraneous overhang. She was big, but solid with it. Her regular gym visits had helped to tighten and firm her up, but she still had not managed to acquire the shape she longed for.

But at least she was fit. Several times since starting out she had found herself having to pull back to allow Simon to catch her up. And when he did, he always needed a moment to catch his breath before continuing, while Laura took the whole thing in her stride.

Simon edged up beside her, his face red and puffy from the exertion. He sank forward, letting his hands rest on his aching knees while he inhaled a great lungful of frosty mountain air.

Laura patted him gently on the back. "How're you doing old soldier?" she asked, caringly. "Ready for a few more miles before we set up camp?"

Simon stood up and looked to the west. The sun had hardly shown itself during the day, hiding behind a thick bank of low cloud. It was only mid-afternoon but dusk was already starting to take over. Simon estimated it would be dark in less than an hour, and by then he wanted to be under cover and as warm as possible.

That was one of the down sides of making this trek in February, the days were so short. Then again, he reasoned that he would not be able to continue walking much more than the present daylight allowed. In fact, he was shattered within the first hour of each trek.

And with the nights being so cold, even inside their tent and cocooned in their double-thick sleeping blanket, all he could think of was being in front of a nice warm fire. It was even too cold for them to make love. Last night they had both been in the mood, but Simon was just too cold to stir himself into action. Laura did not complain. After all, this was her idea and had they have gone with his suggestion of another beach holiday they would have been making love in the cool soft-scented breeze which came off the sea, not shivering together in the freezing cold.

After a few moments rest, they agreed to set up camp in another half-an-hour, which would just about leave them enough light to see by so that they could set up their tent without too much difficulty.

They found a space hidden between two high drifts which helped to cut down the wind velocity.

Once their tent was erected, Laura began making their dinner on the gas stove, while Simon boiled down some snow and ice for water.

They dined on lamb stew with mixed vegetables. Simon made some strong coffee with the water he had boiled up, and finally the warmth started to seep into their bodies.

"Oh that's better," said Laura, draining her mug. "I needed that!"

"I know what I need," replied Simon.

"Oh yeah, and what's that I wonder," said Laura, reaching out with her leg and rubbing Simon's thigh with her sock-covered foot.

"Not that," Simon whined, "it's too bloody cold for that. I meant a drink."

"Oh, now that's just charming," pouted Laura as she slid next to Simon and began rubbing the inside of his thigh with her hand. She laughed as she heard him catch his breath as her hand slipped further up towards his groin.

"Oi, stop that now, it's too bloomin' cold," Simon protested, half-heartedly. He leaned his head back and opened his legs further apart to allow Laura ease of access.

As her hand made contact with his penis she could feel the hardness of it through his trousers' several layers of protective fabric.

She continued to rub harder.

Simon let out a deep sigh of pleasure, "Aaaahhhhhh!"

"Do you still want me to stop?" Laura whispered seductively. She did not wait for a reply as she blew gently into Simon's ear causing him to moan louder. Lost in his haven of ecstasy Simon felt himself losing control as Laura moved her hand back and forth, keeping the rhythm going as she simultaneously traced a line around his ear with the tip of her tongue.

Simon was past the point of no return. He was about to explode and did not care how messy it would be. He could feel his seed rising, gaining momentum, any minute now....!

Laura's movement stopped abruptly as they both heard the wailing howl from outside the tent. A mournful lament carried on the icy wind making it impossible to tell how far away the cry emanated from.

They both looked at each other, equally concerned.

Without speaking they waited.

After a few moments they began to think that what they had heard was just a trick of the wind bouncing off the hillside. They continued to listen intently. The only noise which reached their ears was the moan of the wind battering the sides of their tent.

Then it came again!

This time it was definitely closer than before!

Simon immediately sat up and rolled into a crouching position which was all the enclosed tent fabric allowed. He placed a protective arm across Laura as he moved closer to the zipped entrance.

Laura tried to pull him back. "No!" she hissed, trying to keep her voice down.

"I'm just going to take a peek, might be a lost sheep or something." Laura looked at him incredulously. "How many sheep have we seen today, I counted none?"

Simon could not help but smile in spite of their present circumstance. He did love his fiancée; she always managed to bring a smile to his lips regardless of the situation with her sledge-hammer wit.

He leaned over and placed a gentle kiss on the end of her nose. "I just need to see, I won't be a second."

Simon could tell that Laura was not impressed by his inquisitiveness. He squeezed her hand once more before letting go and unzipping the entrance flap.

Once outside, Simon quickly re-zipped the tent to save Laura from feeling the bite of the wind. The sky was full black now and dotted with stars which seemed to be playing hide-and-seek amongst the scudding clouds.

The snow had stopped and all around him was a shimmering white carpet of unbroken frost. Simon listened intently. The sound did not come again. He waited a moment before deciding which direction to set off in.

Making his way slowly around the nearest drift, he glanced back to ensure that he had not lost sight of the tent. He had watched a documentary once which showed how easy it was in such conditions to lose your bearings. Granted, that was based on Mount Everest, but he did not want to take any chances.

As he reached the edge of the drift he heard it again.

This time it sounded as if whatever was making the noise was right on top of him, but the way it echoed in the air made it difficult to ascertain exactly which direction it was coming from.

Simon was beginning to wish he had stayed in the relatively safe confines of the tent with Laura, but he was not willing to let his bravado abandon him just yet. He wondered if, after tonight, he might be able to convince her to cancel the rest of their adventure and return to more conventional accommodation. There were several huts for rent still available back at the lodge, and they were dry and warm with company near by.

Another howl!

This one was definitely nearby!

Simon accepted the fact that as a townie he was not accustomed to the nocturnal sounds of the open countryside, but this could not be normal. Whatever it was that was making this racket did not sound like anything he had ever heard about or seen on the television.

As Simon slowly edged his way around the drift he noticed that his feet were sinking deeper into the snow with each step. By the time he had moved far enough so that he could see around it, he had to lift his legs out of the snow with each step.

Simon stopped to catch his breath. He tried to slow down his breathing, the icy air hurting his throat. He placed a gloved hand over his mouth and closed his eyes. Simon took several slow deep breaths in through his nose, until he had it under control.

When he opened his eyes he saw the creature standing before him.

It took a moment for the figure to register in his mind, as he had never witnessed such an aberration in his life.

He doubted that anyone else had either!

The Beast stood at well over seven feet tall, and was covered from head to toe in grubby, matted white fur. The eyes were pure black, the nose a small pushed-in snout, barely protruding from the facial hair. The mouth which gaped open was lined with rows of pointed sharp fangs, the incisors in particular were twice as long as the others.

Beast and man stood barely five feet apart. Simon could hear the guttural rattle deep in the creature's throat as it breathed out hot, fetid air. The Beast's enormous chest heaved and fell with each breath. Its arms the size of tree trunks, hung aimlessly by its sides. The edge of the fingers from which elongated claws emerged, almost reached its knees.

Before Simon had a chance to react, the creature lurched forward and took a swipe at Simon's throat, opening his jugular with its razor sharp claws.

Simon instinctively put his hand to his throat to cover the wound as his life's blood spurted between his gloved fingers.

Simon could feel his legs starting to give way under him. He could not scream and there would be no point anyway; Laura would never be able to hear him above the sound of the wind.

Poor Laura. Simon knew the creature would not allow her to live, and there was no way it could miss seeing the tent behind him. Had they been perched on the edge of a cliff Simon would have gladly sacrificed his life for his fiancée by hurling himself at the Beast and taking it with him down into oblivion. But there was nowhere to go, and Simon could feel his strength leaving him as his blood flowed.

As he felt his knees buckle the Beast fell on him, tearing a huge chunk from his throat as Simon blacked out for the last time.

Back in the tent Laura shivered in fear rather than due to the temperature, her arms wrapped around her bent knees for comfort. She had heard the subsequent howls the Beast had made after Simon had left her. She had called out to him twice, but she knew the chances of him being able to hear her were remote at best.

She wished now that she had not let him go. She should have used her stern voice, the one she saved for when Simon needed to know that she was not joking. She only used it sparingly, that way it had maximum effect, and this would have been a perfect situation to bring it out.

Laura wanted Simon back, now!

She wanted to feel his arms around her, comforting her, assuring her that everything was fine and there was nothing for her to worry about.

But she knew that was not the case!

Not now, anyway. He had been gone for too long. He knew how worried she would be and he would not have left her here alone all this time unless he was not capable of getting back.

And what about those howls? They had definitely been getting louder each time, which meant whatever was making them must be coming closer.

She tried to listen intently, but all she could hear was the wind battering the tent.

She decided she could not wait any longer. There was no way she could sit here indefinitely not knowing if her fiancé was in need of help. Perhaps he had fallen into a crevice, or slipped on the ice?

He might be lying outside just a few feet away, injured, unconscious and unable to cry for help.

Laura sat up and put her boots back on. She located the torch in her rucksack, and grabbed the whistle just in case Simon could hear that above her calls. At least then he would know that she was coming to get him.

She checked that the gas stove was off, and then unzipped the entrance flap.

Before the opening was completely accessible an enormous furry arm shot through the fabric and grabbed Laura's leg with one of its mighty hands.

Laura managed to scream once as the appendage dragged her out into the snow. She flailed and kicked wildly as she slid along the ice, until finally she was thrown to one side, landing on her back with the wind knocked out of her.

When she looked up and saw the creature she was unable to react. A scream was lodged deep down in her throat, unable to surface. She could not move, it was as if the fall had paralysed her, though deep down she knew that it was probably the result of fear taking on a physical manifestation.

She wondered how long it would be before her limbs responded to her brain's commands. But the Beast did not allow her enough time to find out before it dropped down onto her and ripped her throat out with its fangs.

CHAPTER ONE

The tyres of the Land Rover skidded on the compacted ice as Steve took the acute bend too fast. Gripping the wheel and gently applying the brake he managed to turn out of the spin without careering into the snow banks on either side of the road. Greg, in the passenger seat, gripped the handle above his head and pressed hard on an imaginary brake as the car slowly came back under the driver's control.

The three girls in the back all yelled in unison at the initial shock of the vehicle losing its purchase on the road. Their panic and fear morphed into anger once they realised that Steve was back in control.

"For the last fucking time, will you slow down Steve?" Sharon, Steve's girlfriend screamed her request from behind him.

"Fucking lunatic!" yelled Carey from the other side of the seat.

Steve looked over at Greg. His concern now evaporated, Greg smiled at his friend and shrugged his shoulders in a 'what's eating them?' show of bravado.

"It's ok Babe, it's all under control." Steve half-glanced back at his girlfriend whilst ensuring his eyes did not leave the road ahead.

"It is not all right!" replied Sharon, through gritted teeth. "If you so much as put a dent in this thing my mother will go spare and she'll probably stop my allowance to pay for the damage!"

Sharon was the 'rich-kid' amongst the group. They were all students in their last year at university and this impromptu break had come about as a result of their university closing for a week for teacher-training, and Sharon's mother and step-father being in America on their first holiday of the year. Their absence had prompted an excuse for Sharon to use her mother's prized Land Rover. Her own little car would not have carried half their luggage let alone her four friends. She did not know why her mother made such a fuss over the vehicle; she could not even drive it properly. And as for parking and manoeuvring! It had once taken her mother the best part of an hour to extricate her car from a tight spot which she had created by straddling two spaces to begin with.

Sharon was an only child. Her father had run off when she was still a baby and her mother was 'off-men' until she went to work for an American oil company and succumbed to the advances of her boss, whom she subsequently married.

He was a lot older than Sharon's mother and had two children from his previous marriage, both of whom lived with his ex-wife in the states. He had already had a vasectomy after his second daughter was born, so Sharon was effectively treated as an only child, which suited her just fine. It was not that she did not like having to share. If anything she was far less spoilt than she could have got away with being. It was more the fact that she did not have anyone to look up to, nor anyone for whom she needed to set a good example, and she liked that scenario.

This trip had been a joint idea. Sharon and Steve had been together for over a year now, and although she occasionally found his behaviour a little juvenile, she reasoned that with work he might be worth holding on to.

Greg was Steve's best mate and they had known each other since secondary school. Carey and Greg were a relatively new item having only got together officially at the Christmas party.

Jan, who was the other passenger in the car, was single for the moment and did not appear-from what she said-to be in any hurry to have a man in tow.

Behind them in the white van were Jenny and Scott. Jenny had always been part of the gang, but Scott was a bit of an outsider. He had started off being one of the team in the first year; in fact, initially Sharon thought that of all the boys he was the most intellectual. But he had fallen into bad company and seemed to be falling deeper on an almost weekly basis.

He had always been a bit of a fitness fanatic, but in the last year he had started experimenting with anabolic steroids, and granted he was now huge with bulging muscles in places most people did not even possess muscles, but he was also prone to severe mood swings and bouts of un-provoked anger.

Jenny had confided in Sharon that Scott had started experiencing erection problems as well, which she had read on the internet were a common side-effect of the type of drugs Scott was taking. But even so, he refused to accept it and on occasion had taken his anger out on Jenny. Fortunately, he had not actually become physically abusive, but Sharon knew that Jenny was worried that things might escalate in the future.

The problem with Jenny was that she was absolutely smitten with Scott, almost to the point that Sharon feared that if he did ever start to get violent with her, Jenny would just put up with it and not say anything.

Though it was only three o'clock, the sun had already started its descent. Jan, sitting quietly in the back, wiped the condensation from the window and gazed out at the uniform whiteness created by the latest snowfall. Winter had always been her favourite season, even as a child. Waking up for school on cold, frosty mornings had always inspired her. Much as she loved the colours of autumn, there was nothing quite like returning home to a welcoming fire and hot buttered crumpets. They just did not taste the same at any other time of year.

And when it snowed, that made everything so much more special. Crunching along the road in brightly coloured wellingtons, building snowmen, having snowball fights, and just seeing everything covered in a thick white blanket enhanced the dullest of views from her classroom window.

Jan firmly believed that it was the effect that snow had on her mood that first peeked her interest in photography. Biology was her calling, she had known that virtually since childhood, but photography was her passion.

That was one of the reasons she had agreed to come on this trip. Being single she knew that she would be playing gooseberry, but it was the scenic attraction and the endless possibility of grabbing some magnificent snow scenes, that and the thought of snuggling under a duvet with the snow piled high outside that enticed her to join in. And besides, she was among good friends, and if the boys became a little too rowdy she knew that Sharon and Carey would bring them to heel. Scott was the only one to cause her any concern. He had changed so much in the last year he was like a completely different person to the one she met at fresher's week. And Jenny had grown more subdued during the passing months, especially in Scott's company. Jan was sure that Jenny was not in control of her relationship, but Jan supposed she would have dumped Scott if she was truly unhappy with the situation.

As they turned another bend the landscape stretched away to their left as far as the eye could see. Jan gazed up at the darkening clouds. She could tell that they were heavy with snow which would probably mean another good downfall before night. She snuggled into her ski jacket in anticipation.

In the distance the far away hills blended with the low cloud, the landscape unspoilt by the tread of man. She felt herself becoming dreamy and lost in the atmosphere of the snow-covered land. For a moment she imagined herself trekking through the Himalayas, the Sherpa's laden down under the weight of their packs leading the way through the drifts, the snow almost up to their thighs with each progressive step, the air crisp and cool, and so thin that breathing was becoming more and more laborious with every breath.

Suddenly she saw it!

There, in the distance, too far away to be distinct but it was definitely there. She rubbed the window again with her sleeve to clear her breath from it.

A man! No, not a man, something bigger, much bigger!

Jan squinted through her glasses to try and make the shape appear more distinct, but it was virtually impossible from so far away. She tried to block out the banter from the other four occupants so she could concentrate, but it was still impossible for her to distinguish exactly what she was looking at.

The man-beast lifted its great arms above its head as if to threaten Jan against provoking it, its great mouth opened in a roar of anger too far away to be heard. She felt herself involuntarily jerking backwards in her seat, slamming into Carey.

"Hey, watch it," said Carey, rubbing her ribs where Jan's elbow had made contact.

Jan turned to her friend. "Sorry Care, look at this."

She turned back to face the window. The Beast was gone!

"See what?" asked Carey, quizzically. She tried to look past her friend out of the window.

Jan waited a moment before responding. There was definitely nothing there now, but she was sure she had witnessed something just a moment earlier. The problem was she did know what!

She turned back to Carey and smiled. "Don't worry, it's nothing, I must be imagining things."

"You need a drink," offered Sharon, passing down a silver hip-flask. "That'll sort you out, at least then you'll have an excuse for seeing things."

Jan laughed and took the flask. She knocked back a swig feeling the warm liquid sliding down her throat. Before handing it back she coughed involuntarily.

"Good stuff, huh?" said Carey, retrieving the flask.

"Hey make sure you save some for us," called Greg from the front.

"You start behaving and maybe you'll get some," replied Carey, taking a shot before passing it back to Sharon.

Jan gazed back out of the window. There was nothing before her but landscape. She tried to concentrate on the spot where she had seen the figure, but there was definitely nothing there now.

As the brandy started to do its work, she could feel her eyelids growing heavy.

Perhaps she had imagined it after all, she wondered. Possibly a trick of the light caused by a combination of the onset of dusk and the snow.

Scott heard the engine revving too fast. He changed up another gear and the van immediately began to pull back. He knew he should never have agreed to this trip, his old van was not up to it and a week out of the gym was going to cause no end of harm to his body. He would never be able to make up for this lost time. He did not care what the alleged experts said about taking a regular break from training to help boost your recovery, they were just saying that so that people like him would not grow bigger than them, but he knew better.

He had made sure he had a good supply of steroids for the week; even if he was not training he would still find some way, even if it was only press-ups on the bedroom floor. He'd packed two huge tubs of protein powder too, as he suspected that the girls had brought nothing but junk food for the week.

Scott had considered portioning individual meals and freezing them so he could liquidate them on holiday and drink down their goodness, but there was no feasible way of keeping them frozen on this journey, cold as it was.

Jenny looked across at her boyfriend. She could tell from his expression that his mood was not a good one. But then it seldom was these days. She smiled to herself as she remembered the quiet, polite, bookish man who had charmed her into bed at the start of their first year. How she longed for his return. In all honesty she did not know how much more of his constant mood-swings she could take.

The trouble was she still loved him, in spite of his behaviour. Deep down she felt confident that she could turn him back into the Scott she once knew, it would just take time and a little patience.

Scott swore aloud as his van struggled to keep pace with the Land Rover. He knew that his vehicle was not built for this terrain, but as he was the only other member of the group with a means of transport he was left with little choice. Jenny would have only sulked if they had to miss out and he could not stand it when she played the poor long-suffering girlfriend.

Mind you, it would be a different matter if his van clapped out as a result of this jaunt. He would not be able to pay for any major repairs and that would mean him losing his weekend delivery job, which in turn would leave him with no money after he had paid for his gym membership and his steroids, to take her out. Then she would have something to really complain about.

Why could she not be more supportive? He had heard some of the other lads at the gym complaining about their other halves too, and the consensus was that unless you went out with a girl who was as much into bodybuilding as you were, you would always have problems. Trouble was, as big and as hard as he wanted his body to be, he wanted his girlfriend to be soft and supple and moreover, hairless. He had seen some of those female bodybuilders and some of them had severe facial hair problems. To him, it would feel like he was shagging another bloke, no thank you!

"How much further is this place?" Scott asked, as much rhetorically as aimed at his girlfriend.

"I don't know baby," replied Jenny, soothingly. "But it can't be much further, Sharon said three hours from when we last stopped and it's been almost that now."

"Don't I fuckin' know it? An' this poor thing has felt every lump and bump along the way." Scott tried to force a gear change without fully engaging the clutch, swearing at the vehicle as it whined and screeched its dissent.

Jenny placed a comforting arm on Scott's shoulder, he did not respond. She leaned over to rest her head on his arm. He let her lay there for a few seconds before shrugging her away. "Not when I'm driving," he barked, still looking straight ahead.

Jenny moved back to her seat, dejected. She had half-expected Scott's response, but it could so easily have been the opposite. That was the problem, she never knew what to expect with him. One minute he was loving and caring, holding her tightly and telling her how beautiful she was and how much he loved her. And the next he was dismissing her out of hand as if she was some star-struck teenager trying to grab the attention of her favourite member of the latest boy band.

Up ahead, she noticed the Land Rover's brake lights flash. Scott pulled over and waited, impatiently tapping the top of the steering wheel with his finger.

"Come on, come on," he growled, "what's the hold up?"

Jenny sat up straight and strained to see out past her friend's car. In the fading light she could just make out a rough wooden sign on the side of the road. She presumed that the group ahead were reading it.

"I think it's the sign for the town, they must be making sure of our bearings," she offered, reassuringly.

Scott tutted and looked at his watch. "Oh hurry up for god's sake," he shouted, knowing full well that no one other than his girlfriend next to him would be able to hear him.

"What's wrong, honey?" Jenny ventured, bravely risking another rebuttal.

"I need to eat, that's what's wrong, and if that lot don't get a move on I'll miss my window."

Jenny knew only too well how particular Scott was about his feeding times. And the longer he was kept waiting the worse he became.

"Don't worry babe, it can't be much longer." Jenny purposely kept her tone neutral and comforting. She had been accused in the past by Scott for not being sympathetic enough to his needs and the hungrier he grew, the closer the next sermon became.

"Is that it?" asked Greg, opening his window low enough to get the best possible view of the snow-covered board.

"I think so," replied Sharon, checking the details on her tablet. The screen kept fuzzing over and going blank. Twice she reset it and twice it flashed momentarily before going down again. She remembered that the man she booked the cabin with had warned her that reception was extremely hit and miss out here, and he was not kidding.

Finally, Sharon gave up with her electronic guide and bent down under the front seat to retrieve the written directions she had made, just in case. She scanned them for a moment before looking back up at the sign.

"Greg, go out and dust the snow off it for me please, I can't be a hundred per cent sure but I think we're nearly there."

"Forget that!" exclaimed Greg from the front, "it's freezing out there."

A sudden smack on the back of his head from Carey persuaded him otherwise.

"Ok, ok, I'm going." Greg removed his gloves from his coat pocket and pulled them on roughly. He knew that clearing away the snow would leave them wet, but it was still preferable to him freezing his fingers off.

Once he cleared the sign, he quickly jumped back in the car, taking off his gloves and rubbing his hands together for warmth.

"How far to go?" asked Carey.

Greg turned in his seat. "You didn't ask me to read the bloomin' thing, just clean it, I don't know!"

"Useless creature!" Carey looked at Sharon and raised her eyes to heaven.

"Hang on," said Jan, squinting through the glass, holding up one hand to block the last remnants of the light from casting a shadow across her viewpoint. "It looks like one mile to go, straight on."

"Lovely," Steve slid the car into gear and pulled away.

"About fuckin' time!" hissed Scott, as he followed on.

CHAPTER TWO

Ten minutes later they finally arrived at the town. The main road was lined with shops, pubs, restaurants and a couple of hotels. The group pulled up outside what appeared to be the largest of the pub/restaurants and Sharon tried to call the proprietor from whom they had rented their lodge. Her mobile signal was down. She tried again but without success.

"Now what?" asked Steve, impatiently.

Sharon fumbled through her bag. "The bloke gave me some instructions on how to get hold of him in case we couldn't get a signal, he warned me how bad it was here." Sharon began passing the contents of her bag over to Carey in an attempt to locate the vital piece of paper which she sought. "Got it!" Sharon called, triumphantly holding up the fruit of her quest.

In the van behind them, Scott was anxiously mixing up a protein shake in his portable blender. Jenny looked on, smiling at him whenever he glanced her way, though the gesture was not reciprocated. She did not mind, she knew how pre-occupied he became when he was trying to concentrate on something, and ensuring he received his daily feed at precise times was always a priority with him.

Jenny gazed over at the Land Rover. She could see that everyone was still in the vehicle and wondered what their plan of action was to be. She took out her mobile and tried to find a signal, but there was not one to be had. Jenny sighed to herself. She could just pop out and go and speak to the others but with Scott's mood she did not feel like mentioning it, best just to wait.

Scott gulped down his protein shake, wiping his finger around the inside of the blender cup to extract any remnants of powder which had not dissolved properly. When he was satisfied that he had consumed every last drop he washed the inside of the cup out with mineral water and threw the liquid out of the window into the snow.

Scott belched loudly, not bothering to apologise for his rudeness.

"Now what are we waiting for?" he asked, clearly irritated by the inactivity from the Land Rover gang.

Jenny shook her head. "I don't know babe," she answered, sweetly, "maybe they're just trying to get our bearings."

"Humph!" Scott grunted, unimpressed with her answer. "Can't you go over and find out?"

"Yep," Jenny slid out of the vehicle without hesitation and walked towards her friends, glad of the chance to escape the atmosphere in the van.

When she reached the side of the car, Sharon rolled down the window to greet her friend.

"Hi you, how's grumpy doing?" She signalled behind her to the van.

Jenny laughed in spite of herself. "Oh, you know," she shrugged. "So what's happening?"

"Well, none of us can get a decent signal, so we thought we would go in here for a drink," Sharon pointed ahead to the bar/restaurant they were parked outside. "Then maybe I can try and reach our landlord using a payphone, he gave me a landline contact."

"Cool," replied Jenny, shivering with the cold. She wished she had taken the time to grab her coat when she left the van, but the truth was she needed to be away from her boyfriend and did not want to let the opportunity slip by.

They all piled into the bar with Jenny and Scott bringing up the rear.

The décor was clearly meant to be based on a western theme, with horseshoes, saddles and other cowboy memorabilia emblazoned around the walls. The bar area was empty save for two old men chatting over a few pints near the hearth, and a group of bikers slumped across one of the sofas at the far end nearest the restaurant.

There was another biker waiting at the bar whilst the barmaid completed his order. The barmaid looked up from her task when the group walked in. She was a slim, sharp-featured woman whom Sharon estimated to be in her mid-fifties. Sharon smiled as she approached the woman, the gesture was not reciprocated.

Sharon waited for the woman to complete the order before she spoke. "Hello, we are looking for a Tom Meadows who rents out cabins near here. None of us seems to be able to get a mobile reception, so I wondered if you have a pay-phone here that we can use?"

The woman looked over the rest of the group before answering. "There's a box around the corner near the toilets, should be working."

Sharon thanked her, but again her response was ignored. The biker collecting the drinks for his group looked at her and smiled. He had a long jagged scar running down one cheek and he reminded Sharon of the Joker from the Batman films.

Sharon and Carey went to make the call whilst the others started ordering drinks.

The phone was one of the old fashioned bright plastic ones attached to the wall. It took Sharon a few taps of the cradle button to finally obtain a dialling tone. As she began dialling, the men's toilet door flew open and a huge biker dressed in black leather with silver studs protruding from his face stumbled into the corridor.

When he saw the two girls he gave them a wide grin, exhibiting several missing teeth with the remainder looking as if they had never seen a toothbrush.

Sharon pretended not to have seen him, but Carey half-smiled back politely before turning away to face her friend.

The big man strode purposely towards them slowly, zipping up his fly as he drew closer. He slapped a large hand with tattoos across his knuckles against the wall by the phone, and leaned in towards them. In a broad Geordie accent he leered, "Well 'ello there pet, 'ow abute the two o' you joining me an' me mates for a little drinkie then?"

The combination of his general lack of hygiene mingled with stale beer which emanated from his mouth and clothes caused both girls to almost gag.

Carey in particular had to make an effort to stop herself putting her hand over her mouth.

"Er, no thank you, we're with friends." Sharon managed to make her reply sound as courteous as possible under the circumstances.

The biker did not take the hint. "Now come on girls, it's jus' one little drink. I'm sure yer mates won't mind!"

"No thank you!" retorted Sharon, more firmly this time.

The biker's grin dropped and was immediately replaced with a menacing scowl. He moved in closer causing both girls to back away.

Sharon held fast to the receiver, deciding that if it came to it, it would make a good enough weapon to defend themselves with.

The biker was so close now that the girls could feel his fetid breath on their faces. Sharon stood in front of her friend as if to protect her. They had moved so far back that the metal chord from the receiver was at full stretch.

The biker moved his eyes over them, as if surveying their bodies for hidden weapons. His eyes roamed up to Sharon's breasts and he stood there leering at them for what seemed to her like an age.

Both girls had considered calling out for help, but each had decided for themselves to save the option as a last resort. They had seen the other bikers in the lounge and presumed that they were all together. The last thing they needed at the start of their holiday was a mass punch-up. And by the look of the man before them, fighting was a way of life for him and doubtless for his cronies as well.

Finally, the man spoke again. This time his voice was low and expressionless, the charm-what little there had been of it-gone! "Suit yersel', yer loss." And with that he turned and shuffled back towards the bar.

The girls both watched him leave before Carey turned to her friend. She had been holding her breath without even realising it until this moment. "Jesus, what did we do to deserve that?"

"Creep!" replied Sharon. "For once I'm glad we have Scott with us, he could be handy if things turn nasty."

Stud Jones, so named because of all the piercings he had surrounding his body, stopped on his way back to his mates and glanced over to where the rest of the group stood at the bar. His eyes quickly scanned the group, focussing on the two girls. He tried to catch their eyes, but both Jenny and Jan purposely kept their gaze averted.

Not wanting to cause offence, Steve advanced a half-nod in the biker's direction, but it was ignored. Scott on the other hand was not at all happy when he thought that Stud was eyeing up his girlfriend, so he leaned away from the bar and stood to his full height, pushing out his massive chest and broadening his shoulders.

Stud did not react and pretended not to notice Scott's confrontational posture. Instead he just swaggered over to his table to join his clan.

Jenny had noticed Scott's demeanour and quickly laid a comforting hand on his chest by way of calming him down. Scott still did not relax, his muscles tight almost as if he was trying to goad the biker into an altercation.

When Stud took his seat the other bikers all crowded round the table, leaning in as if in conference. They kept their voices low so that no one else in the bar could hear them.

"Have you seen the totty at the bar?" asked Stud, the others all smiled and nodded without looking up. As the only female amongst the group, Angel Sommers merely sat back and let the men carry on.

Angel had been "gifted" to Stud as head of this chapter of the Warlords biker gang, by her former lover who was one of the founding members. Not that she cared, it made no difference to her who she rode with, so long as they kept the beer and drugs coming regularly, she was happy.

In truth, though she was supposedly Stud's woman, her duties extended to the rest of the extended family. She was expected to service all the men who rode with Stud, as all the female members of the clan were duty bound to do for their leaders.

They did have some wild parties. When there was a major reunion arranged like the one they had in Reading last autumn, it was basically an excuse for a mass orgy with drink and drugs aplenty to go around. Angel had copped off with over twenty of the gang in one day alone, so servicing Stud's little group was no biggie to her. One night she managed to see to them all within half an hour, luckily most of them only took a few minutes at best. Once they had all fallen asleep she helped herself to their stash-her reward!

They had ridden into town the previous day and were holed up at a grotty motel at the far end of the town. It was cheap and basic but it suited their needs perfectly. They had come down to case a job on a bank in the next town. The big artillery was due to arrive the day after tomorrow, but the heavy snowfall had scuppered their plan for now. Stud was checking daily with their leader for instruction and for now they had been told to just mark time.

Angel was twenty-nine years old, though in truth she had forgotten exactly how old she was having missed so many birthdays due to her tripping out so frequently. She had been on the road since being released from prison after having served two years for mugging an old man for his pension.

Tiny though she was at barely five feet and weighing just over six stone, she had managed to knock the old boy down with one punch. Kneeling on his chest she wrestled his wallet from him and was just about to stand up and give him a boot to the face for good measure when some interfering busybody grabbed hold of her and hauled her off the old man. Before she had a chance to react, more meddlesome members of the public suddenly appeared and together they held her down until the police arrived. She had sworn vengeance on them all, but in truth she had no idea who any of them were and probably would not recognise them if she passed them in the street. But at the time she was mighty pissed off. She had one of her suppliers waiting for her around the corner with some prime gear which she could have cut and made a small fortune on. Instead of which she ended up back at the local station and-due to her previous record-in custody until her hearing.

Angel grabbed her pint and sat back to drink whilst the others listened intently to their master's pearls of wisdom.

"I 'erd one of them birds talkin' about them renting a cabin locally," offered Scarface, the biker who had been up at the bar when Sharon and her group entered.

"Now that's interesting like," said Stud, thoughtfully stroking his chin with a dirty fingernail. "Perhaps we should find out where that is, jus' in case we fancy a get-together later on."

"The big one looks a bit tasty," spouted Weasel, a short painfully thin biker with long greasy hair and a very unimpressive beard. His facial hair had not increased in colour, depth or volume since it first started to sprout on his adolescent spotty face. Ten years later it still looked like peach fuzz. "'e could be trouble if it comes to it!"

Stud turned to him, a look of disdain on his face. "We'll go tooled up, 'e'll be no bother."

The others all nodded their approval.

Skull, a broad-shouldered shaven headed biker with a long black goatee and a skull and cross bones tattoo on the back of his head, took a sip of his beer then said, "'ang on, what about the job?"

"What abute it?" asked Stud, quizzically.

Skull replaced his glass on the table and leaned back in towards the group, keeping his voice down to just above a whisper. "I'm all fer 'aving some fun, but if things get out o' hand it might raise too much attention, 'at's all I meant."

Stud shrugged. "Let's jus' see what 'appens, aye. Fer now, Weasel you go an' lay low roun' the back, an' when they leave, follow 'em, but make sure they don't see yer, understan'?"

Weasel nodded and tried to knock back as much of his pint as he could in one go. By the third gulp the amber liquid was spilling out from the sides of his mouth and staining his already filthy sweatshirt.

He gave up with the glass still a third full, wiped a dirty sleeve across his face and slipped out of the booth towards the back door.

The other bikers sat back with their drinks.

Stud gazed back over towards the group at the bar. He noticed that the two girls he had spoken with outside the toilet were just re-joining their friends. One of them turned momentarily towards him and his gang, he shot her a quick smile which she ignored, pretending she had not seen him.

But he knew that she had.

Sharon and Carey strode over to their friends. Carey kept her eyes straight ahead, though Sharon could not help herself when she peeked at the bikers as she passed. There was something fascinating about them. She had always been a big bike fan though she had never felt the urge to get involved with their style of culture. But still the black leather clothing, the dirty denim and the big boots, not to mention the "fuck-you" attitude, had an irresistible allure which she could not explain.

"How did you get on?" Jan asked, as they reached the bar.

"It's all sorted," smiled Sharon, "Tom is on his way here now to meet us, and he says he will take us up to the cabin himself. His son is already there ensuring that everything is ready for us."

"Excellent," said Steve, sliding a rum and coke along the bar to his girlfriend. Greg passed Carey her gin and tonic and they all "cheered" each other to their holiday.

Jenny gave Scott a side glance as she sipped her drink. She could tell that he was still not happy with the way those bikers had looked them over. She hoped that the cabin owner would get there soon and take them away before any trouble started. In Scott's present frame of mind it would not take much to set him off.

Fortunately five minutes later, before there was a chance of any trouble, Tom Meadows entered the bar. He glanced around for a moment, then seeing Sharon and her group he walked over.

"Hello," he said, cheerily, "would one of you be Sharon Delaney by any chance?"

Sharon moved forward and Tom shook her hand. She quickly introduced him to the rest of the group. Jan was the last in line and when Tom took her hand instead of shaking it he bent down and touched the back of her hand lightly with his lips.

Jan blushed slightly at the gesture, hoping the others did not notice.

Tom winked at Jan with a wicked smile across his lips when he saw her furtively checking to see if anyone else noticed her flush.

Jan estimated that Tom had to be in his mid to late fifties. He was tall and lean with a full head of short-cropped salt and pepper hair, and a matching well-groomed beard.

Jan did not know why, but she took an instant liking to him. He was obviously too old to be boyfriend material, but there was an overwhelming air of protective charm about his manner which made her feel very safe.

Once all the details had been discussed and finalised, Tom suggested that the group follow him up to the cabin. When they went back outside, the sun was on the final leg of its descent, and Jan felt that the town had taken on an eerie almost unworldly feeling. The snow-covered streets were virtually deserted, and it appeared that some of the shopkeepers had already decided to call it a day.

Tom was driving a huge snowplough. He explained that it would make the journey easier for the rest of them if he cleared a decent path for them en route. As they all stood around in the snow, Tom looked over the two vehicles the group had arrived in.

He pointed to Scott's van. "Is that thing a four-by-four?"

"No!" Scott grunted, defensively.

Tom turned to him and smiled, holding up his hands in mock submission. "Easy there big man, I was just concerned about how it will cope on our way up. There's a pretty steep climb we have to negotiate and with this amount of snow things could become dicey."

Scott seemed to be considering Tom's advice. After a moment he looked back at him and asked. "So what do you advise then?"

"Well," answered Tom, thoughtfully, "I could take a couple of you in the plough with me so you can leave your van here until the snow clears a bit, it'll be quite safe. Or as I only live around the corner you could move it outside my place if you like."

"Scott's got all our provisions in the back," offered Steve, "we'd never fit them all in the Rover, the boot's already full."

"It'll be ok," replied Scott, before Tom had a chance to consider another alternative. "I'll take it slow."

Tom could see that Scott had made up his mind. "Alrighty good people, let's go."

As they began to sort themselves out, Jan sidled up to Tom and nervously tapped his arm.

Tom turned; a broad smile covered his face when he saw who it was. "Yes my lovely, what can I do for you?"

Jan pointed to the snowplough. "I've always wanted to ride in one of those, this may be my only chance, would you mind?"

Tom's smile broadened even further. "Not in the slightest, it'll be my pleasure to have you aboard."

Carey, standing between Sharon and Jenny, nudged them both with her elbows and nodded in Jan's direction. Both girls held back a laugh as they moved to their respective vehicles.

CHAPTER THREE

Leading the way with the Land Rover following and Scott bringing up the rear, Tom Meadows cleared a path for the others to follow. From the high vantage point which the plough afforded, Jan looked out across the unblemished snow-covered landscape. Her mind drifted, conjuring up the fantasy that they were on their way to a plush ski resort high in the Swiss Alps, where she would be rubbing shoulders with the rich and the famous, sitting in front of a cosy log fire drinking eggnog.

Jan caught herself glancing surreptitiously at Tom whenever he changed gear. The heavy shift of the gear lever and the way he had to pump the pedal two or three times before forcing it to shift was giving her goose bumps. She did not know if it was the fact that she was on holiday, or the only one of her friends who was not with someone, or just the general warm and protective vibe which Tom seemed to exude that made her feel so protected in his company.

All she did know for sure was that for an older guy he was certainly fit!

But she knew that he had a son and that doubtless meant that there was a wife or a partner somewhere back at the homestead. Or maybe they were divorced or separated. Perhaps Tom had been on his own for a while and was available. Jan had to check herself again before letting her mind wander too far. She reminded herself that Tom was a good deal older than her, and although in this day and age that did not seem to be a negative consideration, the age gap was too wide for her personally to consider it viable.

She decided to just sit back and enjoy the man's company.

"So how long have you lived up here, Tom?" she asked, casually.

Tom averted his gaze from the road ahead long enough for a quick smile before he answered. "Must be coming on for nearly twenty years by now. I moved up here when my marriage broke up. I won't bore you with the details."

Jan felt her heart skip, she chided herself. "Oh I'm sorry to hear that. It's never an easy situation is it; I mean break-ups in general, not that I've ever been married."

"I doubt you've ever been dumped either, gorgeous girl like you."

Jan laughed out loud before she could stop herself. She slapped her hand over her mouth in embarrassment. She could feel her cheeks glowing.

Tom saw her glow and grinned broadly. He felt bad that he had embarrassed her, but he had to admit that it also felt good that a young beauty like Jan would even take notice of what a man his age might say.

Tom waited for Jan's laughter to subside. "What I meant was that I cannot believe that any man in his right mind would dump you, so any relationships that you have had must have ended on your terms."

Jan smiled warmly. "I'm afraid not, so far I've always been the dumpee, rather than the dumper."

"Really?" Tom seemed genuinely shocked. "Well, all I can say is more fool them, if I was twenty-five…" He stopped himself then thought for a second. "No, make that thirty years younger, the others would all have to wait in line behind me before getting a crack at you."

Jan knew he was flirting with her, but somehow she still felt safe enough in his company to flirt back. And she was enjoying it. Men had been few and far between in her life. Not that she dwelled on it, in fact she found most men of her age too immature to bother with. Her sexual encounters too had been sporadic and brief. Not to mention painful and unfulfilling. She knew that there was more from listening to her girlfriends discussing their sex lives, so she had decided to exercise patience and wait for the right time to present itself.

They began the climb up the hill Tom had mentioned earlier. He dropped the vehicle down two gears and gently eased the clutch to make the climb. Tom checked the rear-view mirror to make sure that the others behind them were ok.

He watched as Steve started to slowly climb up the slope.

Tom certainly had not been joking when he said that the going might get tough for Scott's van. Scott could feel the wheels losing purchase so automatically tried to up the revs with the throttle. The tyres began to spin and the van moved sideways rather than straight on. Jenny gripped hold of her seat in nervous anticipation, afraid that they were going to slide into a ditch, or worse, any minute.

Swearing to himself, Scott dropped a gear and hit the accelerator hard. The engine roared in protest and the tyres started to spit snow out from the sides as the lower gear engaged. Scott felt his control of the vehicle start to decline. He did not want to drop any lower, but at the same time he needed a better grip to edge the vehicle forward. In frustration he slammed on the brakes and wrenched up the handbrake. Once the van was at a standstill, he engaged first and gently released the clutch whilst simultaneously easing off with the handbrake. The van started to move forward slowly, whining to be slotted into second gear.

Scott felt the engine start to object at its driver's choice so revved once more before depressing the clutch and slotting the gearstick into second. As he eased off the clutch and pressed home the accelerator the van lurched to one side again, the tyres scrabbling on the ice to gain momentum.

Scott revved the engine harder, shouting abuse at the recalcitrant vehicle, refusing to give in and be beaten. He tried to change down once more to regain his initial grip. This time the van began to roll backwards when he forgot to engage the assistance of the handbrake.

Jenny screamed, genuinely fearing for their safety.

Scott, ignoring his girlfriend's cries wrenched up the brake lever, slipping the clutch as he did so. The engine cut out sending the van into a spin which left them wedged against the offside snow bank.

Jenny, her eyes now closed in fear, took several deep breaths trying to recover her composure.

Scott, after a moment's hesitation, began pounding on the top arch of the steering wheel with his fists. Yelling with each strike as if it gave the action greater impetus. "Fuck…Fuck…Fuck…Fuck…!"

"Woa, that doesn't look so good," announced Tom, gazing in his rear-view mirror.

"What's that?" asked Jan, turning in her seat to try and catch a better view.

"Your friends back there in the white van seem to be in trouble, I should have insisted that they leave it behind, even if it meant making two trips."

Jan squinted past the Land Rover but could only make out Scott's van in the distance parked against a drift. It seemed ok, but she did worry for Jenny's sake if everything was alright. "You could have tried," she offered, "but separating Scott from his van might need surgery, he dotes on that thing."

Tom smiled. "Yes, I kind of got the impression he cared more about it than he does about your friend."

"Very astute," smiled Jan.

"Not just a pretty face, you know," replied Tom, with a wink.

"Mmnn, I'd noticed."

The path was too narrow for Tom to turn the snow plough around, so he continued forward until he reached a sizeable verge into which he could pull over without obstructing the access of the Land Rover.

Leaving the engine running so that Jan could benefit from the heater, Tom jumped down from the cab and approached the Land Rover.

Steve braked slowly and lowered the window. "What's up Tom, everything alright?" the others crowded forward to hear Tom through the rising wind.

"Your friends back there seem to be having a bit of trouble negotiating the incline," The others automatically turned around to look behind them.

Sharon felt guilty that she had not noticed until now that they were having trouble. Not that she could have actually done anything save for getting Steve to stop and signalling ahead to Tom, but anyway she felt she should have kept an eye on Jenny. Should have actually insisted that Jenny travel with them since Jan was happy to ride up with Tom, but she knew she would never have won that argument.

Sharon turned back. "What should we do?" she asked Tom, raising her voice to be heard above the wind.

"Well," he answered, "it's probably better if you all carry on up the road." Tom pointed ahead. "Take the first turning you come to on the right, then it's only about another mile before you'll come to a fork in the road with a sign saying 'Meadow's Cabins' pointing right. Follow that path for about another half a mile and you should see them straight ahead of you. My son Adam is waiting for you, so you should be safe enough." He looked at Steve. "Just keep the speed down, the snow will be a little trickier to deal with as I haven't cleared a path from here."

Steve nodded. He was confident he could reach the cabins intact, the Land Rover was a top of the range model and the tyres were built for off-road travel. Plus it was extremely responsive.

"What are you going to do?" asked Carey, leaning forward.

Tom looked back down the road towards the stationary van. "I'm going to reverse back down the hill and if I cannot convince your friend to abandon his vehicle, I'm going to tow him the rest of the way." He turned back to face the others. "Or at least until we reach the summit of this hill."

"Will that be safe?" asked Sharon, suddenly feeling she needed to quantify her question. "I mean, going backwards in all this snow and downhill as well?"

Tom smiled. "Well it's not ideal I'll grant you, but under the circumstances it seems like the best option."

Sharon looked over at the snow plough. She could just make out the shadow of Jan in the passenger seat. She bit her bottom lip. Not wanting to sound rude, she could not help but worry about her friend. Though she was sure that Tom could manoeuvre his vehicle safely down the incline, the fact was that accidents did happen even to the safest of individuals, and she would definitely feel safer if Jan was with them for the remainder of the journey.

She looked back to Tom. Either he was able to read minds or he recognised the concerned look on her face. "Before you head off," he said, "let me just see if I can convince Jan to go with you. I have done this sort of thing before but I will be better focussed if I've only got me to worry about."

Sharon smiled, visibly relaxed. She suddenly felt great affection for this man who clearly put others before himself. He could certainly teach Scott a thing or two about selflessness.

They waited whilst Tom returned to the plough.

A few moments later he returned with Jan, huddling her under his snow jacket as he escorted her to the Land Rover.

As she extracted herself from his jacket to enter the car, Jan instinctively reached up and planted a gentle kiss on Tom's cheek. There was nothing overtly sexual or even sensual about it, it was more akin to the kind of kiss a youngster might give a visiting uncle, but she noticed Tom blush slightly at the sentiment, none the less; and that made her smile.

Jan climbed into the car and Tom slammed the door shut once he was sure she was clear of it.

He went back around to the driver's side and ensured that Steve had understood his earlier directions.

Tom waited until the Land Rover had pulled safely away. He watched them for a while, long enough to see Jan turn in her seat and wave to him. He waved back, then returned to his plough.

****

Stuart "Weasel" Jenkins watched from behind a huge drift as the wheels of the white van spun furiously, kicking out white tufts from all sides. He had purposely stayed back out of sight, as Stud would not be happy if the occupants of the van as well as those in the preceding vehicles cottoned on to the fact that they were being followed.

Weasel had abandoned his bike around the last bend when he realised that the van was not going to make it any further. It had been difficult enough for him to stay upright in these conditions, and a couple of times he had nearly lost his bike when he hit some hard ice. Though his tyres were relatively new and supposedly all weather-the result of another chapter of the Warlords successfully raiding a supply warehouse last month- in this terrain caution was still the best policy. He was going to need his bike in full working order when they received their instructions on their next job, and again Stud would not be happy if Weasel managed to throw a spanner in the works by smashing his up on a simple tracking mission.

He watched as the van eventually gave up the ghost and jerked to a halt up against a drift. He stayed low and watched, waiting for the occupants to plan their next move. Up ahead he could still see the tail end of the Land Rover climbing the hill, the top of the snow plough in front just visible above it.

Weasel wished he had a telescope or a pair of binoculars. It was hard to fathom what was going on up ahead. It looked as if the other two vehicles had stopped and someone was walking towards the Land Rover. Weasel could not make the figure out from this distance, but he felt fairly confident that it was the tall man who had come into the bar and had left with the group.

He feared that there might be a long wait before anything happened. The icy wind was starting to cut through his leathers. The inner warmth his beer had provided was now waning, so he shoved his gloved hands into his jacket pockets for further protection. He contemplated returning to the bar and telling the gang that the van had become stuck and that he would give away his position if he tried to ride round it to follow the others. But he knew that excuse would not wash with the others and that he would pay for it later.

He decided to wait it out, he had no choice. His place in the gang's food chain was suitably low enough that he was always in line for the brunt of their anger. Which was ok with him, Stud had explained to him when he first joined the chapter that this was the way of things for the first two years. After that, if you stuck it out you were more readily acceptable as one of the gang.

Still, at least he was given a go with Angel, like the rest. She was sweet and never failed to arouse him. Not that he had suffered from erection problems; it was just that some women were so demanding and wanted him to wear himself out making them reach orgasm before he was even allowed to get started. With Angel she was always ready for action. A quick fondle of her breasts, some snogging and she had you inside her before you knew it.

He was not gay, he knew that. Men's naked bodies did nothing for him. In fact the sight of a naked female always made him hard, the problem only started when he tried to insert himself after spending ages satisfying the woman. But never with Angel, curiously. He hoped that one day someone else would come along and take her place as the gang's concubine, then maybe he could convince Stud to give her to him exclusively. But until then, he would just look forward to his turns with her, and savour them as much as possible.

Now as he stood there in the freezing snow, the cold starting to seep through to his bones, he imagined Angel's warm, soft, unblemished skin close to his naked body. Pressing against him, letting him shove his tongue in her mouth, his hardness pushing against her moist cleft as she slid her gentle hand down his body, the tips of her fingernails gently grazing his torso until she finally reached his throbbing organ. Encircling him with her long fingers sliding up and down his shaft before slipping him into her wet pussy.

Weasel caught himself rubbing his erection through his trousers. He groaned loudly at the thought of Angel's fragrant body amalgamating with his own, becoming one.

Reluctantly, he removed his hand from the front of his groin and breathed hard several times as if to release his frustration. Perhaps if he completed his mission successfully, Stud would be pleased with him and grant him a go with Angel. The thought sent a sudden shiver through his body and spurred him on to maintain his vigilance.

Weasel looked back to the van. He could no longer see the Land Rover anywhere in sight. From the look of things, the snow plough was now rolling backwards down the hill towards the van. Weasel watched as the driver veered the huge vehicle gently from side to side as it made its descent, never allowing it to drift too far over one side or the other before bringing it back under control. Whoever was driving clearly knew their stuff.

It took a good fifteen minutes for the plough to reach the van. All the time the air was growing colder as the darkness crept across the sky, bringing with it a biting edge to the wind which cut through Weasel's outfit like a hot knife through butter.

He was still too far away to be seen or heard, so he moved back and stood up. Weasel began stamping the cold ground and rubbing his sides with his hands. It did not seem to be making much of a difference, but he figured it was better than nothing.

He hoped, now that the plough had reached its destination, the wait would not be too much longer.

CHAPTER FOUR

Jenny was glad that Scott had finally stopped slamming his hand into the steering wheel. The initial outpouring of rage abated, she could tell from the redness in his face and the whiteness of his knuckles as he clenched the wheel that he was obviously still fuming at their predicament.

She had to fight the urge to lean over and put her arm around her boyfriend and whisper some comforting words into his ear. She knew from past experience that the gesture would not be welcome.

Jenny was surprised by the fact that the others seemed to have driven off and left them. But then she noticed the snow plough reversing back down the hill, and she guessed that Tom had probably told them to carry on. She hoped that he had a good trick up his sleeve. Maybe there was another way to the cabin that he knew of which would not involve steep hills. But then if that was the case, why had he brought them this way to begin with? He must have known how much Scott would struggle with the climb; after all, he had mentioned it before they set off.

Jenny glanced over at her boyfriend. Scott was still staring straight ahead, his eyes seemingly fixed on the approaching plough. His breathing had calmed down a little, but his overall demeanour was still one of anxiety and stress. And she knew the cause only too well. It had nothing to do with their van being stuck; it was those blasted steroids he kept taking. In the old days before the drugs Scott would have laughed this off and cracked a joke about sending her out to push them up the hill.

She really missed her old boyfriend. The man sitting beside her in the van was not the same one she had fallen for. He had lost all his warmth, compassion and tenderness. Even when they made love now it was totally different to the way it used to be. For one thing Scott had been suffering erection problems which he had never experienced with her before. In the old days she could feel him growing hard just by letting him fondle her as they kissed. Now sometimes it did not matter what she did or how much she tried to reassure him, he remained flaccid. Only a week ago she had sucked on him for so long her jaw began to ache, but still he was not able to maintain a decent erection.

And as usual he had blamed her. His anger and frustration made her an easy target upon which to vent his feeling of inadequacy. She really thought last week that he was going to lose it completely; the look in his eyes was one of pure hatred and malevolence as if everything was her fault.

In truth, Jenny did not know how much more of the new Scott she could take. She had tried on numerous occasions to broach the subject with him, but each attempt had been met with the same vitriolic response. It was obvious to her now that he loved his drugs more than he loved her, and if she gave him an ultimatum she was fairly confident which way he would turn.

Jenny took a tissue from her handbag and blew her nose. She could feel her eyes starting to well up and she did not want to give in to tears. Not that she suspected Scott would notice right this minute, his attention was still firmly fixed on his incapacity to take charge of the situation.

The plough stopped about ten feet in front of them. Tom climbed out of the cab and shuffled through the snow towards the van. Jenny was not sure if it was because he saw the expression on Scott's face or not but Tom made his way to her window instead of his.

Jenny wound it down as he drew nearer.

"Hello you two, are you both ok?" he asked cheerily, the cold air made his breath visible in dense clouds of carbon dioxide.

"We're fine," Jenny spoke up before Scott had a chance. "But we're a little stuck, as you can see. Any chance of a push?" she joked.

Tom laughed. "A push, no, but I've got another couple of suggestions."

"What!" barked Scott, barely turning enough to acknowledge Tom's presence.

Tom ignored Scott's attitude for which Jenny was very grateful. She knew that any confrontational behaviour from Tom would be enough to light Scott's touch-paper. "Well," Tom continued, "You can either leave your van here and I'll collect it later when the snow abates, or I can attach a tow rope from the plough and pull you up the hill." He looked at Jenny, purposely ignoring Scott. "It's your choice, but I have to say my vote goes with leaving the van here."

Jenny smiled weakly at Tom as if to convey her apology that it was not her decision to make. She slowly turned to her boyfriend and they waited for his decision.

With a deep sigh which seemed to Jenny to be more from defiance than exasperation, Scott answered. "Ok, then, I suppose that the tow is the only way we're going to get to the cabin tonight, let's do it."

Jenny turned back to Tom, her expression conveying both her thanks and her apology for her boyfriend's behaviour once again.

"Right you are then," replied Tom, "the tow it is."

Jenny waited for Scott to offer Tom his assistance in connecting up the rope, but he just sat there staring straight ahead once more.

"Would you like a hand?" Jenny asked Tom, hoping that her words might stir Scott into action.

"No thanks, I'll be fine," responded Tom, flicking a quick glance at Scott before looking back at Jenny. "But I do think it's advisable if you travel with me, no offence but the lighter the van the easier the tow will be on the plough."

"Oh," Jenny looked at Scott for approval. When there was no response she just announced. "I'm going to travel with Tom, babe. It'll make the tow go easier."

Scott looked at her and grunted something inaudible.

Jenny pulled on her coat as she exited the van, slamming the door behind her as she stepped onto the frozen ground. Her boots sank in the snow until it almost came over the top of them. She wished now that she had worn her higher ones, the last thing she needed was soggy socks and freezing feet.

She followed Tom back to the plough. From behind she heard Scott bellow something about her not winding the window up before she left. She ignored him and pretended not to hear.

Tom, being a gentleman accompanied her to the passenger side of the plough and helped her up into the cab. He closed the heavy door for her before making his way around the back to fetch the tow rope.

Jenny watched as Tom secured the van. He then went back round to the driver's side to speak to Scott. From the way he gesticulated Jenny suspected that he was advising Scott on the best way to avoid any problems on the way up. From Scott's mannerism he obviously did not welcome Tom's advice. She wondered if he actually felt somewhat intimidated by the older man who, unlike her boyfriend, was able to take charge of a given situation and come up with a workable conclusion, rather than just sitting and sulking like an admonished schoolboy.

From the look on Tom's face when he entered the cab, Jenny could tell that Scott had been anything but grateful for Tom's suggestions.

She reached over and laid a hand on the older man's forearm. "I'm really sorry about him," she said, jerking her head back towards the van. "He really hasn't been himself lately," she lied; hoping that Tom would not detect the dishonesty which she felt must be etched on her face.

If Tom knew that she was lying, he chose not to show it. Instead he gave her a warm smile and brushed the incident off completely.

The plough groaned and wailed as Tom played with the clutch fighting for purchase. As big as it was the machine clearly did not savour the task ahead. It almost made Jenny feel as if it was trying to tell Tom to leave Scott behind, and for a moment she relished the thought of not having to put up with his moodiness for the rest of the holiday. But no sooner had the thought taken hold, Jenny was checking herself for her disloyalty and selfishness. Perhaps this break was just what they both needed. A little fresh country air, some beautiful winter scenery, perhaps even the odd snowball fight and who knows, the old Scott may re-appear full of apologies and remorse.

But somehow she doubted it would all be that easy!

****

Weasel watched as the snow plough struggled to hold fast on the snow-packed hill. The white van edged out of its crash position as the plough tugged at it from above. Finally the van was yanked free and began its ascent. The driver of the plough kept the speed low and from Weasel's vantage point he could hear the squeal of the clutch as it fought to ease the gears in. The van began to slide from one side to the other and for a second it looked to the biker as if it was going to crash over the drift that separated the road from the hillside, but it quickly recovered and settled down to a steadier central position on the icy road.

Weasel waited until he was sure that the vehicle was going to make the climb before re-mounting his bike and starting it up. He waited patiently for the van to clear the ridge before he set off in pursuit. On this wide open snowy-white road it would be easy for him to be spotted with his black leather clothing, so he stayed back as far as possible, even preparing to lose sight of the vehicles he was meant to be following rather than be discovered.

The penalty for failure was severe. So much so that Weasel knew that if he lost his prey and could not tell Stud their final destination, he might as well ride off into the sunset and hope he could disappear without ever being found.

With a sudden lurch the van dipped out of sight on the horizon. In a blind panic, Weasel revved his engine and released the clutch a little too fast. His engine stalled. Cursing, Weasel switched the ignition back on and pressed the starter. The engine roared in protest before finally catching. This time he let the clutch out more slowly and began to climb. He looked ahead, the van was nowhere in sight. Fighting to keep the bike steady on the dicey terrain he edged forward as fast as he felt it safe to do so. The last thing he wanted was to stall the engine again. In this cold weather the next stall may be the last.

As he reached the brow the road before him stretched out for miles with trees on either side and several turnings off the main road both left and right. He could see much further ahead than he estimated the two vehicles could ever cover in the time it had taken him to make the climb. Yet there was no sign of either of them. The snow was just starting to fall again and Weasel lifted the visor on his helmet to try and give him a clearer view.

There was nothing in sight but snow and more snow.

Weasel could feel his heart starting to race. There would be no turning back now. He had no idea where the road ahead led, but anywhere was preferable to going back in shame and disgrace to throw himself on the mercy of his leader. Especially when he knew that his leader had none. He would treat the opportunity as a demonstration to the others of the price of failure. Weasel had witnessed such a scenario once before with another of the chapter leaders, and he remembered thinking to himself at the time that death by his own hands was a far brighter prospect should he ever find himself in the same predicament.

In desperation Weasel dismounted his bike and left it on the side stand with the engine idling. He walked a few steps ahead, the snow covering his ankles and rising half way up his shins as he placed his full weight down.

The headlight from his bike cast a shadow from behind as his body blocked the beam. He removed his helmet altogether and holding it in one hand began to scour the ground for tracks left by the plough or the van in the snow. But the new snowfall was covering the road far faster than he could distinguish what was underneath. Weasel felt the icy blast of the wind cut through his ears. Without thinking he breathed in deeply, regretting it straight away. The sharp wind cut through his nasal passage like a chainsaw leaving his entire head feeling numb.

Weasel tried to put his hands up to his ears to block the wind, but with his helmet in one of them it made the effort unmanageable.

The road began to slope down slightly and Weasel almost lost his footing when he hit an icy patch. The sky was dark, low cloud cover denying him any assistance he might have received from starlight. The uniform white of the ground cover made it almost impossible to distinguish if anything had passed over it recently. Weasel gazed behind and noticed that even his footsteps were quickly being covered over by the fresh snow.

Then he remembered the torch in his back box. He decided that that would be his best option as well as possibly his last hope. He only prayed that the batteries were not dead as he had not had to use it for a while. He made his way back to his bike as quickly as the ground would allow, half walking half jumping to free himself from the rising depth of the snow.

Once he was back at his bike, Weasel remembered that the key to his back box was on the same ring as his ignition key. He had two choices. Turn off the engine and risk it not starting again, or removing his gloves so that he could fumble with the ring to disengage the box key.

He elected to go with the latter.

Biting down on the middle finger of his right glove he pulled his hand free. The cold immediately bit into his fingers turning them red and raw. Weasel tried to uncoil his box key from the ring with the un-gloved hand whilst holding the ignition key steady with the other, but the dexterity needed to free it warranted both hands to be free. Reluctantly he removed his other glove and rubbed both hands together for protection before continuing.

The biting cold left his fingers feeling numb and vulnerable. He watched his mission intently, willing his fingers to respond to the signals he was sending out from his brain. But the cold made his fingers raw and clumsy, and it took him several attempts before he had to surrender and go with plan A.

He quickly replaced his gloves, rubbing his hands together furiously once more before pulling them on. He fumbled the key out of the ignition, hearing the engine splutter and die, fearing it might be for the last time. Weasel opened his back box and removed his torch, mercifully its beam shone brightly as soon as he hit the switch. At least something was going in his favour.

He considered starting up the engine straight away before going on, then decided that with the path being covered more and more by the second he had better deal with the road first.

He aimed his torchlight down on the ground. The result was disappointing; the new snow had covered all but the faintest trace of tyre tracks. Weasel bent down lower to the ground and squinted at the path. He could barely make them out, but the tracks were definitely there. Though for how much longer he could not dare to imagine.

Walking hunched over Weasel followed the grooves in the snow. The going was slow but at least he felt as if he was making progress. An icy blast whistled through the trees giving them an almost human appearance as their branches danced and weaved against the gust.

In the distance Weasel imagined that he could hear a cry. An eerie inhuman howl doubtless caused by the wind reverberating off the distant hills. He ignored it, concentrating on finding the path the van and plough had taken.

As he neared the first bend in the road he struggled to distinguish where the tracks led. Weasel shone his torch back and forth across the ground desperate to see something that resembled tyre marks, but it was impossible to distinguish anything with the fresh snow masking what lay beneath.

He tried to brush some of the fresh snow away with his foot, but all that achieved was a smeared imprint of his own boot.

Weasel raised his head. The snow was falling much heavier now and with the added lack of visibility his task seemed nigh on impossible. He cried out, unconcerned about anyone being able to hear him. A combination of anger and frustration tinged with a small dose of fear. Fear of what would happen to him if he returned to the town having failed in his mission.

The inevitability of it all was starting to hit home in a big way. It was not his fault. Trying to shadow someone in these conditions whilst maintaining enough of a distance to keep your presence covert was enough to tax the most experienced of trackers.

But he knew full well that explanations would be superfluous. There was only success and failure, one to be celebrated, the other merely to be dealt with, severely.

In desperation Weasel turned to walk back to his bike. He decided that he would explore every avenue to try and locate the others, there was no going back. He would ride down each path in turn even it took the rest of the night, but eventually he would find their location.

Bending forward against the driving snow, he trudged on.

Suddenly, he heard it. A wailing cry, low, guttural emanating as if from hell itself. This was no trick of the wind, this sounded far too real.

And far too near!

He looked up, squinting as the snow flakes blasted his face, stinging his eyes and choking him as he tried to breathe.

Which direction had the noise come from?

He could not tell. In these conditions noises were veiled, veering off their chosen path by the wind and snowfall., carried to all corners of the vicinity, merely to bounce off their next obstruction and reverberate somewhere else.

Weasel spun round waving his torch in all directions. Regardless of the circumstances that cry had sounded far too close for his liking. He tried to imagine what could have made the sound. Did they have bears out here? Perhaps it was an escaped animal, a large cat which had broken free from its enclosure at a local zoo, or been let loose by a disgruntled employee from a travelling circus. Left free to roam the countryside, ravenously hunting its prey. Man its only natural enemy, blaming his species for its past incarceration.

He heard it again!

Closer, louder, angrier!

The weak beam from his flashlight was no match for the driving snow. He could barely make out five feet in front of him. The roar was coming from somewhere in the shadows just out of his field of vision. But from which direction he could not establish.

Weasel strode on in the direction of his bike. Whatever was out there he needed to get away from here, now!

Holding his hand in front of his eyes he could just about see the outline of his bike ahead. He tried to focus on it, praying that it would start when he turned the engine over. He kept his eyes fixed straight ahead. Watched as his bike began to rise off the ground as if being hauled up by a giant winch.

He continued forward. What was happening to him? Was his mind going? Was he suffering from some sort of snow-blindness, causing him to imagine strange happenings?

His bike could not be floating in air, it was impossible, just his imagination playing tricks. But there it was, the closer he came to it the less sense it made.

Then he thought he saw it! A huge beast-like creature covered in white matted fur, lifting his machine above its head with its enormous arms. Holding it there, suspended, out of reach. Impossible, nothing on earth could have that much strength.

Weasel did not have time to react as the bike came crashing down on him, crushing his body, smashing his bones and leaving him pinned down in agony beneath its weight.

He screamed, the effort lost in the wind. He felt his mouth start to fill up with a warm metallic tasting liquid. He tried to shift himself, but it was impossible, he could barely feel his own body anymore.

As the creature lurched towards him coming into focus, another mighty roar filled his ears.

Weasel struggled to remain conscious. Mercifully, it was a losing battle.

CHAPTER FIVE

By the time Tom arrived with Scott's van in tow, the others had all unloaded their stuff and settled themselves in. Sharon had purposefully taken the smallest bedroom for herself and Steve. Even though they had agreed on first come first served, she felt bad for Jenny under the circumstances having to tag behind with Scott. Plus which she knew that if they were left with the last choice that Scott would doubtless blame it on Jenny, even though none of it was her fault.

Steve had started to object when she informed him of her plan, but one of her 'looks' soon put a stop to that. Besides, the smallest room was very cosy and still afforded them a good view of the landscape.

Jan and Carey remained in the kitchen unpacking while Sharon and the boys went outside to help Scott unload.

Tom unhitched the van from his plough and reeled in the tow rope. Then he helped carry in the last of the boxes.

Once inside, he asked, "Has anyone seen my son yet?"

All those in attendance shook their heads. Sharon, having led Jenny and Scott to their room was just returning. "What's up?" she asked, noticing her companions all looking at each other as if in anticipation of an answer.

"I was just asking if anyone has seen Adam, my son, yet."

"There was no sign of anyone here when we arrived," replied Sharon. "And there was no vehicle parked outside either."

"I dropped him up here earlier to make sure you had enough wood for the fires."

"Perhaps he finished early and started to make his way back down?" suggested Greg.

Tom shook his head. "I doubt it; he knew I would be coming back up here with you," he scratched his head. "No matter, he'll pop up sooner or later." Clapping his hands together he announced, "Speaking of the furnace, I need to show some volunteers how the genie works."

"The what?" asked Carey, walking in from the kitchenette area.

Tom laughed. "The generator, it's what the lights and the hot water run off. You need to know how to operate it as it can sometimes be temperamental."

"Go on you two," Sharon signalled to Greg and Steve, "follow Tom, and make sure you pay attention, if we end up without lights or hot water you two will be sleeping in the snow."

"Naked," chipped in Carey.

Laughing, the two lads followed Tom back out into the snow.

They found Adam in the outbuilding which housed the generator. He was busy tinkering with the controls and did not hear them come in because of the headphones he was wearing.

He jumped when Tom crept up behind him and whacked him with his gloves.

Adam stood up and removed his headphones from his ears allowing them to dangle around his neck whilst he turned off his music. "Hello," he acknowledged the two men who had entered with his father. "Sorry I didn't hear you come in."

"Some guard dog you'd make," replied Tom, standing with his hands on his hips in mock admonishment. "They've been here ages, unpacked and everything."

"Oh, sorry dad," smiled Adam. "I was trying to get this stupid thing back on the clock," he pointed to the generator, "one of the valves was stuck."

"Sorted now?" asked Tom, hopefully.

"Yeah, I think so, the real proof will be first thing in the morning when the timer comes back on."

Tom sighed. Turning to Steve and Greg he said, "I'd better show you boys what to do in case she shuts down, it's not too complicated, and we're only a phone call away…If you can get a signal that is."

Tom patiently went through the start-up process for the generator, ensuring the two men fully understood each step before continuing to the next.

At Tom's suggestion, Adam went back to the lodge; laden down with some of the logs he had cut, to make sure that the fireplace was stacked.

Having his arms full, Adam nudged open the door to the cabin without knocking first. All four of the girls were gathered around the empty fireplace and they spun around as he entered.

Adam gave them his broadest grin. "Hello, I'm Adam, Tom's son. I come bearing gifts." He shrugged to show off the logs he was carrying.

"Well please come on in," said Carey, "We were just wondering where we could find some of those."

The girls all introduced themselves once Adam had placed the logs on the floor. They took turns at shaking hands. When he reached Jenny, Adam paused as he took her hand. The two of them stared into each others' eyes during their greeting. It was only for the briefest of moments, but the gesture did not escape the other girl's attention. As they broke away, Adam looked up at the ceiling hearing a noise from above.

"Oh that's just my boyfriend," Jenny said, almost apologetically, noticing the crestfallen gaze which flashed across his face at her mention of the word 'boyfriend'.

"Probably doing push-ups or star-jumps or something equally as annoying," added Sharon.

Adam flushed slightly, recovering his composure almost immediately. "Right then," he said, matter-of-factly, "I'd better get started on these fires."

The other girls shared a look which Jenny did not acknowledge. They could tell instantly that their friend fancied Adam, and that the feeling was reciprocated. Adam was the image of his father, just as tall and broad-shouldered but without a beard and with longer hair. The impression he had made on the girls within his first few minutes of meeting them was enough to convince them that he would be a far superior choice of partner for their friend than her present lover. Carey especially, made a promise to herself that she would do everything in her power to force the issue should the circumstances allow.

Having unpacked the coffee, milk and sugar, the girls brewed up a large pot of coffee. Carey called to Adam to ask how he took his. Once prepared, she gave the mug to Jenny and asked her to take it to him, pretending not to notice Jenny's eyes light up when the offer was made. There was definitely a connection there.

At that moment the others arrived from the generator room. The three men stood in the doorway stamping excess snow off themselves.

"Coffee?" asked Jan from the kitchen area, holding up the pot.

"Marry me goddess," replied Tom with a broad grin. "Black with two sugars please."

Jan turned before anyone could tell she was blushing again. The stirring feeling she had in her stomach whenever Tom spoke to her unnerved and excited her in equal measure. No one else in the room seemed to notice her reaction which she was grateful for. Doubtless because of the age gap none of them considered the situation as anything more than harmless banter with an innocent splash of flirtation.

But Jan was beginning to wonder to herself what it was about this man that seemed to be having such a profound effect on her feelings. He made her feel like a schoolgirl with a crush on her teacher, and she liked it. Though she was not prepared to share her feelings with anyone else for now, not even her best friends, she was content to just wait and see where these emotions might take her.

Adam had finished laying the wood in the fireplace. He lit it to a chorus of cheers as the flames licked hungrily at the logs. Snapping and crackling they created an instant arc of warmth which everyone moved in on.

Jenny handed Adam his mug and they clinked before drinking.

"What's all this then!" A sudden boom from the top of the stairs as Scott started to descend. His presence seemed to bring an automatic dampener to the proceedings which everyone felt. Jenny, suddenly feeling very guilty for even standing this close to Adam, rushed over to her boyfriend and took him by the arm, guiding him towards the rest of the group, and Adam especially.

"This is Adam; he's Tom's son and has just built us our first fire." She purposely kept her tone light for everybody's sake, determined not to give Scott an excuse to cause an unpleasant scene.

Adam switched hands with his mug so that he could extend his right one towards the new arrival. "Hello mate, Adam Meadows."

Scott straightened his back as he strode over, trying to boost his height with his rigid stance, but still he was several inches shorter than Adam. He eyed him suspiciously as they shook; he and Jenny had looked far too furtive when Scott arrived for his liking. In his mind Scott was sizing up to his rival. He was trying his best to be subtle but that had never been his forte.

Sharon and Carey both caught each others' gaze as they raised their eyes. Adam did not seem at all fazed by Scott's conduct. Secretly, he actually found the situation quite amusing. Adam was not just taller than Scott, he had also inherited his father's natural broadness across the shoulders, and plenty of outdoor work had put a decent amount of muscle on his frame. He made a point of never using his size to intimidate, but on this occasion he was happy to make an exception whilst still affecting his most charming character.

Once the two men had released their grips, Jenny quickly moved in and veered Scott towards the roaring log fire. "Isn't this glorious?" she said, enthusiastically. "Won't it be wonderful to cuddle up in front of this while the snow is falling outside?"

Scott shrugged. "Suppose," he grunted, in a totally noncommittal manner.

Tom drained his mug and took it through to the sink, grabbing his son's empty from him as he passed. Returning back to the main reception area he announced, "Well now the fires blazing, is there anything you lovely people need before we go?"

Jan felt her heart sink. She really did not want Tom to leave. That schoolgirl crush taking over again.

"Oh could you show us how the hot water is controlled, please," asked Sharon.

"Certainly," responded Tom, "just follow me."

Sharon, Carey and Jan followed the big man back into the kitchen area. Tom pointed to a small rectangular box with a circular dial on the wall.

"This," he began, "is your temperature control, and with it you can regulate the heating and the hot water." He demonstrated how to use the timer and showed them the pre-settings one by one. The girls nodded their understanding as he spoke, and Tom was more convinced that they were taking it all in, than he had been with Greg and Steve earlier when he was showing them how to operate the generator.

"Any questions?" he asked, once he was finished. The girls shook their heads. "Right then, I guess we'll be off." Tom walked towards the door with Adam following. Before leaving he said, "Should you run out of supplies the town boasts several reputable establishments, all of which I can heartily recommend." He had everyone's attention except for Scott's, who had slumped into an armchair in front of the fire.

"I've got your number should we get into any difficulty," said Sharon, "but I'm sure we'll be ok."

"Ah," replied Tom, looking a little awkward, "as I think I may have mentioned earlier, mobile reception is not great around here, it's because of all the hills, you can always try of course but I cannot tell you a specific place it would be best to stand to guarantee reception, but the wifi connection seems fine, I've written the password down on the information board by the front door."

As Tom spoke everyone began taking out their devices to check on the reception. Greg and Steve walked around the ground floor trying for a signal, the others looked on hopefully, but eventually the two lads gave up without success.

"Oh well," said Carey, trying to sound positive. "We said we all wanted a quiet break away from it all, looks like we've got our wish."

"If you need us for anything, we're only about a mile away," offered Adam. "Just follow the road back the way you came and it's the second turning on the right, you can't miss us."

"I thought you lived in town?" said Sharon.

"No, I rent an office in town but we live up here, so if you scream loud enough we should be able to hear you," replied Tom, with a cheeky grin.

****

"Hold on a second," called Adam from the passenger seat of the plough.

"What's up?" asked Tom, slowing down before bringing the vehicle to a complete halt.

"Over there," Adam pointed off to his left. Tom strained to see out of the far side window. A combination of the darkness and the snowfall made his field of view too narrow to see what his son was alluding too.

"What does it look like?" enquired Tom, still letting the machine idle rather than switch it off. He had no doubt that it would re-start straight away, but somehow he did not want to take the risk.

"Not sure," answered Adam. "It's something dark buried under the snow. Might be an animal, but it's hard to tell from here."

"Come on then," Tom ensured that the handbrake was firmly on and the gears in neutral. "Let's go and take a look, just in case."

The two men left the plough and walked towards the dark shape protruding above the latest drift. The wind, though exceptionally cold, could not penetrate their outer clothing; however a biting blast took both men's breath away as they emerged from the vehicle. Adam held his gloved hand over his mouth to assist with his breathing while Tom lifted his scarf to cover his nose and mouth.

As they approached the protuberance both men noticed the dark stains melting into the snow around it. Tom was the first to realise that it was blood, and put his arm out to stop his son getting any closer.

Tom turned and surveyed the immediate area, suddenly apprehensive. Adam, seeing his father's hesitation began to scour the area too. The snow fall limited their vision to no more than thirty feet, but it was enough to reassure them that there was no immediate danger.

Tom moved in for a closer look. He quickly realised that the object was not an animal but an item of clothing. He moved it to one side with his boot, clearing away the top layers of snow. It was a black leather jacket, the type commonly worn by bikers. Upon closer inspection he confirmed that the dark patches were definitely blood, and by the amount he uncovered beneath the snow he could tell that whoever had spilt it had more than a minor cut or injury.

Tom bent down and finding a blood-free corner lifted the garment off the ground. It was then that the two men noticed that the jacket was torn to shreds and what was left of the fabric was absolutely saturated.

They looked at each other for a moment, and then in unison they both turned to survey their surroundings once more. There was no sign of the jacket's owner, and judging from the quantity of blood and the general state of the item they both figured that its wearer could not have been in much of a condition to go very far.

"What should we do?" called Adam, removing his hand from his mouth so that he would be understood.

Tom thought for a moment before replying. "We'd better get the torches and have a look around. Whoever this belongs to might have tried to crawl away to find help and could be lying nearby unconscious."

They both returned to the plough to gather up torches and whistles so that each could signal to the other if they found something or found themselves in trouble. Tom carried the blood-stained remains of the jacket back to the cab and placed it on a plastic sheet he found in the back, being careful not to let any of the blood drip on the upholstery.

Tom decided on reflection to switch off the engine, but kept the lights on full beam to clear a pathway. They set off in different directions each agreeing on how much ground they would cover before starting back to the plough.

They searched the surrounding area for any sign of a survivor, or at least some indication of which direction he or she might have taken. More blood smears in the snow, or another discarded item of clothing would show that they were making progress. But the going was slow. Each followed the luminous halo of their respective torches as they studied the territory, but after thirty minutes neither had found any evidence to give weight to their theory that someone needed help.

Tom climbed over the highest drift so that he could look down the precipice for any sign of a crashed vehicle. He was careful not to edge too close as it was difficult from this point to tell what was solid ground as opposed to built up snow. In the darkness the drop did not reveal anything significant. His torch beam melted away into the abyss blending with the darkness and creating the illusion of a dark morass like some kind of devilish black hole waiting to swallow anyone unfortunate enough to fall in.

Eventually, both Tom and Adam made their way back to the plough.

"Anything?" asked Tom, once Adam was within shouting distance.

Adam shrugged and shook his head, turning off his torch. "What do you think happened to them?"

"Who knows, it might have been an accident and the other driver took the injured one back to town."

Adam thought for a second. "But where is the other vehicle then? If only one person was badly hurt where are the remains of his bike?"

"That's a point," thought Tom solemnly, rubbing his chin through his scarf. "Maybe the other driver managed to put it in the back of his vehicle, somehow." It did not sound especially plausible, even to Tom himself, but the entire situation was strange. Accidents did occur out here, more often than not after a snowfall when the roads had iced over and driving conditions were at their worst. But it was true what Adam was saying, there should have been more evidence scattered around than just one piece of clothing.

"What do you think we should do, dad?"

"Well," sighed Tom, "there's no evidence that there really was anything untoward happening here. The torn and bloody jacket might have resulted from someone having an accident and then discarding it before carrying on their way. As there's no vehicle or body we can only presume that whoever was involved was able to leave, either with help or alone."

"Do you think it's worth reporting?" asked Adam.

"Not really," replied Tom. "I'll keep hold of the jacket just in case anything comes to light further down the line, but as it stands I don't think it's worth bothering the police about."

The two men returned to the plough and set off home for their dinner.

****

The creature watched the two men from up high. Crouched behind a snow-covered boulder it was perfectly masked from view. It could sense their purpose in coming here but it was far too smart to be caught out. The fact that it had not camouflaged the discarded jacket well enough was a lesson it would learn from. It knew now that it should have thrown it over the cliff along with the mangled motorbike.

On the ground beside the Beast lay the crumpled half-eaten corpse of Weasel.

The creature waited for the snow plough to leave the vicinity entirely before it hoisted Weasel's remains on its mighty shoulder and set off deeper into the snow-covered hills for privacy to finish its meal.

CHAPTER SIX

Everyone was exhausted after the day's events. Once the unpacking ceremony was completed the group congregated around the roaring log fire. Sharon and Carey volunteered to make soup and cheese and ham toasties for everyone, washed down with either beer, wine or coffee.

As the evening progressed everyone could feel themselves drifting off. The exertions of the journey, the hot soup and the crackling fire all combined with the alcohol consumed, was a perfect combination to induce sleep.

Sharon drained her glass of wine savouring the last remnants. She was tempted to ask Steve for a refill but her eyes were heavy and she knew she would appreciate the sleep more. She lifted herself off her boyfriend and placed her glass on the table. She was about to announce her retirement when at that moment, the lights went out.

The room was plunged into darkness save for the eerie glow from the fire which cast shadows that flicked and danced around the walls and across the floor.

"Oh, oh," Greg was the first to speak. "That's not a good sign for things to come."

Everyone began to shuffle and move into more upright positions, the darkness making them feel suddenly more vulnerable.

"That's got to be the generator, right?" asked Jan with a slight tremble in her voice which was barely evident through her fatigue.

"Has to be," replied Sharon. "Time for our heroes to go out and earn their crust." She turned towards Steve who was fumbling in the fire glow to ensure that he did not spill his can of beer as he placed it on the table.

It took a moment for Sharon's words to register. "What, you mean go out there, now, in this?"

"In what, exactly?" demanded Carey. "It's only a couple of hundred feet away, what are you afraid of?"

Steve looked at Greg as if in need of support. Greg rubbed the sleep from his eyes. He too had just about been ready to call it a night and like his friend, he did not relish the thought of traipsing out in the snow at this hour. "Can't we leave it until tomorrow babe?" he asked, pitifully. "After all, we are all ready for bed anyway."

"I was going to use my laptop for a while," said Jan. "It's not life and death but I would appreciate it."

"Do you have to plug it in?" asked Steve, trying to keep the irritation out of his voice.

"Yes, the battery's dead, I need to charge it."

"I won't be able to see to take my make-up off," Jenny chimed in.

"Me too," stated Carey, ensuring that Greg received the message loud and clear by jabbing him in the back with her foot.

Greg groaned and looked at his friend. Steve shot a glance skywards and pushed himself off the floor. "All right, all right, we get the message. Come on mate, let's bundle up, it's gonna be freezing out there."

"Oh hark at them," Sharon whined in a mocking tone. "Anyone would think that we were sending them out to the North Pole."

"Feel free to go in our place," offered Steve.

Sharon placed her thumbs inside her mouth and stretched her lips as she poked out her tongue as far as it would stretch. Steve could not help himself burst out laughing. Sharon knew her funny face worked every time, even managing to calm down awkward moments during an argument, so she always used it to its full effect.

While Steve and Greg bundled up, the girls cleared away the debris from the table. Scott ensured that the fire was properly stacked so that there was no risk of any of the logs toppling off while they burnt themselves out. Once he was satisfied he secured the metal guard in place.

Sharon and Carey both kissed their respective partners before shoving them out into the snow, and then everyone began slowly making their way upstairs in the semi-darkness. Jenny clutched Scott's arm to help her balance when her thick socks lost purchase on the varnished wood.

"Oi!" Scott tried to jerk his arm away, but Jenny refused to let go. "What ya'doin'?"

"I nearly fell, help me."

Scott grunted his response and shoved Jenny in front of him, slapping her hard on her bottom as she passed him, causing her to yelp.

The other girls gave each other a knowing look. None of them liked the new Scott, and Jan especially wished that the old Scott would come back before the rest of the group finally gave up on him and started excluding him and Jenny from their group outings. Everyone loved Jenny, but they all knew that it would take an awful lot for her to finally dump him.

Sharon and Carey sat on the bottom step to remove their boots and socks, both deciding that barefoot was a safer bet on the polished wood. Jan was glad she had changed into her pumps earlier. The rubber soles would hold her in good stead.

They all called their "good-nights" before entering their respective rooms. Jan had left her curtains open and now her room was bathed in moonlight shafting in through the trees and casting eerie shadows like talons creeping up the walls. She walked over to the window and gazed out at the snow-covered landscape. It was like a scene from one of those Christmas films her mother always had on the telly while she was wrapping presents. The unblemished snow stretched forward covering land, trees, hills and roads as far as the eye could see. Jan opened the window wide enough to allow her to breathe in the fresh cold mountain air. It filled her lungs with icy tingles which spread down her body towards her tummy. She allowed herself three more deep lungfuls before closing the window and making her way to the bathroom to brush her teeth. She had already decided that the little make-up she was wearing could wait until her morning shower. Unlike her friends, Jan always opted for a more natural look, which complimented her pale complexion.

Once in the bathroom, Jan could hear muffled voices coming from Jenny and Scott's rom. From the sounds of it they were arguing about something, for a change. Jan stood still for a moment and tried to make out the words, but then she decided she did not want to pry on her friends so she continued with her ablutions and tried to ignore the commotion.

Scott stood naked in front of the full length mirror in his and Jenny's bedroom, scrutinising his form as he posed, turning and twisting his torso to allow the moonlight to increase the perspective of each muscle as it was stretched to its full capacity. Jenny was suspicious that he had chosen this room because of the mirror, oblivious to the fact that there were no on-suite facilities and the bed was only a double; unlike the king size ones in some of the other rooms.

Jenny's eyes wandered over her boyfriend's bare body. In truth, she was not a fan of muscles, at least not the hard, lumpy kind that Scott had gained since taking steroids. She actually preferred the old him-in more ways than one. Though he had always had a slight bulge around the middle he was never what you would call fat, just a little cuddly. And he used to have such a sweet personality, caring, loving, and considerate. In fact leading up to his "change" Jenny had started to believe that she had found her soul-mate. Now however, that could not be further from the truth.

Even their love-making had changed so drastically that it was no longer a pleasurable experience for Jenny. Gone was the patient, tender Scott who would ensure that she had reached the height of ecstasy before even considering his own pleasure. These days his erections were so few and far between-not to mention unreliable when it came to maintaining them-that the moment he felt a stirring he expected Jenny to be willing and able.

That was what their argument had been about. As soon as the bedroom door was closed Scott began to strip. In the shadowy light Jenny could see his growing erection and she knew what that would mean, but she was so tired from the journey and the day in general that all she craved was sleep.

Scott, as usual, ignored her protests and began pulling at her clothes. Ordinarily Jenny just gave in and tried her best to become aroused before he entered her. But for once she was not prepared to give in. When he acted like this, Scott was like a stranger to her and making love with him would sometimes make her feel like a rape victim.

When he finally realised that his insistence was not going to bear fruit, in his frustration Scott began his posing routine in silence, purposely ignoring Jenny in an effort to make her feel guilty and as usual, it worked.

Eventually, Jenny slumped off the bed and began removing her clothes. She purposely kept her stockings on because they had always been a turn-on for Scott. Playfully, she crept up behind him and began to rub her hands gently over his bare bottom, working her hands around his waist until she held his hard member between her fingers.

Standing on one foot, Jenny curled her other leg around Scott's, letting it slide up and down so that her stockings rubbed against his naked flesh. She could hear a low moan from deep within his throat as she gently squeezed and released his organ over and over, feeling it throb and tremble in her grasp.

Without warning Scott turned and almost knocked Jenny off her feet. He grabbed hold of her around the waist and unceremoniously hoisted her off the floor and threw her back on the bad.

Scott climbed on top of her and began massaging her breasts roughly. He forced her legs open with his knees and lay on top of her waiting for Jenny to guide him in. The impact of his landing had temporarily knocked the wind out of Jenny and she needed a moment to regain her composure. She tried to take in a few deep breaths, but Scott's weight had her virtually pinned down like a boa constrictor wrapping itself around its astonished victim.

Scott continued to knead Jenny's breasts, harder and harder to increase his arousal. But he could feel his erection starting to go flaccid. Impatiently he reached down and attempted to insert himself into Jenny's cleft, frustrated by his girlfriend's lack of commitment.

At one point he thought he could feel himself enter her, so he quickly pushed forward only to slip out and miss altogether.

Scott grunted his annoyance and keeping his hands firmly placed on Jenny's breast pushed himself up to arms length. The discomfort in Jenny's breast caused by Scott's rough handling increased to searing levels now that she was supporting most of his weight on them.

She cried out in pain but Scott seemed oblivious to her, still focused on his demands alone.

Finally, Jenny called out, "Scott, babe you're hurting me."

Scott switched his gaze from between her legs to her face, and Jenny almost wished that he had not. His eyes were wide and bulging with a look of pure hatred aimed directly at her. Jenny had seen that look before and it always scared her. They were the eyes of a maniac, and she felt as if Scott was about to pull back his arm and start punching her in the face.

Through the strain of trying to breath under his weight and ignoring the pain in her chest, Jenny tried to slip her hand down towards her boyfriend's shaft, realising that once he was inside her it would only be a matter of seconds before he exploded and eventually left her alone. But the response her fingers received when they made contact told her that the moment had passed, and from previous experience she knew that there was no way of resurrecting it.

Even so, Jenny tried gently massaging Scott's ever-shrinking member in a vain attempt to rectify the situation, but it was to no avail.

Suddenly Scott jumped off her with a grunt of anguish. Before she could stop him he kicked over the night table sending the objects on top of it flying against the wall. Fearing the commotion might bring her friends running, Jenny lifted herself off the bed and tried to coax Scott back.

At first Scott wrenched his arm away from Jenny's embrace. She moved closer ignoring his mood and gently started kissing his bare back whilst simultaneously rubbing her hands up and down his buttocks.

After a few moments she felt him relax, so took his hand and guided him back to the bed.

"Come on babe," she breathed seductively into his ear. "I'll make it better."

She guided him back onto the bed and gently pushed him back until he was lying down. She smiled and kissed him gently on the nose before making her way slowly down his torso using her tongue and lips to try and reignite his passion. By the time her head was between his legs she began to feel a more positive response. She decided for the sake of harmony if she could not arouse him sufficiently to enter her she would just use her mouth until he reached orgasm. At least that should satisfy him and finally grant her some much needed sleep.

****

Steve and Greg both looked at each other in exasperation. Each had been firmly of the opinion that they had heard and understood Adam's explanation concerning the re-starting of the generator, but having both had several unsuccessful attempts they were starting to lose faith.

"You'd think they might leave some written instructions," voiced Greg, fumbling for any excuse that might vindicate him and his friend.

"I don't understand it," Steve chimed in, throwing down the crank lever in frustration. "When he did it, it engaged first time, what did he do different to us?"

"Search me, let's leave it and come back in the morning, everything looks better in the sunlight. We could sneak upstairs and get undressed before going into our bedrooms. The girls won't make us get dressed all over again to come back out now."

Steve looked at his friend. "Are you cracked, if we turn up now without getting this stupid thing to work first, Sharon and Carey will throw us back out in the snow whether we're dressed or not!"

Upon consideration, Greg knew that his friend was right. He bent down to retrieve the discarded lever. "Well come on, I don't fancy spending the night in here."

Together they re-traced every instruction they could remember Adam relaying, conferring with each other to ensure that neither of them had missed anything.

Greg cranked the lever over and over, whilst Steve watched the reset dial and punched the start-up button as soon as it reached the top. Still there was no response. The generator just sat there in defiance. From certain angles it appeared to Steve as if the machine had a smiling face with a winking eye, almost as if it had deliberately been designed to wind-up people like him and his friend.

In desperation Greg spat saliva in one palm and rubbed his hands together. He grabbed the lever, this time with both hands, and began furiously to rotate it over and over, waiting for the merest of seconds at the top movement as Adam had instructed before slamming it back down and starting again.

Steve, seeing and feeling his friend's anger, began thumping the start-up button regardless of whether the needle was pointing straight up or not. Together they worked two independent machines with one supreme goal. Their task impossible, their labour unrequited, their opponent completely unresponsive, but they were in this together both knowing that there was no going back without victory.

Suddenly, the machine jolted and hissed steam from somewhere in the back. The men stopped what they were doing and looked from one to the other. All went quiet. Steve lifted his foot back and swung a solid kick at the machine's side. Immediately the generator sprung into life and the bulb above them came on.

Still in shock, Greg looked through the grimy window towards the cabin and he cheered loudly when he saw that the porch light was on.

The two men shook hands then hit a "high five", whooping and jumping with excitement.

They waited another five minutes in the hut just to make sure that the generator was not playing with their sanity, then once they were both convinced that they had earned their stripes, they made their way back out into the snow.

They both stood there for a while taking in the picturesque beauty of their surroundings and breathing in the clean, fresh night air. The only sound was the wind whistling through the trees, and with the protection of the cabin behind them and the hills in front of them, the main force which it whipped up was drastically reduced.

They were just about to turn back for the cabin when in the distance they heard a shrill wail which grew quickly in volume until it sounded as if the maker was directly behind the next hill, and moving closer.

The two men looked at each other and without saying a word both turned and ran for the cabin.

CHAPTER SEVEN

The Beast raised its mighty head and let forth another long cry which echoed into the night. It served many purposes which were instinctual to it. Firstly, it was a warning to any other breed which might stray into its territory. It had found some good feeding here after several weary weeks on the move, staying hidden and foraging wherever it could for food. Finally, out of desperation it had come across the two campers and the hunger in its belly had dictated its final release of that part of it which was remotely human. It had tasted fresh meat, and it had tasted so good. Now nothing else would do.

Having killed both the campers the Beast had dragged their bodies to its latest lair tucked deep within a cavernous fissure in the rocks. There it feasted on the warm, juicy meat until it had had its fill. The remains it buried deep within the snow for another time.

What surprised it more was the speed with which the hunger returned. It had noticed this over time. As a cub it remembered venturing out for food once every two to three days, satisfying its cravings on the carcases of wild or stray animals it caught. A fully grown deer would keep it satiated for several days. But recently the frequency of its hunger seemed to increase with each new kill. When it had come upon Weasel it was not hunting, but the opportunity presented was too good to ignore. So it merely decided to make a kill for another day. But once it smelt the sickly-sweet aroma of the biker's blood its desire to feed was instantly aroused. True, the man's body offered little in the way of sustenance due to the lack of meat on his bones, but the Beast still savoured each morsel until there was nothing left but a few bones it could not be bothered to gnaw on.

That was the second reason for its cry. It was fully satiated and like a wealthy man from days gone by it felt the need to show it by way of an oral emission.

The third and by far the most poignant reason behind its cry was that it sought a mate. From as far back as the Beast could remember it had always been alone. It had no memory of its parents, other kin or friendship from its like, just a vague recollection of wandering the woodland as a cub, searching in vain for comfort and the warm embrace of another of its species. Over time that yearning had manifested itself into an endless unrequited quest which had formed a permanent ache in the creature's heart. Each new moon brought with it the hope that this would be the day that somewhere over the next ridge the Beast would stumble across another of its kind, or better still a community of similar creatures who would welcome it into the set.

But it had come to realise that that was merely a fantasy which would never be. It was alone, and alone it would remain until its final day.

It had learned through experience not to trust man. Having shown itself on many occasions in the early days when it came across campers or trekkers roaming through its terrain it had always been met with a combination of fear and

46

hostility. Unable to communicate with those individuals it came across or properly demonstrate its need for companionship it quickly took to hiding whenever man was near, for fear of unprovoked retribution.

Over time the Beast had learned to hunt and forage, and had become quite adept at camouflage, especially when it was surrounded by snow. But now that it had conquered the threat of man it truly felt as if it were ruler of all it surveyed. There was no need to hide in the shadows anymore, unless it suited its purpose. Man was now its new meat animal and so long as there was a constant supply, the Beast did not feel the need to move on again.

But for all that, it still exercised caution. It had seen the power of man at work when they outnumbered their prey by several to one. They possessed something which made a big bang noise that could drop a charging or fleeing animal from several hundred feet away without exertion. The noise their weapon made was deafening, but only lasted for a second. And the aroma left behind was unmistakable, and one which the Beast had learned to detect on the wind from miles away, giving it ample warning if men were approaching with their weapons of death in their hands.

As the Beast grew in size, stature and years, it had begun to wonder if it would ever be powerful enough to withstand the force of the machines of death. It knew from the reaction of its victims when it first came into their sight that its sheer size could often freeze humans in their tracks, unable to move even as it lurched closer until eventually it was too late and escape was impossible. But still it had never attempted a face to face attack on a human armed with a weapon of death. Its inner instinct still advised caution.

The snow was starting to fall once more. The cold crisp wind whistled through the range, disrupting the settled powder and swirling it up into dust sheets which drifted through the air before settling once more and blending into the latest covering.

The Beast lurched across the most recent drift, its footprints starting to refill with new snow as soon as it moved on. The cold did not cause it any discomfort, for it had a built-in defence system which adapted to all weather conditions.

It knew where its destination lay. It had watched the two men earlier surveying the remains of the biker, and once it had fed, it followed the trail they had made back to the cabin. Through the trees it watched the people inside huddled around the fire, laughing and drinking and finally settling down.

When the two men came out to visit the smaller dwelling nearby, the Beast retreated into the shadows and finally moved away from the compound. But now that night had taken over and all seemed still, it had decided to take a closer look at the inhabitants.

As the Beast approached the clearing it held back to ensure that there was no one stirring either inside or out. Once it was satisfied that the coast was clear it crept out from the protection of its leafy shelter and slowly made its way towards the cabin.

Standing on the fringe of the protection afforded by the surrounding foliage the Beast sniffed the air. There was no scent of man nearby. No fires, no aroma of cooking, no scent left on clothes hung out to dry for morning. It was safe to proceed. Camouflaged by the thick white covering of snow all around it, the creature ventured towards the cabin, its senses keened to react to the slightest movement.

As it drew nearer to the cabin it focused on the gloom inside. There was no discernable movement from within. It surmised that all those inside were asleep. That made them easy prey. Taken by surprise in the dead of night its victims would be despatched before being able to protect themselves.

But first the outer casing would have to be breached. The Beast was more used to attacking those whose only cover came from fabric tents. The cabin was an altogether different matter. With sturdy walls and windows which could give the Beast's presence away to warn those inside, attacking the cabin would only be as a last resort if it was starving. As it was, it was still satiated from the earlier kill, and it knew that it had stored supplies as a back-up.

For now it was more curious than anything else. Inquisitive as to the number of humans dwelling within and, more importantly, to try and discover if they had any machines of death.

The Beast moved slowly around the perimeter of the cabin, the compacted snow crunching beneath its enormous bulk. It kept its eyes peeled, darting from side to side to catch any movement however slight. Even though it felt confident it could handle anything that might come rushing at it from within the cabin, it could still feel the adrenalin coursing through its body tinged with a combination of excitement and anxiety in equal measure.

Ideally, it did not want to be discovered, preferring to merely observe this time. But if the occasion presented itself it was ready to strike, always on the defensive its innermost quest being that of survival.

Having made a complete circle of the cabin and having seen no evidence of any movement from within, it ventured closer to see in through one of the larger windows. There was nothing on display to cause it alarm. Its eyes penetrated the gloom as its hot fetid breath clouded the glass.

Having moved around the building again and peering in through the other windows the creature was satisfied that there were no machines of death inside. Moving backwards it raised its head and gazed up to the second floor. Those windows would also need to be checked to be absolutely sure.

The Beast knew that climbing the cabin would not be a problem. It could scale the tallest trees in a matter of seconds and climb the surrounding mountains at a faster pace than most humans could run on flat ground. But it was still wary of making a noise and disturbing the inhabitants. This venture was about stealth and discovery, not attack and alarm, so caution was still the key.

The Beast stood there thinking, its hulking frame motionless but for the effort of breathing, its white coat blending in perfectly with the snowy surroundings appearing from a distance to all intents and purposes like someone's enthusiastic attempt at a snowman. In the distance a night bird called, its cry was soon answered by others of its breed, a gathering of the species for comfort, protection or just to communicate with others like itself.

The Snow Beast once again felt the stabbing pain of longing. It wanted to let out its own cry to summon others to it, but it knew only too well that it would be in vain. Besides which, its call would alert those inside to its presence, and that was not the effect it desired.

****

Jenny woke from a deep sleep. Her naked body was covered in Goosebumps from the cold night air which wafted in through the window Scott had insisted they keep open. He always insisted on sleeping with at least one window ajar, even on the coldest of nights. It was bad enough back home during the winter but out here in the wilderness the air felt far icier and bitter.

Scott had stolen the duvet, cocooning himself within its warmth leaving her to freeze. It had taken Jenny ages to satisfy him that night. Even with her best efforts he continually kept losing his erection. Jenny tried every trick she knew-as well as a few new ones out of desperation-until eventually his warm thickness spouted over her hands.

Scott's height of ecstasy was equalled by Jenny's overwhelming relief at finally managing to make him reach orgasm. She knew from past experience how impossible Scott's mood swings could be, but they were never worse then when he could not manage it.

Once he was satisfied, Scott turned over and without a word or gesture of appreciation soon fell asleep.

Jenny reached over to the box of tissues on the nightstand to dry her hands. She resisted the urge to go to the bathroom to wash them in case her movement woke Scott. It was best to let him fall into a deep sleep before risking such a venture.

As she lay there her mind drifted back to Adam, Tom's son. She imagined it was him lying beside her, only in this scenario they would have just made love with him refusing to reach orgasm until she was properly satisfied.

Then, once they were both spent, he would gently withdraw himself and roll onto his back ensuring that he covered any damp patches with his own body before gently pulling her towards him and holding her in his warm, tender embrace. There they would lie until they both drifted off into oblivion together.

She released an audible sigh before she could stop herself. Scott stirred, half-rolled back then slumped forward again. Jenny held her breath for a moment in anticipation of Scott waking, and then he began to snore. Finally, Jenny allowed herself to relax once more until she too drifted off.

Now that the cold had woken her up, Jenny knew that she would not get back to sleep without being warm again. There was no point in trying to prise the duvet away from Scott, at the very least she would wake him up from the effort and then there would be hell to pay.

She decided to get up and put some clothes on, that way at least she might be able to drift back off without disturbing Scott.

Slowly she rolled over and eased herself off the bed. The moonlight shafting through the window bathed her nakedness in a silvery glow. For a moment she stood there gazing out into the darkness. She wondered if miles away out of sight there might be another cabin with someone watching her through a powerful pair of binoculars at this very moment.

The thought thrilled her. She imagined the watcher might be Adam. She closed her eyes and licked her lips feeling the soft wet sheen her tongue left in its wake. She began to slide her hands slowly down her taut torso, the friction bringing temporary relief from the cold. As she did so, she imagined that the hands belonged to Adam though his would be rougher, manlier, callused and coarse from all the manual labour he and his Father had to undertake to keep their business afloat.

Though Jenny loved men who were intellectuals, deep down she had a fond respect for those who made their living with their hands. She put it down to the fact that her Father had been a labourer who died in a works accident when she was eight. She could still remember the odour of the dried sweat and concrete dust on his body when he used to come home in the evening and she would run into his arms as he picked her up and held her in his loving embrace.

Yes, there was something about Adam she had decided. Though they had only met briefly she felt sure that he would make a perfect partner. Kind, considerate, attentive, loving, strong, someone who would take charge without making her feel incapable or feeble.

A sudden bout of snoring from underneath the duvet brought her round from her reverie.

Jenny let her hands fall away from her body, her nakedness in front of the large window suddenly making her feel vulnerable.

Tip-toeing to the wardrobe she eased the wooden door open slowly to eradicate as best she could the chance of any unwanted creaks. She chose a pair of woolly socks, some track pants, tee-shirt and a jumper, and carried them out with her into the corridor towards the bathroom on the other side of the landing.

It suddenly occurred to her that if one of the others happened to have woken up to get a drink or go to the toilet they might catch her naked. If it was one of the girls she would not care so much, but the thought of it being one of the boys quickened her pace until she was safely behind a locked door.

Jenny pulled the light cord but there was no reaction. She pulled it twice more as if repeating the gesture might connect the switch, but the room remained in shadow save for the moonlight which lit up the window frame from outside, almost making it look as if it was daylight behind the frosted glass.

Jenny dressed and used the toilet. As she washed her hands, she turned to one side to use the guest towel hanging on the rail. As she did so she caught a sudden glimpse from the corner of her eye of a shadow passing the window on the outside.

Jenny spun around to face the glass.

The shadow was gone. She questioned in her mind if it had ever been there.

She stood there for a moment focusing on the pane, staring intently for any signs of movement on the other side. There was nothing.

Jenny frowned. She was sure that she had seen something, the question was what. She expected to hear all kinds of strange and alien noises being in such unfamiliar territory, but a shadow had to be made by something substantial regardless of where it was. And a silhouette seen out here in the middle of the night was just as ominous as one witnessed back at home, if not more so considering they were supposed to be in the middle of nowhere.

Jenny collected her thoughts. She decided against waking the rest of the household in the middle of the night based on something she was not sure she had seen. And even if she had, there might be a very rational and ordinary reason behind it.

The shadow-if it existed-had moved from left to right, so Jenny fathomed that if she were to make her way along the corridor to the large bay window at the far end, she would have a much better view of the surrounding area, and anything which might be making its way around the house would certainly be visible from there.

Gently, Jenny eased the bathroom door open and began to edge her way along the corridor. Her thick winter socks slid along the varnished floorboards unable to make purchase on the polished wood. A couple of times Jenny was forced to reach out and use the dado rail for balance.

Concentrating on not slipping over, Jenny reached the window and looked out on the snow-covered picture-postcard view below. Edging closer until she could touch the glass, Jenny turned to her right and looked out as far as the angle would allow. She could see the shed that housed the generator and the ends of their cars jutting out from beneath the parapet.

She turned to her left, and saw the face of the Snow Beast staring back at her.

Jenny's initial reaction was to scream, but in her haste to move as far away from the window and the Beast beyond as possible, she slipped on the wooden floor and landed on her rump with a thud, her head barely missing the window ledge as she fell.

The sudden jolt from her landing left her winded. Ignoring the pain that was now searing up from her tailbone, Jenny fell forward and began scrabbling along the floor. She was still barely able to catch her breath but was desperate to get as far away from the fragile glass with the monster on the other side as she could.

Once she felt her breath returning Jenny let out an ear-piercing scream which echoed through the corridor and brought everyone running from their rooms.

The welcoming sight of her friends gave Jenny the strength to look behind her. She knew that the creature had not broken through or she would have heard the glass shatter, but some deep down obtuse voice was telling her that she had to see for herself.

"Jenny, what is it, what happened?" Sharon was the first to reach her. She placed a comforting hand on her friend's shoulder, there was obvious concern in her voice and etched on her face.

Jenny pushed herself up from the floor, Sharon and Jan took an arm each and helped her to her feet. Before either of them let her go, Jenny started to slump forward again, Steve just managing to grab her and support her weight in time.

Jenny fell against Steve, burying her face in his tee-shirt as she began to sob uncontrollably.

Sharon turned to Scott who was standing behind everyone else. "What happened Scott?" She could not help the accusatory tone in her voice.

Scott shrugged his shoulders. "I was asleep when I heard her scream," he offered, defensively. Sharon could tell that he was clearly as bemused as the rest of them. She turned her attention back to Jenny who had pulled herself away from Steve so that she could wipe her eyes and nose.

Jenny was feeling a little stronger now, the initial shock starting to fade. She turned and took another look at the window where she had seen the Beast. Again there was no sign of anything.

Jan immediately picked up on Jenny's reaction. "Did you see something outside? Was someone out there looking in at you?"

Jenny turned to her friend nodding through another flood of tears.

Jan placed her arm around her friend as Steve and the boys strode towards the large window at the end of the corridor. Sharon and Carey watched them go. Carey felt a tremor in her stomach. She knew only too well that Greg would be the first one to go charging in playing the hero, and as usual he would doubtless end up on the receiving end of the worst of it.

The three men scanned the surrounding area from behind the glass. Other than a quick glimpse of some woodland creatures scurrying through the brush there was no sign of anything untoward. They stayed there for a good few minutes before passing a look between each other as if to say that Jenny must have imagined it.

Their mutual expression was not wasted on Sharon who glared at them when they reached her gaze, silently warning them to choose their words carefully before upsetting her friend even more. Once she was confident that she had conveyed her feelings to them she turned back to concentrate on helping Jenny.

"There's nothing there now hon," she offered, comfortingly, "whoever it was has gone."

The men re-joined the group.

"Was it a bloke?" asked Greg, "a peeping-Tom?" He looked at the other two men. "Maybe we should get dressed and take a look around outside, see if the bugger's still there, he might be hiding in the bushes somewhere?"

"Good idea," chimed in Steve, "and if we find him we can lock him in one of the outbuildings until the police arrive."

"Yea," Scott agreed, "after he slips over a few times and smashes his face in."

Carey looked up to heaven. Jan caught the look which summed up exactly how she was feeling too. "Listen," she offered in her calmest voice, "wouldn't it make more sense to all stay together and wait until daylight before charging off half-cocked into the wilderness?"

The girls agreed, but it was clear from their body-language that the men were now officially on a mission. "It might be too late by then," offered Greg. "We need to get out there whilst there's still a chance of catching the bloke."

Jenny let out another huge sob. "It...It wasn't a...Man, I saw...It was....A..." Her words tapered off as her tears returned.

The others all looked from Jenny to one another. The girls agreed without speaking that they should leave their friend to compose herself before continuing.

Scott on the other hand was not prepared to be so patient. "A what?" he demanded, placing his hands on his hips. "If it wasn't a man what was it?"

The girls sighed inwardly at Scott's lack of tact. Before any of them could react, he waded in again. "Come on Jenny, for god's sake, what did you see?"

"Ok, that's enough for now," said Sharon, turning her back on Scott and moving between him and Jenny. "Why don't we all go downstairs and make a hot drink, give Jenny a chance to collect her thoughts."

Scott, evidently not happy at being ignored was not willing to let it rest. "Right, you lot go down and put the kettle on, we're going to get dressed and make a search." He turned to the two other lads who nodded their agreement.

Carey could feel her patience slipping. She wanted to grab Greg and beg him not to go out, but she knew that would not help the situation and would only end up embarrassing him, which in turn would make him all the more determined to go with the others.

Instead she guided her friends towards the stairs, and called back over her shoulder. "Ok, if you boys want to go out and play Rambo, fine. Just remember that you're leaving us girls alone and unguarded, so thanks for that!"

Her words struck home with Greg as she had hoped they would. He looked at the other two. Steve too was now showing more concern, but Scott's face was forming into a mask of growing thunder.

"Maybe we should all just stay together," Greg finally offered, trying hard to sound concerned and not cowardly.

"You might be right at that," agreed Steve.

Scott stood there breathing hard through his nostrils, his face becoming redder by the second. Finally, he threw his hands up in the air in disgust and strode back into his room, slamming the door behind him without saying a word.

The two boys followed the girls downstairs.

Jan brewed up a pot of herbal tea for everyone. The boys fetched blankets and duvets from upstairs as everyone was shivering, including them.

After a while Sharon felt the time had arrived to tentatively ask Jenny what had frightened her. Placing her mug on the table with a quivering hand, Jenny looked up and through a fresh batch of tears, began to speak.

"I know that you'll all think that I've gone round the bend," she began, "and I appreciate that it was the middle of the night and I was still probably half asleep, but I swear that when I looked out of the window I saw a...Monster!"

Jenny looked up at all her friends in turn. She could not blame them for the expressions on their faces. She knew how crazy she sounded and appreciated that if roles were reversed she would probably feel the same.

Even so, she felt comfortable enough with the group to be honest with them. They had known her long enough to know that she was not the type to make up stories or tell lies.

Before any of them could respond, she continued. "Look, I realise how insane I sound, but I don't know how else to describe what I saw."

"What exactly did it look like?" ventured Greg. "I mean, are we talking Vampire, Werewolf, Ghoul?"

Carey shot her boyfriend a stern glance. He shrugged as if trying to explain that his request was in earnest and he was not just trying to make Jenny feel stupid.

Jenny cleared her throat. "Well, if you put it like that, I suppose it looked like what I expect the Abominable Snowman to look like."

There was silence from the group for a moment as they all tried to take in Jenny's words. Then Steve suddenly snapped his fingers as if an idea had struck him out of the blue. "It must have been a bear, you saw a bear. Who knows what kind of wildlife roams these hills."

Jenny wiped her eyes, grateful for the fact that her friends at least were taking her seriously. She wished that she could just reason with what Steve was saying and accept it, but she knew deep down that she would only be lying to herself.

Jenny took another gulp of tea to steady herself. She looked over at Steve and gave him a thankful half smile. "If it was a bear, it was like nothing I have ever seen before in a zoo or on the telly."

"How do you mean?" asked Carey.

Jenny took in a deep breath. "Well, for a start it was covered in white fur, but not like a polar bear, much thicker and more grizzled. And the face," she shivered involuntarily and pulled the duvet around her more tightly. "The face was grotesque. I mean, I know I only saw it for a second or two, but those features were more human than animal. I just remember the nose did not protrude like a bear's and the teeth were just huge fangs. And those eyes," she shivered again. "They were red and so menacing, they looked straight at me as if it just wanted to smash its way in and......" She tapered off as she tried to stop a fresh burst of tears turning into full-blown sobs.

Sharon left the comfort of her blanket and moved over to comfort her friend.

After a moment, Jan spoke up. "You know, considering what Jenny saw outside the window, I've just remembered that on the way up here I thought I saw something far away in the distance." They all looked at her. Jan held her hands up. "I can't be sure what I saw, or even if I did in fact see anything, it might have been snow-blindness for all I know, but for a second I did think I could see something large standing on a ledge far off in the distance."

"Why didn't you say something at the time?" asked Steve, perplexed.

"Like I said, it all happened so fast and was so unexpected, I'm still not sure I actually saw anything. But hearing Jenny's explanation I definitely think we should make some enquires tomorrow."

"Good idea," agreed Steve, "we can ask your boyfriend if he knows anything about it."

Jan threw a well-aimed cushion at him which caught him square in the face. "Ow!"

"Serves you right," laughed Sharon.

The distraction served to break any tension left in the atmosphere.

They stayed up talking for another half an hour, then Steve and Greg re-checked that all the windows and doors were secure before they all went back up to bed.

CHAPTER EIGHT

Because of their disrupted nights sleep, most of the group slept in later than usual. Jenny had spent a fitful night tossing and turning, waking intermittently then trying to relax enough to go back to sleep and preferably not dream about what she had seen. Scott for his part was already sound asleep by the time she went back up to bed, and there he stayed throughout the rest of the night.

When Jenny woke for the last time, she saw that the sun was shafting in through the curtains. Sleepily she checked the time on her phone and saw that it was after ten. She could hear some movement from downstairs so presumed that some of the others were already awake.

Scott was not in bed with her but that was not unusual. Back at home he was forever setting his alarm for an early morning work-out or run, so Jenny simply presumed that he had done the same thing here.

Jenny threw back the covers and pulled on an old track suit. As she made her way downstairs she could smell the welcoming aroma of frying bacon and hot coffee brewing. She found Sharon and Jan in the kitchen finishing off the breakfast.

"Morning," Jan was the first to see Jenny arrive.

"Hi," Jenny looked at her friends somewhat sheepishly. "Sorry again about last night, I guess it ruined everyone's first night of the holiday."

Sharon put down her cup and crossed over to give her friend a hug. "Don't be so daft, you were scared out of your tree, and to be honest if I had seen what you saw so would I."

"Me too," Jan chimed in.

Jenny smiled sheepishly. "Thanks for being so understanding. It all feels like a bad dream now, but it was real enough last night!"

They laid out the breakfast things and Sharon called up to the others to tell them it was ready.

"Has anyone seen Scott?" Jenny asked.

"He went out for a morning run," replied Jan. "He told us not to bother with any breakfast for him, he said he would make his own."

Jenny sighed. "Yes, that sounds like him."

"How was he when you went back to bed?" asked Sharon.

"Dead to the world," replied Jenny. Then as if to justify her boyfriend's actions she added, "He says he needs his sleep to help his body repair from his workouts."

Jan and Sharon just smiled in response, neither wanting to say anything that might upset their friend.

In the background they heard the others coming down the stairs.

During breakfast no one mentioned the events of the previous night. Both Sharon and Carey had warned their other halves not to say anything which might cause Jenny any embarrassment. They both accepted that their partners could both come up short in the tact department at times.

As they were finishing up, Scott arrived from his run. He offered a cursory greeting to everyone without making any effort to single out Jenny, then he crossed through to the kitchen to prepare his post-workout protein shake.

The girls especially wondered how much longer Jenny could put up with Scott's behaviour. In truth they had all been surprised when Scott agreed to come along on the trip. He had grown so far apart from the rest of the gang over the last year that he was only invited out of respect for Jenny.

As they cleared away the breakfast dishes, Sharon took Jenny to one side.

"I've e-mailed Tom and asked if he has any ideas on what you might have seen last night." Sharon noticed Jenny still looking a little sheepish at the mention of it. "He seemed as bewildered as us," Sharon continued, "but he's promised to drop down with Adam and have a look around, just in case."

Sharon could not help but notice Jenny flush slightly, she wondered if it was because she felt guilty for the fuss she thought she was causing, or was it merely the mention of Adam's name? Sharon remembered the instant connection between Adam and Jenny when they had first met, and she knew that she was not the only one to have noticed it.

Before Jenny could reply, Scott called out to her. "I need you to do my back babe, I want to shower."

Jenny merely raised her eyes to Sharon and followed him up. She had told them previously that in order to keep his skin looking taut and smooth she had to shave Scott's back for him at least once a week. Clearly today was the day.

Tom and Adam arrived about half-an-hour later. Jan who had been sitting on the bay window saw their vehicle pull up so she discreetly settled her clothing and checked her pony-tail without the others seeing, before opening the door.

When Tom saw her his eyes lit up. "Morning beautiful," he said, smiling. Jan felt herself blush in spite of herself and punched him playfully on the arm as he entered.

The others gathered around, all except for Scott and Jenny who were both still in the bathroom. The new arrivals declined the offer of coffee and were keen to hear about Jenny's ordeal.

In Jenny's absence, Sharon and Carey filled in most of the details. Tom and Adam listened intently. Incredulous as the story sounded, they took every word at face value. Tom had always prided himself on being the kind of person who could judge another's character within a short time of meeting them. And to that end he was confident that Sharon and her group were not the type to spin tall tales.

"So what do you think it could have been?" asked Carey, eagerly.

Tom took in a deep breath which he let out slowly before answering. "Well, judging by the description I would have to guess at some sort of bear, but the only bears in the vicinity are the ones in the zoo which is over ten miles away. So unless one of them has escaped and the authorities have not reported it, I can't think what it was your friend saw."

"There haven't been any other unusual sightings that you know of?" Sharon shot a quick side glance as she heard Jenny starting to descend the staircase.

"No, nothing like that, least of all not around these parts."

Jenny smiled weakly as she entered the living area. "I take it you're discussing my incident last night?" she asked, tentatively.

Adam caught her eye and smiled warmly. "Yes, your friends were just telling us about it, you must have been scared stiff?"

Jenny laughed. There was a touch of relief that she was not being instantly dismissed as some kind of fruitcake by Adam and his father. "You can say that again, it's lucky I had just used the bathroom otherwise I may have had an unfortunate accident there on the landing."

Everyone laughed at her joke, easing the mood and relieving any last remnants of trepidation Jenny might have had at hearing her tale revealed.

Once the laughter had died down, Jan said, "Tom was just telling us that he is not aware of anything matching what we saw roaming loose in the area."

Tom suddenly looked shocked. He turned to face Jan. "You saw it too?"

Jan felt her face flush. "Well, not exactly, and not as close-up as poor Jenny. I just thought I saw something in the distance on our way up here. I didn't mention it before because I wasn't really sure that I had seen anything, it might have been a trick of the wind causing snow flurries in the distance to look like something was there."

Tom could sense Jan's awkwardness and gave her a reassuring wink.

"So what do you think we should do about it?" asked Sharon. "Should we be contacting the authorities to warn people, do you think it's safe for us to stay here come to that?"

Tom scratched his head. "Well, under the circumstances if you don't feel safe here I'll happily refund your money, I certainly don't want to put any of your lives in danger."

The group all looked at each other, then all eyes fell on Jenny.

"No, please don't cancel our holiday on my account."

"Were not saying that," Carey reassured her, "if we decided to leave it will be a joint decision made by all of us, no one's going to blame you."

"I will," replied Jenny. "Look, I know that I saw something last night, but it was all in a split-second, it could have been anything including some joker in a mask, and the more time that passes the less I am sure of what it was."

"Greg and I had a quick look around the grounds this morning," Steve piped in, "but there was no evidence of any footprints that might give us a clue as to the size of whatever Jenny saw."

"We had a cap of fresh snow falling first thing this morning," offered Adam, "so any useful prints would probably have been covered over."

"Look, I'll tell you what," offered Tom rising to his feet, "Adam and I will make a search of the surrounding area, just in case there's anything to give us a clue. Meanwhile, you can all discuss what your options are, like I say, under the circumstances if you decide you want to leave I'll understand, I won't even charge you for last night."

"That's incredibly understanding of you," said Carey. "We all appreciate it."

There was a general nod from the group, though Tom did notice that Jan looked a little crestfallen. He hoped it might be because of him, but he immediately checked himself for the thought. After all, she was young enough to be his daughter. Not that that seemed to be a concern in this day and age if you believed everything you read in the papers.

"Well you all just think on it," Tom continued, signalling to Adam to get up and follow him. "We'll have a look around and come back in an hour or so. You can tell me then what you've decided, ok?"

The others walked Tom and Adam to the door to wave them off.

Once they were alone again, Sharon began the conversation. "Right then, so what does everyone think? This has to be a joint decision between us all."

Jenny spoke up first. "I would just like to say first off, that I appreciate the fact that all of you are being so considerate towards me and not treating me like some kind of delusional looney, but I do not want this holiday to be cancelled based solely on what I saw, or think I saw, last night."

"We know Jen," offered Sharon, sympathetically, "and for what it's worth if it had been me that saw whatever it was you saw last night, I would have already been packed on my way home by now. I think you're being very brave and positive about all this."

Jenny smiled at her friend. "Thanks Sharon, I appreciate the sentiment, but part of me thinks that had I remained calm and taken a good long look at what was outside the window, none of this would even be an issue."

"Don't be so hard on yourself," reasoned Jan. "You were scared, and rightly so, regardless of what it was outside."

The others nodded their agreement.

After a moment, Greg spoke up. "Right then, I'll put my two-pennyworth in, I would like to stay."

"Me too," stated Steve, in solidarity with his friend. "Whatever it was Jenny saw didn't try to break in, and as none of us are likely to be outside late at night, why should we worry?"

The girls all looked at each other.

Jan spoke up first. "Ok, depending on what Tom and Adam say when they get back, I'm all for staying too."

"We can guess why," said Greg nudging Steve. The two men laughed together. Jan lifted another cushion as if to propel it in their direction. Both men held their hands up in submission. Even Jan could not help but laugh.

Sharon turned to Carey. "What do you say Care?"

Carey shrugged. "I'm with Jan, let's wait to hear what the men say when they get back. On the off chance they've found evidence of a local 'Beast of Bodmin' we can always pack up and leave while it's still daylight. Otherwise, I'm happy to stay."

Sharon turned to Jenny. "I'm of the same opinion, should we discuss this with Scott?"

Jenny gazed up at the ceiling. They could all hear her boyfriend moving about in their bedroom. She looked back at the group. "No, let's just keep all this between ourselves for now, no point in making matters worse."

****

"Was there a reason why we didn't mention what we found in the snow last night?" asked Adam, as he manoeuvred the 4x4 through the snow.

Tom glanced over at his son. "To be honest, I didn't want to spook them anymore than they already are, especially that girl who saw something through the window."

"What do you think she saw?"

Tom shrugged. "It's hard to say. You know what some of the visitors are like when they come up here, their clocks take a while to adjust to the altitude during which time they think they see all manner of things."

Adam laughed. "Yea, remember that woman last year who swore she saw a forest fire over the next ridge, turned out to be the sunset reflecting off the snow."

They drove around for an hour surveying the area for any signs of something out of the ordinary. Anything which might explain what Jenny had seen the previous night. They stopped on occasion to check over any unusual drifts in case there was something buried beneath, but on each occasion they came up empty-handed.

Eventually, they called it a day, having completed a search within a five-mile radius from the cabin without success.

Adam could tell that his father was still not completely satisfied with their efforts, so he suggested that they continue for another twenty minutes or so, spreading out further.

Tom considered his suggestion for a moment, then he shook his head. "No, don't worry; it's just me being over-cautious." He glanced back to Adam. "In fact if it hadn't been for that torn jacket we found in the snow last night, I would probably have dismissed the whole thing."

"What are you planning to do with it?" asked Adam, remembering they still had the torn fabric back at their place.

"Not sure," replied Tom. "I'm still veering towards it just being a discarded old jacket which was probably chucked out of a moving vehicle. But I thought I might keep hold of it until Jed passes this way again."

Jed Solomon was one of the Rangers who covered the local area as part of his patrol. He usually stopped in to see Tom and Adam whenever he was in the vicinity. The last time had been three days earlier, so he was due another visit soon.

Adam looked at his watch. "You haven't forgotten that I promised to deliver those logs today?"

Tom's eyes widened. "Was that today? Hell I did forget," he glanced at his own watch. "You should be on the road by now."

Adam sighed. "It's not a problem, they're already loaded on, and I was planning to stay over anyway so I can always unload them in the morning if I get there too late."

"Come on then," said Tom. "Let's get back to our place, I can e-mail the kids from there and see what they've decided to do." He zipped up his jacket a little further as a sudden unexpected chill ran through him. "If needs be I can always drive back over there later once you've set off."

Adam turned to his father with a quizzical look on his face. "Have you forgotten Dale borrowed the plough this morning?"

Tom pulled a face. That fact had slipped his mind. With Adam using the 4x4 to deliver the logs and his mate Dale using the plough for the next couple of days, all he was left with was his old van which would be far from ideal in the heavy snow, especially when trying to climb hills like the one which led up to the cabin the students had rented.

"Oh well," Tom shrugged. "I'll just play it by ear and see what happens."

CHAPTER NINE

Steve and Greg left the cabin to go and check on the pressure level of the generator. Jenny had informed them that Scott had complained that his shower started running cold towards the end.

Once out of ear-shot, Greg spoke to his friend in hushed tones.

"Do you think we should say anything about what we heard last night?" Steve looked at him quizzically. "You know, when we came out here to start up the generator, remember that howling somewhere in the distance?"

Steve turned as if afraid someone might be behind them and able to hear. He looked back at Greg. "Are you nuts, the girls are already spooked, give them any more ammunition and they'll insist on us packing up and heading home."

They walked into the shed that housed the generator. Once the door had closed behind them, Greg continued. "But I was just thinking that in light of what Jenny says she saw last night..."

"Seriously!" Steve cut him off in mid-sentence. "Look I like Jenny, really, but she has always been a little spacey, don't you think?"

Greg considered his friend's observation for a moment, then nodded. "Yea, I suppose so. But she really seemed convinced last night that she had seen something."

"I know," replied Steve, checking the pressure gauge, trying to remember Adam's instructions, "and I'm not saying that she's lying, I'm sure she did see something."

Greg looked confused. "So if you believe her, why don't you want us to say anything?"

Steve finished with the lever on the valve, then wiped his hands down the front of his jeans to dry off the sweat which had formed on his palms. "Because though I believe she must have seen something, I do not for a moment think that it was some huge bear, or Sasquatch, or the Abominable Snowman. It was probably just a fox or a wild dog or something which took her by surprise in the darkness. She obviously scared the poor thing off when she started screaming, which is why none of us saw anything."

Greg nodded, he knew his friend's logic made sense. And though he had always had a soft spot for Jenny, Steve was right, she could act a little trippy sometimes.

By the time they arrived back at the cabin, Sharon was reading out Tom's e-mail to the others. She paraphrased it for them so as not to have to repeat the whole thing again. There was a moments silence amongst the group once she had finished. Everyone was making an effort to keep their gaze neutral, but Jenny could not help but feel that they were purposely not looking in her direction because they did not want to put any pressure on her to make a decision for the group. But at the same time the general consensus was obviously that she should speak first.

Jenny took in a deep breath and let it out slowly. "Well, as far as I'm concerned I'm happy for us to stay, but if the rest of you want to leave then that's ok with me too."

Sharon smiled at her friend, warmly. "Well Tom has assured us that there doesn't seem to be anything loitering in the vicinity, so that's good enough for me."

"Me too," said Jan, clearly relieved.

"I reckon he's just saying that so that we don't demand our money back if we leave," said Scott, sitting up straight in his chair as if doing so would help him to exude an air of authority.

Sharon and Carey both made as if to object to Scott's assumption, but Jan got in there first. "Tom's already offered us a full refund if we decide to leave, so I really don't think he has any ulterior motive for getting us to stay."

Scott huffed to himself, but did not respond. He just settled back into his chair and continued reading his magazine as if he was not concerned with whatever decision the group ultimately reached.

After a few more moments silence, Sharon said, "Well that's settled then; I'll e-mail him back and say that we've decided to stay."

The others all agreed, except for Scott who remained totally disinterested.

"While you're there, ask him if he knows of a shop in town where I can buy some thick socks?" asked Carey. "My feet were freezing last night!"

"Yea, tell me about it, you woke me up twice trying to warm them on me," said Greg, grinning.

Carey stuck out her tongue at her boyfriend, and he blew her a kiss in response.

Jan offered to make coffee whilst Sharon e-mailed Tom back. Jenny helped her to set out the cups. While they were enjoying their brew, Tom e-mailed back his response.

"Tom says he is delighted that we've decided to stay," Sharon read out loud.

"I'll bet he is," muttered Scott under his breath, not looking up from his magazine.

Sharon ignored him and continued. "He says that if we change our minds then that's fine too, and he will still honour his agreement to give us a full refund." Sharon purposely stopped reading for emphasis. She glanced over at Scott but the effort was wasted as he did not acknowledge the gesture.

Sharon read on. "He says that there is a very good clothing shop in town called "Greenways" but that if we want to go there today we should hurry because it shuts at 4pm and is closed all day tomorrow."

"Nice work if you can get it I suppose," Carey chirped.

"That's why they live longer up here," said Steve, "it's their relaxed way of life,"

Twenty minutes later Steve drove Sharon, Carey, Greg and Jenny back into town. Scott decided to remain at the cabin as he wanted to re-read some training articles he had downloaded before coming on the trip.

Jan was keen to start shooting some snow-scenes with her new camera. When she mentioned the idea she could not help but notice the concerned looks on some of her friend's faces. They knew that Jan was always the most sensible of individuals and that she would not take any unnecessary risks, but even with Tom's reassurance that the area was clear; Jenny's sighting from last night was still a cause for concern.

Sharon cornered Jan whilst the others were getting ready to leave. She felt duty-bound to her friend to mention her concerns. Jan assured her that she would not wander off too far from the cabin, and she reminded Sharon of Tom and Adam's assertion that the area was clear. Neither of the friends mentioned it to each other but in the cold light of day both of them-along with Greg and Steve-were beginning to think that perhaps Jenny had been scared by something quite normal in the wilderness which just took her by surprise when she was half-asleep.

Steve ensured that he kept the Land Rover's gears under control as he negotiated the steep path back down to the town. The most recent fall of snow was still in powder form covering the frozen remnants of the earlier drifts. This made the vehicle's tyres feel slightly unstable on the ground, though nowhere near as unsteady as they would have been had they not been in a 4x4.

Sharon was in no doubt of Steve's capability behind the wheel, but even she felt her heart jump on a couple of occasions when it felt as if the car was going to lose its traction altogether.

They all heaved a huge sigh of relief when the worst of the descent was over. They drove up and down the main street twice before Carey spotted the shop Tom had recommended. Steve managed to find a parking spot almost directly outside and the friends all bundled in.

The shop was relatively small in size, but it was crammed to overflowing with all manner of camping equipment and hiking gear. There were only two staff on duty, a man and a woman both of whom Sharon estimated must be in their mid to late twenties.

Unlike most of the shops back home, the two staff members were both approachable and friendly, and the girls quickly struck up a conversation with the female assistant whilst they browsed. When they mentioned Tom and Adam, the girl knew immediately who they were referring to and told the girls that Tom's cabin was probably the most popular rental in the vicinity.

The girl introduced herself as Joanne, and the male assistant as her partner Colin. She explained that they co-owned the shop and were hoping to renew the lease when it ran out in a year's time as they both loved the area and camping and hiking were shared passions for both of them.

Joanne explained that they always closed the shop early once a week so that she and Colin could make a trek out somewhere in the surrounding hills and camp overnight. She told them that tonight they planned to camp just a couple of ridges over from where the group was staying. Jenny joked that she and Colin could always pop over for a cup of sugar if they ran short.

Once they had made their purchases the group said their goodbyes and went outside to load up the car. It was just after midday and the sun was at its peak directly above the high street. Standing in the warm glow took the edge off the wintery sharpness, and helped to entice the group to go for a wander around the town before heading back.

They strolled aimlessly in and out of some of the shops, the girls in front with Steve and Greg bringing up the rear. As they walked, they drew the odd glance from some of the locals who naturally recognised them as not being from around there. They stopped at a local supermarket and replenished some of their supplies for the cabin. Sharon and Carey offered to play cooks for the evening and promised a spaghetti bolognaise complete with home baked garlic bread.

All the talk about dinner was making everyone hungry, and when they realised that it was almost two o'clock, the group agreed to stay in town for lunch. The others could all see that Jenny was looking guilty at the idea of them going out without Scott, but she did not say anything. Chances were that he would probably have complained that their food choice was not healthy enough for him anyway.

Even so, Jenny tried to text Scott just to let him know why they were taking so long, but she could not receive sufficient reception to send it, so after her third attempt she finally gave up.

They decided to go back to the bar that they first went into upon their arrival the previous day. Some of them had glanced at the menu whilst they were waiting for Tom to arrive, and they agreed that the food looked good as well as being reasonably priced.

The bar was just across the road from the car, so first they unloaded their groceries before going in to eat. Even though they had picked up some dairy produce which needed refrigerating they determined that the weather was cold enough to allow them the luxury of eating first before they took everything home.

The bar was far more crowded than it had been yesterday, but fortunately there appeared to be more staff on duty. The group were only kept waiting for a few minutes before they were seated. Their waitress was a young girl called Sophie, according to her name badge. She looked to be in her late teens and had long curly ginger hair swept back and pinned on top of her head. Sharon noticed that she had tried to mask her acne with copious amounts of foundation but it did not quite seem to have the desired effect.

They all ordered their drinks straight away and Sophie disappeared behind the bar to fetch them.

"What do you fancy?" asked Steve, glancing at Sharon before immersing himself back into the menu.

Sharon switched her gaze between the burgers and the pizza section. She was tempted to go for the lasagne, but as they were having the spaghetti that evening she decided that something slightly less Italian might be a better choice. Even though she was aware that pizza originated in Italy, she always associated them with America, so that made them a feasible choice for today.

"I think I'm going to go with the chicken and tomato pizza, with a side order of salad," she replied, biting her bottom lip as she quickly looked over the dessert menu.

"Sounds good," said Jenny. "I think I might go with the same."

The boys both went for the house speciality monster burgers with extra cheese and bacon, while Carey opted for fish fingers and chips with baked beans and bread and butter from the children's menu. Greg gazed up to heaven with a smile when she made her choice. He was used to her doing that whenever they went out to dinner and fish fingers were on offer. It was an association back to her childhood and that simple meal always left her feeling warm and safe inside.

Still, Greg did not mind, it made her a cheap date.

They chatted animatedly during their meal. Everyone could feel how calm and relaxed the atmosphere was, and everyone knew that it was mostly down to the fact that Scott was not there to dampen the mood. If asked, even Jenny would have to admit that that was a fact, though none of her friends would have knowingly put her in that position. Certainly not in company, though as her best friend, Sharon had often contemplated speaking to Jenny alone. She hated to see her friend being so badly treated by her boyfriend, and could not understand Jenny's reluctance to finish with him or at the very least give him an ultimatum.

Jenny's entire demeanour seemed to change whenever she was around Scott. The bright, witty, confident Jenny seemed to fade into the background and was replaced by a shadow of her former self. That was why it was so good to get her away from him like this, even if it was only for a couple of hours or so.

After they finished eating, the girls excused themselves to use the toilet whilst the boys took care of the bill. They left Sophie a good tip, which in fairness she had earned due to her excellent service. But even so, part of the reason for the gratuity was because the boys found her very cute, in spite of her bad skin. And Greg especially had to check himself on more than one occasion during the meal when he found himself watching her pert behind sashaying across the floor.

Sharon and Carey finished up and called to Jenny to say they would see her outside. Jenny finished up and washed her hands. The towel machine was stuck when she tried to pull the fabric down, so she used the wall dryer instead. She allowed the machine to run through two cycles before she was satisfied that her hands were dry.

As she went to leave the bathroom a group of girls burst through the door almost knocking her off her feet. She received a few half apologies as the group were obviously too engrossed in their conversation to take any notice of their surroundings.

Jenny grabbed the door as it swung back on its hinges and in a moment's confusion turned left instead of right. The door before her led to the alleyway behind the bar where all the food bins were located.

Before she could react to her mistake, the door swung shut behind her leaving her locked out. Jenny swore under her breath and tried to pull the door open, but it was locked, the bolt on the inside having secured once the door slammed to. She was about to start pounding on the door to try and gain someone's attention, when she suddenly heard the sound of groaning and moaning coming from behind the wrought iron wheelie bins.

Being the kind and trusting soul that was inerrant in her make-up, her immediate thought was that someone was hurt or had had an accident and was lying in the alley and obviously in pain.

She glanced around her. There was no one around. She honed in on the noise and decided that it was definitely emanating from behind the municipal bins. Slowly, Jenny edged her way past the bundles of cardboard and paper which were tied up and obviously awaiting disposal. The closer she came to the bins the louder the moans became. Someone was obviously behind them, and doubtless in need of assistance.

"Hello…Are you ok…? Do you need any help?" Jenny asked cautiously as she neared the bin area. The moaning did not stop. No one called back in response to her. Her concern for whoever was making the noises grew. Her mind began to work in overdrive. Could this be a mugging victim who had been dragged into the alleyway, beaten, robbed and then left to die out of sight?

Did such things happen out here? After all, this was not London.

"Hello?" Jenny spoke louder as she peered around the first bin. "Do you need any help?"

The sight that met her took Jenny completely by surprise.

Behind the bins, lying on his back on a mattress of folded cardboard was a man. Jenny thought that she recognised him as one of the bikers they had seen in the bar when they first arrived in town. He had a thick mass of jet-black hair which had been shaved at the sides to resemble a Mohawk. Down the left-hand side of his face was a deep purple scar which swept down towards his mouth, there to be swallowed up by his beard.

The man was fully clothed in black leather, and above him stood the woman that Jenny was sure she had seen the day before drinking with the bikers. She too was fully clothed in jeans and biker's leather jacket with matching boots. Her right foot was firmly placed between the biker's legs pressing down on his crotch as she twisted her boot back and forth whilst holding onto the side of one of the bins for balance.

The man had his eyes closed and was obviously lost in ecstasy as the woman pleasured him from above.

Before Jenny could retreat, the woman turned and looked straight at her. For a moment the two of them merely locked gazes. Jenny half-opened her mouth to speak, but the ridiculous nature of the circumstance stopped any words forming in her mouth.

The woman continued to twist her foot on the biker's groin whilst she stared at the intruder. With his eyes closed and him lost in his own world, the biker was still oblivious to Jenny's presence.

Jenny was about to back away and mouthed an apology to the woman for her intrusion, when the woman promptly stopped moving her foot and removed it from the man's genitals. She stood there with her hands on her hips staring directly into Jenny's eyes, her brow starting to furrow.

Before Jenny could respond, the woman called out. "Hey, Scarface, looks like we have a voyeur in our midst."

The man, now conscious that the woman had ceased pleasuring him opened his eyes and quickly took in the situation. He jumped to his feet and stood towering over Jenny who was suddenly feeling very vulnerable and scared.

Through the tightness of his leather trousers the man adjusted the bulge between his legs. Jenny could not help herself but follow the movement with her eyes, then quickly snapped back to look up at his face, her own cheeks flushing hot.

A slow grin started to spread across the man's face, forcing his scar to stretch to one side along his jaw line.

He glanced over to the woman beside him. "What do yer reckon Angel, think she wants to join in the fun?"

The woman did not speak at once but began to move around Jenny as if sizing her up. Before she realised it, Jenny found herself hemmed in with the man and woman on either side of her and one of the larger metal bins against her back.

Jenny cleared her throat, afraid that otherwise she would not be able to speak clearly. "Listen, I'm really sorry that I disturbed you both," she glanced quickly from one to the other, "but I thought that someone was in trouble and needed help."

The man moved in. "Oh, I could do with some help alright, with this." The man grabbed his groin and gave his bulge a quick shake.

Jenny spontaneously pulled a face.

Scarface noticed. "Oh, so I'm not good enough fer yer, eh?"

Jenny tried to shake her head in denial, but only managed a feeble half-shake before Angel cut in.

"I reckon little miss perfect 'ere reckons 'er shit don't stink." Both of them moved in closer, cramping Jenny right up against the bin. She was now completely trapped and would have to physically push past the two of them to make her escape.

Scarface leaned in close to her until she could smell the alcohol and weed on his fetid breath. Jenny closed her eyes in terror as she felt his slavering tongue lick the entire side of her face. She felt herself gag. Jenny thrust her hand up against her mouth to stop herself from bringing back her lunch. She wanted to scream but her throat was heaving too much from the effort of keeping down her food.

"Jenny!" A familiar, friendly voice. Jenny opened her eyes and saw Sharon standing next to the bins.

Sharon looked at the three of them and immediately assessed the situation.

"Steve, Greg, get here. Now!" She bellowed.

There came the sound of running feet from further down the alleyway. Scarface and Angel exchanged glances then moved away from Jenny allowing her to leave and go to Sharon.

Tears were starting to run down Jenny's cheeks, the fear and anger of her situation finally taking hold. She wiped her eyes with her palm, then using the back of her hand wiped away the trail which Scarface's tongue had left on her cheek.

Steve and Greg arrived, closely followed by Carey. The friends now completely outnumbered the bikers and both of them knew it. Scarface and Angel backed away a little further from the group but were conscious of the fact that their escape route was blocked by several large bins behind them. They had specifically chosen this location for their tryst because it was shielded from the rest of the alley. Now they both regretted that decision as they would have to fight their way out.

"What the hell's going on here?" Steve aimed his question at Sharon, but the bikers knew that it was really aimed at them.

Jenny looked over at Scarface and Angel. She could tell from their expressions that they were expecting a confrontation. Scarface had his right hand behind his back as if he was about to pull something from his back pocket. Jenny suspected that whatever it was, there was a chance that one of her friends might get hurt if she did not put a stop to this now.

"It's all right," Jenny blurted out, still looking at Scarface. "I heard these two behind the bins and thought that someone was in trouble." She quickly glanced at her friends, then looked back to the bikers. She was afraid that if her friends saw the look in her eyes that they would know immediately that she was lying.

"Scared the hell out of us, I can tell you," said Angel, trying to sound calm and matter-of-fact. "We thought it was the Police coming to bust us, didn't we?" She turned to look at Scarface who, though a little slower on the uptake, eventually caught on and nodded, almost with a smile.

"I'm sorry about that," responded Jenny. "I should have called out first before just barging in like I did."

Sharon was convinced that her friend was covering up and that something far more sinister was taking place before they arrived. But she understood her friend's reluctance to cause a scene, so decided to help her keep the situation under control.

"That's what you get for being such a girl scout," said Sharon, gently rubbing her friend's arm.

The boys too were not convinced by Jenny's assertion. But neither wanted to create an unnecessary scene, especially as it was clear that Jenny was unharmed and willing to let things drop.

"No hard feelings then," said Angel after a moment's silence, moving forward and extending her hand towards Jenny.

Jenny took the offering and they shook briefly.

Steve and Greg both shot a glance at Scarface as the group turned to leave, it was an unspoken warning conveying their animosity and the fact that one word from their friend and they would have both been upon him.

Scarface held their stare without expression, until they turned their backs and followed the girls back along the alley.

CHAPTER TEN

Jan set off from the cabin shortly after the others had driven into town. She packed herself a thermos of hot soup and some sandwiches and strapping her new camera bag over her shoulder said goodbye to Scott who was too involved in his reading or just too rude to respond.

The air outside was cold and crisp, with the sun beating down on the harsh whiteness making it almost impossible for Jan to keep her eyes open through the glare. She slipped her sunglasses on, pushing the arms under her woolly hat to keep them in place.

Within an hour she had reached the summit of the nearest hill. Though it was one of the smaller ones the view from it was still breath-taking. The land stretched for miles around her in all directions, interrupted only by more hills, each one as magnificent as the next.

Jan stood there for a moment taking in a huge lungful of fresh mountain air. The sharpness caught in her throat for a split second which made her feel as if she had swallowed an icicle, but the sensation soon dissipated as the oxygen warmed inside her.

The snow which clung to the hillside reflected the sun's power giving the surface a sharp blue metallic hue which pierced the vista causing Jan to squint. She fumbled in her bag for her sunglasses, instantly appreciating their benefit once she slipped them on.

The warmth she felt from the exertion of her climb was already starting to wane now she was standing in one place, but the view was so magical Jan desperately wanted to take some pictures before moving on.

Jan stamped her feet to boost her circulation; her boots dislodging the snow compacted on the ground beneath her.

Once she felt a little warmer Jan took off her rucksack and squatted on the ground to remove her camera and stand. She had to remove her gloves temporarily to set up the tripod because the thermal lining made it impossible for her to manoeuvre the wheels and cogs into place.

Finally she was ready. Using the light refractor to reduce the sun's glare, Jan began firing off shots. The tripod allowed her to move in a perfect arc so she could complete a series of photos covering the surrounding area.

Once she was satisfied that she had enough, Jan picked up the tripod and moved a little further towards the edge of the hill. The sweeping view of the valley below with its unblemished white covering made for a breathtaking series of shots which from this angle could quite easily have been mistaken for some taken from an alpine ski lodge.

The wind was starting to pick up and an icy chill blast shot through her, slicing its way through her thermals and causing Jan to shiver involuntarily. Jan decided to take a break before continuing. She squatted back down and retrieved her thermos flask from her rucksack. The hot coffee would suffice for now and should hopefully allow her to continue for a while longer. She had certainly not anticipated the chill factor when she set out and made a mental note to add a few extra layers if she ventured out again tomorrow.

Again she had to remove her gloves, this time to get a proper grip on the stopper of her flask. Her hands were shaking with the cold as she twisted it free. Holding the plastic mug with her bare hand Jan started to pour the steaming liquid out. A sudden shrill cry from somewhere in the distance caused her to look up, momentarily taking her concentration away from the job at hand. Before she realised what she had done she felt the scorching hot liquid pouring over her bare hand.

Jan screamed and simultaneously dropped the cup causing its contents to splash down the front of her clothes. In a panic she tried to grab the falling cup and in doing so managed to lose her grip on the flask. Conscious of the fact that she was now about to be splashed with its entire contents, Jan quickly moved to one side and managed to catch her foot on one of the tripod's stands. Before she could regain her balance, Jan fell to one side, her arms spinning in mid air reaching out for something which was not to be found.

Jan felt herself falling over the side of the precipice before she had a chance to react. She managed a final scream before she hit the floor below, then everything went black.

****

"I'm telling you Stud...they were definitely part of that group you sent Weasel... after yesterday," Scarface was still flushed and heaving for breath after running to the hotel from the pub's car park to tell the others the news.

Angel, younger and fitter than the biker was, stood behind him nodding her consent to the others.

Stud Jones scraped the back end of his machete across his unshaved chin while he thought. "Did you check which way they went?" he barked, half expecting a negative response.

Scarface having now caught his breath, continued. "I saw the car they all went for, that's why I ran here, they were piling all their stuff in so they might still be there if we hurry."

Stud moved to the window and looked down the street in the direction of the pub. "Can you still see them from here?" he called behind him.

Scarface moved up beside him and pressed his head sideways against the glass, squinting to get a better view. He was quiet for a moment and Stud suspected that there was no sign of them. The stupid bugger should have followed them and then reported back. If it had been either Skull or Axe he was confident that they would have acted on their own initiative, but unfortunately Scarface was only about one or two levels of stupidity above Weasel, and he knew better than to ever show his face again after running out on them.

Suddenly, Scarface started pointing frantically and jumping on the spot as if he needed to use the toilet. "There, there, there they are just coming down the road, see I told you."

Stud followed his subordinate's gaze and saw the Land Rover slowly edging its way down the street. "Are you sure that's them?" he asked, without taking his eyes off the vehicle.

"Definitely," replied Scarface, a trace of desperation in his voice as if it would mean everything to him if his boss believed him.

"Right," said Stud, not turning from the window. "Get after them and find out where they're staying." Before Scarface had a chance to move, Stud swivelled round and caught the biker by his lapel. Bringing his face to within an inch of his own he growled, "And don't let me down!"

Scarface pumped his head up and down in a desperate act of compliance. The moment Stud released him the biker scurried from the room grabbing his crash helmet as he left.

Stud stared back through the grimy window and watched the Land Rover slowly make its way down the street. He waited patiently, his breath misting up the glass. After a minute there was still no sign of Scarface. Stud leaned against the window and tried to see as far down the road as possible, but the Land Rover was now out of sight. "Come on you stupid twat, where are you?" he said, rhetorically.

Finally Scarface's bike roared into action, skidding around the corner of the hotel and almost causing Scarface to lose his purchase on the snow. He managed to swing the machine back and catch it on the return to keep it, and him, upright.

There was a loud bang and a cloud of black smoke emanated from the back of his exhaust pipe, before he roared off in the direction the Land Rover had just taken.

Stud watched until Scarface was out of sight before he turned away from the window and looked at the others. "I need to make a phone call, then I need a drink, come on." The others laughed to each other as they followed him out of the room.

****

Jan slowly opened her eyes. As they came into focus she gradually began to remember what had happened. She was lying on her back and the warm afternoon sun warmed her face. She pulled off her glove and touched her cheek; she was feeling a little flushed. She wondered how long she had been lying there. Evidently long enough to start getting a tan. As someone who was normally very careful about overexposure she wondered how her pale skin would cope. But that was not her main concern. Right now she needed to make sure that she was in one piece and mobile so she could find some help.

As she tried to lift herself off the ground, Jan felt a blast of pain shoot through her right foot and ankle. She slumped back to the floor with a pitiful cry. Looking down her leg there was no obvious sign of anything out of the ordinary, but considering she was shod in thick socks and hiker's snow boots there really was not much that she could tell from here, other than the fact that she was in severe pain when she tried to put her foot down.

Turning, Jan tried to put pressure on her left foot. That seemed fine, which made her think she must have landed awkwardly on her right side. Now she thought about it, there was a dull ache seeping up through her right hip leading almost to her arm-pit.

Without thinking, Jan let out a cry for help. Her voice came out high-pitched and squeaky and she surmised at best she would only attract the attention of someone standing directly in front of her. She cleared her throat and took a deep breath; the cold icy air filled her lungs making her feel as if she had just swallowed an ice-cube. She let out a far stronger more controlled cry for help this time, her voice echoing around the nearest hills. She waited for the faint echoes to die down, listening for any call or reply. There was none.

Struggling, Jan lifted herself up on her left side and tried again. The only answer came in the form of some wild birds which flew overhead and away into the distance.

She slumped back down on the snow-covered ground and heaved a huge sigh. This was a fine pickle. She glanced around her, suddenly remembering her backpack with her mobile in it. It was nowhere to be seen.

The area of ground she was sitting on was perfectly flat and sloped away gently to what looked to her like a road. She wondered if by some miracle the road was the same one her friends would drive along on their way back from town. Was that too much to hope for? Leaning forward she tried to get a better look. The snow covering the road appeared unblemished. Had her friends used it this morning there would undoubtedly be tracks still visible from their car tyres. Her heart sank as she considered she had no idea where she was in regards to the location of their cabin.

Turning, whilst being careful not to aggravate her right foot, Jan tried to see above her to the cliff edge from which she had fallen. She surmised the ledge was about twenty to twenty-five feet high and she counted her blessings that she had not suffered further injury as a result of the fall. The soft padding of the snow was doubtless the main reason for her uneventful landing.

Squinting through the sun's radiance as it bounced off the snow she thought that she could just make out the strap from her pack dangling over the edge of the cliff. There was no way that she would be able to reach it, certainly not in her present condition.

Just then, Jan's hand touched something in the snow. Looking down she discovered her sunglasses peeking through the whiteness. Retrieving them she was grateful to discover that they did not seem to have been damaged during the fall. Putting them on she immediately felt the benefit of their protection from the sun's rays.

Jan strained to listen for any signs of life, but all she could hear was the wind buffeting against the hills and trees, and the squawk of birds. She felt a slight rumble in her tummy. Food was the furthest thing from her mind at this precise moment in time, but her body's survival instinct was reminding her that she needed sustenance. She glanced back up at the ledge where her pack was just out of sight and she could almost taste the sandwiches and hot soup she had prepared for this trip. She tried to concentrate on being rescued to take her mind off her stomach. Her food might just as well have been a hundred miles away as on the ledge above her. Either way it was inaccessible.

She felt completely helpless and alone, out here in the middle of nowhere with no way of communicating her position or seeking assistance.

Through the bitter chill of the wind she felt the hot sting of tears as they rolled from her eyes and down her flushed cheeks.

****

Scarface managed to catch up with the Land Rover, but only after having to double-back when he initially rode past their turning. He could feel the anticipation rising in him even now. Stud had told them that if all went to plan they would have time to enjoy themselves with the students and still have plenty of time for their heist.

Scarface had worked out the maths, only three blokes against the four bikers. Even without Weasel it would be a pushover. Only one of the students looked a bit tasty and Scarface was confident that Skull could probably take him alone. And if the girls became a bit too excited, Angel, small as she was, could handle her own with the best of them.

Just thinking about the female biker was enough for Scarface to feel his erection stirring. She had promised him a blow-job after lunch but then she had gone and ordered a spicy chilli burger, and he was not about to let her put her mouth around his cock with chilli on her lips. That was why he had settled for her wanking him off in the car park with her foot. It was still good. Not as nice as a blow-job, but still exciting in its own way. Angel had introduced him to foot-jobs. The way she managed to manoeuvre, twist and glide her foot over his stiff cock, even through his leathers, made him ejaculate in next to no time.

Scarface removed his hand from the handlebar and adjusted himself. He smiled; perhaps he would have time to collect that blow-job before they had their choice of the girls. He had already picked out his selection, the little one with the dark-brown hair which she had worn in a pony-tail today. She looked as if she could pass for a schoolgirl, which was fine with him; he had always liked them young.

Scarface edged his bike slowly up the gradient. The snow beneath his tyres was quite firm, which was good in one respect, but it made the surface more slippery and harder to negotiate. The grip of his snow tyres was holding for the most part, but he was still wary having nearly lost the bike earlier on a sharp bend.

He made sure that the Land Rover was far enough ahead so as not to arouse suspicion from its occupants. His all black outfit contrasted sharply against the snowy surroundings making him stick out like a sore thumb, and the last thing he wanted was for the students to blow his cover.

At one point he felt sure that they had noticed him, so he waited back pretending to be pre-occupied with something on his bike, until he saw them round a corner. Again he nearly lost his purchase when he let his clutch out too soon. The bike swung one way then the other as Scarface pulled it over, only just managing to keep it upright.

As he neared the turning Scarface slowed down, half-expecting the students to be lying in wait for him. But his suspicions evaporated once he made the turn- the Land Rover was nowhere to be seen.

His immediate instinct was to panic. If he had lost them Stud would not be pleased, and Scarface did not relish the prospect of having to go back to the town and report his failure. He could understand why Weasel had disappeared, doubtless more afraid of confronting Stud than setting off on his own. In that respect Weasel was braver than him. Scarface had been a member of the Warlords for far too long now for him to contemplate a life on the road alone. Much as he feared the wrath of Stud and the fact that their leader would doubtless make an example of him, anything was preferable to not being part of the gang.

Scarface turned off his engine and tried to listen out for the sound of the student's car. He thought for a moment that he caught something, but then a flock of birds overhead blocked out the sound. He cursed them, straining to hear above their squawking. Finally, he picked up a distant tremor. He strained to hear but the noise was growing fainter. He decided to take a chance. After all, nothing would be gained by him just sitting there, and if it turned out not to be them then he would spend as long as it took to try and locate them before returning to explain his failure to his boss.

Scarface edged gently forward keeping his bike in a low gear to allow him to ascertain the direction the distant engine noise was coming from. He hoped the sound belonged to the student's Land Rover, otherwise he felt sure he had lost them for good, and that would not be a conversation he would relish having with Stud.

Eventually, he reasoned that the noise was coming from just over the brow of the nest hill. Scarface eyed the gradient and decided that there was no possible way he could ride up it without announcing his arrival. Instead he switched off his engine and moved his bike to the side of the road, leaning it on the stand.

He climbed off and leaving his helmet and gloves on began the climb. As he reached the brow he could hear the sound of talking and laughing, young voices. He felt confident that this had to be them, but he needed to make sure. Moving out of the road and verging onto the bank, Scarface lay down on his front and strategically crawled forward using his elbows and knees to propel him. Once he reached the apex he could see the familiar sight of the Land Rover through the foliage.

He waited for a while, watching as the group unpacked their car before going inside. Once the door was closed, Scarface considered venturing down to explore the surrounding area so he could give Stud a more comprehensive report. But on reconsideration he decided that there was not enough cover and the students could easily see him just by looking out of the window. Furthermore, contrasted against the snowy white background his black leathers afforded him no camouflage whatsoever, and he would stick out like the proverbial sore thumb.

Deciding that discretion was the order of the moment, Scarface slid back down the slope until he was confident he could not be seen, then he stood up brushing the snow and foliage from his front before making his way back to his bike. He freewheeled down the road a bit before starting up his engine. Carefully he manoeuvred the machine away from the cabin ensuring that he did not allow the bike to gain too much speed, on this surface, that would doubtless result in a tumble when he applied the brakes.

Once he felt that he was far enough away to be safe, Scarface hit the starter and the bike roared into life.

At the same instant, Scarface thought he heard a roar of a different kind somewhere nearby. He stayed where he was for a moment and switched off the engine. Removing his helmet he listened intently for the noise to come again, but all he could make out was the sound of the wind whistling through the trees.

Shrugging to himself that he must have imagined it, Scarface replaced his helmet and re-started his bike.

As he sped away into the distance he was blissfully unaware of the Snow Beast watching him from behind a clump of trees.

CHAPTER ELEVEN

Jan opened her eyes. It dawned on her that she must have fallen asleep at some point, doubtless exhausted from all the crying and shouting she had been doing. She looked around her; there was no one else to be seen. She gazed down at the road; there were still no tracks in the snow as evidence of someone having passed whilst she was out. In many ways she felt that that was a good thing, at least she had not missed a chance of rescue.

The air had grown much colder. The sun was already starting its descent in the western sky and Jan started to face the reality that if no one came this might be her last night on earth. There was no way she would survive a night out in this temperature. She was dressed for a walk in the winter snow, not an overnight stay.

Jan tried once more to put weight on her ankle. She cried out as the pain shot through her foot and slumped back on the ground. It was fruitless; the pain was far too severe to allow for movement. Jan gazed up longingly at the strap of her rucksack which was just visible, dangling over the edge of the ledge from which she had fallen.

She searched the area around her, desperate to locate a fallen branch she could use to snag the end of the strap and bring her possessions down to her. Her food, her hot soup which had probably lost most of its heat by now she surmised, those thermos flasks were never as good as the adverts led you to believe. And her mobile. Oh if only she could manage to reach that, at least then she could try and call for help.

In desperation at the hopelessness of her plight, Jan could feel the hot sting of tears starting again. She had always prided herself on being able to stand on her own two feet and cope with whatever life threw at her. Now for the first time, quite literally as well as metaphorically, she was unable to do that; and she felt completely helpless.

Even though Jan had been raised a catholic she had never followed the doctrine. The over-zealous attitude of her teachers at her all-girl secondary school had in effect caused her to turn her back on the faith. Now, for the first time in a long time she could hear herself starting to pray.

From memory she could recite the words of the confessional, though she had not realised until this moment that she still could. She closed her eyes tightly as the words came flooding back. As she spoke them, Jan could not help but feel like a complete fraud, but she reasoned this was what people did in such circumstances, and what is more she meant every word she was speaking.

Through the sound of the wind buffeting against the trees and the hillside Jan could hear the faint roar of an engine. At first she was convinced it was just her imagination clutching at straws, but as she tried to hold back her sobs to make listening easier she knew that it was not all in her mind.

Excitedly, without thinking Jan tried to raise herself up, but the moment she put pressure on her foot the pain reminded her of her predicament.

Jan slumped back on the ground, her prayers forgotten for the moment; her full concentration was now on the sound of that engine. She strained to listen trying to ascertain whether it was getting closer or moving farther away. Jan held her breath. It was definitely getting closer.

Jan frantically looked around her for something she could use to attract the driver's attention. There was nothing close to hand. She considered making a super-human effort once the vehicle came into sight by trying to stand up and wave her arms wildly, but she knew the slightest pressure on her foot was agonising and with the best will in the world she would not be able to support herself unaided.

The vehicle was very close now, it sounded as if it was just around the next turning. It had to come her way, please god make it so! Jan knew that being so far back from the side of the road and with the failing light there was still a chance that the driver may not see her. She realised that her voice would not be able to penetrate the sound of the engine, plus there was a good chance that the driver would have their music blaring, or even be speaking on their mobile lost in conversation. Her only chance was to be seen at the vital moment.

Jan frantically started trying to take off her jacket. As cold as it was it was the only item she could think of that she could wave like a flag to draw attention. She rolled over on the floor trying to remove one arm from its sleeve. Once it was free, she rolled back over to release the other one.

The ice-cold chill sliced through her body the moment the garment was removed. For a split second Jan actually feared that she would freeze to the spot and be unable to move at all.

At that moment the headlights from the approaching vehicle cut a swathe through the dusk to her left and Jan found the inner strength to raise her arm above her head and swing her heavy coat back and forth whilst simultaneously screaming in competition with the wind and the engine's roar.

For a split second Jan's heart sank as the van came into view and carried on along the road in front of her without slowing down. She was pragmatic enough to realise that life was not always fair and that bad things often happened to good people, but something inside told her this would not be her end.

With an inner strength born of desperation and a will to survive, Jan took in a lungful of freezing air and let out an ear-piercing scream which even she did not recognise as coming from her mouth.

The driver slammed on the brakes. The tyres skidded on the compacted snow but the driver managed to keep the vehicle on the road as it came to a complete stop.

Jan could feel her heart pounding in her chest. For a split second her mind could not compute the fact that she was about to be rescued. In that same second it dawned on her that the driver of the van might be a homicidal maniac who scoured the countryside looking for fresh victims, the dismembered limbs from his latest prey still freshly wrapped in plastic in the back of his van.

But the moment Jan saw Tom emerge from the driver's seat; she breathed a prayer of thanks. Unable to control her emotions Jan fell back on the ground, her tiny body wracking with sobs.

In a moment Tom was kneeling beside her in the snow, the expression on his face was one of fatherly concern. Before he had a chance to speak, Jan shot up into a sitting position and wrapped her arms around him, burying her face in his chest and soaking his jacket with her tears as she hugged him close to her.

Tom gently kissed the top of Jan's head as he cradled her in his warm embrace. After a few moments Tom wrapped Jan's jacket around her shoulders to keep her warm.

"What happened to you?" he asked, soothingly.

Through her tears Jan could barely speak. "I…I fell…from up there," she indicated the ledge above with a movement of her head. "I was…taking pictures…and…I think I've done something to my foot…I can't stand…my rucksack with my mobile is still up there…" Her words trailed off as another flood of sobs began to fall.

Tom scooped her up in his powerful arms and carried her over to his van. Once he had settled her comfortably in the passenger seat he cocooned her in a blanket and then switched on the engine, turning up the heater and directing the flow of warm air onto Jan's legs.

"There you go," he said, reassuringly, "you'll soon start to warm up now."

Jan smiled, weakly. Her tears had dried. She felt as if she could start again at any second but she tried to maintain her composure. She imagined her face must already be red and puffy and not in the least bit attractive, which made it all the more special when Tom leaned over and kissed her gently on the end of her nose.

Tom swung the van around and headed back in the direction he had originally come from. Jan was completely disorientated now as far as direction was concerned. She did not know whether he was taking her back to the cabin, or into town, or back to his place and to be honest, she did not care right now. She felt safe and protected in Tom's company and after her ordeal that was all that mattered.

Upon reconsideration, she hoped that he was in fact taking her back to his place. She felt in need of some TLC and right now Tom was at the top of her list as the one to administer it.

They drove on for about ten minutes in silence. Jan could feel her eyes growing heavy abetted by the comfort of the warm air blowing on her.

When she woke up she found herself alone in the van. Tom was nowhere to be seen, but she presumed that he could not be far away as he had left the engine running, doubtless so that the heater could remain on to keep her warm.

She glanced over her shoulder to see if Tom was behind the van, but there was no sign of him. Jan snuggled back down beneath the blanket. A moment of panic passed her by, but she knew that Tom would not desert her. He was bound to be close by.

Just then she saw him appear from behind a ridge to her left. He trod carefully down the slope, his legs sinking into snow almost up to his knees as he descended.

Jan noticed that he was carrying something in one hand. As he drew nearer she realised that it was her camera, and over his shoulder swung her backpack. Tom's thoughtfulness touched her. Jan had already resigned herself to the fact that she would probably never see her possessions again, and here was this wonderful man traipsing through the snow to bring them to her.

Tom placed Jan's things on the seat between them. He shivered involuntarily as the warm air from the heater hit his body.

"There you are," he said, smiling. "I think that's everything."

Jan leaned in, restricted by the blanket which Tom had wrapped around her. She hoped she had moved close enough for Tom to take the hint, and he did. Jan pressed her lips against his, the bristles from his moustache and beard gently tickled her. She had never kissed anyone with facial hair before. It was an odd sensation, but not in any way unpleasant.

They both let their lips linger past the stage of being merely a glancing kiss of friendship, but neither tried to take it any further.

"Thank you," said Jan, when they finally pulled themselves apart. "I really thought I'd lost them for good. I wondered where you were when I woke up; I thought you'd abandoned me."

Tom laughed. "Never," he said, reassuringly. "I didn't want to risk driving the van up the hill so I thought it best to trek over to see if I could retrieve them. I only came out in the van because I was checking something in one of my other cabins; I've got some guests who just booked in for next week."

"Well I'm certainly glad you did, otherwise I'm not sure I would have survived much longer out here, you probably saved my life," Jan looked Tom directly in the eyes. "Lord knows how I'm ever going to repay you."

To her shock and amusement, Tom blushed. "That's ok," he said, obviously feeling his own embarrassment. "That kiss was payment in full."

Let's just call it a down payment, Jan thought to herself as the van pulled off.

On route, Tom tried to receive a signal on his mobile, but to no avail. He knew it was probably a fruitless exercise but he felt he should at least try.

Tom replaced his phone back into the dashboard holder. "I tried to see if I could contact your friend Sharon so I could let her know you are alright, but there's no signal out here," Tom explained.

"Not to worry," replied Jan. "How much longer until we reach the cabin?"

Tom looked a little sheepish as he replied. "Well, to be honest I don't want to risk trying to get this baby up the hill. I could really do with the 4x4 but Adam is using it for an overnight delivery and typically I loaned the plough to a mate of mine who collected it this morning. So I'm afraid we'll have to e-mail Sharon from my place and see if one of them can drive over in the Land Rover to pick you up."

Outside the window Jan could see the first signs of a new snowfall starting. The flakes were quite large and were already settling on the glass enough to cause Tom to switch the wipers on.

Tom gazed up at the sky. "This doesn't look so good," he said.

"How can you tell?" Jan asked, quizzically.

"The formation of the clouds," replied Tom, slowing down the van to avoid what looked like a patch of black ice. "There's definitely snow in those clouds and judging by the colour of them we might be in for some of the deep stuff."

Jan thought for a moment before offering, "Do you think it will be safe for Steve to drive out to your place if it gets any harder?"

Tom sighed. "That depends on how quickly it starts to really come down. The last thing I want is him getting lost or stuck half-way between the cabin and my place."

"Would it be easier if I just stayed at your place tonight?" Jan asked, casually. "As long as you don't mind, that is."

Tom turned to her and smiled. "It would be my pleasure, but you have to remember Adam and I are two bachelors neither of whom is particularly house-proud, so you'll have to take the place as you find it."

Jan faced front so Tom could not see the cheeky grin starting to spread across her face. "I'm sure that won't be a problem."

****

Scarface caught up with the rest of the gang in the pub. They were occupying their usual corner at the far end of the bar, and there were already the remnants of several pitchers of beer dotted around the table by the time he arrived.

Scarface slumped down on one of the seats next to Axe. He grabbed a spare glass into which, even though it appeared none too clean, he tipped the contents from one of the jugs. The golden liquid gushed out so quickly it left him with a glass half full of foam. Regardless, Scarface knocked back the contents in one go, leaving a rim of froth around his mouth.

Before he could speak he let forth an almighty belch which caused half the pub to glance over in his direction.

"Well?" Stud demanded, clearly annoyed that Scarface had elected to quench his thirst before making his report.

"I found it!" Scarface announced with obvious pride. "It weren't easy; them roads are all slippery slidey, but I managed to keep track of them all the way home."

"And they didn't see you following them?" Stud narrowed his eyes when he spoke. He made no attempt to hide the obvious suspicion in his voice.

"No...No way," Scarface spluttered, unable to hold his leader's gaze. In truth, he was not completely sure if he had been noticed or not, but there was no way he was going to admit it. In fact, if he was honest, he would not have admitted it even if he had been sure that he was seen. Scarface had witnessed Stud's anger against other gang members who had let him down or disobeyed a direct order in the past, and he had no intention to join that sorry bunch.

Clearly unimpressed, Stud returned his attention to his beer. The others all did likewise. Angel in particular looked disappointed. Secretly she enjoyed the violence that ensued whenever there was a bust-up. Her biggest thrill was when there was a clash of rival gangs and she was more than happy to launch herself into the melee and take her chances. The rush she would feel afterwards could sometimes last for days, during which time she would get as drunk as possible and sleep with as many surviving members as she could. The Warlords were notorious amongst biker gangs for their violence which was the main reason Angel had set out to join them in the first place.

Scarface leaned over and poured himself another glass of beer. There was a general buzz of activity from the patrons in the restaurant section which was separated from his group by a thick frosted glass and wood panel. The scattering of drinkers at the bar appeared completely unfazed by the biker's presence. Even so, Scarface took the precaution of leaning towards his leader before speaking. "So are we going to visit them tonight then?" His voice barely rose above a whisper.

Stud shook his head in response. "Nah, I got a call from Reaper this afternoon, e's coming in tomorrow so we'd better behave for now. Can't risk doin' anything which might jeopardise the raid." The others all nodded solemnly. "Besides," he continued, "Reaper might fancy a bit of action himself, an' we can't afford to ruin his fun now can we?" The others all started laughing loudly in unison. This time they did cause a few concerned looks from some of the bar staff.

CHAPTER TWELVE

When they arrived back at Tom's house, Tom carried Jan inside from his van. Even though she offered a minor protest, Jan was grateful for the attention as her foot was really throbbing. When they reached the front door Jan was impressed with the way Tom managed to support her full body weight with one arm whilst he fumbled for his keys.

Once inside, Tom placed Jan down gently on the sofa and brought her his laptop so that she could contact her friends and tell them she was alright. For the next ten minutes Jan had an e-mail conversation with Sharon whilst Tom attended to Jan's foot. As carefully as he could he removed her boot and sock, then he gently squeezed and prodded her swollen flesh trying to evaluate the potential damage.

Once he was satisfied Jan had not broken any bones, he put together a make-shift cold-press using a freezer bag and some ice and cocooned in a tea towel which he then tenderly wrapped around her foot and ankle, releasing the pressure every couple of minutes or so to help with her circulation.

Jan had never met a man so attentive. When she thought back to some of her past boyfriends she could not imagine any of them taking so much care if the need arose.

Once the ice started to melt, Tom gently placed Jan's foot on a cushion then he cupped the bag in the towel and took it back to the kitchen. As the door swung open and closed Jan's nostrils were suddenly assailed by the most marvellous aroma. Her stomach grumbled loudly before she had a chance to try and stop it. Luckily Tom was already inside the kitchen so she comforted herself that he could not possibly have heard her. Even so, she felt her face flush.

When Tom came back in the room he was carrying a tablespoon which he brought straight over to Jan and held it in front of her mouth. Cupping his other hand beneath the belly of the spoon in case of spillage, he told her to blow gently on the contents before he tipped the spoon towards her mouth.

Without asking what was in it Jan closed her eyes and eagerly tasted what Tom had placed before her. The flavour was incredible. The combination of succulent slow cooked beef with onions herbs and thick meaty gravy made Jan realise again just how hungry she was.

"How's that?" asked Tom, expectantly.

Jan opened her eyes whilst savouring the tender morsel. "Mmmnnn," she moaned, before swallowing. "That's delicious!"

Tom grinned broadly. "My world famous beef casserole, it's been slow cooking all day. Hungry?"

"Famished," replied Jan, licking her lips to savour the residual flavour.

"Ok then, dinner in ten minutes," said Tom, lifting himself off the sofa. On route to the kitchen Tom stopped to put on some music. It was classical, and Jan was pleasantly surprised by his choice. She recognised the piece though for the moment she could not put a name to it.

Jan eased back on the sofa and could feel the stress of the day starting to ebb away. Were it not for her foot, everything would be perfect. As the wind howled and moaned outside Jan snuggled down letting the warmth from the log fire crackling behind the grate engulf her. Tom had put the heater on full in the van to help Jan recover her circulation and though it had certainly helped, it did not compare to the warm embrace from a real fire.

Jan almost felt herself starting to drift off when Tom emerged from the kitchen again with two glasses of red wine. He walked around the sofa and handed one to Jan after she propped herself up a little to make drinking easier.

"I don't know what made me do it," said Tom, indicating towards the glasses, "usually I make do with a beer, but something told me to decant this before I left this afternoon, so it should be good and ready by now."

Jan took her glass and placed it beneath her nose, breathing in. One of her uncles had been a keen enthusiast when it came to wine and he was forever demonstrating the correct way to fully appreciate the grape's bouquet.

The scent of plum and apricot filled Jan's senses. She looked up at Tom, smiling, and then she held her glass forward for them to clink. As they drank they both held each others' gaze as though neither of wanted to break the magic of the moment.

Tom looked away first, a slight flush coating his cheeks.

Jan continued to look directly at him, a cheeky grin almost escaping.

After a moment Tom could not resist gazing back at her. He was pleasantly surprised to find she was still looking at him, but still he hesitated. He had always considered himself an honourable man, especially where women were concerned and he was all too conscious of the fact that Jan might find the whole scenario a little overwhelming.

After all, he had just rescued her from might have been a tragic accident, and here she was now, helpless because of her foot, caught in the romantic glow of the fire with tranquil music playing and him plying her with alcohol.

Tom held himself fast. Though he was incredibly attracted to Jan there was a tremendous age difference between them and he knew that if things went any further, he, as the more mature and supposedly responsible adult, would have to take the full blame. And he really did not think he could live with the thought of Jan hating him for letting things get out of hand.

Just as he was about to push himself away, Jan wrapped her hand around the back of his neck and slowly began to pull him towards her.

Unable to resist, Tom allowed himself to be drawn closer until their lips met.

They kissed gently at first, then more eagerly as both placed their wine glasses on the floor so that they could use their arms to embrace fully.

After a moment they pulled apart, just far enough for each to catch their breath. They could both tell from the expression on the others' face that neither regretted their action.

As Tom slowly lowered himself towards Jan again, they both heard a loud *ping* from the direction of the kitchen.

Tom stopped himself mid-way and sighed. "Dumplings are ready."

They ate together at the kitchen table.

Tom placed a spare chair with a cushion on it in front of Jan so that she could rest her foot on it. Even though the swelling had gone down since Tom placed his homemade ice pack on it, Jan's ankle still had a dull throbbing ache which was alleviated somewhat when her ankle was elevated.

Jan was starving, and each mouthful of Tom's casserole and dumplings tasted like heaven. Tom had even baked his own bread, and Jan managed to consume two thick slices of it slavered in butter to soak up the remaining gravy on her plate.

They emptied the decanter and polished off the best part of a second bottle during their meal. Afterwards, Tom carried Jan back over to the sofa and cleared away the dishes before he poured them both a large cognac.

Jan was already starting to feel the effects of the wine. Her ravenous appetite had also caused her to drink much faster than she did normally. But like the food, the wine tasted so good, and she felt so comfortable in Tom's company it just seemed natural to throw caution to the wind and just relax and enjoy herself.

Before bringing over their drinks Tom placed more logs on the fire and changed the CD. The high, clear strains of Aker Bilk's clarinet filled the room. Jan recognised the piece immediately, it had been one of her father's favourites and she remembered as a child when sleep refused to come she would creep down the stairs and listen to her father playing his music whilst he worked on his accounts. On several occasions she had fallen asleep sitting on the stairs propped up against the banister, only for her father to discover her on his way up to bed some time later. She would wake the next morning tucked up in her own bed warm and safe.

It was strange, but the familiar sound of the music she associated with that childhood memory now mingled perfectly with the subdued lighting and the fire's glow to recreate for her the same feeling of warmth and safety she had experienced all those years ago.

The fact that Tom was the one who had rekindled those feelings made her want him even more.

Jan smiled up at him as he passed her the cognac. "Are you trying to get me drunk?" she asked, cheekily. "I think that wine has already gone to my head."

"I thought a night-cap might help with the pain," replied Tom, gently lifting Jan's legs so that he could sit down and rest them on his lap.

Tom held out his glass so that they could clink.

They both took a sip. The smooth, peppery taste of the special port trickled down Jan's throat increasing the internal glow left by the wine.

"Did you enjoy dinner?" asked Tom, savouring his drink.

"Mmnn, it was the most delicious casserole I've ever had."

"Speciality of the house," Tom beamed.

"Well then I must come here more often," said Jan, meeting Tom's eyes and holding his gaze as she took another sip from her glass.

****

Joanne Canton and Colin Pratt trudged hand in hand up the steep slope. The snow crunched beneath their weight as their snow boots sought purchase on the fresh drift. On more than one occasion one of them had to grab hold of the other to stop them falling as their legs were swept out from underneath them as they skidded on the slippery ground.

Colin groaned inwardly as yet again he could feel his grip on the road give. As much as he loved hiking, these weekly trips of theirs up into the hills seemed to be growing more hazardous with every outing.

In truth, when they had originally moved up here it was as the direct result of them loving every minute of a two week hiking tour arranged through a club they had joined. Then when they managed to secure the lease on the shop it seemed as if it was a dream come true for both of them, allowing them the opportunity to roam the hills and mountains almost at will with all the creature comforts of home back in the town.

But these weekly jaunts of theirs had taken most of the fun out of the experience for Colin. There was no spontaneity in coming out at the same time on the same day every week. And as both of them needed to be back at the store the following morning they were restricted as to how far out they could travel before having to camp down for the night.

Granted the view was still wonderful, and the sight of a full moon in a sky clustered with stars with the snow-covered hills as a backdrop was breath-taking. But it was the combination of having to revisit the same areas every month or so and not being able to stay anywhere for more than one night that was starting to irritate him.

Colin had always loved camping from as far back as he could remember. As a child, coming from a large family where money was scarce, the majority of their family holidays had centred around camping. When he was six or seven, his parents had purchased a run-down campervan which quickly became the main focus of their weekend trips and summer holidays.

Colin and his siblings loved the thought of boarding the vehicle outside their home and magically being transported to another part of the country within a few hours; traffic allowing.

More often than not, if they were going anywhere for more than a weekend his parents would purposely ensure that they stayed at several locations throughout their break. They would encourage their brood to relish each new location and savour the different views and surrounding areas.

As he grew older Colin took up hiking, in his view a natural compliment to camping. That was when he discovered his true passion. From that point on he spent every available holiday trekking around the country. In his view the pastime had the best of all worlds. It was relatively inexpensive once you had the right equipment, and there were virtually no limits as to where you could go and what you could see.

To find like-minded individuals with whom to share his passion, Colin had joined several hiking clubs and it was through one of them that he had met Joanne.

For him, certainly, it was love at first sight.

Their group was on a ten day tour of the Lake District. Joanne was one of the group leaders from the club and Colin was very proud of the way he surreptitiously managed to manoeuvre himself into position when the leaders were choosing their teams, so that Joanne could not possibly ignore him without making it look obvious.

Once in her team, Colin ensured that he stayed mainly in the background. Some of the other single men on the hike were making very clumsy, obvious attempts to catch Joanne's attention, so Colin played it cool and kept his cards very close to his chest. He became quite adept at looking at her sideways whilst making out he was staring off into the distance, then turning to catch her eye and smile when he noticed her looking in his direction.

On a couple of occasions he even made her blush when he caught her eye.

And that to him was a very positive sign.

Each evening as the volunteers to help set up the tents were growing thinner Colin was always there, tools at the ready and enthusiasm at full speed.

By the end of the jaunt, Colin and Joanne had grown considerably closer. They discovered they shared a similar sense of humour, and as well as a passion for hiking and camping they admitted to each other that they were closet horror film fans.

At the last second Colin almost lost his nerve and could feel the perfect moment to ask Joanne for a date ebbing away. Luckily, Joanne saved the day by suggesting that they join some friends of hers who had bought tickets for an all night showing of five classic horror films at one of the big cinemas up in town.

Colin jumped at the offer and by the end of the production, having stolen several sneaky kisses in the darkened cinema, they were officially together.

That had been almost a year ago and with each passing day Colin fell more and more in love with Joanne. There was nothing about her that he did not like. Even her little quirks and foibles-like the way she demanded that all the cans in the cupboard faced the front so that the labels could be clearly seen, or the way that she insisted that everyone should eat chocolate bars the right way up-Colin found far more endearing than annoying.

"Oh look at that!" Joanne exclaimed, excitedly. They had just reached the summit of the steep slope and the view before them, Colin had to admit, was glorious.

The moon was almost full and much bigger than it had looked in a while. The valley below them swept down towards a series of smaller hills and ridges and everywhere was covered in a perfect blanket of fresh snow.

The reflection of the moonlight on the snow cast everything in an eerie metallic-blue hue which transformed the valley before them into a magical winter wonderland.

Colin moved up beside Joanne and put his arm around her shoulders.

Joanne snuggled up against him still keeping her eyes fixed on the scene in front. Their breath, laboured from the climb, mingled in a cloud of carbon dioxide which dissipated within a few feet of their mouths.

Joanne appeared to be mesmerised and her excitement and wonder were infectious to Colin. Suddenly it did not matter that they had only recently stood in this very same spot and marvelled at the wonders of nature. Her squeals of delight always reminded him of a child fervently unwrapping their Christmas presents.

Colin leaned in and kissed her gently on the side of her head. "Come on," he said, rubbing his hand up and down her arm, "let's set up our stuff before it gets too late."

****

Jan could feel herself being carried gently up the stairs. She opened her eyes and stared up into Tom's loving gaze. He had obviously picked her up from the sofa and, without waking her, cradled her sleeping form in his arms as he carried her up to bed.

She felt like a child being taken up to bed by her father after falling asleep watching the television.

But she was no child, and the feelings she had for Tom were definitely not those of a daughter to a father. She wanted him. Longed for him. Her body actually ached with desire, a feeling she had never experienced before for any other man.

Jan had never had a long-term relationship. Her first sexual encounter had been a very disappointing experience with a young lad in the back of his car after her friend's seventeenth birthday party. There had been three other men in her life since then. The longest had lasted barely three months. Jan had even considered that there might be something wrong with her. After all, her friends all seemed to be able to have stable relationships. She tried not to feel envious, but every so often she felt the little green monster give her a dig.

The main problem Jan had decided was that she found most men of her own age to be too immature. She had often heard that women matured faster than men and if that were so then she supposed it made sense. She had never really given the matter any serious thought, until now.

Jan smiled up at Tom's handsome face as he carefully manoeuvred her around the railings ensuring that he did not bump her injured foot against the banister.

They held each others' gaze for a long moment.

Jan wondered what Tom's intentions were. She knew how badly she wanted him and they had shared that passionate kiss before dinner, but even so she did not want to take anything for granted. Tom was certainly a gentleman but he was still a man and she was a woman. A woman who could now feel some very familiar moisture emanating from between her legs.

Jan decided that when Tom placed her on her bed-or his for that matter-she would pull him towards her and see where things led. She felt so warm and secure in his arms she surmised she might have to fight against the onslaught of sleep in order to get things started, but it would be worth it.

As they approached the top of the stairs Jan rolled her head against Tom's broad shoulder and slipped back into a deep sleep.

CHAPTER THIRTEEN

"What was that?" Joanne sat up with a start.

Beside her in the tent, Colin stirred momentarily before turning back over to continue with his sleep.

Joanne listened intently to the night sounds outside their fabric cocoon. The wind had picked up quite a bit since they had dropped off and she could hear it battering the side of the tent.

Otherwise there was silence.

But she knew that she had heard something!

Something happening outside the tent had woken her up!

Joanne was never one to cause an unnecessary fuss regardless of the situation, so she was not yet prepared to shake Colin awake until she was positive there was a good reason for it.

Shuffling to one side Joanne slipped her hand up and grabbed hold of the zip at the side of her bag. She carefully pulled it down not wanting to snag it on the fabric. Once it was down far enough she eased her legs out from under the cover. Even fully clothed as she was, and with the added protection of the tent's surround, she immediately felt the cold air penetrate her body.

Ensuring that she did not disturb Colin, Joanne slid forward until she could reach the zip on the tent's outer wall. She began to slowly pull the metal tog down; still not sure what sight might be waiting to greet her on the outside.

As the opening grew, the frosty air swept in, blinding her vision. Joanne tried to squint against the onslaught of wind and snow but it was useless, she could not see enough to make out what might have caused the noise she heard earlier.

Turning, she fumbled in her pack for her goggles. She was sure that they were the last thing she packed away before retiring, but somehow they had managed to slip further down into her pack.

Joanne groped in the darkness trying to ascertain which item was her goggles from the various shapes and forms her hand made contact with. Nothing felt right. Reluctantly, she removed her torch from her coat pocket and covered the end with one hand before turning it on so as not to disturb Colin.

In the tunnel of light given off by the torch Joanne retrieved her goggles from her pack and turned off her torch. She placed her goggles on her head and she edged further towards the entrance. Though she was now able to keep her eyes open behind the protective plastic the swirling snow outside the tent made it virtually impossible to see further than a few feet in front of her.

Joanne strained to make out what lay beyond her peripheral field of vision. The entrance flaps of the tent still limited her view of the outside. Pulling her bobble hat down further to cover her ears, Joanne leaned outside the tent flaps to get a better look.

Other than the swirling snow and the scudding clouds nothing else seemed to be moving. Joanne glanced around surveying the vast expanse of land and hills before her but her overall vision was still badly impaired by the snowflakes buffeting her face.

Joanne crouched down as low as she could to try and improve her overall visibility. Her feet were just inside the tent. She knew that to enhance her observation she would have to go outside the tent and stand up. But that would mean putting her boots on and she was beginning to think that the effort was not worth it.

In her mind she had already begun to doubt that she had heard anything of any note. As it was, she was woken from a deep sleep so the noise may have actually been in her head as part of a dream.

She could not even remember what kind of noise it had been.

A distant roar, or perhaps a howl.

More than likely a wild bird or a fox, she reasoned. She had heard foxes making love before and remembered the first time how the screeching had made her think the poor animal was being tortured.

Whatever it was, it seemed to have stopped now.

Joanne shivered as another icy blast swept into the tent opening.

She was just about to pull back into the tent and zip up the flaps when she saw them!

She leaned forward straining her eyes to improve the view. Even with the wind whipping up the snow all around her she was sure that she could make out some kind of tracks in the snow in front of the tent's entrance.

The harder Joanne looked, the more imprints she noticed.

They did not look like man-made prints. For a start they were much bigger than any human could make.

Joanne had often heard that footprints left in deep snow would change and grow as the snow began to freeze and thaw, but these could not be hers or Colin's surely.

It was no good, she would have to investigate further or she would never be able to fall back to sleep.

Shuffling back inside the tent, Joanne sat down and slipped on her boots ensuring that the laces were tightly crossed. She pulled on her parka checking the side pocket for her torch. Before exiting the tent, she glanced down at the sleeping form of Colin who remained blissfully unaware of what was going on around him.

Joanne zipped up the parka until it covered her nose, readjusted her goggles, and then flipped over her hood before venturing out into the open.

Once outside she re-closed the tent flaps so that she would not return to find a blanket of snow covering the groundsheet.

The air outside the tent was crisp and clear. Joanne took in a huge lungful as she stood, and even with the parka's protection the chill still seeped through her nostrils giving her the sensation of having swallowed a large ice cube.

The wind whipped around her causing huge flurries which obscured her vision. In between them, Joanne could barely make out any conceivable shapes in the distance. The land and sky before her almost seemed to blend into a uniform white making it even harder to ascertain if anything was amiss.

Joanne turned. The tent was directly behind her and fully visible. She edged forward slowly, stopping every few steps to ensure that she could still see it. The last thing she needed was to get lost out here and end up wandering around half the night trying to find her way back. They had heard stories from some of the locals about tourists and intrepid campers who had wandered off into the snow at night never to be seen again. A combination of rough weather and losing your bearings could make the terrain around here hostile and very unforgiving.

After a dozen or so steps, Joanne felt as if she had ventured far enough away from the tent. It was still visible but now somewhat obscured by the violent drifts rushing past.

Joanne stood in place and turned a full circle, slowly.

There was really nothing untoward to be seen. Certainly nothing to account for the noise which had woken her up. She was growing more and more convinced that perhaps she had imagined it after all. Failing that, it could possibly have been a wild animal passing by, or for that matter, even one several miles away, their cry carried on the wind over the hills making them sound so much closer.

She was glad now that she had not bothered to wake Colin. Though he would have grumbled and moaned under his breath, she knew that he would have succumbed to surveying the area for her peace of mind. And when he returned to the tent with nothing to report she would have felt very guilty for sending him out in the first place.

Joanne stood in place and took one more turn to look out at the distant hills.

Even with her goggles fogging up the scene before her was beautiful.

She took in one more huge breath and rubbed the snow from her goggles as she turned to make her way back to the tent.

At first her mind would not allow her to focus properly on what was before her.

She could see the tent quite clearly, but behind it was what appeared to be a huge creature covered in thick, white fur.

She stared for a moment, straining to see what was there, still convinced that the snow and the light were uniting to play tricks on her.

At first the thing did not move.

Joanne needed to get closer to see what was there, but her legs seemed frozen to the spot with fear.

Finally, she willed herself to take a few unsteady half steps forward, her eyes never leaving the huge shape behind the tent.

By the fourth step, Joanne could make out a slight movement from the thing. She stopped.

Its enormous upper body was heaving slowly up then back down again.

Was it breathing? She wondered. If so, it must be alive!

Fear like no other she had ever experienced gripped her. Once again she found herself unable to move.

She desperately wanted to call out to Colin, to warn him that something was behind the tent and to get out before it was too late. But her tongue along with the rest of her body was frozen in place by fear.

Joanne's mind raced through a jumble of potential scenarios to explain away the situation.

Possibly, someone was playing an elaborate joke on them; some of Colin's friends from back home had followed them up here to give them a scare. Or a film crew nearby was making a wildlife documentary; or perhaps just an inquisitive camper passing by whom the darkness and the snow made look ten times larger than they actually were.

There had to be some sort of logical explanation, surely!

Suddenly, the creature lifted its head and let forth a huge roar which seemed to Joanne to make the entire valley shake.

Still unable to move herself, Joanne could see some movement coming from inside the tent. Colin was awake. Who could possibly have slept through that noise?

For a moment Joanne felt herself relax. Colin would know what to do. As big as the creature looked from here chances were that once Colin appeared it would turn tail and leave the area. Whatever it was it doubtless did not want to risk a confrontation with a grown man. Joanne surmised that it had probably come across men before and had learned to leave the area and hide itself away.

She saw the tent flaps start to move as Colin wrestled with the zipper.

As his head emerged from the protective fabric, Joanne found her voice.

"Colin!" she screamed, as loud as her lungs would allow. The icy cold air rushed into her mouth as soon as she opened it causing her to half-choke. Her voice, distorted by the wind, fell short of its intended target.

Colin pulled himself free of the tent and crawled forward on all fours. Even from this distance Joanne could tell that he had not bothered to dress first before investigating where the howling was coming from, though at least he had the presence of mind to pull on his walking boots.

Through the obscurity of the driving snow Joanne watched as Colin began to rub the sleep from his eyes so as to focus properly on his surroundings.

Joanne instinctively covered her nose and mouth as she took in a massive lungful of freezing air before letting forth another scream of warning.

This time she seemed to reach her mark.

Colin looked straight towards her, covering his eyes with his arm in an attempt to keep the rushing snow out. From behind the tent the Beast stood motionless, watching the scene before it with great intensity. Its eyes focused on the newly arrived form of Colin and it knew that its hunger would soon be abated.

Colin, still blissfully unaware of the danger behind him, started to wave to Joanne, calling to her. Instead of attempting another warning shout, Joanne began to jump up and down on the spot pointing frantically behind him.

Before Colin could register the warning, the Beast grabbed hold of the top of the tent and ripped it from the ground with one almighty jerk.

The metal tent pegs all went flying in different directions from the sheer force of the action. One of them caught Colin on the back of the head sending him sprawling to the ground where he landed with an immense *humph* on the compacted snow.

Seeing her boyfriend attacked in this manner gave Joanne renewed courage. She bounded towards Colin's prone figure with enormous strides, heaving and grunting as she fought against the deep snow which made it harder for her to pull her feet free with every step.

Before she could reach him, Joanne lost her footing and fell.

Unable to react in time to break her fall, Joanne landed face first in the snow. She closed her eyes for fear the goggle's plastic glass might shatter upon contact with the ground. The glass held but the plastic frames dug into her nose and forehead as she landed.

With her face immersed in the snow, Joanne could no longer see or hear what was going on around her. The landing had knocked the wind out of her and as she tried to inhale, the snow clogged her nose and mouth causing her to choke.

Forcing herself onto her back Joanne coughed, sneezed and spat out the freezing snow whilst trying to take in a decent breath.

From behind her she heard Colin start to scream.

Joanne lifted herself onto one arm to support her body weight which allowed her to turn sufficiently so that she could see what was happening to her boyfriend.

The sight which met her eyes made her wish that she had not bothered.

The Beast had hoisted Colin into the air and was holding him aloft as if to demonstrate its great strength.

Instinctively, Joanne tried to scream, but once again her voice was lost in the gushing wind. She could feel a cold icy blast shoot down her throat and placed her arm over her mouth and tried to breath past the material of her parka in the hope that it might warm the air before it entered her lungs.

She looked up just in time to see the creature balance Colin across its massive shoulders before grabbing him by the neck and ankles and pulling down with all its might.

Colin had the chance to scream once.

Then there followed an audible *crack* as the creature broke Colin's back.

Joanne looked on in stunned silence as Colin's lifeless body slid down the Beast's shoulders and landed in a heap on the ground.

She gazed at him for a moment. Even from this distance and through the snow, she could tell that he was dead. His head was twisted towards her with his tongue lolling out of his open mouth. The angle of his shoulders compared to that of his hips made him look as if he had been put together back to front like some shop mannequin incorrectly assembled.

She could not believe that what now lay crumpled at the feet of this creature had once been her boyfriend. Colin's broken, twisted form sprawled in the snow as the first signs of blood seeped from the corner of his mouth and splashed on the ground in front of him.

For a second, Joanne believed that if she could just get to him and scoop him up in her arms she could perhaps kiss away his pain and bring him back to her. For he could not possibly be dead! Not her Colin! Wounded possibly, unconscious definitely, but by no means dead!

Only sleeping!

The sudden savage roar which emanated from the mighty Beast and echoed throughout the surrounding hills brought Joanne out of her reverie.

She stared straight ahead, her eyes wide open in a feral stare of insanity, her lips spread in an insane grin as the Beast retrieved its kill from the ground and frantically began tearing away at Colin's clothes until his bare flesh poked through.

Once the wrapping had been removed, the creature lifted Colin to its mouth and sank its gnashing jaws into his flesh, tearing out bloody strips which it barely took time to chew before swallowing.

Joanne watched transfixed as Colin's lifeblood stained the creature's fur around its nose and mouth.

She stayed there, at first unable to move as the creature tore chunk after chunk from Colin's lifeless form. All the time the creature appeared to be looking directly at Joanne as if taunting her that she would be next.

Suddenly, Joanne found her legs.

She wrenched herself up off the ground and turned away from the grisly scene playing out in front of her. Without looking back, she began to run.

With each step she could feel the snow trying to trap her, but she kept on going, pumping her arms to aid her escape.

Though she fell over several times her internal survival mechanism forced her to keep going.

As she ran further and further away from the Beast, its menacing shrieks and howls grew more distant.

Even when it was no more than an echo, Joanne still refused to turn.

She just kept running.

CHAPTER FOURTEEN

Jan yawned and stretched her arms as she brought herself back into the land of the living. It took her a moment to realise where she was and consider how she came to be here.

She remembered Tom carrying her up the stairs and her feeling all warm and cosy in his strong arms. She remembered the sumptuous meal he had prepared them, the wine, the music, the log fire...*Their passionate kiss!*

Jan's heart sank.

They were going to make love. At least, she was sure that that was the intention. It had certainly been hers. But she had fallen asleep at the threshold of their union. She realised, much to her chagrin, that she only had to stay awake for a matter of moments before Tom would have brought her into the bedroom, then she would have pulled him down on top of her and everything would have been all wonderful.

Jan checked herself.

Things like that never actually worked out in the real world.

But the setting had been so perfect. From the time Tom rescued her right up until she had fallen asleep in his arms, what would have been more idyllic than for the two of them to end the night in each other's embrace?

Jan sighed out loud.

Too late now, the moment had passed. But she could not get the image of his arms wrapped around her and their bodies entwined sliding against each other in a perfect rhythm, out of her mind.

Was it really too late?

What was stopping her from climbing out of bed and making her way towards his bedroom, stripping naked, leaving her discarded clothes on the floor then gently sliding in beside him and caressing his naked torso until he woke?

My busted foot for one thing! She thought to herself.

How was she supposed to make her way to Tom's room with her injured foot without making a racket? She remembered him telling her during the evening that the entire house was covered with floorboards, so there was no way she could hop to his room and still not manage to wake him up.

And as for undressing seductively on one foot...

Forget it!

But Jan's body still ached. Thinking about Tom's strong lean body next to hers had excited her and now she wanted him more than ever.

She considered just making her way to his room regardless of how much noise she made and just throwing herself into his arms when he came to see what all the fuss was about.

How romantic!

But what was the alternative? Just lie here and regret the fact that she could not stay awake long enough to entice Tom into her bed?

Now Jan was really getting frustrated.

She considered just relieving herself. At least that way she could think of Tom whilst she was doing it. Naturally, it would not be the same, but it was a viable substitute that she had relied on several times in the past.

Jan slipped her hand down towards her crotch. It was only then that she realised that she was still fully dressed. Tom, being the gentleman that he was, obviously had not tried to undress her. By the look of it, all he had removed was her sock from her uninjured leg then covered her over with a duvet.

Oh why did he have to be such a gent? If only he had stayed to remove her clothes she might have woken up, and then they could have had some fun.

Jan threw back the quilt and swung her legs out of bed. She tried to place some weight on her injured foot, but the pain caused her to wince so she quickly lifted it off the floor.

Undoing the button, she shrugged herself out of her jeans and let them fall to the floor. She pulled her jumper over her head, and managed to catch the band that held her pony-tail in place, with her finger. She continued to pull the garment as the band fell free. Once off, Jan let her sweater fall to the floor beside her jeans.

As she began to unbutton her shirt, Jan suddenly felt the need to go to the toilet.

Great!

Jan looked around the room for something she could use as a make-shift crutch, but nothing appeared to be viable.

She wondered for a moment if she could hold it in until morning, but the more she thought about it the more her bladder cried out for release.

Using the headboard for support, Jan hoisted herself into a standing position ensuring that she kept her weight off her swollen foot. Once she was upright she let go of the headboard and steadied herself before attempting to hop her way to the bathroom.

The going was slow, and try as she might Jan found it impossible to make any headway without occasionally allowing her bad foot to take some of her weight. She realised that by using it she was probably doing it more harm than good, but her other need was by far the more urgent at this present moment in time.

Jan part hobbled part hopped as far as the bedroom door. It was only when she reached it that she realised that she did not know where the bathroom was on this floor. Earlier in the evening Tom had helped her into the downstairs toilet when she needed to go, but now looking at the doors along the corridor, none of them gave any indication as to which one was the right one.

Jan bit her bottom lip as she glanced along each side of the landing. Finally, she decided to go right for no reason other than it housed a greater choice of rooms than the left did.

The first door she hobbled to turned out to be a storage cupboard. The second was a shower room. Third time lucky, she found it.

By the time she sat down, her foot was throbbing. She could really have done with some more painkillers but the thought of trying to make it downstairs was not even worth considering. She decided she would just have to make her way back to bed and try and get some sleep. And if she could not sleep she would pleasure herself thinking about Tom.

Finishing up, Jan flushed and then washed her hands, drying them on a towel hanging behind the door.

As she steeled herself for the journey back to bed, Jan steadied herself on the door handle as she opened the door.

The unexpected sight of Tom framed in the open doorway caused her to topple backwards in shock.

Tom leaped forward and grabbed Jan by the arms, his firm but gentle grip saving her from crashing backwards onto the hard, wooden floor.

Once he was sure that he had a firm grip on Jan and that there was no chance of her falling, Tom stepped towards her. "Gotcha," he smiled.

Jan's heart was still racing from the initial shock. Now with Tom holding her in such close proximity she could almost feel it missing a beat.

"You scared me!" It came out far more like a whine than Jan had anticipated.

Tom could not help but smile. "I have that effect on women sometimes, I really don't know why."

Instinctively Jan wrapped her arms around Tom. He was wearing a towelling dressing gown which felt soft and comforting against Jan's cheek.

She was suddenly conscious of the fact that besides her shirt she had nothing else on except her underwear. But rather than feel embarrassed the realisation thrilled her. As Tom was so much taller than her, Jan could feel his growing member starting to poke her in her stomach. It was obvious he was not wearing anything under his gown and Jan could not help smiling as she gazed up into his brooding eyes.

She pressed herself closer to him, pushing her tummy into his erection. Tom actually started to blush which made Jan laugh out loud.

"Well?" Jan asked, finally. "Are you going to see me back to my room, or do I have to limp there in agony?"

Without replying, Tom effortlessly lifted Jan off the ground and swept her into his arms. As he walked towards her bedroom door they gazed at each other intently. A silent message passed between them and they both smiled.

Tom gently lay Jan down on top of her bed.

If he was having second thoughts Jan was not going to let him get away with it. Before Tom had a chance to let go Jan reached up and grabbed hold of his lapels and pulled him down on top of her.

As their lips pressed together Jan kissed him, hungrily. Tom responded in kind. He pulled on the belt of his robe releasing the garment and shuffled out of it whilst still in Jan's embrace.

Jan could feel his nakedness pressing against her. She needed to be naked too. Her impatience rising, she was about to rip open the buttons of her shirt when Tom slipped his hands in between their bodies and worked each button free before helping Jan out of her shirt and discarding it on the floor next to his gown.

Jan pulled away and turned onto her front. Before she had a chance to undo her bra Tom was already on the job. Once the straps were free Tom began to kiss

Jan's back sensually, starting from the nape of her neck he slowly moved his lips down her spine until he reached the top of her panties.

Gripping the band with his teeth, Tom carefully began to remove the last garment to cover Jan's modesty. Once he had it over the smooth mounds of her soft white cheeks he used his hands to assist in removing it altogether.

Tom travelled back up Jan's nakedness using his tongue as a guide and stopping every few seconds to kiss and nibble her soft flesh. She squirmed as he left a moist slippery trail up the back of her legs. By the time he reached her shoulders, Jan could feel his erect member rubbing and prodding against the top of her legs and she could wait no longer.

Jan flipped herself over onto her back and reached down to caress Tom's manhood. He moaned softly as she clasped it gently in her palm and began sliding her hand up and down its shaft.

Without hesitation Jan guided Tom inside her, raising her knees to allow him deeper entry.

Once she could feel him fully inside her, Jan wrapped her legs around Tom's body and just about managed to cross her ankles behind his lower back.

Their two bodies entwined, and began to move together as one.

Tom's torso, though hard and rough with callused skin and matted with thick salt and pepper hair, felt warm and protective to Jan and she let her fingers explore all his crevices and ridges while they made love.

Jan felt every fibre in her body tingle as she reached orgasm. Moments later, Tom shuddered as he too reached his. Jan felt the warm flood of his semen squirt inside her and wrapped herself around him more tightly to prolong the sensation.

Not wanting him to leave her, Jan moved her hips in an effort to re-stimulate his ardour. It worked, and she could feel his organ stiffening again.

They stayed locked together until both of them had been fully satisfied.

When they finally parted, their bodies drenched in perspiration, Tom rolled onto his back. He rubbed his hands up and down his face to clear away the excess perspiration and to stop it from trickling into his eyes and stinging.

Without him on top of her, Jan suddenly felt the night's chill and shivered involuntarily.

Tom retrieved the duvet which had slipped onto the floor during their union and covered them both with it.

Gazing across at Jan, he said, "Thank you."

Jan looked at him quizzically, and then smiled. "No," she replied, "thank you!"

They both laughed in unison before drawing closer for another long, hard kiss.

CHAPTER FIFTEEN

"Eh'up gang," Madge Skinner announced as she crashed through the main doors of the "Lone Traveller" bar and restaurant. The three members of bar staff on duty all looked up to acknowledge their boss' return.

"How was the conference Madge?" asked Joan, cracking a half-hearted smile as she finished pouring a pint for one of their customers. Joan was two years younger than her employer but to look at them you would never guess it.

Joan had been a big shot in the city for years until she suffered a nervous breakdown and moved to the country for a change of pace. It was rumoured around the town that no one had ever seen her smile since she had arrived.

Madge had met Joan through their local ballroom dancing club. At first she had offered Joan a job because she was short of bar staff and Joan had told her that she was growing increasingly bored with sitting at home looking at the four walls all day. As it turned out, Joan was a solid, loyal member of staff who, if not exactly conversational with the punters, understood the benefit of good customer service.

Madge had never regretted taking her on and over time had come to rely on her to run things for her in her absence.

Madge had owned the 'Traveller' outright ever since her husband Geoff had passed away three years earlier. At the time, Geoff had been a part-owner along with his friend Conrad Munt, but when years of excessive living finally took its toll on Geoff, Conrad decided that it was time to move on. Fortunately for Madge, Geoff had a good life insurance policy which more than gave her enough to buy Conrad out, which is just what she did.

Though Geoff had travelled the world during his time in the armed forces, Madge was a local girl and had never wanted to live anywhere else. Though she loved and missed Geoff, since his death Madge had found a new lease of life, and at fifty-three she still felt young and glamorous enough to party with the best of them.

"Well," replied Madge, "I s'ppose as conferences go it weren't that bad. The food at least was good, but some of the speakers were pretty rubbish."

Joan handed the customer back his change. "Well a conference run by a brewery is hardly likely to provide the most scintillating of conversationalists."

Madge laughed. "You're right there Joanie, I think most of 'em were there for the piss-up." Madge signalled behind her. "Including 'is nibs back there."

Joan looked past her boss through the window at Darren, Madge and Geoff's only child. At seventeen he was proving to be more of a handful than Madge would have liked. She told herself that his problems stemmed from the loss of his father, but she knew in truth that his rebellious nature had been a problem long before she lost her husband. Geoff had always been too soft with the lad, making excuses for him and saying it was all part of growing up and that he would make good in the end.

Of course, Geoff had never lived to see that day.

By fourteen, Darren had already been expelled from two schools, and at sixteen he was finally given a custodial sentence having previously been issued with several anti-social behaviour orders, all of which he had breached.

Now Madge was determined to get her son on the straight and narrow and keep him there, whatever it took.

"Did Darren play up then?" asked Joan, watching as he wrestled with the luggage from the back of Madge's 4x4.

Madge shrugged. "No more than I should've expected I s'ppose. 'e got his face slapped by one of the girls they had hired to show people round the place."

Joan shot her eyes up to heaven. "That sounds familiar, what did he do?"

"Usual, got too frisky when 'e was tanked up on free booze. I had to intervene to stop 'em calling the police. I had to promise the organisers that I would keep 'im under lock and key, otherwise they wanted us out."

"So what did you do?" Joan enquired, her curiosity only mildly peeked.

"Well I gave him a thick ear an' a dead arm for starters, and then I told him if he dared to leave his room without me as an escort he'd be walking home. That seemed to do the trick."

Just then Darren came crashing through the doors juggling three suitcases with a holdall around each shoulder. He was panting for breath and it was obvious to anyone looking on that he was struggling.

Madge just stood there shaking her head at him.

Finally, she asked, "What did I tell you about not trying to carry 'em all at once?"

Darren just grunted in response.

"Oi," shouted Madge. "Tweedle-dumber, I'm talking to you!"

Darren flushed. "I didn't wanna' take two trips did I," he answered, avoiding Joan's gaze. He hated it when his mum embarrassed him like this, but she would not be told.

Madge looked back at her friend. "If 'e had half a brain 'e'd be dangerous this one."

Darren did not wait to hear any more and struggled to the far end of the bar to the door which led to the staircase.

As he approached the door, Pat, another member of the bar staff emerged from the kitchen. She laughed when Darren tripped over one of the bags and bumped his head against the door jamb. Darren shot her an angry look.

"Sorry," Pat apologised, "I didn't mean to laugh. Do you need a hand up the stairs with those?"

"No!" Darren grunted, angry with himself, his mum, Pat and the stupid luggage. He barged through the swing door and made his way toward the stairs.

"Sorry I spoke," said Pat, half under her breath. She, like the other staff, were used to Darren and his moods so she did not take any offence at his remark.

Just then, some of the bikers strode in and took up their usual corner of the bar.

Madge eyed them, suspiciously. She turned to Joan. "Where did that lot blow in from?" She asked, under her breath.

Joan leaned in towards her manager. "They've been here a couple of days now off and on."

"Any trouble?" Madge mouthed the words without actually making any sound.

Joan shook her head. "Nope, and they have done no end of good for the bar takings."

Madge watched as Pat went over to where the bikers were seated to take their first order. Straight away Madge did not like the way the men looked Pat up and down as she scribbled away on her pad. In Madge's experience they still looked like potential trouble, even though Joan had told her that they had behaved themselves so far. Even so, when a couple of them glanced in her direction, Madge made sure that they knew that she was keeping an eye on them.

There would be no nonsense in her establishment!

Upstairs, Darren crashed his way into his mother's bedroom, carelessly bashing her matching designer luggage against the door frame before dumping the cases onto her bed. One of them bounced off the mattress from the force of his throw and landed with a loud smack on the wooden floor.

Grumbling to himself, Darren dropped his bag where he stood and made his way around the bed to retrieve the suitcase. The fall had caught the edge and scuffed it. Darren heaved it back on the bed and then spat on the stained corner and rubbed it vigorously with his sleeve.

The effort paid off. Most of the scuff marks vanished and only a few stubborn ones remained.

As far as he was concerned it was his mum's own fault for buying such light-coloured luggage in the first place. *Who the hell buys canary yellow suitcases just because they have a designer logo on them?*

Darren swivelled the suitcase so the damaged area could not be seen from the door, hoping his mother might not notice when she unpacked.

As he re-emerged onto the landing, his mother's voice caught him off guard and nearly made him drop his own case.

"What the bloody 'ell are you doing up there, boy?" Madge's bellow from downstairs reverberated around the corridors and seemed to fill the entire top floor.

"Nothin'!" Darren yelled back. "Just sortin' out the luggage."

"Well make sure you unpack and put your dirty stuff in the basket before you come down, ok!"

"Yea," Darren mumbled back under his breath.

He managed to take a further two steps towards his room before his mother screamed back up at him. "Did you hear me?"

"YES!" This time Darren made a point of yelling back as loud as he could before he entered his room. He knew that his mother would have to have the last word, and sure enough a second later it came.

"And don't you shout at me you bugger, or I'll give you the back of me 'and!"

Darren slammed his door in defiance. He listened, half expecting to hear the sound of his mother's footsteps stomping up the stairs, but there was none.

As a youngster, that was the familiar sound he would hear after slamming his bedroom door so as not to have to listen to anymore of her screeching. Up she would race, bursting into his bedroom, usually red in the face and panting for breath, a slipper or wooden ruler or whatever she could lay her hands on gripped tightly in one hand, ready to give him a walloping.

Sometimes, if he was quick enough, Daren would scoot around her and if he made it to his father he would often escape his beating.

That in turn would cause a row between his mum and dad, but as far as he was concerned that was not his problem.

Darren tipped the contents of his bag onto his bed and began choosing items for the washing basket. Sniffing several of them he decided which ones could last another wear before being discarded to the washing pile.

Checking his mobile, Darren noticed a missed call from his friend Cecil Jackson, who since school had always been known by his peers as "Jax".

Darren hit the speed dial button. After a moment his friend's voice came on the line. "Hey Jax-man, 'ow's it hangin' man?"

"Further down than yours, gay man." They both laughed. Jax, like Darren had had his share of run-ins with the law, but as he had never risen to the dizzy heights of actually being incarcerated he looked up to his mate with a certain amount of pride and hero-worship.

"So listen," Jax continued, "me Nan's not well so mum and dad have driven out to see her for the night, they won't be back until tomorrow afternoon."

"Sweet," Darren gushed, already the rest of the day was looking up considerably and after what he had been made to endure over the past week, he desperately needed some fun-time.

"But wait," Jax interjected, "there's more to come. Dad's only gone an' left the keys to his cabinet behind."

At the other end Darren's eyes lit up. "You mean, the one with his porn DVD's?" he asked, eagerly.

"The very same," Jax beamed. "But not only that, me brother came over for a visit at the weekend and he had some terrific weed, 'e let me try some, I was out of it all night," he continued, excitedly. "So anyway, when 'e was leaving I managed to lift some off 'im, I've still got it, there's enough here for two massive roll-ups man, what d'yer say?"

Darren almost screamed out loud with excitement. Suddenly, his day had completely changed direction and now he had a wonderful night to look forward to. He turned and looked behind him at his closed bedroom door, just in case his mum had sneaked up from downstairs and was standing there in the open doorway waiting for him to finish.

Assuring himself that he was alone and out of earshot, he went back to his call. "Listen, I'll tell you what," he continued, excitedly, "when it's quiet downstairs I'll nick a couple of bottles of the good stuff and meet you over at yours." Darren could hear his friend whooping with delight on the other end of the line. "Just don't start the party without me," he warned.

****

Jan was woken up by the sound of the toilet flushing. She reached over and checked the time on her watch, it was 11.25am. Though she had never been the type for late lie-ins, on this occasion she was happy to make an exception.

She listened as Tom washed his hands, and then waited for him to return to bed. She was disappointed to hear him go back into his own room from the toilet.

Jan waited patiently. She considered the fact that Tom may not have realised that she was even awake yet, so perhaps he just needed to do something next door before returning to her.

Eventually, she heard him emerge from his room and within a few seconds he appeared in the doorway. To Jan's chagrin, Tom was fully clothed.

He looked over at her. "Morning," he said, almost sheepishly. "Can I tempt you to a cup of coffee, another speciality of the house?"

Jan held out her arms towards him. "First," she said, a cheeky grin spreading across her face, "I want some more of the real speciality of the host."

Tom could not help but smile, in spite of himself. He sloped into the bedroom and came over and sat beside Jan on the bed.

Jan, her arms still outstretched, leaned forward and Tom slipped in between them, putting his around her slim frame to hold her.

Jan knew instinctively that something was wrong with Tom.

She presumed that whatever it was it must have had something to do with last night as he was obviously not as happy as she was this morning, and it hurt a little.

Jan decided to test the water. They were hugging each other with their heads side by side, so she manoeuvred Tom's around to face her and before he could object she planted a firm kiss on his lips.

Tom did not pull back, so Jan was pleased about that. As they kissed, she parted her lips and began urging him to do likewise.

Eventually, Tom gave in and their kiss grew more passionate.

Though Tom was fully dressed, Jan was still naked, the duvet having slipped away from her as they embraced. Jan guided Tom's hand towards one of her bare breasts. Immediately he began to play with it. Rubbing the soft white flesh with his palms he gently massaged it with his fingers before flicking her erect nipple gently with his thumb.

Jan began to moan in his ear.

She wanted him, and she knew the feeling was mutual.

Jan tried to slip her hand inside Tom's shirt to unbutton it, but to her astonishment he slid back out of her reach.

Jan could not disguise the hurt in her eyes, and she knew that Tom saw it too.

They were still gazing into each others' eyes when Jan asked. "What's wrong, Tom?" She kept her tone soft and undemanding; she still hoped that the moment could be saved.

Before he answered, Tom stood up and moved around the bed towards the window.

Jan waited patiently for his answer.

Finally, after what seemed to Jan an eternity, Tom turned away from the window and looked back at her.

Jan could tell from the sombre expression on his face that whatever he was about to say she probably did not want to hear. She raised her knees making a small tent with the duvet, and then wrapped her arms around them to support herself. She was conscious that her bare breasts were now resting on her bended knees almost as if she was putting them on offer to Tom, inviting him back to bed to fondle them.

Jan managed a weak smile.

Tom rubbed his face vigorously with both hands. It appeared to Jan as if he was struggling to find the right words to start.

Eventually he began. "Jan, listen honey, I don't want you to take this the wrong way, but what we did last night, I should have been more in control and stopped before things went too far."

Jan hugged her knees closer. It was about what she was expecting Tom to say, but that did not make hearing it any easier.

Jan thought for a moment before replying. "So, in different circumstances this would be the part where you leave and tell me that you will call me, without actually intending to?"

Tom moved closer to the bed. "No, nothing like that," he assured her, "the last thing I want is for you to feel used."

"Good, because I don't feel used at all," Jan beamed. "So what else is bugging you?"

Tom released a loud sigh. Jan could tell from his body language that he had visibly relaxed now that this conversation had started; the question now was what she would have to do to try and bring back the carefree Tom of last night.

Tom moved over to the side of the bed and sat down. He reached over and took one of Jan's hands in his own. Jan immediately felt her heart flutter. At such close proximity all she wanted to do was pull him towards her, but she realised that the present situation could not be resolved so easily, more was the pity.

Tom lifted her hand to his mouth and gently kissed the back of it. He could feel his cheeks flush. This was stupid; here he was a fully grown man acting like a teenager on a first date.

"Well?" Jan asked, tenderly. She felt one of them needed to break the elongated silence before things between them grew too awkward to be righted.

Tom kept his gaze down as if he was concentrating on Jan's hand. Jan could feel that he was on the verge of speaking so she looked directly at him waiting to catch his eye when he finally looked up.

When he did, and saw Jan looking at him, his cheeks flushed again. "Oh Jan," he said, sheepishly. Jan was just relieved that he had started talking again. "Look, I appreciate what you said about not feeling used, because just so you know, I had no intention of...You know, using you," it was obvious to Jan that Tom still felt as if he had to somehow justify his actions, and no reassurance from her would change that.

"But?" Jan offered.

Tom let out a deep sigh. "I should have shown more restraint."

"Oh, I see," Jan could not help but smile to herself. "So, in effect, I'm to blame for being too sexy for you to resist, fine, I can live with that!"

Tom laughed in spite of himself.

He wagged his index finger at Jan. "You wanton woman."

"Wantin' you right now," Jan smiled, gently trying to pull him towards her, but she could feel that there was still resistance on Tom's behalf, but definitely not as much as before.

Jan continued to tug on his arm playfully.

Eventually, Tom gave in and slid over for a kiss.

When they broke away, Tom still had a perplexed expression on his face. Jan reached over and tickled him under the chin.

Tom squirmed, and smiled back.

"Still not convinced, huh?" Jan asked, propping herself up on her elbow for comfort. "You know, some women might actually take offence at being dumped this early on in a relationship."

Tom's eyes widened. "That's what I mean darling, how can we possibly have a relationship?"

"We're both adults," Jan reasoned.

"Only just in your case," Tom ventured, with a wry smile creeping across his face.

Jan leaned back and grabbed a pillow which she then threw at him, hitting him square on the head.

Jan held out her hand. "Come here you, no more arguments," she demanded, with mock sternness in her voice.

Tom took her hand, but still seemed unwilling to go any further. "But I'm a zillion years older than you," he ventured. "Where will this all end?"

Jan tugged at him harder, bringing him closer towards her. "Well, for an old man you certainly showed me some moves last night," she chuckled.

Tom's defence was down.

He moved in closer for another kiss, this one more passionate than the last.

Jan lay back and kicked away the duvet, uncovering her legs. The movement reminded her that her foot was still very sore and uncomfortable, but she was not about to complain now.

She manoeuvred Tom on top of her. Before they continued making love she looked him directly in the eyes and said, "This ends when it ends and both of us should be happy for our time together, no matter how long or short."

The wisdom and maturity of her sentiment made it impossible for Tom to find any argument to offer.

CHAPTER SIXTEEN

Stud Jones felt his mobile vibrate whilst he was pulling up the zip on his jeans in the bar's toilet. Without bothering to wash his hands he rubbed them down his leather jacket before retrieving his phone from his inside pocket.

He checked the screen. It was a text from the Reaper stating that he would arrive in town within the next thirty minutes. Stud smiled to himself. With the Reaper's arrival the fun would really start. Reaper should be bringing the firepower for the robbery with him, so the heist should take place in the next couple of days, the news of which would motivate the rest of the team.

Stud knew that this job was not the biggest the gang had ever pulled off, but it certainly was the largest haul his little troop had been trusted with, so that in itself would increase their notoriety amongst the rest of the Warlords. And the fact that Reaper trusted them with such a big job also made a statement concerning Stud's team in the overall pecking order.

It was a shame they had lost Weasel as technically they were now a lookout short, but he had become increasingly annoying over the last few months so in a way Stud was glad that he was not around anymore. Not to mention the fun they would have with him if he ever tried to come back, or was seen by another member of the gang.

No one ever left the Warlords and lived long enough to tell the tale!

Stud made his way out towards where the other members were seated in the bar. He leaned in closely to get their attention and checked the area around them to make sure that no one else was in ear shot before he began talking.

"Reaper's on 'is way," he growled in a hushed tone. "I'm gonna meet him 'round the back, the rest of you stay put until I return."

The others all nodded in agreement. Though the men were excited to see what firepower Reaper was bringing them, they all knew better than to question their leader's instructions.

Once he had acknowledged their response, Stud drained his glass and then swaggered out of the bar and into the street.

The sun was just about managing to penetrate the clouds as he walked towards their hotel. The reflection of the rays on the snow forced Stud to have to squint in order to see ahead properly.

The snow on the pavement, having been trodden down and compacted, was beginning to ice over and Stud had to steady himself a few times to prevent himself from slipping.

There was a wide alleyway at the back of their hotel which screened their view from the main road. It would be excellent for their purpose so Stud had directed Reaper to meet him there.

As he turned into the alleyway, Stud heard a loud roar and a vehicle honking from behind. He turned to see one of the familiar black lorries that the Warlords used for transporting their weapons, bikes and equipment around the country.

Stud waved his acknowledgement to the driver and carried on walking, leading the way around the side entrance to the hotel to the enclosed alley.

There were no other vehicles parked behind the hotel so the driver pulled up directly outside the back entrance.

Stud waited, patiently.

He knew from past experience that Reaper would not exit the vehicle until he was good and ready. It was one of his foibles to have those in the front cab check for prying eyes before he would venture out.

Finally, Stud saw the vehicle lurch to one side. That could only mean that Reaper was ready to disembark.

The lorry continued to rock as Reaper's massive bulk moved towards the back doors from within.

The driver came around from the cab and acknowledged Stud as he began to unfasten the back doors. Once they were unlocked, the driver swung them open and Reaper stepped out into the daylight.

He was certainly a sight to behold!

Standing at almost seven feet tall with shoulders almost as broad as his height, his frame completely blocked the view from inside the vehicle. His black beard had been laced into a plait and hung down almost to his navel. His mop of black hair cascaded around his shoulders and covered his face in front so that, unless he chose to push it back, you could not clearly see his eyes.

His face, when it was uncovered, was a different story again. The scars from countless battles were all clearly visible and only enhanced his reputation amongst the other gangs for being one of the most feared and respected bikers throughout their fraternity.

Reaper's right ear was only a fragment of what it had once been, the rest having been ripped off when he became entangled in a barbed-wire fence whilst trying to break out of prison.

His left eye was almost permanently shut as a result of nerve damage after having that side of his face caved in by a rival gang leader swinging a sledgehammer at him. Notoriously, Reaper still won the overall battle by ripping out his rival's vocal chords with his teeth.

The end of his nose was missing having been bitten off by another rival in a fight to the death over some drug-related turf war. Naturally, Reaper came away the ultimate victor.

The crisscross of scars which were mapped across the rest of his face were merely reminders of some lesser adversaries he had disposed of in his time.

No one in the gang actually knew where Reaper had come from and his ascension to overall Warlord had become the stuff of folklore and legend. Rumours of him suffering from some form of rare genetic disorder whereby he could no longer feel physical pain remained just that, rumours. No one ever dared to ask him if the stories were true.

In all the time that Stud had been a member of the gang only one other biker had been stupid enough to challenge Reaper's authority as leader. And everyone knew that that man had never lived to tell the tale.

As far as everyone else was concerned Reaper was their leader for a reason, and no one else wanted to challenge his authority.

Unless they had a sudden death wish!

Stud walked around the lorry to greet him. Reaper yawned and stretched out to clear away the stiffness in his joints which had been caused as a result of being cramped in the back of the van throughout the journey.

"Alright Stud?" He enquired; taking his fellow biker's outstretched hand. "'ow's the gang?"

"They're all good Reaper, thanks for askin'," Stud looked away sheepishly before adding, "'cept for Weasel, 'e's done a bunk."

Reaper eyed Stud suspiciously. "Any trouble?"

"None that I knew of. The others seem bemused by the whole thing as well. He seemed 'is usual self when 'e left to check somethin' out for us, then 'e never came back." Stud shrugged his shoulders as if he did not have anything further to offer on the subject.

Reaper stroked his beard appearing to be lost in thought momentarily, before adding. "Did yer send anyone after 'im to see what 'appened?"

Stud nodded, enthusiastically, "Oh yeah, when I realised 'e wasn't comin' back I sent Scarface up after 'im, but when 'e got there there was no sign of 'im."

Reaper nodded, slowly. "Oh well, stranger things 'ave 'appened an' all that."

From behind him the others began to emerge from the lorry.

Stud recognised the two men at the back of the vehicle who were busily un-strapping Reaper's Harley. And of course Reaper never went anywhere without his number one girl.

Deedee had lived most of her life in Germany where she was born, but she spoke near-perfect English though with a very strong German accent. Though she was nowhere near as tall as Reaper she was still five feet ten inches in her bare feet, and a good six feet in heels.

Her looks were often described as striking by those who saw her for the first time. Her skin was a pale milky white and completely without blemish. Her cheekbones were high and her eyes a piercing blue which seemed to look straight through you. Her short cropped blond hair would have given most women a boyish appearance, but not Deedee; she was every inch a woman without a doubt.

She had been Reaper's number one since she first joined the gang.

At the time, Reaper had three other girls all of whom had "done the rounds" with the other gang members as was the norm, before catching Reaper's eye. Once Reaper chose a companion the rest of the gang knew to keep their hands off. And besides, there was always plenty to go around.

But Deedee was not prepared to share. She made her intentions plain and challenged the other three girls to a fight in order to become Reaper's one and only. One of the girls backed down and was happy to go back to just being one of the gang. But the other two tagged up against Deedee and tried to beat her off.

Deedee left both of them flat on their backs within seconds and joined Reaper to the cheers from the rest of the assembled gang.

Behind Deedee, two blond girls emerged from the lorry, blinking in the daylight like small animals emerging from hibernation.

Stud did not recognise either of them, but they both caught his eye.

He smiled, weakly and the two girls smiled back before sidling past Reaper and Deedee and making their way around the lorry to check out their new destination.

Both girls were dressed in black leather cat-suits which emphasised their faultless curves to perfection as they sashayed down the alley.

Reaper caught Stud looking after them and smiled. "A little somethin' for the boys," he growled. "Help to keep their minds on the job."

Stud's grin widened. "Thanks Reaper, the boys will appreciate that." He turned his attention back to Reaper; his face took on a more serious countenance. "But don't worry, everyone is on the clock. They're all ready to take the job on," he said, reassuringly.

Reaper swept back his hair with his hand, exposing the myriad of scars beneath. He placed an almost comforting hand on Stud's shoulder, before saying in a low voice barely above a whisper. "Yeah, we need to talk about that!"

A look of concern suddenly spread across Stud's face. "There's nothin' wrong, is there?" he asked, the concern in his voice matching his look.

"Let's go upstairs an' talk," Reaper replied, "walls 'ave ears yer know."

****

Darren Skinner crept down the staircase trying to remember which one of the boards made the loudest creak. He could hear his mum bellowing at the kitchen staff, as usual. He wanted to sneak past without her noticing so that he could get down to the cellar and make it back with a couple of decent bottles of scotch.

He had promised Jax that he would supply the liquor as he was supplying the pot and the porn.

As he emerged from the hallway, Darren could see the kitchen door was shut, which did not stop his mother's roar penetrating the wood panelling, but at least she would not be able to see him pass.

Once he reached the cellar, Darren edged open the door as carefully as he could, before entering and closing it behind him. Once downstairs he quickly managed to locate the crates of single malt, and removed a bottle from two different crates so as not to arouse suspicion if the bar staff checked.

On his way back up he listened at the cellar door. His mother was still going, but now her voice had calmed somewhat and from what he could tell she was regaling them all with tales from the conference.

Darren snuck past the kitchen door on his way to the pub's back entrance as stealthily as he knew how. Once outside he quickly made his way to a dilapidated outbuilding across the courtyard where he often stashed contraband he did not want his mother to find. The outbuilding had originally belonged to the old lumber mill which closed down a couple of years earlier, and apart from being used as a refuge by the odd tramp, was usually uninhabited.

Darren checked over his shoulder that no one had followed him from the bar. Once he was satisfied he was alone, he slid open the ramshackle door and walked in.

He tucked his cache behind one of the old partitions so that it would be out of sight to anyone who happened to venture in.

As he turned to leave he came face to face with Angel Sommers.

The shock of seeing her there made Darren jump back and he was glad that he was not still holding the whiskey as the sudden movement might have caused him to drop both bottles.

Angel eyed him, suspiciously. "Who are you?" she demanded. "And what are you doing in here?"

Darren opened his mouth automatically, but no sound emerged. The combination of being startled by Angel's sudden appearance and the fact that she was probably the most beautiful woman he had ever laid eyes on was enough to stun him into temporary silence.

"What are you, a fly catcher?" asked Angel, planting her fists firmly on her hips as she glared at him like a snake surveying its prey before attacking.

In response to Angel's comment, Darren shut his mouth so fast that he managed to catch the end of his tongue between his teeth.

"Ow!" he squealed, slapping his hand across his mouth.

Angel laughed at him without trying to disguise it.

Darren could feel his face flush.

Without speaking, Angel moved forward and placed a tender hand on the side of Darren's hot cheek. The gesture took him by surprise and caused his blush to deepen even further.

Angel gently rubbed her hand up and down Darren's cheek.

When he looked up at her she was smiling, warmly.

"Sorry," she said, "I shouldn't have laughed, that must have hurt."

Darren nodded, dumbly.

Finally, he found his voice. "That's ok, it's my own fault."

Angel turned her head slightly to one side. "No, I believe it was more my fault than yours. I scared you didn't I?"

"Oh no, no, no," Darren flustered, "it was nothin' really."

Angel looked behind him. "So what's the big secret?"

"How do you mean?"

Angel's smile broadened. "What have you just secreted behind that panel so carefully? Some sort of hidden contraband?"

Darren half-turned then immediately swung back to face Angel as if there was not anything behind him worth mentioning. "Oh, nothin' much, just somethin' for later on, that's all."

"Let me see?" Angel coaxed as she moved to pass by him. Instinctively, Darren blocked her way. His movement was far more confrontational than he had intended and he almost stepped aside again, but on reflection he decided to hold his ground.

Angel stopped short in front of him. They were now barely a few inches apart. Darren had never been this close to such an attractive woman before and had to fight an overwhelming instinct to grab hold of her and try to kiss her.

Angel too was not prepared to give any leeway. She held her ground, refusing to step backwards. Darren was much taller than she was, but that did not intimidate her. She looked up into his eyes and smiled to herself as she saw him starting to crumble.

"If it's nothing special," she offered, "then why can't I see it?"

Darren could feel his resolve starting to melt away. He gazed down into Angel's beautiful eyes and again could feel his face redden.

This was so embarrassing!

At seventeen he should be more adept at dealing with girls, or women as in Angel's case. But the truth was that he had minimal experience with them. Though he often bragged about past conquests to his mates, and they boasted straight back, he was convinced that they were lying every bit as much as he was, if not more.

At least he tried to keep his embellishments to an acceptable standard.

Darren had in fact managed several under the top fumbles with various girls from school, but alas that was as far as they had allowed things to go.

He could feel his knees starting to tremble with Angel so close to him. From this distance he could smell the aroma of her freshly washed hair and the sweet smelling soap she had used to bathe with. He longed to move even closer, but knew that he dare not. She did not seem the type of girl to welcome uninvited intrusions.

Lost in thought, Darren did not notice as Angel leaned in close enough for her lips to almost brush against his earlobe. "Let me see, and I'll give you a kiss." She whispered.

The shock must have registered on Darren's face as Angel could not stifle another laugh when she pulled back and looked at him.

Darren's eyes widened as Angel's offer filtered through.

Before he could reply, Angel nodded at him as if in response to his unasked query.

At last, he said, "You're 'avin' me on."

"No I'm not," Angel assured him. "You show me what you're hiding behind there and I'll give you a big kiss as your reward."

Darren did not need more than a moment to consider her offer.

He turned on the spot and went to retrieve the two bottles he had stashed there earlier.

Darren held them up for Angel to see.

"Ooo, single malt, the good stuff," Angel cooed, moving in closer for a better look. "Now what does a girl have to do to get a shot of that?"

They were now barely a couple of feet apart.

Darren placed the bottles behind his back. "Oh, sorry, no I can't, I promised my mate we could share them later."

Angel smiled and without saying a word walked slowly up to Darren until she was directly in front of him.

With both his hands behind his back shielding his liqueur Angel had a free reign. She curled a hand behind his head and pulled him down so that their lips could meet. Before Darren could respond, Angel slipped her tongue in between his lips and started to snog him.

It only took a few seconds for Darren to respond in kind, but he was annoyed with himself that because he was holding the bottles he could not use his hands to make the experience even more pleasurable.

After a while, Angel pulled back. "That was for showing me what you had," she informed Darren. "Now for a taste of your wares…" as she spoke she slid her hand down Darren's stomach and allowed it to rest between his legs.

She could feel him starting to grow hard and revelled in the low moan that escaped his lips as she played mercilessly with him, sliding her hand up and down over his bulging denims.

"What'd'yer say, mmnnn?" she purred. "Perhaps you had better put those somewhere safe before we have ourselves a little accident."

CHAPTER SEVENTEEN

The heavy snowfall from the night before had inspired the group to take part in some outdoor snow-themed activities. Sharon, Carey and Jenny had struck upon the idea over breakfast. It was too nice a day to spend indoors, and even though Steve's Land Rover could probably have coped with the snow, none of them seemed too bothered by the prospect of staying by the cabin for the day.

Initially, it was just the girls taking part.

Steve and Greg were engrossed in some video game Greg had brought with him and were apparently at a vital point in the proceedings and far too busy to consider outdoor activities.

Scott, being his usual self was upstairs in his bedroom thumbing through a body building magazine. Jenny tried as optimistically as she could to make him take part, but it became apparent after a while that he had no intention of being disturbed.

Sharon and Carey could both see the all too familiar expression of disappointment on Jenny's face as she descended the stairs and both of them passed a silent comment to the other regarding the state of their friend's relationship.

They endeavoured to cheer her up with their snowy pastimes.

First on the agenda was a snowman.

The girls rummaged through the outbuilding that housed the generator to find shovels and scrapers to assist them with their task.

When they began they were all muffled up to the brim with scarves, hats, gloves and thick coats. But within a short time the work was making them so hot that one by one they started to strip off, until eventually they were only clad in jumpers and gloves; the snow being far too cold to handle without at least one protective layer.

Once they had finished their labour they found some old sacks in one of the sheds to help dress their snowman. They used an old bucket for a hat, pebbles for the eyes and mouth, and a twig for the nose.

They decided to call him Bertie.

Whilst in the process of trying to find Bertie suitable attire, they came across some oval plastic seats which had been discarded at the back of one of the sheds. They had presumably once been part of a larger article of garden furniture, possibly a swing or a recliner.

Carey had the idea that if they cleaned them up they could perhaps use them as sleds. The area directly behind the cabin had a steep slope which carried on for a couple of hundred yards before petering out to a flat surface. It provided an ideal condition for sledding.

Using some old rags and torn towels they found next to the log pile they set about cleaning up the dipped section of each of the carriers as these would make ideal seat units for their sleds.

Once clean, they carried the seats to the peak of the slope behind the house. Looking down however, the girls were suddenly unsure of the safety of their venture. The climb appeared far steeper than they had remembered, and the prospect of having no way of stopping once they had reached the bottom, gave then all cause for concern.

The slope evened out, so in theory the momentum should eventually slow them down sufficiently to stop. But from up here the prospect still seemed a daunting one.

Finally, having accepted responsibility for having the idea in the first place, Carey stepped up to the plate and took the plunge.

Both Sharon and Jenny held their breath as their friend started her descent. But Carey's shrieks and whoops of laughter on her way down allayed their fears.

Sharon followed soon after with Jenny bringing up the rear.

The steep climb back up the hill was more than compensated for by the thrill of sliding back down again.

After playing follow-my-leader for a while they decided to all start off together and race each other. As the afternoon wore on the races became more and more competitive as each of the girls learned how to master the art of sledding.

Using their own bodyweight to turn and manoeuvre their crafts became second nature after a while. Even so, there were still occasions when one of them would shift their body the wrong way, causing them to collide with one or both of the others, leaving all of them rolling and tumbling down the slope until they eventually lay at the bottom in a great heap of bodies and upside down sleds, laughing so hard that they could almost not catch their breath.

Finally, Steve and Greg, feeling the stiffness of too much inactivity spent all day in front of a screen, decided to investigate what all the commotion was about. Seeing the fun the girls were having they went in search of boards for themselves. Unable to find any more plastic seats, they both settled for some old rusted dustbin lids and as they were not so concerned for their clothes they did not bother to clean them up first.

The races continued, but because they boys were heavier than the girls it gave them an unfair advantage, speeding their descent.

After a while, to put things on an even keel, the boys would give the girls a slight head start, taking even more delight if they still passed them on the way down.

The girls in retribution for the boy's smugness, having had longer to train and perfect their expertise, formed a barrier by skimming down as close to each other as possible without knocking each other over.

Steve and Greg began to experiment with different kinds of stunts to better the girls, but this usually resulted in them taking a tumble before reaching their goal.

After a while their exhilaration and enthusiasm gave way to fatigue.

The climb back up the hill was becoming more and more exhausting, and seemed to be taking longer with each attempt.

In the end they called a halt and put their makeshift sleds back into storage.

As they made their way back to the cabin, Scott suddenly emerged from the front door.

For the first time since their arrival he was not wearing his usual frown.

"So here you all are," he said, cheerily. "I came downstairs and thought perhaps you'd all abandoned me and gone into town."

"As if we'd leave without asking you along," replied Sharon, trying to keep the mood light.

"So what have you all been up to?" asked Scott.

Jenny, hopeful that her boyfriend's new found mood might hang around for a while, sidled up to him and put her arms around his waist. "We've been tobogganing," she answered gleefully, pecking him on the cheek. "And, we made Bertie," she half-turned so that she could point to their snowman.

"Nice work," Scott nodded approvingly. "He looks like he could handle himself if things got rough."

Scott placed his arms around his girlfriend and planted a gentle kiss on her forehead. "So what's next on the agenda then?" he asked, smiling down at her.

"Next!" cried Carey. "We're all in, now."

"And besides," Steve piped in, looking at his watch "it's almost beer o'clock."

Scott nodded his understanding, and then suddenly he swept Jenny to one side and pointed excitedly behind the others. "What the hell is that?"

They all spun around in unison, holding their breath and scanning the area in front of them.

Scott's words had set all their nerves on edge, especially in view of Jenny's experience from the other night.

Sharon and Carey moved in closer to their respective boyfriends instinctively feeling the need for some comfort and protection.

The sun had already begun its descent behind them and the view ahead had taken on a misty eerie quality which they had not noticed until this moment.

Each of them strained to see what Scott had been alluding to.

A sudden gust of wind shook some loose snow free from the trees to one side of them. The movement caused them all to turn as one.

They waited, scrutinising the land before them.

The first snowball hit Steve squarely on the back of his head where it exploded showering the others in cold wet ice.

The initial shock took a moment for them all to register what had just happened.

Slowly, as the reality of the situation dawned on them they all looked at each other before turning to see Scott's grinning face. He was now holding two freshly rolled snowballs which he then hurled in their general direction before they had a chance to move apart.

The balls hit their targets sending the four friends scattering to each side.

Before Scott had a chance to re-load, both Steve and Greg had gathered up their own ammunition and started firing off balls in Scott's direction. Unfortunately for Jenny several of their missiles missed their target and landed on her, so Jenny started gathering up her own and fired them back.

Before long the other girls had joined in too, and a mass snowball fight ensued.

The game continued until everyone was too exhausted to continue and held up their hands in unison to reflect surrender.

Once back inside the cabin the boys volunteered to fetch drinks and prepare dinner, leaving the girls to crash out and relax.

Even Scott seemed happy to help, even though he would have to prepare his own food separately.

Greg made up a fire in the hearth and the girls eased back to chat and listen to music whilst their meal was being prepared.

"Have you heard anything more from Jan?" Jenny asked Sharon. There was a slight edge of concern in her voice although the other two girls knew that she was trying to hide it. Jenny had expressed her unease the previous evening when Jan first e-mailed Sharon to tell her about her accident and subsequent rescue by Tom.

Jenny knew that the other two girls did not share her apprehension at leaving their friend alone with a man they hardly knew, but in the end she felt forced to acquiesce as both Sharon and Carey seemed fully confident that Jan could take care of herself.

Sharon swallowed a mouthful of her wine before answering. "She sent me an e-mail before we went out. Not much new to say except that her ankle was still killing her and she was going to stay with Tom at least until Adam comes back tomorrow, because he has the 4x4."

"Oh, right," replied Jenny, sheepishly.

Sharon and Carey gave each other a sly look. They could tell that their friend was still was not happy with the situation so Sharon decided to allay her fears, somewhat.

"To be honest," she said, lowering her voice as if to prevent the boys in the kitchen from hearing, "I got the distinct impression that our Jan and Tom were......" She allowed her silence to hang in the air for a moment before looking back over her shoulder once more to check for eavesdroppers. "You know?"

Carey almost choked as she swallowed her wine.

She spluttered twice before Sharon leaned over and slapped her on the back.

Jenny's mouth was wide open, almost as if she was unable to close it on her own.

Carey managed to clear her throat before stating. "What, you mean she and Tom are...?" her eyes widened in disbelief as she stared at Sharon.

"Sleeping together!" Jenny finally blurted out, much louder than she had intended.

"Ssshhh," chided Sharon, ensuring once more that none of the boys were close enough to hear. "I don't think she'll want it broadcast even if it is true. I may be totally wrong, after all she didn't come right out and say it, and I didn't ask, I was just reading between the lines."

"So what did she say?" Carey leaned in closer, unable to hide her eagerness to know more.

"Well, it was more the fact that she seemed to be leaving the obvious details out," Sharon replied, still keeping her voice low. "She mentioned how Tom had carried her back to his place and tended to her wounded ankle. Then she let slip that he carried her up to bed, then the next thing she mentioned was how hungry they both were this morning, after last night."

The other girls both looked at each other. Carey stifled a giggle, Jenny still appeared shocked.

"You need to find out the juicy details," Carey insisted, "you can't just leave us hanging like that"!

"No," replied Jenny, "it's really none of our business, it'd be like prying."

"Nonsense," Carey shot back, defensively. "We're just showing concern for our friend's wellbeing."

Sharon looked at her. "And who are you trying to kid?" she challenged. "You just want to know if Jan got any last night, that's all you're concerned with?"

At this, all three of them began a fit of giggles, feeding off each other.

****

"Jax, I'm tellin' yer mate, I'm on the level." Darren was almost at the point of pleading having been trying for the last ten minutes to convince his friend to change their plans for the evening. If what Angel had promised him earlier in the bar was true, they had a much more exciting time ahead of them than simply staying in at his place and watching porn.

In the outbuilding, true to her word, Angel had brought Darren up to the height of ecstasy. She allowed him to snog her and let him fondle her breasts while she stroked him between his legs.

At one point Darren actually thought that she was going to let him have full intercourse with her, but before he had the chance to see how far she was prepared to let him go, her groping and stroking caused him to ejaculate into her soft palm.

Even then, as she removed her hand from inside the front of his jeans she lifted it up to her mouth and slowly licked the remains of his eruption from her fingers, moaning seductively as if she was savouring the flavour.

Darren let Angel keep one of the bottles of single malt. It seemed to him a very small price to pay for the service she had just rendered.

He felt foolish asking her to keep it out of sight so his mum would not become suspicious and investigate the stock in the cellar. But Angel seemed to understand perfectly and said that she would not want to be the cause of any unpleasantness, so she took it back to the hotel before re-joining her fellow bikers.

Back in the bar Darren walked right into his mother. She demanded that he perform some chores for her before he went out for the night. She reminded him for the umpteenth time the bar did not run itself and he needed to pull his weight to earn his keep.

For once Darren did not argue. Angel's handiwork had left him feeling completely relaxed and satisfied, so a few menial errands was a small price to pay considering he still had his evening with Jax to look forward to.

Jax was going to be so jealous when he told him what had happened.

Darren saw Angel re-enter the bar from the hotel, minus the bottle of single malt, and when she blew him a kiss he blushed, involuntarily.

It was while he was mopping up some spilled beer behind the bar that Angel approached him. The other bar staff were at the far end busy with customers so Darren was confident that whatever she wanted to say to him would remain private.

Angel stood on the foot rail to raise herself up, and leaned over the bar towards him. Darren followed her lead and turned his head to offer her his ear.

"I've just been talking to the rest of my lads," she whispered. Darren could feel the soft warmth from her breath brush against his earlobe. Being at such close quarters with Angel again was intoxicating. "Seems like we're going to have a bit of a party back at the hotel tonight," she continued, checking to ensure that no one else was in earshot. "Some of the other girls from the gang are going to join us, so if you and your friend want to come along we can have some more fun like we did outside."

Hearing her words, Darren almost choked as he swallowed.

Before he had a chance to answer, Angel said, "Of course, to make the party really go with a bang, we could do with another couple of bottles of the good stuff, and your friend's pot, of course."

As she pulled away, Angel could tell from Darren's wide-eyed stare that she already had him convinced.

She gave him another sly wink and slid back down the bar to the floor, before making her way back to her friends.

As soon as Darren could get away he raced up to his room and called Jax.

To his astonishment, his friend was being much harder to convince than he had anticipated. It was obvious to Darren that Jax thought that he was being wound up. In all honesty, Darren himself found the situation too good to be true, but after Angel's performance in the outbuilding he had no doubt about how brilliant the night ahead was going to be.

"Jax, come on man, what's the matter with you?" Darren could feel the exasperation seeping into his own voice. "I'm telling you there's gonna be some seriously hot babes at this place, and they're gonna put out for us, big time."

From the other end of the phone Jax let out a huge sigh. "And you know this how, exactly?"

Darren had wanted to save telling his friend about his little adventure with Angel until later, but now he was feeling pressured into throwing everything he had in his arsenal into the mix to get the job done. "Alright, alright, I was gonna tell you later anyway," Darren muttered. "One of the girls already gave me a hand job in return for a bottle of my mum's whiskey, so I know we're on a definite promise if we turn up with more booze and your gear."

"What!" Jax gasped. "Some girl just gave you a hand job? Bollocks!"

"I'm telling you mate, why would I lie? Darren was finding it harder by the second to keep the exasperation out of his voice. "Come down 'ere and I'll show 'er to yer, she's gorgeous!"

"If she's so gorgeous why's she bothering with an ugly bastard like you then?"

"Very funny," Darren sneered. "Look, if you aren't interested I'll jus' go alone; it'll be your stupid loss."

Darren was starting to regret even bothering with Jax, but the truth was, without his mate's weed he was afraid that he might not be made so welcome at the party.

And tonight may turn out to be the best night of his life!

He decided to give it one more push.

"Listen mate," Darren said, calmly, "if you really wanna miss out on the chance to have it off with some gorgeous sexy women, then that's up to you, but don't say I didn't offer you the possibility."

There was a long sigh on the other end of the line followed by an even longer pause, before Jax replied. "Alright, alright, I'll come. But I'm warning you, if this is a wind-up…"

Darren let out a sigh of relief. "Trust me mate, this could be a massive night for both of us," he said, with conviction. Then as an afterthought he added, "Just don't forget the stuff!"

CHAPTER EIGHTEEN

Tom lay back on the sofa with Jan nestled against his chest. The soothing sound of classical music filled the air, mingling with the crackle of the logs on the fire to create a romantic setting similar to the one they had enjoyed the previous evening.

The main difference between now and last evening was that this time they lay together as lovers to appreciate the ambience.

Also, unlike last evening, neither Tom nor Jan wanted to be parted long enough for Tom to prepare one of his fantastic dinners. And since Jan could not stand for long enough to help him in the kitchen, they decided to just have something from the freezer for convenience.

Tom had suggested going out for dinner as an alternative, but neither of them really wanted to leave the warmth and comfort of his home on such a cold and inhospitable night.

After they had made love that morning, Tom fixed them a delicious breakfast of scrambled eggs, crispy bacon and strong coffee. As Jan was still somewhat immobile due to her foot, Tom set up a DVD player in the bedroom so that they could lie back and watch a film. He apologised to Jan for the limited selection as most of them belonged to Adam and were action films, but Jan confessed a secret fondness for such movies so they decided on one that they could both enjoy.

Afterwards, Tom ran a hot, soothing bubble bath for Jan to relax in and help with the pain in her foot. When he carried her into the bathroom and laid her gently in the tub she convinced him to join her, which he did gladly, and the two of them stayed there until the water grew too cold to enjoy.

Tom found Jan a set of oversized clothes that she could change into, and then he carried her back down and placed her on the sofa where they stayed for the remainder of the afternoon, listening to music, talking, kissing and cuddling.

Tom let out a deep sigh.

Jan moved her head slightly so that she could see his face. "What was that for?" she asked, bemused.

"Oh nothing," replied Tom, unable to cover the lie convincingly enough to fool her.

"No come on, tell me," Jan persisted. "That was not a *nothing* sigh."

Tom leaned down and kissed the top of her head, tenderly. "Don't worry about it; it was just me being stupid."

Jan turned even more now so that she could see his entire facial expression while he talked. "Well now you've got to tell me!" she demanded, her lips turning up at the ends into a cheeky smile.

Tom gazed down at her. Jan could see a far away look in his eyes which conveyed a sadness she had not seen before. It made her want to hold him closely until his sorrow went away.

Tom could tell he was not going to get off so lightly and part of him regretted not keeping the mood brighter.

Finally, he replied. "It's just that we've had such a wonderful day together, at least I have," he said, quickly, feeling he had to justify his statement without taking anything for granted. "And now it's almost over...well, it's all been over too fast."

Tom waited nervously for Jan's reply.

As each second passed he regretted his little speech more and more. He knew that he should have kept his feelings to himself, and now that they were out, there was no way of winding them back in.

After what seemed to him like an eternity, Jan reached up and pulled him in closer for a kiss.

When they parted, she said, "I would never have had you pegged as such an old romantic."

Tom smiled, sheepishly. "Yeah, old being the operative word there."

Jan smacked him, playfully. "That's not what I meant and you know it full well, Tom Meadows."

"Do I?" His voice was playful again, but his eyes betrayed his real feelings.

Jan kissed him again, this time more passionately.

"And what do you mean by it's over?" Jan asked, suspiciously. "Am I being chucked over now, out into the snow with the rest of the unwanted trash?"

Tom could not help but smile. "Never," he said, reassuringly. "You could never be anything but *wanted* by me."

"And wanton, as I recall," chided Jan, wagging a finger.

"Oh yes please," Tom agreed, holding her closer.

They stayed silent for a while, letting the gentle strains of the music flow over them until the CD ended. Neither of them felt any inclination to stir, so for a while they just lay still, the silence only being interrupted by the occasional crackle of a log on the fire.

Finally, Tom made the move. "Come on you," he said, playfully, "I need to check on dinner and lay the table."

Jan moaned, and reluctantly lifted herself off Tom to allow him to move.

Tom slid out from underneath her and ensured that she was securely propped up before he ventured into the kitchen.

After setting the table and selecting another CD, Tom came back over to the sofa. "Ok my lady," he announced, "dinner is almost ready and your table awaits."

Jan shuffled herself forward then Tom swept her up into his arms and carried her over to the dining table in the kitchen.

"And what would you like to drink?" he asked, before suddenly snapping his fingers. "I've just remembered," he said, excitedly. "I've got a couple of bottles of champagne still in the back, how about it?"

Jan's eyes lit up. "Oh yes please, I haven't had that for ages."

Tom went out to the garage and returned with the two bottles. He put one in the fridge for later and set about opening the other. The cold temperature in the garage meant that the first bottle was already adequately chilled and ready for serving.

Tom filled up two flutes and handed one to Jan. "Well," he asked, "what shall we drink to?"

Jan gazed straight into his eyes. "Us, of course," she replied.

They clinked, and drank.

****

Joanne felt the icy blast as the wind whipped around the corner of the rocks and penetrated the extremely inadequate protection which the alcove afforded her.

She had no idea how long she had been asleep. But now she could see that night had fallen again and with it, the temperature had plummeted.

When she first started to run from the Beast, her mind had lapsed into a kind of catatonic shock, unable to process the fact that she had just witnessed her boyfriend being torn apart in front of her very eyes.

With the depth of the snow impeding her progress, Joanne ran with sheer abandon, not caring how fast she was moving or in which direction she was heading. Her only goal was to put as much distance between herself and the creature as possible.

On and on she ran, stumbling, falling and scrabbling to get up, the soles of her boots often refusing to make purchase on the icy surface. With her legs pumping desperately she would continue to try and run even when she was in the midst of another tumble.

Behind her, she could feel the creature gaining.

The ferocity of its rage bore down upon her; its thunderous roar growing louder it seemed with every passing second, carried on the wind as the Beast gained more ground, its progress unhindered by anything which lay in its path.

Joanne refused to look back even once, throughout the chase. She was afraid that if she did the mere sight of the creature almost upon her would cause her legs to give way for the last time, leaving her exposed and defenceless at the mercy of her pursuer's ravenous appetite.

Each time she fell, lying there prone with the wind knocked from her body, her face buried in the snow, her mouth open trying to regain her breath against the freezing ice which assailed her nostrils, she would still not give in and she forced herself to carry on.

With every effort she would strive to regain her composure, all the time expecting one of those huge, hairy, blood-stained paws to grab her by the neck and seal her fate.

There were times when she could almost feel the Beast's fetid breath penetrating through her clothing and warming the back of her neck. The hot rancid stench of the thing's saliva as it escaped from between those bloody fangs, Joanne imagined dripping and splashing onto her head and shoulders from high above her.

And with each new repulsive emanation Joanne knew that her moment of death would surely follow!

But it never did!

Whether she managed to out-distance the Beast forcing it to give up the chase, or it had never tried to follow her in the first place, she did not know. But eventually, exhausted and unable to continue any further, Joanne fell forward for the last time and lay in the deep snow awaiting her doom.

She turned her head to one side so as to be able to hear the final cry of victory from her attacker, but it never came, and eventually she passed out.

When she came to, Joanne could see that the sky was starting to grow light.

The snow had stopped falling and she was covered with a thin veneer of white camouflage.

She stayed still for a moment, listening. The only sound she could hear was the wind, but still she waited. She was afraid to move in case the action caught the eye of her pursuer, as she still sensed that the creature was nearby, waiting.

Eventually, she could wait no more.

If this was to be her end then she was ready. She would not run anymore, she would not fight or try in any way to protect herself. She was there for the Beast's taking.

There would be no defiance in her final action.

Surrender!

Summoning what was left of her strength; Joanne placed her hands beneath her shoulders and forced the ground away from her, lifting her torso up into a kneeling position.

She waited.

Nothing!

Wearily, she hoisted herself up to her full height and stood knee-deep in fresh powder. Joanne gazed around her, surveying the horizon.

There was no sign of the creature.

She stood there for what seemed an eternity.

At any second she expected the Beast to appear in the distance and make a beeline for her. She had already conceded that her life was over before she passed out, so this was merely a waiting game. There was no point in running. There was nowhere to hide. She might as well stay put and await her fate.

After a while, Joanne's mind began to do battle with itself. Part of her wanted to stay where she was, resigned to her end. But another part of her sensed a chance for escape. As the two sides raged against each other in a conflict of will, Joanne began to feel one side growing stronger, outwitting the other.

Her sense of reality started to return. Yes her situation was precarious as she had no idea where the Beast might be lurking, but it was not completely hopeless.

She was still alive and in full command of her faculties. She did not have to just stay here and await her destruction. She still had a chance of escape.

Almost as if in autopilot Joanne lifted one leg free from the snow and placed it forward. She continued with the other foot, one step at a time. Her progress was slow with the compacted snow and ice hampering her progress, but at least she was moving.

She began to feel alive again.

She felt more and more in control with each laborious step.

As she slowly managed to pick up the pace, Joanne could feel her heartbeat racing. She still had no idea in which direction she was heading, she could in fact be walking directly into the Beast's lair. For all Joanne knew the creature might be laying camouflaged straight ahead of her, but that did not matter right now.

She was moving, and that by itself equalled progress.

Joanne walked for over three hours.

In all that time she never saw nor heard the Beast.

She walked until she felt she could not go on anymore without rest.

Finally, she came across the tiny alcove buried behind some large rocks. The protection it offered her was minimal, but it was still better than being completely exposed and out in the open.

Joanne huddled herself against the rock face, squeezing her body in as far as she could for cover and concealment.

The protection afforded her by the recess sheltered her from the worst of the wind, and only someone passing directly in front of her would be able to see that she was there.

She felt as safe as it was possible for her to be under the circumstances.

Within seconds Joanne had fallen asleep.

Now awake again, under the cover of darkness, she wondered if this might be her best and only chance of escape.

There was no way of knowing from her hideaway if the Beast was anywhere around. Her view from within the alcove was limited to the space directly in front of the opening; everything else was masked behind the outcropping of rocks.

Joanne strained to listen to any sound above that made by the wind.

There was nothing!

Cautiously she began to lean forward to give herself a better vantage point. Her legs were stiff from the cold and sore from having been in the same position for too long. As she moved Joanne gave an involuntary *squeal* as the cramp in her legs took hold. She pushed against the pain forcing herself to stand erect to ease her suffering.

She stamped against the frozen ground to restart her circulating.

Joanne hopped and jumped forward away from the protection of the alcove and out into the vast expanse of the snow-covered hills and mountains that surrounded her.

She looked around her in all directions. There was no immediate indication as to exactly where she was or how far away from the nearest form of civilisation she might be.

Her tummy rumbled. Joanne surmised it may well be twenty-four hours since her last meal, though food had been the furthest thing from her mind until this moment.

But she was hungry. And thirsty. And she needed to go to the toilet.

She looked about her for a reasonably secluded spot where she could relieve herself. There was a dark cluster of trees about four hundred yards straight ahead of her.

That would do.

Joanne was about to move towards them when all of a sudden she became aware of how exposed she was.

If the Beast was anywhere in the vicinity it would soon spot her in her dark coloured clothing sticking out from the white background like the proverbial sore thumb.

Gripped by a sudden panic, Joanne slowly edged her way back into the alcove.

Forcing herself back into her crouched position she sat there alone and afraid. She was shivering, but not so much from the cold as from the fear of discovery.

Her terror had taken control of her logical thought pattern once again. It was if she could sense the creature's approach. Its massive body moving effortlessly through the snow as it salivated in anticipation of its next feed.

Her!

Joanne lifted her knees up to her chest and bent her head down to meet them as she awaited the creature's approach.

She began to rock herself slowly back and forth, until eventually she drifted back off to sleep.

CHAPTER NINETEEN

Darren managed to sneak Jax into the bar through the back door without his mother or any of the bar staff noticing. Having already given Angel one of the bottles he had smuggled out from the cellar earlier, Darren decided that the bigger the offering he and Jax brought to the party, the more they were likely to receive in kind.

Naturally, he could not make the theft appear too obvious, which was another reason why he needed Jax to help him. Darren knew that the way the booze was stacked in the cellar, the crates at the bottom of the pile probably would not even be accessed for another couple of months, by which time he could blame the theft on any bar staff his mother had recently fired. And knowing his mother, there was bound to be several candidates.

Jax, for his part, was at first reluctant to act as an accomplice. He had always had a soft spot for Darren's mother. She was one of the only people besides his own mother who he did not mind calling him Cecil. So even though he was not adverse to a little thievery whenever the occasion presented itself, it did not sit right with him when it was Mrs Skinner who was the intended victim.

Darren finally managed to persuade Jax by pointing out Angel to him from behind the door. It was obvious that Jax had not believed his friend when he told him how gorgeous she was, but once he had seen her in the flesh his reluctance to play the part of an accomplice all but disappeared.

They waited in Darren's bedroom until the evening rush started. That way Madge and her staff would be too busy to notice them coming and going.

The ideal opportunity arose when a large booking turned up for dinner. Darren and Jax surreptitiously slipped down the stairs, closing the door behind them to muffle any noise that they might make during their endeavour.

The racket coming from the kitchen above the cellar also helped to mask their enterprise, and there were even a couple of alcoves for them to hide in should anyone come down to the cellar whilst they were there.

From his earlier expedition Darren knew where the latest deliveries had been housed. The plastic crates the spirits were stored in were stacked five high, with each crate holding twelve bottles.

They made their way over to the first stack of single malts.

"Right then," Darren whispered, "we'll take off two crates at a time and nick a bottle from the last one, then put the others back and no one will be any the wiser, ok?"

Jax nodded, though his heart was still not fully behind their little scheme.

They both took the strain and lifted the first two crates off the stack and placed them to one side, then they repeated the task until the last one was exposed. Darren retrieved a bottle from the middle section so that the theft could not be seen by anyone passing the stack.

Once they replaced the crates they carried out the same manoeuvre to salvage a bottle of vodka from a different stack, then a third of rum from another.

Having had the foresight to wear his big overcoat with the deep inside pockets, Darren shoved two of the bottles inside out of sight, while Jax wrapped the third one in his leather jacket and tucked it under his arm.

They crept up the stairs with Darren in the lead. Once they reached the door he placed his ear against it and tried to gauge the optimum moment to make their getaway.

Once he was sure that the coast was clear, Darren gently opened the door and ushered Jax out onto the passage.

They eased their way cautiously past the kitchen without being seen, and then they walked along the corridor past the toilets towards the door at the far end leading to the outside yard.

As Darren twisted the handle and yanked the door open they both heard a voice bellowing at them from behind.

"And where exactly do you two think you're off to then, I'd like to know?" It was Madge, standing by the kitchen door with her feet wide apart and her chubby fists planted firmly on her hips.

As he turned, Jax almost lost his grip on his jacket under his arm. In a moment of panic he felt the bottle secreted under it starting to slip from his grasp. By sheer good fortune he managed to grab the neck of the bottle through the fabric and avoid an almighty explosion.

Darren, when seeing his friend stumble, took in a huge lungful of air and held it until the danger had passed; and then he released it unconsciously in an enormous gush which did not escape his mother's attention.

Madge's eyes narrowed in an all too familiar expression of suspicion as she began to walk slowly and purposely towards the boys.

As she approached, Darren surreptitiously unbuttoned his coat allowing the flaps to fall apart and help conceal the contents of his inside pockets. He stared directly back at his mother, knowing from past experience that that was the best way to allay her suspicions.

Jax on the other hand reacted more like a frightened rabbit caught in the headlights of an oncoming vehicle. Try as he might he could not relax his stance and try to appear more nonchalant. Besides which, it was harder for him than it was for Darren to appear calm as he had far less experience than his friend had of dealing with his mother's suspicions. That and the fact that he was still holding onto the bottle for dear life made his demeanour appear precarious at best.

Madge was no fool and she knew instinctively that her son was up to no good. But exacting the truth she knew would take guile and fortitude on her behalf, so she decided to play things cannily.

As she drew alongside Jax her expression immediately changed to one of kindness and sincerity. "Cecil dear, how are you?" she asked, tenderly. "We haven't seen you around 'ere for a while. Where 'ave you been hidin'?"

Jax immediately dropped his gaze as if he was studying Madge's shoes. He unconsciously squeezed the bottle harder against his side. Panic gripped him as he felt the bottle begin to slide again, but he managed to address his posture and secure his hold before disaster struck.

Jax coughed into his fist pretending that that was the reason for his sudden movement. "Oh, I'm fine thank you Mrs Skinner."

Madge moved in closer and put her arm around Jax's shoulder. "Now come on Cecil, I've told you before luv, it's Madge not Mrs Skinner, you're a grown man now."

Jax could feel himself blush. Even though there was nothing remotely sexual about Madge as far as he was concerned, whenever she came this close to him he would always feel himself growing shy and awkward. It was almost as if she had some kind of provocative allure which he could not help but respond to.

He was glad at least that he had his baggy trousers on. Once, about a year earlier, he remembered Madge coming to watch him and Darren play football, and after the game she came up to him and gave him one of her massive hugs for playing so well. Jax remembered only too well the embarrassment he felt as his erection grew spontaneously as they made contact. It stuck out proudly through the flimsy nylon of his football shorts like a badge of honour.

He remembered too thinking that Madge must be able to feel his hardness as she held him close, pressing his puny torso against her voluptuous frame, with his head wedged between her more than ample bosoms to the extent that she restricted his breathing.

Jax was sure that he noticed a very knowing look from her when she finally released him. It was almost as if a secret had passed between them which only they knew about.

Since that incident Jax had always turned red whenever Madge was close by. Even the most innocent of gestures made him flush, and he was quietly suspicious that Madge revelled in his embarrassment.

Finally, after what seemed to him an eternity, Madge removed her arm and stood away. "Right then," she demanded, "what are you two rogues up to tonight?"

Jax shot a quick glance at his friend then immediately looked back at Madge's shoes unable to answer for fear of blowing the game.

"I'm jus' goin' round Jax's to watch a film," explained Darren, confidently.

"What're yer doin' about dinner?" Madge asked, obviously not convinced by the lie but unable to fathom what was going on.

Jax, still struck dumb, looked up at Darren, willing him with his expression to make the lie work.

"Don't worry about us," Darren piped up. "We'll get fish and chips on the way."

Madge nodded. "I see, so your parents aren't at home then Cecil?" She enquired, trying not to make it sound too suspicious.

Jax, realising he had been backed into a corner, raised his head to answer but Darren jumped in first. "They've gone out to see some friends, but they'll be back later."

Madge noticed Jax's red hue deepening. She knew only too well that lies poured out of Darren's mouth like running water from a tap, but Jax on the other hand lacked her son's ability to embellish the truth without the fear of his conscience pervading.

Even so, she had to admit defeat. If she could not entice Jax to open up then there was no point firing off more questions in the hope of catching Darren out.

Madge decided to accept the loss graciously. "Well you boys have a nice time, an' don't go gettin' into any trouble."

"We won't," Darren assured her.

As the two of them turned away from Madge to head back to the door, they each gave a huge sigh of relief.

But their reprieve was short lived. Before they had managed to take one full step towards the door and freedom, Madge called out. "Just a second."

Darren and Jax both froze where they stood. They were convinced that Madge had somehow sussed out what they were up to.

Slowly, they both turned. "What now, mum?" Darren asked, his bravado starting to waver.

Madge closed in on them.

In unison, they both drew in a sharp intake of breath as she reached for Jax's coat which was tucked under his arm.

Jax instinctively tightened his grip. He had to fight the reflex of moving away from the advancing woman; otherwise his actions would appear both rude and suspicious. He knew that the game was up. Both of them did, but unlike his friend, Jax was not able to bluster his way out of it.

His heart missed a beat as Madge finally grabbed hold of his jacket.

"What're doin' mum?" Darren's tone managed to convey irritation, but some of the confidence had left his voice.

Madge looked at her son. "It's freezin' out there," she replied, casually. "Cecil will catch 'is death!" she turned her attention to Darren's petrified companion. "Come on love, let me 'elp you on with it."

Realising that all was not lost, Darren jumped straight in. "Fer god's sake mum, we're not five," he protested. "If 'e's cold he can put 'is own coat on once we get outside."

With that Darren gently tugged Jax's other arm towards him, mindful not to make too sudden a movement for fear that his mate would lose his grip on their prize.

Fortunately for them both, Madge released her hold and Jax, pretending to be carried by the force of his friend's wrench, moved away from her and towards Darren.

Madge replaced her hands on her hips. "Well I'm sure I don't know. You make sure that you wrap up Cecil, I don't want your mother calling me up accusin' me of not takin' care of you."

"I will Mrs Ski…Madge," Jax spluttered, his forehead coated in perspiration. "I'm just a little warm at the minute, but thank you anyway."

Madge watched as the two boys scuttled through the door and outside into the snow.

Once outside, Jax slammed the door shut and leaned against it, heaving a huge sigh of relief. He mopped his forehead with the back of his free hand and wiped the displaced sweat down his trousers.

"There," said Darren, gasping as a result of inadvertently holding his breath for too long as they made their escape. "Told you it would be a piece of piss!"

His friend stared at him. "You speak for yerself, your mum scared the shit out of me!"

Shivering from the sudden change in temperature, Jax carefully eased his bottle out from under his coat and passed it to Darren. Once his hands were free he struggled into his coat, appreciating the immediate warmth. He pulled a pair of leather gloves from his pocket and slipped them on. They would serve a dual purpose of keeping his hands warm and securing a firmer grip on the bottle.

Once he was ready, Jax collected his bottle from his friend and the two of them made their way to the outbuilding to retrieve the one Darren had left there earlier after his encounter with Angel.

The snow was starting to fall again as they made their way to the biker's hotel.

CHAPTER TWENTY

Toby Coates had been the manager of the Stag Hotel for over thirty years. At sixty two, he had accepted his lot such as it was, and had no inclination to consider any changes.

The job came with free room and board and enough money for him to indulge in his many vices. A keen gambler and friend- due mainly to the amount of money he had paid to them over the years- to the many bookies in town, Toby's other main vice was whiskey. Everybody knew that he kept a bottle under the counter from which he drew sustenance throughout the day, and usually by late afternoon most regulars knew not to stand too close to him if there was a naked flame in the vicinity.

The hotel's owner lived abroad and seemed content enough with the state of play so long as a regular amount of a certain sum reached their account each month.

The hotel itself was on the verge of dilapidation due mainly to the lack of care and attention that it had received over the years. Most of the paint on the walls was cracked and peeling and the linen was only changed when someone complained. Most of the rooms were en-suite with the pipes amalgamating in the basement before running down to the sewer. This often resulted in the toilets backing up when the main pipe became blocked which subsequently resulted in Toby having to pull on his rubber waders and industrial strength gloves to go down and clear the waste.

Several of the windows were either cracked or broken and patched up with tape and plastic sheeting, and the heating and hot water worked sporadically, usually after Toby went downstairs and hit the generator several times with a spanner to start it up.

But for all that, the Stag still had a relatively regular clientele amongst travelling business types who wanted to save on their expenses and pocket the difference by claiming that they had booked into more extravagant accommodation.

Beside the passing trade, the Stag was also a regular haunt for the working girls in town. Though almost everyone knew what was going on, Toby ensured that he kept a plausible façade by allowing the girls to come and go via the back entrance through the alleyway.

The girls for their part would pay Toby in cash for their occasional use of the rooms at the back of the hotel whilst he ensured that any passing genuine trade was only ever booked into the rooms facing the front street.

Toby also had a special arrangement with a couple of the girls whereby he allowed them the use of the rooms at a reduced rate in return for a couple of free sessions with each of them every week. It was an equitable arrangement which suited all parties concerned.

Toby glanced up from his *Racing Times* when he heard the familiar squeak of the main door leading to the lobby, opening. He recognised one of the two young men who entered as being the son of the woman who owned the bar and grill down the road. He did not like her much. She had once tried to charge him the full bar price for a bottle of scotch.

Toby wondered what her son might be doing coming in to his ramshackle hotel when he already had somewhere to stay five minutes away.

He wondered if perhaps he had had a fight with his mother and she had thrown him out. Or perhaps the bloke with him was his secret lover and they needed somewhere discreet to hang out without attracting too much of the wrong kind of attention.

Toby laid down his paper as they approached the desk. "Yes gentlemen, and what can I do for yer both this evening?"

Darren and Jax passed a nervous look between them before Darren spoke up. His voice quivered as he tried to find the right words. "We've been invited to join some of your guests for the evening," he mumbled, unable to look Toby square in the face.

Toby eyed them both, suspiciously. "I think you'll find that *those* guests use the back entrance in the alley, yer'll need to arrange your business with them before you come in."

From the puzzled expressions both men had on their faces it soon became apparent to Toby that they were not here for business with the girls, after all.

Jax was relying on his friend to do all the talking, so when Darren looked at him for inspiration Jax merely shrugged his shoulders and motioned for him to start speaking up.

Before Darren found the right words, Toby jumped in. "So if you're not looking for the girls, who exactly are yer here to see?"

"You've got some friends of ours, bikers," Darren stuttered, trying to compose himself. "They've invited us 'round for a drink."

Toby could tell by the way the two of them were trying to hide it that they both had something secreted beneath their outer clothing. He suspected from the *clinking* noise that they made as they walked that it was bottles of booze. Probably purloined from the bar the boy's mother owned. Toby smiled. Perhaps that was why they both looked so guilty.

He grabbed a toothpick he had discarded earlier from the counter in front of him, and wedged it in the corner of his mouth. He chewed at it slowly, enjoying how he seemed to be making the two men squirm by keeping them waiting. They were obviously up to something in his opinion. But if it was not business with the working girls, and they did not want a room for themselves, then Toby could not imagine what else it might be, unless that stolen booze they were trying so hard to conceal was to sell to the bikers for a quick profit.

Either way, neither of them looked particularly menacing so Toby was willing to give them the benefit of the doubt that they were not here to cause trouble. And if it was the bikers they were here to see, then that was fine with him.

Although he had been wary of them when they first arrived, the bikers had proved themselves to be solid guests. They paid their bills up front and in cash as well, which allowed Toby to skim a little off the top before he made his deposit for the owner at the bank.

They kept their noise to an acceptable level, cleaned up their own rubbish, and did not complain about the accommodation, so in many ways they were perfect clients.

Toby looked back at his paper. "Top floor," he announced, not bothering to look up to see whether or not his words caused the two of them to finally relax and stop looking so guilty.

Darren murmured an inaudible "thanks" as they walked past the desk.

Toby waited for them to reach the lobby before he called after them. "Lift's out, yer'll 'ave to use the stairs."

Darren and Jax groaned to each other as they turned away from the lobby and made their way to the large flight of stairs which led to the upper floors.

As they began their ascent, Toby reached down beneath the counter and grabbed a half-finished bottle of whiskey. He spun the stopper off with his thumb and, still watching the staircase, he took a large swallow.

He took another big gulp before replacing the stopper.

When Darren and Jax finally reached the top floor they were both breathing heavily from the climb. The fact that they were both bundled up in their coats to protect the bottles hidden underneath did not help their cause.

Catching his breath, Jax turned to Darren. "What room number do we want?" He asked, excitedly.

Darren shrugged his shoulders. "Dunno, the bloke downstairs didn't say."

"What!" Jax could not believe his friend's answer. "You mean to say you don't know, and you still didn't bother to ask 'im downstairs?"

Darren shivered. "Bloke gave me the creeps," he replied by way of explanation.

Jax sighed. "So what do we do now, just start knocking on doors?"

They both looked up and down the corridor. There were roughly eight doors leading down each corridor from the left and the right of where they stood. At the end of each corridor the path appeared to turn out of sight past the end rooms, which both men presumed would lead to another set of rooms down each side, and probably another row at the back for good measure.

After a moment, Darren decided to take the lead. "Come on," he said, "let's try down this way first and see what we can find out." He indicated to his left, signalling Jax to follow him.

They made their way down the first corridor, stopping outside each room to see if they could hear anything from inside. The doors did not appear to be especially thick, so it made sense to Darren that if there was a party of any description taking place behind one of them they should be able to hear something from outside.

By the time they reached the final straight without success, Jax was ready to suggest that one of them go back down and ask the desk clerk.

Just then, the faint sound of music wafted down the corridor towards them from the far end.

They both looked at each other and smiled. This had to be it!

As they neared the door in question they could hear the muffled sound of voices and laughter from within, mingling with the music.

Darren placed his ear against the wood of the door in an attempt to hear if he could identify the sound of Angel's voice, but there was too much commotion going on to be sure. Darren leaned in a little closer.

Just then, the door swung open causing Darren to lose his balance and fall against the person holding it ajar. His head smacked against the leather-clad chest of Axe, who grunted loudly from the impact but managed to keep his posture upright, unyielding from the blow.

Darren stumbled backwards, trying to regain his bearing without appearing to look too much like a cartoon character who had just stepped on a banana skin. Eventually, seeing his friend's distress, Jax came to his aid and helped to steady him.

They both stared at the formidable sight of Axe as he stood framed in the open doorway. Axe was well over six feet with a broad barrel chest and a protruding girth to match. His long, greasy hair hung down over his shoulders with strands of it disappearing inside his open neck leather top where they matted together with his coarse black chest hair.

He had a drooping Mexican-style moustache and when he parted his lips to sneer at the new arrivals, several gaps in his teeth became visible.

For a moment both Darren and Jax were stunned into silence by Axe's menacing appearance. Darren, already feeling foolish after his stumble, was starting to feel the trickle of perspiration slide down his face. Suddenly the thought of another fondle with Angel seemed too high a price to pay for this encounter.

Before either of the boys could find their voice, Axe took a step forward completely blocking out their view of the room behind him.

Both boys took an automatic step backwards

Then Axe spoke. "Yeah, what do you two want?" His voice was gruff and unwelcoming and matched his persona perfectly. Instinctively, Darren reached out and grabbed the shoulder of his friend's jacket. Although it appeared that he was reacting in order to stop his friend from running away, in reality it was more to steady himself as he felt his knees begin to give way under Axe's threatening gaze.

"Well!" Axe demanded, his eyebrows knitting closer together as if his patience was fast running out.

Finally, Darren found the resolve to speak. "We...we were invited here by...miss Angel...she said that there was a party."

As he spoke, Darren undid his jacket and produced the bottles of rum and whiskey he had stolen from the bar. Taking it as a signal, Jax did likewise with his booty.

Axe's eyes widened at the sight of the bottles, and a broad grin crossed his face when Jax brought out his bag of weed.

Axe stood to one side and ushered the two friends in.

Even with the change of the biker's demeanour, both boys gulped a nervous swallow before they moved forward, almost as if they knew that once they entered the biker's lair there was no way out.

The scene inside was like something from an old porn movie.

There were several male and female bikers, all in various states of undress cavorting with each other, some on the floor and others draped over the sparse furniture.

The floor was littered with crushed beer cans and empty bottles of liqueur, several of which must have lost some of their contents on the carpet judging by the stale odour contaminating the air.

Darren and Jax were both frozen to the spot as they surveyed the melee before them. They looked at each other nervously and passed an unspoken contemplation that they both felt completely out of their league in the present company.

At that moment, had it been an option, they would both have turned and run from the room and not stopped until they reached the comfort and security of Madge's bar. Even if it meant leaving their ill gotten gains behind, that too was ok, they just wanted out!

But leaving was definitely not an option with the sound of the door being slammed shut behind them, and the sturdy figure of Axe looming over their heads.

They both flinched as they felt Axe's big broad-fingered hands slap down on their shoulders. "Come on lads," he chuckled, "join in and 'ave some fun, the night is still very young."

Darren made a nervous sweep of the room. He was not exactly sure what he had expected to find after Angel's invitation, but now that he was here he decided that his libido must have taken hold of his senses. It was one thing to be alone with her, or even to have one of her girlfriends tag along for Jax, but this scenario was way out of his comfort zone and being surrounded by all of these bikers he was far too intimidated to do anything other than fantasise about spending more time with Angel.

The situation grew worse as all eyes in the room slowly began to focus on the two new arrivals and the murmur of conversation dissipated.

The two boys both felt obliged to offer some form of salutation, but neither of them appeared able to make such a gesture.

Darren caught sight of Angel in the far corner. She was naked from the waist up and was in the process of rubbing her bare breasts back and forth against a biker's open mouth. When she noticed Darren, she pushed herself away from the recipient of her charms and rushed over to greet him.

Angel threw her arms around Darren's neck and kissed him full on the lips. His instinct, even in the present company, was to hold her close to him but with the bottles in his hand he decided to err on the side of caution.

"Hey babe," Angel said, cheerily. "You made it; I thought you had stood me up."

Darren tried his best to at least keep his exterior composed, though inside his heart was racing at the thought of Angel's naked bosoms right before his face.

"Found them loiterin' outside the door," Axe interjected from behind. "I thought that they wus trespassers or summit."

Angel released her hold on Darren. "No," she replied, "they're my guests for the evening." She turned towards Jax who was making a conscious effort not to stare at her bare breasts. "And who might this be?" she asked, eyeing Jax up and down.

Finally, Darren managed to stutter out a response. "This is my mate, Jax…you said it would be ok to bring a friend."

"Oh it's more than ok," Angel smiled as she sidled up to Jax and pulled him towards her for a kiss.

Darren felt shocked and hurt that she was kissing Jax so passionately right in front of him. He could feel his face turning red with anger at his friend for taking advantage. After all, this was no way of repaying him for bringing him to the party in the first place. They were supposed to be best mates and Darren had already told Jax how much he liked Angel.

But then before he said or did anything stupid Darren managed to calm down and take stock. In all fairness to Jax it was Angel doing all the kissing and snuggling.

And what's more she had hardly been merely chatting to that other biker when they first came in.

But even so!

Darren still felt a twinge of jealousy as he watched the two of them kiss.

Finally, Angel tore herself away from an astonished Jax and seemed to focus her attention on the ill-gotten gains the two teenagers were carrying.

She relieved Jax of his pot. "Ohhh," she purred, holding up the plastic bag for all to see. "Now this looks like something we can use to really get this party started."

Angel handed the bag over to Axe. He opened it and held it up to his nose inhaling deeply. "Oh yes," he whooped, holding the bag aloft as if displaying it to the rest of the gathering. "Now this is good shit, I can really make something of this!"

The others in the room cheered and clapped as Axe made his way over to a table at the far end of the room. From their vantage point, Darren and Jax could see several mounds of various coloured substances spread across the wooden top.

As Axe busied himself mixing and combining the various ingredients, Angel guided the boys over to where Reaper sat sprawled sideways across a large armchair with Deedee perched on the end of his knees.

Angel introduced them. Reaper gave Deedee a hard slap to the rump to get her to move. When Reaper stood to shake their hands, both boys automatically offered their trembling hands to be rung tight.

Neither of them had ever been so close to anyone so big or so menacing-looking. The smile that crossed Reaper's face as he shook with them seemed to be genuine, but at the same time it also conveyed a message of warning, as if to let them know that they were in his territory now and the rules-whatever they might be-needed to be obeyed.

Angel introduced the two of them to the only other girls in the room, Stacy and Kim, who both helped to relieve the boys of their coats and bottles.

They received a combination of nods and the odd thumbs-up as they were introduced to the rest of the bikers and Darren felt disappointed that the men outnumbered the girls. If this night was going to end in an orgy-which he still hoped for-then the last thing he wanted was a bunch of hairy sweaty bikers crawling over him to gain access to one of the girls.

The thought made him shiver, involuntarily. Angel noticed the action and took it to mean something quite innocent. "The two of you must be cold from the walk over here, come on and let's fix you boys up with a drink."

Stacy and Kim began pouring drinks for everyone from the bottles supplied by the new arrivals. When everyone had a refill, Angel lifted her glass to toast Darren and Jax. As everyone else tossed their drinks down in one go, the boys felt obliged to do the same so that they would not been seen as wimps. Kim had poured them both very generous amounts of neat brandy so as the two of them tried to take it down in one swig they both choked and spluttered then dribbled some of the alcohol down their chins.

Jax managed to recover the fastest, but Darren had to take several gulps of air before he could properly clear his throat.

No sooner were their glasses empty then Stacy and Kim began a second round.

Darren looked at his friend through tear-stained eyes, almost as if he were begging for him to come up with a plausible excuse for them not to drink anymore for the moment, but Jax was in the same boat and reluctantly held out his glass for Stacy to refill.

Everyone downed the second round almost as quickly as the first, so this time the boys took things a little slower to try and avoid another episode like the first one.

By now, both of them were starting to feel the effects of the burning liquid and they each wished that they had suggested eating before coming over.

Fortunately for them, by the third drink the pace had slowed down. The others merely took a sip and continued with their various conversations.

Darren saw Angel whisper something in Kim's ear and the girl smiled and nodded in response before passing the message on to Stacy. Stacy too nodded, and then the two girls made their way over to Darren and Jax and linked arms with them both and guided them over to one of the larger sofas in the room.

As they slumped down both boys almost spilled their drinks, but that did not seem to deter the two girls who pressed themselves on top of them and started kissing them.

The boys, both too drunk by this point to protest even if they had a mind to, did nothing to stop the girls slipping their outer clothes off and sliding their hands over their bare torsos.

Both of them barely managed to lower their glasses safely to the floor before they were swept away by the power of lust. As the four of them cavorted and entwined themselves around each other, the rest of those present looked on as if watching some kind of live stage show.

After a while, both girls began to remove their partner's jeans and, almost in unison, began to stroke and fondle the teenager's growing erections.

Though still aware of where they were and those around them, both boys merely slid forward and moaned and writhed as they were played with.

They were vaguely aware that Axe was now passing around joints of various sizes which he had been busy creating since confiscating Jax's stash. When Axe reached the sofa where the four of them were frolicking, he handed one to Stacy. She managed to tear herself away from Darren long enough to take a huge drag on the joint. She held the smoke in her mouth as long as she could before blowing it in Darren's face.

Darren began to cough and splutter, much to the amusement of all. But when Stacy handed him the roll-up he took it willingly and drew the potent mixture into his mouth. Though he tried, he was unable to hold it in as long as Stacy. As he began to exhale Stacy grabbed him and held her open lips against his so that his smoke blew directly into her mouth.

Kim reached over and grabbed the joint from Darren. She took her turn before passing it to Jax for his. Jax had far more experience than his friend of using dope, but even he found the strength of the concoction overwhelming.

Between the copious amounts of drink that was forced upon them, and the extreme strength of the pot which seemed to reach both their turns very rapidly, Darren and Jax were completely out of it within an hour of arrival.

As the night progressed they both began to experience an 'out of body' sensation as they watched various naked and partly clothed bodies of both sexes slide and writhe over them. By this point, neither appeared particularly concerned by what was happening around, and to, them.

They could vaguely feel a combination of experiences from alcohol being poured into their mouths to it being replaced by tongues, searching and exploring them both inside and out.

Through the haze of smoke which hung in the air like a huge storm cloud preparing to unleash its fury, they could both see a frenzied parody of bodies moving back and forth, and voices which seemed to drift in and out of their subconscious as they both sank deeper and deeper into their drug-fuelled serenity.

At some point Darren noticed a pair of beautiful naked female breasts just in front of him. At least, they seemed within reaching distance. Unable to feel the movement he managed to lean forward far enough to wrap an arm around the owner of the bosoms and pulled her towards him as he fell back onto the sofa.

The force of the movement brought one of the nipples directly to his mouth, so he took hold of it with his eager lips and began to suck on it gently, rolling the nub back and forth with his wet tongue.

Suddenly, the nipple retracted and he felt a stinging slap across his face!

Though shocked and stunned by the attack Darren was still too high to let it register properly. Then as he tried to recapture the pink nub a huge hand grabbed hold of his outstretched arm and yanked him to his feet.

Darren found himself staring up at the threatening gaze etched on Reaper's twisted face.

Still too out of it to realise the position he was in, Darren merely smiled lopsidedly at the massive biker and tried to pass a witty comment which came out as little more than a slurred unrecognisable garble.

Even when Reaper threw Darren across the room and sent him crashing into a corner unit the seriousness of the situation still did not register on his foggy grasp of reality.

Everyone else in the room stopped what they were doing and watched in silence. Other than Darren and Jax, they all knew that a cardinal rule had been broken, one from which there was very little hope of survival.

YOU DO NOT MESS WITH REAPER'S WOMAN!

Some of the bikers sat back with huge grins spreading across their stoned faces. They had seen Reaper kick off before and they knew that there was no stopping him once he had been riled. Someone was going to pay for the disloyalty that Darren had shown, and they were all just glad that it was not going to be one of them.

Angel for her part felt a twinge of guilt for being the one to invite Darren and Jax to the party. Although, there was no way that she could ever have envisioned what was going to take place. She realised that both boys were obviously not accustomed to partying as hard as the rest of them, so maybe she should have kept a closer watch on how much drink they consumed and how many times they accepted the spliffs on offer. But in fairness to her, they were hardly children, and anyway, they had brought most of the stuff with them.

Angel knew that only a fool would attempt to stand in Reaper's way, so what was done was done. Now it was just a question of sitting back and waiting until Reaper had decided that he had made Darren suffer enough for his heinous crime.

Darren's one saving grace, Angel surmised, was that he appeared to be so far gone that his substance abuse might act as a buffer to whatever pain Reaper was about to inflict on him.

Before she could react, Angel saw Jax hoist himself off the sofa and launch at Reaper. He too was only barely cognisant of what was happening, so it must have been instinct more than bravado that caused him to act.

Jax managed to hit Reaper once with a wild haymaker to the chest before the big man looked down at the scrawny shivering wreck before him and, grabbing him by the throat, lifted him a full six inches off the floor before hurling him into his friend.

The two teenagers hit each other with such force that they knocked each other out.

CHAPTER TWENTY ONE

Having enjoyed the lavish dinner of hotdogs, potato salad and bread rolls the boys had lovingly prepared, all washed down with beer and wine, everyone was ready to call it a night. That was until Carey suggested that they all go outside and look at the stars.

It was true that out here there was none of the light pollution that they were used to back home, so the sky appeared much more expansive and the stars even more illuminating than on the clearest night in town.

After some initial groans at the thought of leaving the comfort and warmth of the lodge, the gang were won over by the picturesque clarity of the sky once they stepped outside. The moon was almost full and hung frost-free above them with a myriad of stars twinkling and glistening against the midnight blue of the night sky.

For a while they all stood together, huddled against the cold night air, captivated by the glorious aura.

However, after a while even Carey, bewitched as she was by their striking surroundings, began to feel the chill wind intruding upon her enjoyment of the blissful serenity.

Even with their parkas and ski jackets zipped up tight, soon everyone was starting to shiver loudly enough for the others to hear. Eventually, Sharon decided to take the lead. She looked over at Carey, and through chattering teeth she reluctantly asked: "Have you had enough yet?"

Carey sighed. "Oh, but it's lovely, look at that sky," she indicated around them with a sweeping arm. "You don't see sky like that back home, we should savour every minute of it while we can."

The others passed glances between them.

No one seemed to have the heart to spoil Carey's enjoyment, and they knew that she would not stay out for much longer on her own if they abandoned her for the shelter of the cabin.

Greg for one would not have the heart to leave until his girlfriend was ready. And for that matter, Sharon could not envisage disappointing her best friend either.

Oddly enough, it was Scott who came up with a winning suggestion. The rest of the group was still getting used to the newly arrived helpful, amicable, friendly Scott, so it came as a surprise when he suddenly announced that they should make a bonfire to keep them warm while they appreciated the ambiance of the place.

Having heard Scott's suggestion, everyone made themselves busy setting the scene. Steve remembered seeing some firelighters in the outbuilding which housed the generator. Whilst he sought them out, Greg and Scott gathered newspaper and kindling from the wood pile which Tom and Adam had left for them.

The girls meanwhile fetched enough garden chairs for everyone from the storage shed behind the cabin.

Once the fire had been constructed, they all sat around in anticipation of the warm glow as the boys took it in turns to try and light it. After several failed attempts Jenny stepped in and re-arranged the combination of wood, paper and firelighters before setting the pile ablaze.

The flames took immediately and licked their way hungrily up the wooden tent she had created, snapping and crackling as the timber caught.

Once she was satisfied that her efforts had born fruit, Jenny wiped her hands down the front of her jeans and stepped back to take her seat along with the others. Having sat down she suddenly noticed that everyone was looking at her; their expressions belied their obvious disbelief at how adept she had been at making up the fire. In response, Jenny just held up her hands. "Girl Guides camp merit badge winner first class," she announced, matter-of-factly.

Everyone fell about laughing, much to Jenny's amusement.

When everyone had calmed down the boys volunteered to fetch some drinks. Once they were out of ear-shot, Carey could not help but mention what she knew the rest of them were thinking. "Scott seems like his old self tonight!" She made a point of stating the fact openly without looking directly at Jenny, even though it was obvious that she was the intended recipient.

Understandably, Jenny blushed. "I know," she quickly looked over to make sure that the door to the lodge was still shut so that the boys-Scott especially-could not hear her. "I hope he stays like this for the rest of the holiday," she said, almost apologising for having made the comment.

"For the rest of his life would be better," stated Carey, emphatically.

Sharon shot her a look.

Carey shrugged. "What! I'm only saying what the rest of us are thinking, Jenny knows that!"

Jenny certainly did. Although hearing it from one of her best friends was still a little tough to bear. She lowered her head as if in shame. She could feel her cheeks growing red from embarrassment. The group all knew that Jenny was in no way responsible for Scott's frequent mood-swings and outbursts, but because they had been together for so long Jenny had grown accustomed to apologising on his behalf and still feeling guilty for it.

Carey leaned in and tenderly placed an arm across Jenny's shoulders.

Jenny looked up and smiled, although she looked to Carey as if she was on the verge of tears.

Carey kissed her gently on the side of her head. "Come on Jen, you know I don't mean it as a criticism of you. Lord knows we all think you're a saint for putting up with it."

Jenny wiped away a tear before it had a chance to brim over.

She turned to Carey. "I know," she replied, barely above a whisper. "It's just that when he's like this he's so wonderful and kind that I feel myself falling in love with him all over again." She offered Carey a 'what can I do' expression.

Sharon decided that now the ball was rolling she would add her weight to the argument. "We know what you're saying Jenny, it's obvious to anyone who's seen you together how much you care for him, but…" She trailed off as she heard the men approaching from the other side of the door.

Jenny took out a tissue from her pocket and blew her nose to cover for her tears. She even managed a cheer when the drinks arrived.

The group sat around the roaring fire chatting and drinking, laughing and joking. Jenny had been nominated as the chief fire starter, so it was her job to ensure that the flames did not die down.

Together they discussed their plans for the rest of their break in between several re-fills of wine. Greg had come up with the brainwave of wedging several bottles of white wine in the snow to keep it chilled and to avoid having to run back to the kitchen every so often.

They had done the same thing with their cans of lager, and Steve had made sure that they had a refuge plastic bag for their empties; otherwise he knew he would have been nagged by Sharon about keeping the countryside tidy.

As the alcohol flowed, the jokes seemed to grow funnier. Especially the ones attempted by Sharon, who had an uncanny knack of either forgetting the punch line, or slotting it in too soon before realising her mistake. Eventually they reached the stage where the minute she would start to tell one, everyone else would fall about laughing.

In the end, she became frustrated that the laughter was so loud that no one could hear her jokes, and that too made everyone else laugh even more.

By the time the jokes had finally run out it was almost midnight.

Even so, there was a general reluctance to end the evening as everyone was enjoying themselves so much. Sharon felt a slight twinge of guilt that Jan was missing out on what was the best night so far of the holiday. But she comforted herself with the knowledge that she believed that her friend was enjoying Tom's company far more than she would theirs.

The talking and laughing lulled to a point where the only sound was that made by the crackle of the kindling in the fire and the odd hoot from an owl somewhere in the distance.

"I wish one of us had a guitar," Carey suddenly announced.

"Can anyone here play?" Greg asked, taking a long swig from his tin.

Everyone shook their heads in response.

"We could all pretend it was a piano and just sit around it, wishing one of us could play," chuckled Scott. The others joined in.

"I can strum a few chords," Carey shot back, defensively.

"What were you thinking of?" asked Steve, trying to keep from laughing until after he had finished speaking. "A couple of choruses of *Cumbyar*?"

Carey joined in the laughter in spite of herself. "No, I was thinking maybe *Country Roads.*"

"Oh, I love that one," Jenny piped up. And before she-or anybody else-could stop her she began to sing. *"Country roads, take me home, to the place, I belong…"*

Carey joined in, followed by Sharon. Their voices were not exactly matched in harmony but they were pleasant enough so as not to make anyone pull a face.

The boys took a little more persuading, but eventually Greg chimed in, keeping his voice low so as not to lose the key. Both Steve and Scott shook their heads, neither one wanting to reveal how good or bad their singing voices were.

They all mixed up the words to the verses, but that did not matter. When the chorus came around again they all sang louder and with abandon as they rocked from side to side in time with their music.

All of a sudden, from out of the night they all heard an emotive cry, emanating from the darkness.

The group stopped their merrymaking in unison.

They sat there for a moment as if waiting for someone else to move or speak.

The cry had been more plaintive than aggressive, but it had still managed to put the wind up the group.

Steve and Greg turned to each other, both remembering the sound they had heard on their first night after venturing out to start up the generator.

Jenny was in no two minds as to what had made the sound. Her mind raced back to the creature she had witnessed leering in at her from outside the lodge in the early hours, and before she could help herself she abruptly stood up and let out her own terrified scream.

As if spurred into action, the others all rose and huddled together as a group. The boys moved around so that they could comfort their partners, and they all stood with their backs to the fire, staring out into the pitch black wilderness, almost as if they were waiting for another cry to prove to themselves that they had not imagined the first.

Scott wrapped his huge arms around Jenny, who by now was shaking and sobbing with fright.

They all stayed like that for a moment, but when no other cry came, Steve suggested that they make their way back inside the safety of the lodge.

He and Greg doused out the fire with snow as the others made their way to the door. Scott scooped Jenny up into his arms and whispered words of comfort to her as he carried her in.

Once they were inside, Sharon stayed with the door open waiting for the boys to follow. Steve and Greg ran to the door having ensured that the fire was out. Once inside the porch area Greg ushered his friend in, and then took one more look behind him before closing the door and double-locking it.

Both boys heaved a huge sigh of relief once the inner door was closed. Scott had placed Jenny down on the large sofa and was sitting by her, holding her and gently brushing her hair away from her tear-stained face.

Carey and Sharon were both secretly relieved that Scott was treating Jenny with the warmth and sensitivity she obviously needed so desperately. They had both initially had their doubts about what Jenny claimed to have seen through the window so now, having heard that roar in the distance, the pair of them felt guilty that they had not been more inclined to accept their friend's word at face value.

Sharon especially felt the urge to go over and give Jenny a big hug by way of an apology, but at the moment she felt that Jenny would appreciate Scott's attentions more.

"We need to do something." It was Greg who broke the silence. The others all turned towards him as if seeking inspiration. "Call someone," as he said the words he remembered the lack of reception from the lodge.

"I could send Tom an e-mail," Sharon suggested, helpfully. "But I'm not sure what he could do right now. His son Adam has his 4x4 and won't be back until the morning."

"He could contact the local police for us, or the Rangers, or Troupers or whatever they have out here," offered Carey. "Maybe they could send someone out to check the area for us."

Steve shook his head. "They'll probably just laugh at us. A bunch of townies who were scared by a noise in the woods. That won't be at all embarrassing."

Greg turned to his friend. "Well we need to do something."

"Yeah," said Carey, supporting her boyfriend, "if the thing that made that noise is the same thing Jenny saw then I would rather be safe than sorry, no matter how ridiculous we seem."

"What do you say Scott?" Steve looked over at his friend who was still trying to comfort Jenny.

Scott thought for a moment before saying. "Well, whatever it was we haven't heard it since, so presumably it hasn't come any closer."

"Or it has decided to stay quiet to try and catch us unawares," offered Carey, obviously not convinced.

"Look, why don't we just make sure that all the doors and windows are securely locked?" Steve suggested, looking at Greg. "Once we are sure that the place is secure, we can decide what to do next."

The idea obviously appealed to Greg who nodded thoughtfully, though Steve noticed a concerned look pass between Sharon and Carey. Steve walked over to Sharon and put his arm around her shoulders, holding her close to him.

Sharon looked at him and after a while nodded in agreement.

"Ok," announced Steve, clapping his hands together. "We'll go and sort out the upstairs, Scott do you want to come with us?"

At the mere mention of Scott leaving her side, Jenny buried her face in his chest and squeezed him tightly.

Scott looked back at the lads. "Can you manage without me on this one?" he asked, apologetically.

"No bother," replied Greg. He gave Scott a reassuring wink as if to let him know that he appreciated the situation he was in.

The four of them left Scott and Jenny alone on the sofa whilst they made a complete check of the ground floor. They checked and double-checked every window and door ensuring that they were all locked and bolted.

Sharon volunteered to make coffee. She anticipated a long night for them all and she figured that the caffeine would help to sober them up, though in truth the sound of that creature howling had already done the trick for her.

Carey stayed back while Steve and Greg made their way upstairs to start the second floor checks. They decided to split up to speed up the process, neither wishing to admit to the other any trepidation about being on their own.

They made their way from room to room repeating the process of double-checking the window locks. Neither could resist the chance of staring out of the windows for any sign of movement as they worked, but with the thick foliage so close to the lodge their vantage was minimal at best.

They had both just completed the last check of their rooms when, without warning, the lights went out!

They heard a scream from downstairs, one of the girls. It did not matter which one, they both scrabbled through the darkness towards the top of the stairs and, using the banister and wall for balance, quickly made their way back down trying not to trip each other over in their haste.

The only light available was the dying embers from the log fire which they had lit earlier in the evening, plus the shadowy glow of the moonlight shafting in through the windows.

As the lower floor came into view the boys could see the forms of Sharon and Carey emerging from the kitchen. Scott appeared to be still on the sofa huddled over Jenny who was crying fitfully. Both Steve and Greg presumed that it had been Jenny's scream that they had heard from upstairs.

They both moved closer to their respective partners. Though neither of them would admit it, the sudden lack of light left them both feeling a little vulnerable. And seeing Scott being so protective towards Jenny reminded them of where their responsibilities lay.

The three couples held onto each other for a moment in the darkness.

Other than the faint crackle from the logs in the hearth, all was at peace.

After a while Carey broke the silence. "Now what?" she asked, rhetorically.

Steve and Greg looked at each other. Though they were fairly close to each other it was too dark for either to see the other's expression. However, in the circumstances they each seemed to know what the other might be thinking.

"I suppose we need to go out and re-start the generator again." It was Steve who lent his voice to what everyone knew was the obvious answer. Even so, once the words were out, both Sharon and Carey gripped their men instinctively, as if willing them not to go anywhere.

"No!" The objection came from Jenny. She pulled Scott closer to her until, even in the darkness, he could see the abject terror in her eyes.

Scott kissed her tenderly on the forehead and tried once more to calm her down. "It'll be alright babe," he said, in his best assuring tone. "We'll only be gone a few minutes; Sharon and Carey will be here with you."

But Jenny seemed inconsolable. She clung on tightly to Scott as if he were the only lifebelt left on board a sinking ship. She had been crying almost constantly since they came back in and now Scott could feel the moisture from her tears starting to penetrate the fabric of his shirt.

Scott let out a deep sigh.

Both Steve and Greg picked up on their friend's predicament, and neither wanted to make the situation feel any more awkward for him than it already did.

Greg gave Carey another squeeze, then eased himself away and moved closer towards where Scott and Jenny lay. He placed his arm on the back of the sofa and looked down at Scott. "Listen mate," he began, tentatively, using the most reassuring tone he could muster. "One of us should stay back with the girls, you know, just in case."

Scott was about to protest just as Steve came over and stood next to Greg. He held his hands up to stop Scott in his tracks. "Greg's right, Scott, and it makes more sense for us to go out as we've re-started the stupid thing before, so we know what we're doing."

Scott backed off. As much as he felt that he needed to do his bit, a part of him was quietly relieved that he did not have to venture out again.

Greg made his way over to the fireplace and fetched a couple of pokers for Steve and him to use as weapons should the occasion arise. Steve accepted his gratefully, and the two of them made their way over to the front door, closely followed by Sharon and Carey.

Trying to keep the fear and panic out of her voice, Sharon hugged Steve and told him to keep his eyes open, and to run back if they saw anything approaching them from the woods.

Carey re-iterated her friend's instructions and gave Greg a kiss and a playful punch in the arm.

Just as they were about to set off, Sharon remembered the torches. "Hang on," she said, reaching over to the shelf where they had placed them earlier. "Don't forget these; you'll need them out there," she handed one to each of them.

Both lads nodded gratefully and taking a deep breath, they made their way through the porch and tentatively out into the night.

They waited just in front of the lodge to get their bearings.

The torches made a tunnel of light which faded to a mere glimmer before reaching the trees which surrounded the lodge.

The night air seemed colder and sharper than it had when they first left the comfort of the camp fire to go back inside.

Greg shivered and pulled the zip on his jacket right up to his chin. He wished now that he had remembered his gloves. The cold iron of the poker made his fingers feel numb, but he was not about to turn around and go back inside to look for them.

After a moment they both looked at each other and, without speaking, they slowly started to make their way towards the shed which housed the generator.

As they walked, both men listened out for anything which might indicate that the architect of the horrendous cry they all heard earlier was anywhere in the vicinity.

As they walked, the snow beneath their feet crunched loudly as if it was purposely trying to prevent them from hearing their assailant's approach. They took slow, measured steps to try and combat the noise, but it seemed that the harder they tried the more of a racket they made.

When the reached the entrance to the shed both men stayed put, neither relishing the thought of being trapped inside if the Beast suddenly appeared from the darkness.

Indicating towards the door with a nod of his head, half joking, Steve asked, "Do you wanna toss for it?"

Greg could not help but laugh at his friend's gesture. "No, you stay out here and keep guard, I'll go in."

Steve nodded and took a firmer grip on his poker.

Once inside the shed, Greg shone his torch around to ensure that he was alone. Once he was satisfied he walked over to the generator and began the re-start procedure which Adam had shown them.

Being back inside the shed reminded him of the last time he and Steve had had to complete the same task, and the roar that they had heard as they were leaving to go back to the lodge. In his mind it had to be the same creature that they had all heard earlier. And if that was also the thing that Jenny had seen-the result of which had now left her a quivering wreck-then Greg could well do without coming face to face with it. Whatever it was!

He could hear Steve stamping on the ground outside, presumably to keep warm, and he wished that his friend would not make so much noise in case it masked the approach of the enemy.

Still, he knew that Steve would be keeping a watchful eye out and that whatever might come at them he knew his friend would not desert him.

The levers and cranks on the generator were frozen to the touch and Greg's hands were still numb from the cold outside, so he blew hot air into his cupped hands and rubbed them together vigorously to try and revive his circulation before continuing.

On his third attempt, the apparatus caught. As the pump started whirring Greg held his breath as if waiting for it to stop again, but it continued working so he let out a sigh of relief before making his way back out to Steve.

Once outside, Greg could see the lights inside the lodge had all come back on. He closed the door to the shed and held up his hand for Steve to high-five him.

As they turned to make their way back to the lodge, they heard the Beast roar again!

The two of them stopped dead in their tracks.

This time the cry seemed louder which meant that the Beast must be closer than it had been earlier.

Far too close!

They both turned towards the direction from which the cry had come, but it was difficult to tell out here in the open where sound was carried on the wind and distorted before it reached the ear.

The men shone their torches in wide arcs straining to make out any significant movement coming from the surrounding bushes and trees, but it was impossible to distinguish anything specific in the weak half-glow their lights afforded them.

They waited for what seemed to both of them, an eternity.

Their eyes darted from side to side covering every inch of ground before them. Each new gust of wind was followed by a subsequent movement of the surrounding foliage, which in turn caused both men to shiver and take a stance in anticipation of a subsequent attack.

But after a few seconds without incident the fear would pass, until the next strong gust came along and started the ball rolling all over again.

After a while, Steve whispered, "I think we should start making our way back, what d'yer think?"

"Sounds good to me," Greg could not hide the relief in his tone.

They continued to scan the area before them with their torches as they started to take their first tentative steps backwards. Steve almost lost his balance as his foot hit the bottom of the stairs leading up to the porch door, but Greg reacted in good time and saved him from a fall.

At the top of the stairs, before they entered the porch, Steve turned to his friend. "Shall we keep it to ourselves again about…what we just heard?"

Greg nodded. "Yeah, no point in spooking anyone more than they have been already."

They entered the porch. Closing the door behind them Greg quickly turned the key in the lock as if the safety offered by the simple bolt could protect them against whatever was out there.

They both took one more look back before entering the lodge and locking that door too.

CHAPTER TWENTY TWO

The tyres on the biker's lorry fought hard for traction on the snow-impacted road. The tread on some of the wheels was fast approaching a stage of wear which would make them illegal and subsequently unsafe on the driest of roads, so having to contend with such icy conditions made the driving precarious at best and downright dangerous at worst.

That, plus the fact that the nominated driver was an alcoholic and a drug addict who had been high on weed for most of the day, meant that the chances were that even the most ardent gambler would not wish to bet on the odds of the group making it to their final destination in one piece.

Inside the vehicle scattered amongst the mixed debris of tools, chains, spare tyres and assorted spare bike parts, Darren and Jax sat slumped on the floor with gags in their mouths, and their hands tied behind their backs.

The others all sat at the back of the lorry blocking the doors, just in case either or both of them decided to try and make a run for it. Not that either of them was in any fit state to attempt an escape.

The combination of the neat alcohol and pot had left both men feeling dazed, confused and sick, but at least it had helped to block their pain sensors for the beating that Reaper had dished out on them.

After Darren's accidental fondle with Deedee, Reaper had wasted no time in showing him that he had just made the biggest mistake of his life. Having discharged his initial fury by bouncing Darren and Jax around the room like rag dolls, Reaper finally calmed down and stopped his onslaught long enough to take stock of the situation and decide what punishment would be adequate for such an unforgivable breach of trust.

Once Reaper had waded in, the other bikers in the room-most having borne witness to previous outbursts from their leader under similar circumstances-half expected to be spending the rest of their night cleaning up and disposing of the dead remains of the two men, once Reaper had satisfied his craving for their blood.

But instead, in what might appear to some a rare moment of mercy on Reaper's part, he decided to leave their fate to Mother Nature and the elements.

On Reaper's command the rest of the gang had forcibly dressed Darren and Jax, partly for the sake of modesty but mainly so that their appearance would not cause any unwanted attention if they were seen leaving the building.

The two teenagers could barely stand unaided, so the theatre of trying to pull their socks and trousers on for them was a farcical performance interspersed with raucous laughter from the bikers and giggles from the girls who joined in for their own amusement.

Darren and Jax themselves offered little resistance, both still experiencing exhilarating highs and crashing lows as a result of the drugs they had both partaken of earlier in the evening.

Once they were dressed, the teenagers were dragged down the back stairs of the hotel and into the alleyway, where they were forcibly bundled into the back of the waiting lorry and driven off, still blissfully unaware of the precariousness of their situation. On Reaper's orders some of the gang bound and gagged the two of them just in case either decided to scream for help or make a break for it. Whilst being restrained, Jax suddenly felt a surge of power and bravado and before anyone could stop him he swung his arm in a wide arc catching Skull squarely on the nose with his clenched fist.

Skull's nose exploded in a spray of blood which splattered across his face and dribbled into his goatee. The sound of the impact caught everyone's attention and they all turned to look at their comrade.

Scarface grabbed hold of Jax's loose arm which was still swinging wildly though without an actual target to aim for, and twisted it behind him before binding it tightly to his other one.

Skull, finally reacting to Jax's blow, rubbed the back of his broad hand across his face smearing his own blood, leaving him with a crimson mask covering his features. If the force of the blow had caused him any pain, Skull did not show it. Instead, he merely turned to look at Reaper who, after a moment's hesitation, nodded his consent.

Upon his signal, Skull began kicking Jax hard in the ribs. Just as before when Reaper had been dishing out the punishment, Jax was still too far gone to realise how much pain he was in. As he fell against his friend, the two of them tumbled forward, neither being able to support the other.

With each subsequent kick Skull's aim became less precise, to the point that he treated the two teenagers as one target unable to distinguish which body he was making contact with, and not caring either way. As far as he-and the rest of the gang-was concerned, their days were numbered anyway.

During their second beating of the night, Angel could not help but feel a slight twinge of guilt. After all, she was the one who had invited both teenagers to the party. However, she relieved herself of any responsibility by remembering that Darren's behaviour had been of his own doing and that no one had forced him to grope Deedee. And how was she to know that they could not handle their drink and drugs?

After all, they were the ones who had brought them!

If they wanted to play in the big league, then they had to suffer the consequences.

Angel would not lose any sleep over whatever became of them.

And besides, what could she do anyway?

She knew that if she even tried to intercede on their behalf that the chances were that she would be on the receiving end of a beating, and she might even end up worse off than them by the end of the night.

Eventually, the effort of swinging his leg back and forth at the boys became too much for Skull and he slumped to the floor, exhausted. The sound of the groans coming from the two of them brought him a rare smile of contentment. He could still feel blood dribbling from his broken nose seeping into his beard, so he wiped the back of his hand across his face once more and then rubbed it clean against his faded leather trousers.

When the lorry finally made the incline, the driver pulled over and cranked up the hand brake as far as it would go. As a precautionary measure he also slipped the gear lever into third to help prevent the vehicle from sliding backwards.

Once he was satisfied that it would hold, the driver jumped down from his seat and walked around to the back to let the others out. Before releasing the catches, he scanned the area to ensure that they did not have an audience. When he was sure that the coast was clear, he flung open the doors and waited for the gang to disembark.

After Reaper, Stud and the girls were safely on the ground, the others dragged Darren and Jax's unresponsive bodies off the lorry. Skull jumped down first, and when Axe and Scarface passed over their charges, instead of hoisting them from the lorry he just let them fall straight off, unconcerned about which part of their body made contact with the ground first.

Both teenagers had the air knocked out of them as they landed on the snow.

Neither one was in any fit state to complain, not that it would have been wise for them to do so even if they had been fully conscious.

As instructed earlier by Reaper, Axe retrieved a long length of rope from the back of the lorry before joining his colleagues on the ground.

Amid howls of laughter and whoops of delight, the bikers took turns in dragging the two teenagers across the snow, following their leader. The effort was far more than any of them had bargained for and in hindsight Skull wished that he had not left the two of them so incapacitated from his beating.

Reaper strode across the snowy landscape leaving huge craters behind in his wake. The girls, suddenly aware of the freezing conditions since exiting the lorry, huddled together against the sharp wind which whipped towards them as they walked. Those who had had the foresight to bring bottles with them passed them around to help ward off the chill.

Eventually, Reaper stopped beside a large oak tree which stood alone far away from the surrounding woods.

He pointed at the base of it. "Here!" he commanded.

Without requiring further instruction, the bikers hauled the two wasted teenagers towards the tree and shoved them both down on either side of it so that they were seated on the ground with their backs leaning against the trunk.

While Skull and Scarface held them both in place, Axe looped the rope around the tree and then proceeded to pass it back and forth between the others to ensure that both boys were held firmly in place and unable to move.

The biker left enough rope to fasten the two ends with a double knot.

When they were sure that their two victims could not move, much less escape, the bikers stood up and moved away to allow the others a prime view of their prey.

The gang passed around the various bottles of booze whilst they stood there laughing and snorting at the helpless forms bound to the tree. None of them was at all concerned about the amount of noise that they were making, because they were confident that they were alone, miles from anywhere and anyone, out in the wilderness.

Finally, having had his fill, Reaper knelt down in the snow between Darren and Jax. Without speaking, he slapped each of them in turn across the face with his huge, shovel-like hand, until he received a response from both of them.

Still groggy and barely conscious, both teenagers began to open their eyes, not fully, but enough to satisfy the big man that they were paying attention.

The rest of the gang grew silent and stood around watching and drinking, waiting with eager anticipation for their leader to make his announcement.

Reaper watched amused as the two teenagers tried to focus on the big man squatting before them. Though he had always been able to move quite quickly for such a big man, having waded through the snow, Reaper was breathing hard and his breath left his mouth in large clouds of air as his massive chest rose and fell. He waited to make sure that both Darren and Jax were aware of his presence before he started to speak.

"Now then," he growled his voice low and husky. "I want both of you to know that after what you done at the 'otel you should both be pushin' up daisies by now!"

There were a few quiet sniggers from the watching audience.

Reaper saw the spark of realisation start to flicker in both teenagers' eyes and he smiled to himself, happy that his message was not falling on deaf ears.

He continued, "'owever, bein' the reasonable sort that I am, I'm willin' to believe that you gropin' my woman was a result of you not bein' able to 'old yer drink."

Darren was starting to focus on Reaper's voice. He knew that the remark was aimed at him; after all, he had been the one who grabbed Deedee's breast. But the whole incident, like the entire night, still seemed like a distant dream. It was almost as if he had been watching the scenario unfold on a shaky old 8mm film.

As his hazy memory faded in and out of reality he wanted to speak up. He wanted to apologise to the big man and his girlfriend in the hope that his gesture would somehow make everything alright. But his tongue felt very large and heavy in his mouth and he was afraid that the effort of trying to talk might make him choke on it.

From the other side of the tree Darren heard his friend trying to speak up. His speech sounded slow and his words were slurred, but at least he was making himself understood.

"Listen mate... wee'rre really sor...sorry for what we did, but it was....an accident yer know....no harm...done...come on now...stop messin'"

Darren shuddered as he heard Reaper's palm strike Jax another heavy blow across the head.

Reaper leaned forward until his mouth was so close to Jax's face that Jax felt himself turn away, automatically.

"Do I look to you like a fuckin' comedian?" he growled, menacingly. Spittle sprayed from his mouth as he spoke and landed on the side of Jax's cheek. Unable to wipe it away due to his confinement, Jax felt himself gag. For a moment he thought that he was going to vomit all over himself, but fortunately he managed to keep control and staunch the eruption.

Darren felt his head loll forward, uncontrollably. As his chin touched his chest he swung it back up too quickly, smashing the back of his head against the tree. The pain from the impact sent a spasm through his head. He could feel himself starting to slip back into unconsciousness so he shook himself to stay awake.

For a moment he felt as if his brain had become detached inside his cranium. Darren sat still, convinced that if he tried to move he would feel his brain collapse in on itself. Slowly his senses returned to normality. It took him a while to focus, but through his dazed state he could hear his friend trying to reason with Reaper, unsuccessfully.

Suddenly, Darren felt a stinging pain as Reaper slapped him again on the side of his head.

"Are you listenin' ter me?"

Darren's weary eyes tried to focus on the big man's face as it hovered directly in front of his own. He managed a half-hearted nod which seemed to appease the biker.

"Now, like I wus sayin', ordinarily we'd be out here burying yer corpses by now, but out of the kindness of me 'art I've decided to give yer a fightin' chance."

Darren felt his spirits lifting slightly as Reaper's words started to sink in.

At least he and Jax were not going to be murdered and left buried in shallow graves out here in the middle of nowhere. Perhaps their punishment would only be that they would have to find their way back to town. Yes it was cold and dark, and it might be a long trek, but after one of his mum's speciality breakfasts and a couple of hours sleep they would both be back to full strength.

Darren vowed to himself never to allow drink or drugs to cloud his judgement to this extent again!

He had learned his lesson well and truly and he suspected that Jax had too.

The worst of it was that he had been banking on getting his leg-over with Angel or at least one of the other biker girls at the party. And even though he had a vague recollection of getting naked with some of the girls, he was pretty sure that he had not gone all the way with any of them.

At least that would have been something to make the night seem worthwhile.

Darren's mind wandered back to earlier in the day when he had first met Angel in the warehouse behind the pub. He remembered the smell of her hair, freshly washed and infused with the scent of vanilla and cherry, as he buried his face in it moaning softly while she gently slid her hand inside his jeans and began to stroke him.

The way she caressed the back of his neck with her other hand as she allowed him to taste her, and how, just as she brought him to ecstasy, he had to fight not to bite too deeply into the tender flesh of her neck as he shuddered and writhed with pleasure, squeezing her soft warm body against his own.

Even now, in his present predicament, at the very thought of it Darren could feel himself growing hard.

He gazed up at the bikers who were all standing a few feet away in the snow and found Angel in the crowd. He attempted a lop-sided grin at her, hoping that in some way it might send a telepathic message to remind her of their earlier encounter.

But Angel did not reciprocate. Instead she just stared down at him as if he meant no more to her than a chunk of roadkill left half-buried in the snow.

His smile faded as Angel turned away and accepted a bottle handed to her by Scarface.

Darren turned his attention back to Reaper who, fortunately for him, had not noticed the disrespectful way that Darren had been ignoring him in favour of Angel.

To his horror, Darren saw Reaper remove a large carving knife with a dark wooden handle from his belt. The big man waved the blade through the air back and forth between the two bound teenagers. Convinced that he was about to be gutted like a fish, Darren tried to pull away from the biker's blade, but the restraints holding him would not yield so much as an inch.

Certain of his impending doom and the pain that would surely precede it, Darren heard himself starting to whimper like a stranded puppy. He wanted to apologise to Reaper for not paying attention to him, positive that his lack of reverence was partly to blame for what was about to happen to him and Jax, but his mouth would not form the words he wanted so desperately to express.

A squeak of fear escaped Darren's lips as Reaper threw the knife down.

It landed with a soft *whump* in the snow beside him buried up to the hilt.

Reaper heaved his massive bulk up to a standing position and stood there for a moment with his hands on his hips looking down at the sorry state of the two quivering teenagers.

"Right then, as soon as one of you can reach that knife you can cut yerself an' yer mate free and toddle off home to your mummies."

The other bikers did not try to disguise their amusement at their leader's choice of words. Axe walked over to Reaper and handed him a half-empty bottle of whiskey. Without acknowledging the gesture, Reaper threw his head back and downed most of the contents in one go before handing what was left back to his devoted follower.

Reaper let forth an almighty belch which seemed to echo throughout the surrounding area. Once again the other bikers could not contain their amusement.

Bending down at the waist, Reaper's eyes narrowed as he gave the two bound friends a suspicious stare. "An' if either of yer tell anyone about us, we'll bring yer back 'ere an' skin yer both alive, understand?" he snarled.

Darren and Jax both nodded their understanding.

With that, Reaper stood up and moved off back towards the lorry, closely followed by his entourage.

Even at this late stage Darren still hoped for a nod or a wink from Angel as she passed.

But it did not come.

The two teenagers craned their necks to watch as the bikers piled back on to the lorry. They waited until it had driven out of sight before trying to move.

****

Joanne edged out a little further from the sanctuary of her secluded crevice.

She had heard the lorry when it first arrived, the roar of its diesel engine reverberating around the surrounding hills, shattering the peace and tranquillity of the night.

At first she was too scared to move, afraid that the arrival of the vehicle might bring the Beast out from its lair; so she stayed put and listened intently for any indication of its approach.

But when she heard the raucous laughter and shouting from the passengers on board, she became a little less wary and began to edge her way out into the open to see what all the fuss was about.

From her vantage point, Joanne witnessed the scenario which took place between the bikers and their prisoners. Her initial instinct to run to them and beg for help gave way to caution when she realised the implications of the scene unfolding before her.

So she stayed hidden, and watched.

Once the lorry had driven off she waited to see what the two bound teenagers proposed to do. Having witnessed them both being tied to the tree Joanne surmised that they had been abandoned for a reason. She considered that it might be some kind of student prank or initiation, but the bikers who had brought them did not look like any students she had ever seen.

She had watched the biggest one throw something down in the snow next to the bound teenagers, but she was too far away to see what it was.

Under normal circumstances her first instinct would have been to offer her assistance. After all, it was freezing tonight and the two young men did not appear to be appropriately attired for such shenanigans.

But then her circumstance was anything but normal. Joanne was not out here on a camping trip anymore. Nor was she just another back-packer tromping through the woods that happened to stumble on this scene.

No. She was hiding in fear of her life! Afraid to venture out from behind her place of concealment for fear that the Beast would return and do to her what it did to her boyfriend. And if it meant that she was to spend the rest of her life crouched and hidden in her tiny hole then so be it. Anything was better than meeting such a grisly end.

But there was still a part of her petrified mind that remained rational, and fantasised about a chance of escape. She desperately wanted to return to her little shop and continue to serve the good people of the town with their camping and outdoor apparel.

But now she would be running the place on her own, without Colin, and she knew that it would never be the same.

Joanne could feel tears welling up in her eyes as she thought about her dead boyfriend. She allowed them to trickle down her cheeks without bothering to wipe them away. Nothing would ever be the same again now that Colin was gone. The saddest part for Joanne was that she never realised before he died how much she was in love with him. And now of course, it was too late to tell him!

Colin would not want her to die out here alone, she decided. Not if there was a chance, however slim, of escape. And those two young men tied to the tree might very well provide that all important chance.

Urged on by the thought of Colin watching over her, Joanne switched to survival mode and crept forward onto her belly ready to start edging her way towards Darren and Jax.

CHAPTER TWENTY THREE

Whether it was due to the freezing conditions, the length of time since they had had either a drink or some weed, the beatings they had endured or a combination of all of those things, Darren and Jax were both starting to come back down to earth with the stark realisation of their situation.

Of the two of them, Jax, possibly due to his more sustained use of pot over the years compared to his friend, appeared to be the more cognisant of the pair. Rationalising the situation as best he could, he surmised that if he could just free his hands-or even one of them-from the restraints which tied them together behind his back, he could then manage to work his way out from under the rope which bound both him and his friend to the tree.

Failing that, with just one hand free he might be able to reach the knife which Reaper had left them, and use that to cut them both free.

He thought about the problem for a while trying to work out the best path forward. He had seen in films where people managed to slip their bound hands underneath their bodies and then wriggle free by bending their knees and bringing their feet back through the ropes.

But as with most things, those acts always looked far simpler on the screen than they actually were in reality.

Jax planted his feet on the floor and pushed against the ground for leverage. The snow offered only minimal purchase and he kept slipping each time he tried to take the strain.

Undeterred, Jax shoved his feet as far beneath the snow as he could until he was sure that he was on solid ground, and then he took a deep breath and pushed again, this time placing his weight on the front of his feet to gain maximum traction.

He could feel the ropes digging into his chest as he heaved himself up. From behind him he heard Darren scream as the rope tightened against him at the same time. He ignored his friend in the hope that if he managed to manoeuvre himself into position the pain he was causing them both would be over soon enough and they would be able to break free.

But on his third attempt his feet lost traction and he slid back down the trunk landing hard on his rump, out of breath and really feeling the delayed soreness from the rope cutting into his body.

"Owww, what the hell are you playing at?" Darren yelled from behind.

"I'm trying to get us free you fucking idiot, what d'yer think?" Jax shouted back, venomously.

"Well it fuckin' hurts, whatever you're doin'" Darren whined. "Can't you try something else instead?"

Jax was quickly losing his patience with his friend. "HURTS!" he bellowed back at the top of his voice. "I'll tell you what fuckin' hurts shall I? Being beaten up by that gorilla Reaper and then being kicked about by that other wanker in the back of the lorry, before being dragged across the fucking frozen wasteland to this shitty tree, before being strung up against it and slapped about some more for the amusement of those other tossers…THAT'S WHAT FUCKIN' HURTS!"

"All right, all right," replied Darren, surprised by his friend's verbal attack. "There's no need to 'ave a go about it."

Darren could hear Jax take in a huge lungful of air before he retorted.

"Have a go! Have a go! Are you having a fuckin' giraffe or what?"

"What d'yer mean?" Darren asked with genuine ignorance. "I don't like this anymore than you do Jax so it's no good screaming your lungs out at me!"

"Are you kiddin' me?" Jax cried, trying to turn as best he could to see his friend, without success.

"What!"

"It's all thanks to you that we're in this situation in the first place!"

"No one forced you to come to the party," Darren responded trying to keep the hurt out of his voice. "I asked you along because you're supposed to be me mate and I thought you'd enjoy it."

"I was!" Jax called back, unable to keep the irritation out of his tone. "But then some stupid twat decided to grab hold of the tits of the boss man's woman, and then suddenly, surprise surprise, I wasn't enjoying meself anymore!"

Darren opened his mouth to respond, and then thought better of it.

They sat there in silence for a minute, neither wanting to be the first to speak.

Finally, Darren decided that it was his place to make the peace before it went too far and their friendship was ruined forever. "I'm sorry mate," he offered, apologetically. "I think it must've been all the booze. And that weed was definitely mixed with something."

Jax felt himself calm down with the sincerity of Darren's apology. "Yeah, I think that bloke back at the party must have had some bad skunk and used my gear to boost its kick, fuckin' dickhead!"

They sat there a moment longer in silence.

The wind was starting to gather force, whipping around them as they huddled against the tree.

"What're we gonna do?" Darren asked, sheepishly.

"Make it out of here before we freeze our nuts off, I hope."

Darren stared down at the knife handle sticking up through the snow. Reaper had thrown it too far for either of them to reach in their present situation, doubtless on purpose.

Darren stuck his leg out just to see how close he could get to it.

The knife handle was still a good couple of feet away from the end of his boot.

Straining against his binds Darren tried to edge himself closer in the direction of the knife. But the knot was too tight and held him fast against the tree. So instead, he attempted to slide down the trunk, his idea being that if he could manage to scoot down far enough the rope might slip up his chest and once past his shoulders he might be able to manoeuvre his body underneath it.

But once again the rope refused to yield its grip on him, and the more he tried to shift underneath it the tighter it seemed to become until finally he started to feel as if he was having the life squeezed out of him by a boa constrictor.

His chest heaved, attempting to fill his lungs, but the tightness of the ropes prevented his ribcage from expanding sufficiently.

Reluctantly, he gave up the struggle and pushed against the icy ground with his feet to relieve the compression.

"What are you doin'?" Jax cried from the other side of the trunk. "You're crushin' me ribs!"

Darren was still breathing hard from the exertion of trying to reach the knife.

Sucking in a lungful of air through his mouth, he replied, "I was…trying to see…if I could…reach the knife."

"Any luck?"

"Nah…too far…away." Darren closed his mouth and tried to concentrate on breathing properly through his nose. The cold air rushing in through his mouth was starting to hurt his throat to the extent that it was painful for him to swallow.

Jax could hear Darren's laboured breathing from behind. He did not have the heart to have a go at him for making the rope so tight as he knew that Darren was only trying to get them out of this situation.

Jax craned his neck to see the knife himself. He could tell straight away that it was way too far for him to reach.

He needed to think.

Jax had heard of escapologists being able to dislocate their shoulders in order to escape from straightjackets and the like. He remembered watching Mel Gibson doing it in one of the Lethal Weapon films. He had made it look easy but Jax knew that that was just acting. His brother had dislocated his shoulder once as a result of a rugby tackle and Jax remembered him screaming the place down when the doctors were trying to slot it back into place.

As desperate as things were, that was not an option that Jax was willing to consider.

Why did Reaper even bother to leave them the knife when he knew that there was no way that either of them could get to it?

Was it merely to taunt them? To make them suffer even more by leaving it just out of reach?

Or was it perhaps to give them a fighting chance should someone happen to pass? After all, the ropes had been tied so tight that without the knife even the most willing and compassionate individual would have a hard time trying to free them.

Then a thought suddenly occurred to Jax.

Perhaps the bikers had parked up around the next bend and were now hiding just out of sight watching them, making them suffer a little bit more before they came back to free them.

Maybe, they were even feeling guilty about the way that they had mistreated him and Darren, and once they had set them free they intended to take them back to the hotel to let the two of them continue partying with the girls.

Now there was an idea!

The thought gave Jax some comfort and even seemed to warm him up a little. He hoped that if such a scenario was the plan that it would not be too long before the bikers gave in and showed themselves.

Encouraged by the prospect, Jax strained his eyes in the direction that the lorry had disappeared to see if he could make out any movement from the bikers crouching out of sight. He decided that if they were there, that they would not be able to resist cadging a peak to see how he and Darren were coping.

But with the wind picking up and constantly sweeping snow across his path of vision Jax soon realised that his task was fruitless. So instead he strained to hear any sound from that direction which might give them away. But again, due to the wind howling in his ear, it was a thankless venture.

Eventually, Jax gave up. He decided that if the bikers were just playing a cruel trick on them they would just have to wait until they were ready to reveal themselves.

He just wished that it would be sooner rather than later.

Sitting on the snow-covered ground Jax could feel his legs starting to go numb as the icy powder penetrated through his jeans. Travelling back in the lorry with sodden clothing was going to be no picnic, but at least once they reached the hotel they could warm up again. And maybe just a smidgeon of alcohol would help to warm them both up from the inside.

But definitely no more pot!

At least not for Darren. Jax had decided that his friend obviously could not handle it, and if he had to he would tell him so even if it meant embarrassing him in front of the others.

Anything was preferable to a repeat performance of earlier on.

"What's that?"

Darren's voice suddenly broke through Jax's train of thought.

He tried to look behind at whatever his friend was indicating to, but the ropes restrained him.

Finally, his frustration took over. "What's what?" he demanded.

There was a further moment's pause before Darren answered his friend.

"There's someone moving towards us through the snow," he announced.

Jax was livid that he could not see what his friend was talking about. "What do you mean by someone?" he called. "Is it one of the bikers?"

"I don't think so," Darren sounded vague, distracted, as if he was trying to concentrate on something else whilst still talking.

"So who is it?" Jax could feel himself starting to panic. The fact that he was tied to a tree in the middle of nowhere with no way of defending himself made him feel very vulnerable. And not being able to see who it was just made everything seem ten times worse.

"I...I think it's a girl." Darren did not sound completely confident about his observation, but Jax could tell from his friend's voice that he was not concerned by whomever it was approaching them, which gave Jax a moments relief.

"What's she doin'?" Jax asked, trying to keep any trace of trepidation out of his voice so as not to alert his friend to the fact that he was feeling so helpless and exposed.

Through squinted eyes Darren tried to focus in the darkness at the figure making its way towards them. He was reasonably confident from the build and shape of the body that it was a female but he could not see the face clearly enough to be sure. The approaching form was laying face-down on the snowy ground, propelling itself forward by pushing away at the ground with its legs whilst moving its forearms one over the other like a solider on manoeuvres.

"Well?" Jax was clearly at the end of his tether unable to control his annoyance at the fact that he had no way of seeing what Darren was alluding to.

"Yes," announced Darren, excitedly, "it's definitely a girl, not one of the bikers either. She's crawling towards us through the snow."

"Crawling?" Jax asked, quizzically.

"Yeah, I think she's coming to help us...Over here!" Darren yelled.

"Help us!" Jax joined in, unable to contain himself. He felt foolish shouting for help from someone he could not even see, but their present predicament called for desperate measures.

Joanne edged forward through the snow heading directly towards the two teenagers. All the time she was making progress she kept shifting her gaze from left to right convinced that the Beast would suddenly appear from behind one of the ridges surrounding them. Due to the wind battering against the side of her parka hood she could not trust her hearing alone to alert her to the creature's presence. Then again, a part of her could not forget the terrible cry it made when it attacked Colin, and in her mind the noise was constant and refused to cease.

She was twenty feet away from her target and closing in. Joanne briefly looked up to try and study the faces of the two men she was about to rescue. She could only see one clearly from this angle and she thought for a moment that she recognised him, but she could not remember from where.

The other teenager was too far around the other side of the tree for her to get a decent look at his face.

She continued forward. Fifteen feet and counting.

The expression on the face of the one that she could see held a combination of panic and urgency. She wondered if they too knew of the potential impending danger which may or may not be lurking around the next bend. Or perhaps, she considered, it might just be the fact that they had been marooned out here in the freezing cold without any means of escape. Save for her.

Ten feet and counting.

Joanne realised that she had not considered how, once she reached them, she was going to free the captives. The biker who had tied them looked tremendously big and strong from her vantage point, and he presumably meant business when he fastened the knots.

Joanne surmised that she would doubtless have to remove her gloves before trying to squeeze her fingers through the criss-cross of ropes before making any headway. In this cold she did not relish the prospect, but she knew that with them on she would not have sufficient dexterity for the task.

Five feet and counting.

As she crawled to within reaching distance of the teenager whose face she recognised, he suddenly began to gesture frantically to his left using his head.

"Over there, over there," he nodded. "In the snow."

Joanne stopped in her tracks and followed the direction of his gesticulation. It took her a moment before she saw the handle of the knife protruding from the snow.

Joanne turned to her right and crawled over to it.

As she plucked the knife free, in the distance they all heard the roar of the Beast!

Joanne froze to the spot. The knife in her hand and the plight of the two teenagers in front of her were suddenly forgotten. All she could think to do was get away and try to make it back to her safe haven before the Beast found her.

Darren and Jax too were now both rigid with fear.

"What the hell was that?" Jax screamed, his momentary relief at impending freedom had now evaporated only to be replaced with another kind of fear.

Darren swung his head from side to side, desperate to try and see from whom or what the howl had come. But there was nothing to see.

He turned to Joanne, anxiously willing her to start cutting at the ropes so that he and Jax could escape whatever was over the hill.

But Joanne was no longer looking in his direction. She had flattened herself against the freezing ground and buried her face in the snow.

Before Darren had a chance to call out to Joanne, the Beast cried out again.

This time it sounded closer than before!

On impulse, Joanne's entire body shivered with fear at the sound of the Beast's call. She immediately forgot the reason that she had left the relative safety of her enclosure, the two helpless teenagers before her, even the knife that she clutched in her hand.

All that she could think to do now was bury her face in the snow and pray!

Both Darren and Jax began frantically wrenching their bodies left and right in a futile attempt to break free of their confines. As each one of them leaned forward the other felt the ropes stretch even tighter across their upper body. Whenever the two of them happened to move forward in unison, the effect was twice as bad for both of them. But even then, as neither could see the other from around the tree, they still continued pulling and heaving at random, their desperation for freedom overpowering any sense of logical thought.

"Please help us, cut the rope!"

Darren's scream brought Joanne back to reality.

She lifted her face from the snow and looked straight up at him. Her vacant stare told Darren that her mind was elsewhere. Though it had been his cry which brought her around, he was pretty sure that he still had not managed to capture her attention.

Darren looked directly into Joanne's eyes. "Please," he pleaded, "you can't leave us 'ere."

Mechanically, Joanne moved forward until she was next to the tree.

Holding the blade of the knife against the nearest rope she began slicing at it with a sawing motion.

The blade edged back and forth as she worked, all the time she listened out for any signs of the Beast's approach. Her concentration was definitely not on the job at hand, and several times the knife slipped and cut away at empty space.

From his angle Darren could just about make out what Joanne was doing. He could feel the blade against the rope rather than actually see it, but that was enough to give him hope.

"What's goin' on?" cried Jax from around the tree. His voice sounded to Darren as if he was close to tears. In all the years Darren had known his friend, he had never once seen him in such a state. He had always looked up to Jax as the leader of their little partnership, but now Darren felt as if he had to take the reigns for the sake of his friend.

"She's sawin' through the rope, won't be long now."

"Jus' tell 'er to hurry the fuck up, before whatever made that noise finds us!"

Somewhere in the fog of her mind Joanne heard Jax's words and she attacked her task with renewed vigour.

Unfortunately, even though she was now trying to concentrate on what she was doing, she still did not realise that the knife she was using was making very little progress against the sturdy line securing the boys to the tree.

Joanne gripped the handle with both hands and pressed down as hard as she could against the rope. But it was to no avail. The dull blade had not even begun to make any headway.

Though none of them realised it yet, the blunt knife was Reaper's final joke on them, just to add insult to injury.

Again the stillness of the night was shattered by the Beast's cry.

Only this time it seemed much closer than before!

Virtually, over the next ridge!

Joanne stopped moving and snapped her head to the left. She could feel the Beast's approach even though she could not see it.

Unaware of the futility of her sawing action, Darren begged her to carry on trying to set them both free.

But his words fell on deaf ears!

For a moment, Joanne stayed frozen to the spot. The knife, still held out in front of her was resting against the rope she had been trying to cut, but her attention was fixed on the area the Beast's cry had emanated from.

Darren could see from the look on her face that Joanne would not respond to anything either he or Jax might suggest. It was futile to even try asking. And yet, she was their only hope of escape from whatever was making its way towards them.

Out of a combination of fear and desperation Jax screamed out and started thrashing around against their unyielding binds.

His shriek seemed to shake Joanne from her reverie.

She glanced back over at Darren. The look in her eyes conveyed a message of sorrow and regret.

Darren shook his head slowly, his lips forming one last desperate plea.

But before he could utter the words, Joanne shuffled around in the snow until she was facing back towards the direction she had originally come from, and without making a sound she began to scuttle back to the safety of her hide-away.

Jax, still oblivious to the fact that they had been deserted, continued to yell and struggle against the ropes, whilst Darren, fully aware that they had been abandoned by their last hope, slumped back against the tree and began to sob.

Joanne did not look back. Keeping her gaze firmly fixed on her destination she moved through the snow on all fours, her feelings of guilt at having left the two teenagers to their fate outweighed by the sheer terror which gripped her heart at the sound of the Beast's approach.

Once back inside the protection of her cavity, Joanne closed her eyes and held her hands tightly against her eyes; trying desperately to block out the sound of the carnage she knew would follow.

The boys did not have to wait long!

Darren had barely lost sight of Joanne in the snow when the head of the Beast suddenly loomed over the nearest ridge.

Darren watched transfixed as the creature paused for a moment and sniffed the air before setting its sight firmly on its prey.

Darren realised that he could not scream.

As he watched the monster approach he knew that his time was up. There was no going back from here. No running home to safety, no being able to lock himself in his room and hide under the bed.

This was it!

Jax, still blissfully unaware of the creature's advance, futilely continued fighting against his restraints.

As the Beast drew nearer to the tree it fixed its gaze on the helpless Darren, and looking up at the night sky it let forth another huge roar.

The sound echoed through the surrounding woodland and shattered Darren's trance-like state. He looked up as the enormous monster drew closer, now barely twenty feet away and closing fast. He could see its malevolent eyes boring into him; regarding him as nothing more than a tender morsel waiting to satiate its hunger.

Behind him, Jax was still screaming and wrenching at the unyielding ropes.

Darren managed to let out an almighty scream of his own before the Beast was upon him.

Raising one of its gigantic arms it swiped down at him, its extended claws severing the rope as if it were merely twine being cut by a carving knife.

Darren's throat suddenly felt restricted as if there were a scream inside which could not find its way out. His eyes bulged and his tongue lolled out from between his lips as he slumped forward. With the ropes no longer offering any resistance, Darren tried to lift his arms to protect himself from hitting the ground, but just like his voice they refused to respond to his brain's command.

Darren hit the snow face first and rolled onto his side. With his head bent forward he was just able to observe the river of blood which gushed from the deep striations the Beast's claws had made across his stomach. He stared unblinking as his life's blood soaked into the snow changing the colour from white to red to form some kind of hideously grotesque slush-puppy.

As the Beast grabbed him and hoisted him into the air, Darren could barely feel his body at all. The sound of the creature's next roar sounded much further away than it should have, considering the closeness of their proximity.

Mercifully, Darren was already dead before the Beast plunged its razor sharp jaws into his exposed flesh.

Jax felt the restraints loosen sufficiently for him to turn around and see what was attacking them.

One look at the Beast motivated him to re-double his efforts to escape. Now that his binds were gone he managed to scrabble away from the tree on all fours. He glanced back just in time to see the creature lift up his friend's lifeless body and sink its huge fangs into him, before ripping out a massive chunk of flesh.

It was a vision he knew would never leave him.

Unwilling to stop moving away from the Beast even for a moment, Jax groped and fumbled his way along the ground on all fours trying desperately to make it up to an upright position so that he could start running.

His limbs ached and his legs felt like lead weights as a result of being slumped in the cold snow and tied to the tree. Even so, he continued moving forward as fast as his body would allow, willing himself on towards the surrounding trees and the possibility of some relative protection.

Finally, Jax managed to run upright. But after only a few steps he slipped and fell headlong onto the ground. Even though the thick carpet of snow helped to cushion his fall he still had the wind knocked out of him when he landed.

Unable to catch his breath, Jax mechanically tried to regain his bearings but out of desperation to get away his legs were moving so quickly his feet could not gain purchase on the slippery ground and again he found himself flat on his front.

Jax pushed against the floor and managed to get to his knees without falling over. Shaking his head from side to side he spat and sneezed out the clumps of frozen ice which had lodged in his mouth and nose when he fell. His eyes too had started to sting as a result of making contact with the snowy ground so he rubbed them with the back of his gloved hands to try and alleviate the discomfort.

Still on his knees and with his eyes clamped tightly shut, Jax heard the Beast roar from behind.

It sounded much too close considering how much ground he had covered since he broke free, but he surmised that it was probably just his imagination running riot.

Even so, he ignored the stinging in his eyes and forced himself to stand once more. As he continued to run, he glanced back over his shoulder. To his horror the Beast had discarded his friend and was now bounding straight towards Jax, its gigantic strides allowing it to gain ground much faster than Jax could make headway.

Jax turned back around to concentrate on where he was going. The trees still appeared too far away for him to reach before the creature would be upon him.

He re-doubled his efforts. Putting his head down he pumped his arms and legs as fast as he could, cursing the slippery ground beneath him whenever he slipped or stumbled.

The Beast seemed to have no such problems, judging by the speed with which it was gaining on him.

Jax could sense the creature was virtually on top of him. He was sure that he could feel its foul breath warming the back of his head as he ran. When the snow in his hair began to trickle water down the back of his neck, Jax was convinced that it had to be saliva dripping down from the Beast's drooling maw.

In a last ditch attempt at escape, Jax remembered the advice of his junior league football coach. Feigning a swing to the right, Jax turned and moved left just as the creature lunged forward at him.

The rouse bought him a few precious seconds, but alas not enough to escape altogether.

Though duped by Jax's manoeuvre, the Beast quickly regained its balance and with renewed malevolence chased after the fleeing teenager.

Jax did not want to scream. Instead he tried to save his breath for running, but in the end it did no good. In less than a minute the creature was upon him.

Jax felt the swipe from the side without seeing the blow coming.

The strike propelled him into the air and sent him crashing down into the snow several feet away.

Jax's initial instinct was to keep moving. He tried to lift himself off the ground but in doing so his right arm gave way under his weight.

Unable to fathom why, Jax glanced to his side. To his horror he saw that what had been his right arm was now a bloody stump which hung disjointedly from his shoulder.

Jax did not realise it but he was in shock. Such was the effect of it that the pain he was in did not register. He sat there open mouthed gazing down at what used to be his arm as what was left of it swung uselessly back and forth.

He began to look around him, frantically trying to locate his missing limb. It made perfect sense to him that in such frozen conditions his arm would remain preserved so that a surgeon could re-attach it at some later date.

With his attention focused elsewhere, Jax did not notice the Beast looming over him.

With another swipe of its huge paw it sliced Jax's head clean off his shoulders.

CHAPTER TWENTY FOUR

Sharon and Carey exchanged a weary glance as they listened to the shouting and screaming from upstairs. It was mainly Scott's voice that they could hear ranting, about what, they did not know. But the one thing they could be sure of was that poor Jenny was receiving both barrels full blast.

Both couples had been woken up by the sound of Scott's voice resonating through the walls that morning, accompanied by Jenny's much quieter tones trying to calm him down.

As loud as he was, none of them could actually make out what he was complaining about. But then, as they all had come to accept with Scott, there did not need to be a specific reason these days.

Carey slid the last piece of French toast on top of the pile and put the plate in the centre of the dining table so everyone could help themselves.

Just at that moment, Steve and Greg came in from outside each with an arm load of logs for that evening's fire. They put them down carefully next to the grate, with Steve grabbing hold of the loose ones which tumbled off the pile and replacing them properly.

They could both smell the pungent aroma of the French toast, bacon and freshly brewed coffee.

Greg led the way into the kitchen. "Mmnn, something smells good," he announced, reaching over the table to grab a slice of crispy bacon.

"Ah, no!" hollered Carey, leaning over and slapping his hand away before he could reach the plate. "Wash your hands first; they're filthy from those logs."

Greg pulled a face for the benefit of Sharon and Steve which produced laughter from them both.

"Please don't encourage him," sighed Carey. "You'll only make him worse."

Steve did not wait to be told, and he joined his friend at the sink.

From upstairs they could hear Scott raising his voice again, although from down here it just sounded like a monotone droning.

Steve looked over to the girls. "Those two still at it?"

Sharon raised her eyes while Carey nodded, silently.

"We should try and get them on Jeremy Kyle," Greg piped in, drying his hands on the front of his jeans.

Carey threw a dishcloth at him, partly to dry his hands properly and partly as a result of his remark.

They all sat down to eat.

"Do you think we should see if they want to join us?" Carey asked, gazing up at the ceiling.

"I was thinking about that," replied Sharon, "but there's no telling how Scott will react, seeing as he's in such a mood." She looked over to her friend. "Besides, I don't want to make things worse for Jenny."

"All the more for us," said Greg, cheerfully sticking his fork into another rasher of bacon.

"Pig," Carey shot back.

"Don't worry," Sharon smiled, "I can always make more if they decide to join us."

Just then, they heard a door upstairs open and slam shut.

The next second Scott came thundering down the stairs with a face like thunder. He ignored the four of them eating breakfast and stormed out of the front door, leaving it to crash back against the panelling before it swung shut with a loud bang.

The four friends all looked at each other for a moment before Sharon announced, "I think that might be my cue to go and see how Jenny is doing."

"Come on," Carey added with a supportive smile, "I'll come with you."

The two girls made their way up the stairs towards their friend's room. As they drew closer to the landing they could hear the muffled sound of sobs coming from Jenny and Scott's room. They looked at each other as if each were trying to gauge the other's opinion as to what they should do next.

Finally, Sharon shrugged her shoulders with a "Come on" expression on her face, and they both walked over to the closed door.

They waited a moment before Sharon knocked gently on the wood.

They could hear Jenny from inside trying to compose herself.

"Just a second," she called, trying to sound as cheery as she could. They could hear her move from one side of the room to the other, and then came the sound of trumpeting as she blew her nose, forcefully.

A moment later the door opened.

Both Sharon and Carey stared in disbelief when they saw their friend's face.

Through the puffiness of her crying, both girls could clearly see a large swelling just below Jenny's left eye. She had made an effort to mask it with make-up, but the evidence was still there for all to see.

Scott had obviously hit her!

With Carey following, Sharon guided her friend over to the window so that she could see the state of her face reflected in the daylight.

Jenny allowed herself to be led, but once they reached the window she dropped her head so that they could not see her bruising.

With the caring tenderness of a loving parent, Sharon placed a hand beneath her friend's chin and gently lifted it up. At first, Jenny kept her eyes closed, too ashamed to see the expression on her girlfriend's faces.

Eventually, she opened her eyes. Through the blurriness of her tears, Jenny could tell that both her friends were horrified having seen the extent of her bruising. She could feel herself blush with embarrassment.

When Sharon cupped Jenny's face in her hands she felt a fresh flood of tears brimming over. Sharon pulled her friend towards her and hugged her, kissing her gently on the side of her head.

Carey placed a gentle hand on Jenny's shoulder for added support.

For the next few minutes Jenny's sobs came in wracking fits and bursts.

Sharon could feel her friend's hot tears penetrating through her jumper where Jenny's head lay on her shoulder. In response, Sharon just held her tighter.

After a good ten minutes or so, Jenny finally managed to get control of her emotions and she stopped crying. Reluctantly, she pulled away from her friend's embrace and Carey offered her some fresh tissues which she retrieved from the open box on the dressing table.

Jenny took them gratefully, managing a half smile as she daubed her eyes and wiped her cheeks.

Both Sharon and Carey waited for Jenny to speak, but she stayed silent, making a meal of wiping her eyes and blowing her nose until eventually, the silence only served to emphasise the proverbial elephant in the room.

In the end it was Carey who took the plunge.

"So I take it the bruise on your cheek is not the result of you tripping over the bed during the night?"

Sharon winced. Carey's words sounded harsh to her ears, but a part of her also felt that the time for dancing around the subject was well and truly over. Maybe this was exactly what Jenny needed to see the reality of the situation.

To both girls' surprise, Jenny laughed at her friend's statement. It was good to hear her laugh. Sharon wondered if it was just a nervous reaction on behalf of her friend, but regardless it served to break the ice.

Sharon, not wanting to lose the momentum of the conversation now that Carey had so skilfully opened the door, pressed on. "So how long has this been going on for then, Jen?"

Jenny let out a deep sigh before replying. "This was the first time," she offered, reluctantly.

"Really!" Carey demanded. "You want us to believe that he has never touched you before?"

Jenny looked at Sharon as if for support, but none was offered. Even though Carey's "cruel to be kind" approach was not something Sharon would normally employ, on this occasion it seemed to be doing the trick, so she decided to let her run with the ball.

She could always comfort Jenny again once the worst was over.

"Well!" Carey's tone was sharp; she was obviously in no mood to play around.

Jenny looked from one girl to the other. The hurt in her eyes was almost palpable. She took in a deep breath to try and staunch another deluge of tears. With a shaky voice, she finally answered. "It's true; Scott's never hit me before, not like this."

"So what suddenly made him lose his temper?" Carey continued. "Last night he was the life and soul of the party."

Jenny's bottom lip began to tremble. "It's those damn drugs he's taking," she blurted. "They give him horrendous mood swings, but every time I try and tell him about it he just explodes."

"And now he's started taking his aggression out on you?" Sharon tried to sound as soothing as she could, almost playing off Carey in a *good cop, bad cop* style scenario.

More tears came. Jenny could not help herself. She knew deep down that everything her friends were telling her was true, and she had always made herself a promise that if Scott's outbursts ever became physical then she would have no hesitation but to leave him. But now that it had finally happened, she could almost feel herself making excuses for his actions.

Carey pulled some fresh tissues from the box and gave them to Jenny, who accepted them gratefully. Carey put her arm around her friend's shoulders and gave her a gentle squeeze. She had not meant to attack her in such a manner, but it really infuriated her that it almost sounded as if Jenny was making excuses for Scott's actions.

After a while, Carey continued, but this time in a softer tone. "You know that you cannot carry on like this Jen. It must be like going to bed with Dr Jekyll and waking up next to Mr Hyde."

Jenny laughed again, in spite of herself.

Sharon took her cue and moved in. "You know we'll all be here for you."

"Of course we will," Carey reiterated. "Scott has always been one of us, but none of us are prepared to sit back and watch him treat you this way."

Jenny sniffed into her tissue and nodded her head, reluctantly.

"Where's he gone?" asked Carey.

"He said he was going for a run to clear his head," Jenny replied. "I'm sure when he gets back he'll be full of apologies."

"Too late for that!" Carey snapped, pointing with her index finger as if to emphasise that she was not prepared to accept any concession on Jenny's behalf.

"Carey's right Jen," offered Sharon. "He's crossed a line, how can you ever trust him again?"

Jenny looked at her friends, almost pleadingly.

They could both tell that she did not feel strong enough to split up with Scott, but that was mainly due to the fact that he had worn her down over time and sapped all of the confidence out of her.

Sharon could not help but feel sorry for her friend and wished that there was something more that she could say or do to make things easier for her.

Carey on the other hand, was fighting the impulse to grab her friend by the shoulders and shake some sense into her. She could not fathom why someone would want to stay with a man who beat them. And the fact that Jenny was such a good friend made it even harder to stomach.

Carey had never considered herself to be naïve; she knew that there were masochists in the world who derived pleasure from being hurt. But she knew that her friend was not one of them, and she deserved better.

Sharon could tell that they were at an impasse. The decision had to be Jenny's and no matter how much they tried to convince her, there was no point in bullying her to leave Scott.

Sharon noticed Jenny's eyes starting to well up again. She moved closer and put a comforting arm around her shoulder and decided that it was the right moment to change the subject. "Why don't you wash your face and come down for some breakfast?" she suggested.

"Good idea," agreed Carey, quickly catching on to her friend's idea. "We made French toast and bacon, if the boys have left any that is."

"Not to worry," said Sharon. "I can make some more." She gave her friend a final squeeze before removing her arm. "What'd'yer say Jen?"

Jenny nodded, though she could feel another stream of tears on their way.

"That'a'girl," Carey chimed in, rubbing her friend's arm. "We'll see you downstairs."

The girls left their friend to wash away her tears and made their way back downstairs.

As they suspected, the boys had managed to polish off most of the breakfast, but at least they had washed up.

The girls busied themselves preparing another round for Jenny. The boys were sitting in the living room watching something loud on the television, so at least they were out of earshot.

"Should we tell them about what Scott did to Jenny?" Carey whispered.

Sharon looked up to make sure that they could not be overheard. "I don't know," she shrugged, "they are bound to notice her face before too long no matter how much make-up she uses to hide the bruising."

"You don't think they'll say anything in front of her do you?"

Sharon looked up at her friend. "Well, I know for a fact that Steve won't." She allowed her sentence to trail off, hoping that Carey would take the hint.

After a moment, the penny dropped. Carey had been with Greg for a long time by the standards of most of her relationships, but she appreciated Sharon's candour, he did have a bad habit of speaking first and thinking second.

Not that he would say anything hurtful to Jenny on purpose, she knew him better than that, but there was still a chance that the initial shock of seeing Jenny's face might spur an awkward remark and once it was out it would be too late to *un-say* it.

The question was what to do for the best.

If Carey spoke to Greg, Sharon would have to tell Steve too. Otherwise, Greg would only let it slip to Steve and then he in turn would wonder why Sharon had not trusted him with the truth.

The trouble was neither of the girls felt comfortable talking about their friend behind her back, but the alternative might prove to be too uncomfortable all round. Not to mention more than a little embarrassing for Jenny.

Before the girls had a chance to make a definitive decision they heard Jenny coming down the stairs.

Carey turned to Sharon with a concerned expression on her face.

"Too late now," whispered Sharon, as she turned the rashers over in the frying pan.

A moment later, Jenny entered the kitchen. Both Sharon and Carey could tell straight away that their friend had covered her face in foundation and lavished her cheeks with blusher, doubtless to try and conceal the bruising, which had sort of worked.

Ordinarily, Jenny tended not to wear make-up unless they were going out. She had a very natural fresh-faced complexion so when she did apply some it really showed which was probably not the look she was trying to achieve today of all days.

Jenny smiled nervously. "What do you think?" she asked.

"You look beautiful," Carey assured her as she ushered her to the table. "Come on sit down, breakfast is nearly ready."

****

Stud, Axe, Scarface and Skull climbed off their bikes and without removing their crash helmets, rushed into the bank.

Once inside, they all removed the sawn-off shotguns they had concealed beneath their jackets and with Skull guarding the main door, the other three aimed their weapons at the customers and staff inside.

As the weapons were revealed, there followed an immediate cacophony of noise made up of both customers and staff panicking, shouting, screaming and begging for their lives.

Axe screamed a warning to everyone to get down on the floor and stay put adding for them not to make any sudden movements if they wanted to make it through in one piece. Meanwhile Stud and Scarface rushed over to the counter area and aimed their guns directly at the staff behind the desks. They ordered them not to touch the alarm buttons, *or else!*

Both men swung the holdalls they had been carrying over their shoulders onto the main counter, and then Scarface, aiming both barrels directly at the trembling girl sitting in front of him, demanded that both bags be filled immediately.

Stud lifted his weapon and scanned the dozen or so workers in the back to make sure that they were all complying with his instructions. He looked back when he heard Scarface scream even louder at the poor girl on the other side of the desk to get a move on.

The girl, who was no more than eighteen or nineteen in Stud's opinion, was physically shaking and starting to cry. Frozen to the spot, she was clearly incapable of carrying out the biker's instructions.

To speed the process up, Stud picked out a middle-aged employee who looked to be in charge, and aimed his gun directly at him. The man immediately raised his arms even higher above his head, but from his facial expression he still looked to be in control.

"Get over 'ere and 'elp her!" Stud growled.

The man lowered his arms and dropped the papers he had been carrying on a nearby desk as he passed, keeping his eyes fixed on Stud as he manoeuvred himself around his colleagues and made his way to the front.

Taking his eyes off the big biker, the man leaned over the young girl who by now was crying hysterically and tried to calm her down, but his efforts only resulted in her screaming even louder through her tears.

To prove that he was not time-wasting, the man grabbed the first of the bags and placed it to one side, then he removed a large bunch of keys from his trouser pocket and fumbled for the one he needed to open the till drawers.

Once he had the correct key he realised that he could not get access to the lock with the cashier in the way. He tentatively tried to move her swing chair to one side, but as soon as he did she screamed again.

In desperation the man turned to another of his colleagues for assistance.

Without speaking, the female colleague who had been sitting a few desks back came over to assist him with the hysterical girl.

The woman looked to Stud to be around forty. She was tall, blonde and extremely attractive with a small waist and long legs. Though she was obviously in fear for her own life, the woman managed to exude an elegance and grace in her deportment as she rushed over to assist her colleague. This was an attribute Stud found extremely appealing.

Once the sobbing girl had been whisked away to safety, the man frantically began to fill the holdalls from the till drawers in front of him. In his haste he dropped several bundles of notes, some of which ended up on the floor, but he did not bother trying to retrieve any of them and simply concentrated on completing his task with whatever notes he could grab from the drawers.

Once he believed that he had stuffed in as many bundles as physically possible, he zipped up the bags and shoved them across the desk towards the bikers before lifting his arms back above his head.

Just at that moment there came a huge bang which echoed throughout the small branch. This was immediately followed by a fresh spate of screaming and crying from those held captive.

Stud turned around, slowly.

Axe was standing over the bleeding body of a young man. Smoke poured from the barrel of his gun.

Stud could feel his anger rising behind his helmet. They had been warned no shooting unless it was life or death. Stud looked over to Axe, demanding an explanation.

Before Axe had a chance to speak, there was another blinding crash from behind Stud. He turned back to see Scarface pointing his gun at the manager who had just filled their bags for them. The man was sprawled back in his chair, a wide-eyed look of shock on his face, and a large patch of red on his chest which slowly spread across his chest. He managed to look down once at the increasing crimson circle before he slumped down to the floor.

There were more screams, though this time they were louder and came mostly from the staff behind the counters.

Stud could feel his gang losing control.

He looked up at Scarface who muffled through his helmet. "He was reaching for the panic button…I had to."

Stud, now ready to explode himself, ordered Scarface to collect the bags filled with money. Scarface grabbed both at once and criss-crossed the straps over his shoulders to balance himself out.

Stud yelled a final warning to everyone not to try anything stupid as the bikers backed away towards the door to make their escape.

As he passed, Stud looked down at Axe's victim. He too had a large pool of blood seeping out through the holes Axe had left in his chest. The man was not moving. His eyes were open wide, staring lifelessly at the ceiling.

Skull stood guard with his gun barrel sweeping the room, as his fellow gang members exited the bank. Once outside, as arranged, they all mounted their machines and sped off in pre-determined different directions.

From across the street, Peter York or "Pete the snake" as he was known in the biking fraternity, watched the raid from the comfort of the lorry. Once he was confident that Stud and the rest of the gang had accomplished their mission he knocked three times on the panel behind his head and waited for one of the gang from inside the vehicle to pull it back.

After a few seconds, Angel opened the shutter.

Hearing it slide open, Pete glanced back. "Tell Reaper it all went to plan," he said, with a wink.

Angel turned back and, moving away from the shutter, disappeared into the darkened interior of the vehicle. Pete nonchalantly turned back and continued watching the bank for any sign of action. In the distance he could hear the faint wail of a police siren. He smiled to himself, the gang had timed the raid to perfection and Reaper was bound to be pleased.

Angel reappeared at the opening. "Reaper says to wait for a while to see what the police do."

"Ok," replied Pete, keeping his eyes forward so as not to attract any unwanted attention from passers by. The commotion caused by the arriving police cars was obviously an event for the citizens of the town. Within minutes countless numbers had spilled onto the streets from their various shops and offices to see what all the fuss was about.

Pete heard the shutter slide back into place behind him.

He made himself comfortable to watch the show.

CHAPTER TWENTY FIVE

Tom stood at the upstairs bedroom window with Jan in front of him and together they watched Adam in the 4 x 4 making his way up the winding driveway towards the house.

Tom put his arms around Jan and gave her a light kiss on the back of the head.

She turned around to face him keeping her body close to his so that he did not have to break his hold.

She gazed up at him. Although he was smiling, his eyes conveyed a sadness she had not seen in them before.

Jan wrinkled her nose. "What's that face for?" she asked, quizzically.

Tom sighed. "Oh nothing, it's just with Adam back now and the swelling in your ankle going down, there's no excuse not to take you back to the lodge to be with your friends."

Jan pulled a face. "You can't get rid of me that easily, Buster," she said, with fake exasperation in her voice.

Tom leaned down and kissed her gently on her forehead.

"Come on," he said, "let's go and welcome back my son and heir."

"Are you going to tell him about us?" Jan asked, curiosity getting the better of her.

Tom thought for a moment. "He'll probably figure things out for himself when he sees you here, smart boy that one, bit like his old man." Tom winked.

Jan gave him a playful punch to the ribs as they set off downstairs.

"Home again, home again," called Adam as he entered through the front door, negotiating his way around the frame with two bags of shopping in each hand. He shut the door using his elbow to save having to lay his burden down.

As he made his way to the kitchen he glanced up at the sound of footsteps on the stairs. He was unable to disguise the look of astonishment and shock on his face when he saw his father descend with Jan behind him.

His expression was not wasted on Jan, who caught herself blushing and averting her gaze to the ceiling as she followed Tom down.

"How was your trip?" Tom asked, cheerily.

"Fine," Adam replied, recovering his composure quite expertly. He did not know why in fact he had been momentarily taken aback by seeing his father with Jan. After all, this was not the first time. His father was still a handsome man and women of all sorts found him attractive.

Many a time the two of them had ventured into town for a drink when they had been approached by a couple of women more Adam's age than his dad's. In fact, Adam remembered on one particular occasion a girl, no more than nineteen or twenty at most, had been eyeing them both up all evening. But when Tom excused himself to go to the toilet and the girl finally made her move, it was only to ask Adam about whether or not he thought his *'friend'* might be interested in her.

As they reached the bottom of the stairs, Jan mis-judged the last one. She called out as she felt herself fall. Tom reacted swiftly and managed to catch her and support her weight before her bad ankle took the brunt of it.

Adam was too far away to react in time, but he was very impressed by his father's reflexes. "Are you ok?" he asked Jan, anxiously.

Grabbing onto the banister rail with one hand and leaning against Tom with the other, Jan managed to right herself. "I am now, thanks to your dad." She grinned.

"Nice going dad," said Adam with genuine admiration in his voice.

Tom shrugged, modestly, and in his best John Wayne voice said, "It's all in the reflexes kid."

"Oh my god, seriously?" said Jan, not even trying to keep the incredulousness out of her voice.

"See what I have to put up with?" said Adam, raising his eyebrows to emphasise his suffering.

"Everyone's a critic," laughed Tom, pretending to be hurt, but soon realising he was not about to receive any sympathy from either quarter.

Adam turned back to the kitchen and began to unload the shopping. He was dying to know how Tom had managed to persuade Jan to come over, but he reasoned that that was a conversation for when they were alone.

Tom and Jan followed him in while he unpacked.

"So how are things at the lodge?" asked Adam, whilst placing items from his bags on the counter.

"Ok, so far as we know," replied Tom. "To be honest, we were waiting for you to come back so that we could take a trip up there." He indicated to Jan who was standing beside him. "Jan hasn't seen her friends in days; I think she's feeling lonely."

Jan decided that she had better try and explain the situation to Adam. She presumed that he must be curious to know how she happened to be there and she did not want there to be any awkward silences if the topic were raised, even accidently.

"In case you're wondering," she began, looking straight at Adam, "I had a nasty fall over a high ledge whilst trying to take some photographs. Luckily for me your dad came along," she patted Tom gently on the back, "and saved me."

"Wow, are you ok?" There was genuine concern in Adam's tone which Jan found quite endearing. Obviously his father's son.

"Yeah," replied Jan, lifting her leg off the ground. "I gave my ankle a nasty jolt, but thanks to Tom's nursing skills I think I'll live."

"I didn't want to risk taking the van up there," Tom chimed in, pleased that Jan had taken the lead in explaining things. "There have been a couple of hefty snowfalls since you left."

Adam nodded. "I take it then that Dale still has the plough?"

"Yep, and knowing him we won't see that for a while."

"So have you been in touch with the rest of the gang up there?" Adam asked, purposely not directing the question at anyone specific.

"I've sent a couple of e-mails," Jan replied. "There's been no reception so I just wanted to let them know that I was ok."

"No more signs of anything untoward then I take it?" Adam purposely did not look up when he asked the question. He did not want to embarrass Jan, after all, Jenny was her friend. He hoped that they had found some kind of explanation for Jenny's sighting. He quite liked Jenny. Shame about her boyfriend.

"Not that we're aware of," answered Jan, quite matter-of-factly. "We may find out more when we go back there, who knows."

"Why don't you come over with us when we go?" Tom suggested to Adam. "Unless you're too tired from your trip."

Adam considered his father's idea for a moment.

He was somewhat exhausted from the early start and the long drive, and he certainly could have done with some shut-eye. But the thought of seeing Jenny again made the idea a very tempting one.

"Great," he replied, removing a packet of bacon and one of sausages from a carrier bag and holding them up with one hand. "Time for a spot of brunch first?"

"You bet," said Tom, licking his lips.

"Yes please," Jan chimed in.

****

Jed Solomon had worked for the Forestry Commission as a Ranger for over twenty years. He had fallen into the post virtually by accident having spent the earlier part of his working life as a second generation tree-feller. Though independently employed he managed crews on several contracts for the government and had gained a reputation for his honesty and integrity towards both the people on his team, and those who employed his skills.

Though a keen sportsman in his early years, when he hit his forties he suffered the onset of hereditary arthritis, first in his knees then spreading to his hips. By forty-five the pain had become far too intense for daily physical labour, and though his wife, Jean, suggested that he step back and merely manage the contracts he was bringing in, Jed had always been more of a hands-on sort of man and so he did not relish the idea of just sitting in an office and shuffling paperwork.

It was as a result of a chance conversation whilst negotiating for one of his contracts that the prospect of the Ranger position was put forward.

Initially, it still took some persuading from Jean, but once he had accepted the fact that his doctor had nothing new to offer except more painkillers, Jed took up the post and soon came to relish his new position.

Jed had always preferred the outdoors lifestyle and being a local boy he had spent many a happy holiday hiking and camping around the hills and mountains. His parents had always tried to find the most remote spot to pitch the tents, far off the beaten track, and sometimes they could go for days or even weeks without seeing another soul pass by.

The vastness of the area had always possessed a magical quality in Jed's eyes, and he really could not imagine living anywhere else in the world. Each season held a special allure for him, and winter was by far his favourite. Having worked outdoors for so many years Jed had built up an immunity to the cold, and even his arthritis did not seem any worse in the winter, than it was in the summer months.

His mother had always said that he was one of Mother Nature's children, and being out on such a fine, bright, crisp day as this, always made him feel at one with the earth.

The narrow pass before him wound back and forth through the mountains, and all around him, the area was covered in a dazzling white. It almost seemed a shame that he had to cut a sway through the fresh snow leaving his tracks behind in his wake.

The going was slow due to the icy conditions, but Jed was in no hurry. Enjoying the scenery and drinking in the ambiance was all part of the beauty of being on patrol.

Yes, today would be a good day.

As Jed swung the van around the next bend he was suddenly confronted by the motionless figure of Joanne blocking his path.

Jed slammed on his brakes, the van veered sharply to one side as the tyres fought to keep their grip on the frozen ground. For a second Jed could feel them losing traction. He pulled the steering wheel back to try and turn away from the slide, but it felt as if the tyres beneath him had their own agenda. The van lurched and swerved violently, bringing Joanne directly back in its path.

Jed willed her to move out of his way, but Joanne remained steadfast, her eyes staring straight ahead of her, watching the oncoming vehicle completely nonplussed by the prospect of being run over by it.

Out of sheer desperation Jed began to pump the brake pedal. He could feel the tyres lock, then slide, lock, then slide again as they tried desperately to gain purchase against the snow-covered surface.

Finally, he felt them hold and the van screeched to a halt less than six inches from where Joanne stood.

Heaving a huge sigh of relief, Jed slipped the gear stick into neutral and applied his handbrake before turning off the engine. For a moment he just sat where he was catching his breath, whilst studying the young girl in front of him.

Even from this distance he could not see Joanne's face due to the hood of her parka being zipped up past her nose. But he could tell from her overall posture that she was female. The bonnet of his van had stopped so close to her that he was only able to see her head and shoulders from where he was sitting and he began to wonder if perhaps she was already dead and had somehow been propped up in the middle of the road…perhaps by her killer!

Jed considered calling the situation in to his base before venturing outside, but then he decided that he needed to determine exactly what he would be calling about. Several scenarios began to run through his mind.

Was this perhaps some sort of student prank?

Perhaps this girl was part of a gang and the rest of them were lying in wait to attack him when he left the relative protection of his van.

Jed turned around in his seat and studied the surrounding territory as far as he could see. There certainly did not appear to be anyone lying in wait. Then he reasoned that they would hardly be standing out in plain sight if they intended to jump him. He considered re-starting the engine and driving away from the area before anyone had the chance of attacking him.

Instead, Jed checked himself for allowing his imagination to run wild.

Whoever the girl was she obviously needed his help and he knew that he would not be able to forgive himself if he abandoned her without at least finding out what she was doing out here all alone.

For all he knew she might be the victim of an attack.

Jed opened the driver's door and cautiously checked behind him. Once he was satisfied that there was no one waiting to pounce on him, he eased himself out of the van, wincing as he pushed against the ground with his right leg. Of the two, his right knee was by far the most painful, but it was awkward trying to alight from the driver's side without putting pressure on it.

As he walked around to the front of the van, Jed continued to survey the area around him, just in case of ambush. He cursed himself for having planted such a seed to begin with, but now it had taken root and try as he might, he could not stop it niggling away at him.

Only when Joanne was completely in view did Jed notice that she had a knife clutched in her right hand.

Instinctively, he froze.

He waited for Joanne to make a move. He was convinced now that he was about to be set upon by the rest of her mob, who undoubtedly, would emerge into view any second from behind the surrounding boulders and trees.

He held his breath in anticipation.

But no one else came.

Still anxious, Jed moved forward towards Joanne, his gaze shifting from her face to the knife and back again. As he moved to the side of her she made no effort to face him or monitor his movement.

He was conscious of the fact that he was now within reach of the knife, and though he had begun to relax a little he was still aware that with a swift and practised move Joanne could make a stab at him before he had a chance to defend himself.

The compassionate side of him decided to give her the benefit of the doubt.

"Hello," he said, tentatively, "my name is Jed, I'm a Ranger." There was still no response from Joanne. She just stood perfectly still with her gaze fixed on the road behind the van.

Jed took another careful step towards her.

He was now close enough to touch her arm, though not the one still clutching the weapon.

He took a final sweep of the area before turning his full attention back to Joanne.

"Are you hurt?" he asked, keeping his tone neutral. "Would you like me to take you somewhere, or call someone to come and get you?"

Still there was no response.

Jed extended his arm slowly and touched Joanne on the elbow.

Her sudden scream took him completely by surprise.

Jed backed off a couple of steps, this time convinced that she was about to lunge at him with her knife. He could feel his heart thudding in his chest as he braced himself for the attack.

But Joanne merely stayed where she was and continued staring straight ahead of her as if totally unaware of his presence.

By now, Jed had convinced himself that the girl before him was definitely in need of his help. Although the knife in her hand still gave him cause for concern, he was now more intent on taking Joanne to a place of safety, than anything else.

The question was, how?

After a moment's thought, Jed decided that the situation called for desperate measures. He carefully edged his way behind Joanne, being careful not to make any sudden movements which might cause her to react in panic.

When he was in position, Jed flung his arms around her, pinning her arms by her side and thus ensuring that she could not strike out with her weapon.

Joanne instinctively screamed and began to lash out, but Jed's embrace was too strong to allow her any chance of fighting back. She twisted and turned her body using every ounce of her half-starved diminished strength to try and break free, but her efforts were futile.

Jed put one foot back to steady himself as Joanne kicked out at the van in front of her for leverage. Jed managed to stay upright and pulled her back, away from the vehicle to stop her thrusting them both back into the snow.

Jed supported Joanne's full weight as she continued flailing and kicking her legs in mid-air, presumably unaware that she was too far away from the van to make contact.

In frustration she began to scream again.

Jed was no longer fazed by Joanne's shrieking and squealing, in fact he had expected her reaction to be somewhat similar to the first time he had made physical contact with her. She was obviously traumatised by whatever had happened to her so he had to do whatever he could to try and help her. Ideally Jed would have preferred some help, but as he only ever patrolled alone preferring his own company to having a partner, occasions such as these meant that he had to make the best of it by himself.

Finally, Joanne's kicking and screaming began to subside.

Jed was careful not to release his grip on her, fearing that it might be a ruse on Joanne's behalf to escape, and as Jed did not relish the prospect of having to chase her through the snow he felt that discretion was the better part of valour, so he kept his grip tight.

In his most soothing and calming voice, Jed began an attempt at calming his captive down.

"It's ok," he proffered, calmly. "No one is going to hurt you, I just want to take you somewhere where you will be safe."

Jed felt his words starting to work as Joanne began to relax in his grip. Her screams and protestations had finally given way to pitiful sounding whimpers, moans barely above a whisper.

"It's all going to be ok," continued Jed, grateful that his tone and manner seemed to be having the desired effect.

Still holding Joanne firmly with his right arm across her body, Jed allowed his left hand to gently slide down her arm until he could feel the knife. Joanne's fingers were still wrapped tightly around the wooden handle, so Jed had to prise them off carefully, one at a time, until the weapon finally fell to the floor with a soft thud.

Leaving it where it had landed, Jed began to guide Joanne towards his patrol vehicle, keeping her calm with soothing words and gentle persuasion.

He could just about tell from the gap in her parka hood that she was still transfixed by the road ahead of her. Jed could not imagine what it might be that Joanne was expecting to see, but whatever it was it had obviously caused her enough anxiety to virtually paralyse her with fear.

Eventually, Jed managed to slide Joanne onto the passenger seat and slot in her seatbelt.

He took a moment to survey the surrounding area once more before climbing back behind the wheel.

Once back in the car Jed looked over at Joanne. Her initial trepidation at being confronted by the Ranger seemed to have passed, and now she sat strapped into her seat, her overall demeanour was much calmer and more subdued.

Jed noticed that she was shivering, so he turned on the ignition so that the warm air could penetrate the inside of the vehicle and help restore Joanne's circulation. Jed himself was also feeling the effects of the drop in temperature and he had only been outside the van for a couple of minutes. He had no idea how long his passenger had been out in the elements but he was encouraged by her reaction to the warm air as it blasted out of the grate.

As Joanne leaned forward to get closer to the source of the heat, Jed leaned over to the back seat and retrieved his flask. He poured out a mug of steaming coffee and offered it to Joanne. She took the cup gratefully and was about to drink when Jed called over, "Careful, blow on it first, it's boiling hot."

Joanne took his advice and then slowly began to sip the steaming liquid.

The coffee burned her throat but she did not care. She gulped down the hot beverage as slowly as she could, blowing on the surface between each swallow. It had been so long since she had tasted anything other than snow that the sensation almost seemed alien to her.

Joanne felt the steaming liquid spreading its warmth throughout her insides and slowly she began to feel human again.

From his pack on the back seat Jed offered over a couple of sandwiches he had brought with him to see him through until dinner. Joanne's eyes widened at the sight of the food and Jed gently relieved her of the remnants of coffee left in the cup so that she would not spill it on herself whilst tearing open the wrapper to get access to the sandwiches.

Joanne ate voraciously, taking one bite after another without leaving time to chew her food properly.

"Take it easy," Jed advised, smiling warmly. "It's not going anywhere."

After a while Jed tried his radio to call his base camp. The receiver crackled and whined in his hand, but there was no audible response from the other end. This was not uncommon at their present location and Jed had often been cut off from radio reception by the surrounding hills.

Placing the handset back in its cradle, Jed poured Joanne another cup of coffee as she demolished the second of his sandwiches. She took the cup gratefully and poured the hot liquid down her throat while her mouth was still full of bread and ham.

Once she was finished, Joanne pulled her hood off and looked over at her rescuer. Jed was encouraged by the fact that she no longer had the same expression of sheer terror in her eyes that she had when he had first walked up to her.

"Is that better?" Jed asked.

Joanne nodded. "Thank you," she replied, her voice shaking. Although the hot coffee had warmed her inside, her face still felt the effects of the freezing weather she had been exposed to for so long.

Jed was relieved to finally hear Joanne speak. He was starting to fear that whatever had caused her trauma to begin with might have also destroyed her capacity to communicate.

He held his hand out. "My name is Jed," he offered, warmly.

Joanne was too afraid to remove her glove in case her fingers might freeze and break off. "Forgive my glove," she explained, slightly embarrassed. "I'm Joanne, Joanne Canton, thank you so much for finding me; I thought I was going to die out there from exposure or..." her words trailed off as she began looking around her at the landscape outside.

Jed could tell that Joanne was not completely out of the woods and that whatever had frightened her was still very much on her mind.

Jed was curious to dig deeper, but he decided that he did not want to push the issue and risk sending Joanne off the deep end. He was no expert on the subject but he surmised that it did not take a psychiatrist to see that she was too fragile to start pumping for information.

The important thing was to take her somewhere safe and warm and, most importantly, away from here.

Jed shook Joanne's hand loosely, then let go. "My pleasure," he responded. "And now I think we need to leave."

Joanne looked back at him. "Where are you taking me?" she asked, a sudden spark of fright flashed across her eyes.

Jed started up the engine. "Ideally, I'd like to get you to hospital to have you checked over, but the nearest one is a couple of hours from here, so there's a friend of mine who owns a lodge about an hour's drive away. Once we're there I should be able to make radio contact with my office and they will be able to send an ambulance over to meet us there."

Joanne considered Jed's words for a moment and then seemed to visibly relax.

Jed took that as an encouraging sign so he slipped the van into gear and drove away.

CHAPTER TWENTY SIX

When Scott returned from his run he went straight upstairs to shower without bothering to acknowledge any of his friends in the lodge. Even Jenny, who he almost collided with at the bottom of the stairs, did not receive so much as a nod when he passed her.

Sharon and Carey merely shook their heads in disgust at Scott's behaviour.

Jenny waited until her boyfriend had reached the top of the staircase, still hoping that he might change his mind and at least turn to smile at her, or better still come back down and apologise for earlier. But deep down she knew that the chances of that happening were next to nothing.

This time she really believed that there might be no going back. A line had been crossed, and though she would not openly admit it to her friends, she would still forgive Scott if he apologised and at least look as if he meant it.

However, deep down Jenny felt that Scott wanted to push her away and end their relationship. And since she seemed oblivious to his uncaring behaviour and indifference towards her feelings, perhaps he had hit her as a final straw, hoping that she would now use the incident to break it off with him, thus saving him the effort of having to do the dirty deed himself.

Jenny placed her foot on the bottom step and was about to hoist herself up when Carey caught her arm. She turned back to look at her friend.

"What do you think you're doing?" Carey demanded, keeping her voice just above a whisper so that Steve and Greg would not hear.

Jenny looked at her friend with doe eyes. "I'm just going to talk to him," she replied softly, looking over her friend's shoulder to ensure that the boys were not listening.

"To tell him where to go, I hope?" Sharon asked, moving in closer to help keep the conversation intimate.

Jenny's expression looked pained, as if she was desperately searching for the right words to satisfy everyone without causing her friends to lose their temper with her.

She shrugged her shoulders, dejectedly. "Yeah, I suppose so, if it comes to that."

From the lack of conviction in her voice, plus the fact that Jenny was unable to hold their gaze, Sharon and Carey knew instantly that their friend was about to do no such thing.

As Jenny turned back to ascend the stairs, Carey moved in and placed a gentle but firm hand on her shoulder. When Jenny turned back there were fresh tears in her eyes. She wiped them away with the back of her hand before they had a chance to brim over and run down her cheeks.

"Oh Jen," said Carey, with genuine concern in her voice. The anger and frustration that had been building up inside her due to her friend's lack of gumption faded the moment she saw her fresh tears.

Sharon also moved in closer and between them they had a group hug.

When they broke apart Jenny looked at her friends and with a half-smile said, "Wish me luck," before she turned around and made her way up the stairs.

From above they could hear the sound of Scott in the shower.

Sharon waited for Jenny to be out of earshot before she looked at Carey and asked, "What do you think?"

Carey continued to look up until Jenny had disappeared around the corner, and then she turned back to her friend and quietly replied, "I think under the circumstances we need to tell the lads," she nodded towards where Steve and Greg were watching television.

Sharon's brow furrowed. "Why?"

Carey sighed. "Because I have this horrible feeling that when Jenny confronts Scott there will be an almighty eruption and then the boys will be asking all sorts of questions." She bit her bottom lip while she thought, then continued. "If we tell them now, it will be less embarrassing all round when things get sticky."

Sharon considered her friend's reasoning, then nodded. "Yes, I suppose it will be for the best, long term." She looked over at their boyfriends. "Come on then, let's get it over with."

****

Jenny waited patiently on the bed while Scott was showering. Out of habit she began to fold his discarded running attire, and placed it neatly in a pile ready for washing.

She dreamed to herself that when Scott emerged from the bathroom that he would sweep her up in his arms and hold her close to his naked body, apologising and begging for her forgiveness as he kissed her both gently and passionately alternating between the two until their fervour got the better of them.

But more than anything, Jenny just wanted the man she fell in love with to come back. The pre-steroid, roid-rage Scott who was always so happy and playful, kind and compassionate.

Last night had given Jenny a glimpse of the Scott she once knew. But in hindsight it had been a cruel twist of fate proceeding as it did his behaviour this morning.

She heard the water stop and the screen slide open.

Jenny held her breath as Scott's footsteps approached the shower room door.

When he emerged into the bedroom, Jenny managed to greet him with a warm smile, but her gesture was not reciprocated. Scott glared at her as if she were a stranger on a train blocking his way. He walked straight past her without bothering to acknowledge her presence and proceeded to dry himself off.

Jenny watched his taut torso twist and turn as Scott towelled himself dry. In truth, she had preferred the old skinny Scott to this manifestation, but no matter how many times she told him so, he would never believe her. He often remarked at how other girls at the gym and in the street gave him admiring glances which they never would have had he remained as he was before.

If he was merely saying it to make Jenny jealous, then it did not work.

In truth, it was his constant striving for perfection which had taken over his life, leaving little or no time for Jenny or anyone else for that matter.

Finally, the strained silence was making Jenny feel very uncomfortable, so she decided to take the higher ground and speak first, even though it was him who owed her an apology.

"Scott," she said, timidly, "why are you being like this?"

"Like what?" he spat back, not bothering to glance in her direction.

Jenny sighed. "Like this!" She gestured with her hands for emphasis, but it was futile as Scott still refused to turn around.

Once he had finished drying himself, Scott began to dress.

Jenny waited until he was almost finished. The subtle approach was obviously having no effect on her boyfriend, so she decided it was time to make a decisive move to try and save the day-as well as their relationship.

Jenny slid off the bed and walked over to Scott. He still had his back to her while he was rooting around in a drawer for a jumper.

Jenny wrapped her arms around his waist and leaned her cheek against his back. She immediately felt Scott stiffen as if he had been grabbed from behind by an unknown assailant and he was preparing himself for retaliation.

Unperturbed, Jenny rested her head in the groove between Scott's shoulder blades and began to slide her hands gently up and down his torso.

Without warning Scott grabbed her hands and forced them away from his body. At the same time he stuck out his rear forcing Jenny to stumble backwards, almost losing her balance altogether.

Scott spun around to face her; his face was a twisted mask of contempt. Such was the look of malevolence in his eyes that Jenny feared that she was about to strike her again. "What the hell is the matter with you?" Scott roared.

Jenny could feel the tears coming. She bit her bottom lip in an attempt to keep them at bay. Nothing she could say or do seemed to be able to placate Scott right now, though why he was being so mean to her she still did not know.

Scott turned his back on her again and continued shuffling through his drawer.

Even at this stage Jenny would have been elated if Scott came to her and held her in his arms. She would forgive him instantly for the way he had been acting during this trip; even the fact that he had hit her this morning would be forgiven.

But deep down, though she was desperate not to have to accept the fact, she knew that that time had passed. Their relationship was over. Jenny needed to storm off downstairs without looking back to retain some dignity and self-respect for herself.

Instead, she burst into tears.

Upon hearing her blubbering, Scott wheeled around again, that same look of disgust on his face. "Oh for god's sake, can't you just shut up with your sobbing and crying, it drives me nuts!"

His words hit Jenny with the force of a sledgehammer. He really did not care for her feelings one bit. Now she was desperate to leave the room, but her legs would not carry her. Jenny was genuinely afraid that if she tried to walk away she would collapse on the floor in a sobbing heap.

Jenny slumped back on the bed. She gazed up at Scott through bleary eyes. There was no recognition left of the loving, caring, sympathetic man who would do anything to make her laugh.

Still, Jenny needed to know. "Why are you being so nasty?" she pleaded through gasping sobs, her chest heaving up and down as she spoke, her words almost lost on her breath.

Scott let out a grunt of exasperation. He grabbed his suitcase from on top of the wardrobe and began throwing his clothes in, not caring that he was mixing the clean ones with the dirty, sweaty ones from his run.

Jenny tried to get a hold of herself. "Where are you going?" The question was almost unnecessary as she felt sure that she already knew the answer. But deep down there seemed to be a masochistic part of her that needed to hear it from his lips.

Without looking up from his task, Scott replied. "Away from here, and away from you, I've had enough!"

Even though Jenny was expecting an answer along those lines, the minute she heard them a fresh batch of sobs erupted.

Scott finished packing his case and zipped it closed.

He retrieved his keys from the dresser and, turning, threw them on the bed by Jenny. "Right, I'm going for a piss; now get your stuff out of my van 'cos I'm leaving in five minutes, got it?"

Jenny picked up the keys. "But how am I supposed to get home if you go now?" she asked, her voice shaking with emotion. "There isn't enough room for all of us in the other car."

"Not my problem," Scott hissed. "Just make sure you get your stuff out or I'm throwing it out before I go."

With that, he left the room and made his way along the corridor to the toilet.

Jenny felt desolate.

Regardless of how horribly Scott was treating her she could not simply switch off her emotions and stop caring for the man who, at one time, she thought she might be with forever.

But she realised that the present situation was hopeless.

Scooping up the van keys from the bed, Jenny wiped her eyes with the backs of her hands and walked over to the mirror. She gazed at her reflection and knew instantly that her friends would be able to see she had been crying, there was no hiding it.

Not that it mattered anymore. Scott was leaving and that was an end to it.

The problem concerning getting home would be an issue she would have to deal with later. She knew that her friends would not abandon her, but the reality of the situation was that Sharon's mum's car could only legally seat five, and now there were six of them who needed a ride.

Jenny blew her nose and wiped her eyes again before making her way to the top of the staircase. She descended slowly, trying to compose herself before having to face her friends.

As she reached the bottom she noticed that they had all gathered in the kitchen area. She suspected that they had done so to try and save her any more discomfort than was absolutely necessary. Doubtless they had heard Scott's shouting and realised that they were witnessing the end of what was once a beautiful relationship.

Before she headed for the door, Jenny turned towards where her friends were standing. The boys were looking away, pretending to be engrossed in conversation, but they were not fooling anyone.

Sharon and Carey both tried to give their friend encouraging glances, and Jenny even managed a slight smile before she turned away and walked towards the front door.

Jenny pulled on her coat and tried as best she could to stay strong as she slid back the bolt on the door.

She could not remember if she had even left anything in Scott's van, but after his warning she thought it was best to check, just in case.

As she opened the door, the leering face of Reaper stared back at her.

CHAPTER TWENTY SEVEN

Before Jenny had a chance to react or shout out to her friends, Reaper had clamped one of his huge shovel-like hands over her mouth and forced her back inside the lodge.

The rest of the bikers barged in behind him, with Deedee and the girls bringing up the rear.

Once they were all inside, Reaper let go of Jenny who, too scared to scream, merely backed away from the gang towards the kitchen where her friends were.

Jenny had only taken a few steps backwards before the bikers began to close in on her again. Scarface, Axe and Skull were all brandishing their shotguns and Jenny could see that several of the others, including some of the girls, also had firearms, knives and other assorted weapons jutting from their belts.

Before she had the chance to raise the alarm Jenny heard the others emerging from the kitchen.

After the initial gasps of shock and surprise, Greg was the first to speak up.

"Who the hell are you?" he asked, trying to sound authoritative and in control, but unfortunately for him he was unable to prevent his voice from cracking.

Reaper stood in the middle of the room with his hands on his hips as some of the others converged menacingly on the five friends.

Instinctively, Sharon reached out and grabbed Jenny, pulling her closer to the rest of them for protection. As the three frightened females huddled together, first Steve and then Greg moved in front, nervously trying to act as a human shield preventing the bikers from gaining access to their girlfriends and Jenny.

Scarface moved in ahead of the others, a sinister smug smile creasing his lips. He swung the barrel of his weapon towards Steve and Greg and revelled in the way both the men's faces registered their terror at seeing the gun.

Both Skull and Axe circled around their comrade to prevent the students from breaking free should any of them consider the possibility.

Feeling trapped and completely inadequate in the present circumstance, Steve and Greg took a step back towards the girls, each still holding their arms out to their sides to perform a protective barrier, both realising that their efforts would prove completely ineffectual should any of the bikers decide to use their weapons.

With his gang members covering their charges, Stud sauntered over and placing his hand on Skull's shoulder looked down at their captives.

When he spoke, his voice was gruff but still calm, and he exuded the bearing of someone completely in control of the situation.

"Well hello there," he drawled, taking his time with each syllable. "I trust that none of you mind us dropping in unannounced like this?" There was a spate of giggles and titters from behind him. "But you see," he continued, "we need somewhere to crash doggo for a while, just until things outside calm down."

Steve and Greg exchanged glances as if each was hoping that the other might have an idea what to do. Both of them were more concerned with the girls' welfare than anything else, but they realised that neither of them was in any position to make demands.

Even if Scott joined them, it would still be only three of them against the five bikers, and the biggest one looked as if he could take all of them on by himself without even breaking sweat.

Added to that, they were armed, and they all appeared as if they would have no qualms using their weapons, if any of the lads fancied their chances.

Even the tall blond woman standing behind the large biker looked as if she could handle herself pretty well if push came to shove.

Just then, Scott appeared at the top of the stairs with his suitcase in one hand and his backpack in the other.

Everyone in the room turned their attention towards the new arrival. It was obvious from the look of surprise on Scott's face that he had not heard the bikers arrive, but it only took a moment for him to grasp the situation.

Dropping his bags, Scott began to make his way down slowly, one step at a time. Even those bikers holding loaded weapons still took a step back when they saw the purposeful look on Scott's face. With his arms hanging by his sides he began to clench and release his fists as if he was preparing to go into battle.

Reaper seemed to be the only biker who was not in the least bit phased by Scott's demeanour. Even Deedee appeared to move back farther behind her boyfriend as if she felt in need of more protection.

As Scott reached the bottom of the stairs, Jenny ran over to him and made an attempt to grab hold on him as if to stop him going any further. Without even acknowledging her, Scott pushed Jenny aside with one arm as he continued to move forward towards the armed men. Jenny, clearly not expecting the gesture, lost her balance and started to fall backwards, but fortunately for her Steve was able to react swiftly enough to race over and catch her before she fell.

"That's far enough big man!" It was Stud who decided to break the spell of the moment that Scott seemed to have created. He held out his hand at the approaching figure by way of reinforcing his command to Scott. The futility of the gesture reminded Sharon of the story of Canute trying to stop the waves from reaching the shore.

When the other bikers realised that Scott was ignoring their leader's command they raised their guns and pointed them directly at him. Skull made a point of cocking the hammers on both his barrels for effect. The gesture worked.

Scott stopped dead in his tracks, his eyes now focused on the collective barrels pointing in his direction. He stood there for a moment, his hands still balled into fists, his mighty chest heaving and lowering as he took several slow steady breaths. The veins on his arms seemed fit to pop as he struggled to keep his composure. From the look in his eyes, the bikers were in no doubt that if it were not for the fact that they were all armed, Scott would have not hesitated to take them all on, possibly even Reaper.

Stud moved forward, closer to Scott but still safe in the knowledge that his gang had him covered. He held up his hand in a gesture designed to calm things down, but Scott's stance did not alter or relax, he kept his gaze focused on the men in front of him, snorting like a bull about to charge.

"Now why don't you just calm down old son," offered Stud. "If you all do as we tell yer, perhaps no one needs to get 'urt."

Scott's reply astonished everyone in the room, not just his friends.

"I don't give a fuck what you do with them, just let me go, I need to get away from this dump!"

Even after all he had done and said to Jenny, she was still hurt the most by Scott's words. "Scott!" she cried. "What are you saying, these are our friends."

Scott spun on the spot and advanced towards her and the group. Jenny instinctively cowered, afraid that he was about to strike her again, this time in front of everyone.

Instead, Scott reached out and tore his van keys from Jenny's grasp. With everything else that was going on Jenny had forgotten that she was still clutching them in her hand. She yelped as Scott ripped them free, wrenching her knuckle in the process.

Scott turned back to face the bikers. "Look, I don't care what you lot are up to or what you've done or what you intend to do, I just need out and I'm going to leave right now." He spoke with determination in his voice, and no one doubted his sincerity.

Stud held out his arm and raised his weapon so that both barrels were pointing directly at Scott's face. From such a close distance there was no way he could miss if he decided to pull the trigger.

Axe, Scarface and Skull all followed suit so that they all had their guns trained on the unarmed bodybuilder.

Jenny, Sharon and Carey all drew back and closed their eyes in anticipation of the loud blasts they expected to hear any second.

Steve and Greg found that neither of them could look away, they were both transfixed with a morbid fascination for what they believed was about to take place. Their friend had pushed things too far with these men who clearly had no problem using their weapons to kill another human being.

Greg was shocked to see a smile start to crease the lips of one of the dark-haired biker girls at the back. She was obviously relishing the situation and from her facial expression seemed to actually be willing her men folk on to obliterate Scott.

The two blond girls next to her obviously did not share her enthusiasm as Greg could see them huddling together and turning their heads away so as not to see the carnage erupt.

Scott continued to hold his ground. Although he was in no doubt that the bikers meant business, there was a rage building up inside him which would not let him back down. He had often felt it before and it often arose in the most unlikely of situations, but he had come to accept that the feeling controlled him, rather than the other way around.

No one moved.

It was almost as if the bikers were waiting for one more excuse to open fire on Scott, and any second now it felt to the others as if Scott was going to give it to them.

But miraculously, instead, he relaxed. His shoulders slumped and he released his fists, letting his van keys dangle from his fingers.

The bikers continued to hold their position for fear that it might be a trap and that Scott was just trying to lull them into a false sense of security. He was definitely close enough to charge them, and though they had the advantage of their weapons, at this range there was a chance that Scott could still take them all down if he hit them square on.

The bikers finally began to relax when Scott took a step back.

Stud, without realising it, had been holding his breath, but once Scott moved away he let it out and allowed his breathing to level before speaking.

"Well, now, that's very sensible of you, no need for any unwanted bloodshed is there?" He spoke calmly, like someone who felt fully back in control of the situation. Behind him he heard Reaper grunt as he took a seat in an armchair with its back to the wall. Deedee moved alongside him and perched herself on the armrest, taking up her usual position as if she felt the need to let their three female hostages know that Reaper was spoken for.

The two blond girls, Stacy and Kim, also seemed to relax visibly now that the imminent feeling of someone being shot had passed.

Stud lowered his weapon slightly as a token to show Scott that he was no longer under threat having made the right decision.

Just at that moment, there was a knock at the front door.

Stud spun around, automatically lifting his gun again and aiming it towards the front door. Stacy and Kim, who were closest to it, shuffled away back into the room until they were close enough to Stud to feel protected.

Stud looked over to Reaper. The big man pulled a handgun out from inside his jacket and signalled with a nod of his head for Stud to investigate.

Stud called back over his shoulder. "Watch 'em," as he slowly walked towards the nearest window which looked out onto the front porch.

The three bikers kept their weapons aimed at the six friends while their leader investigated.

Both Greg and Steve watched Scott closely, wondering if he really had calmed down or was just waiting for the chance to launch an attack. Regardless of what he had said to the bikers about them, both men were convinced that it might be part of a ploy to catch their captors off guard.

The girls on the other hand were convinced that Scott was just being an idiot. After the way he had treated Jenny that morning and the fact that he had already packed his bags ready to go, they were more inclined to believe that he really did not care what happened to any of them, and he was in fact more interested in leaving than anything else.

Sharon and Carey suddenly both noticed their respective boyfriends casually changing their stance. To the girls it appeared as if they were manoeuvring themselves into a more favourable position in order to launch an attack at their captives.

Both girls instinctively reached out and grabbed their partners by the arm and gently but firmly pulled them closer. The boys, realising what the girls were doing, reluctantly allowed themselves to be guided back. Between the two of them, they stood facing Scott's back, reforming their human shield to protect all three girls should Scott provoke the bikers into using their firearms.

From the window, Stud suddenly lowered his weapon.

"It's ok," he called out, reassuringly, "it's only Snake." Stud walked over to the door and welcomed their driver in.

Pete "the Snake" entered carrying a large cooler bag which was bulging under the weight of its contents. He acknowledged Stud as he crossed the threshold; he then quickly surveyed the scene in front of him, before walking over to Reaper to make his report.

Reaper looked up at the new arrival through the long strands of greasy hair covering his face. "All done?" he asked, in a low growl.

Snake nodded, carefully placing his burden on the floor beside him. "Yep, all the bikes safely on board an' I hid the lorry behind a dense clump of trees about a quarter of a mile away. No one will be able to see it from the road."

Reaper nodded his approval and then signalled to the cooler bag.

Without needing further instruction, Snake opened the bag and took out several bottles of beer. He handed one to both Reaper and Deedee, then he began to pass the others around to the rest of the gang.

Skull took the bottles for his two comrades and placed his shotgun under his arm to pop the caps whilst they continued to cover their hostages.

After taking a long swig from his bottle, Scarface held it out towards the group as if offering them a drink, though it seemed as if he was directing his offer towards Jenny.

They all shook their heads, and Steve spoke on their behalf.

"No thanks, we're ok."

Scarface continued to drink; his eyes seemed to be boring into Jenny making her feel very uncomfortable. She looked away, first at the floor and then randomly around the room, anywhere but back at the biker.

Stud strode back over to his gang, his half-finished bottle in one hand, and his gun loosely carried over his other arm with both barrels facing the floor.

"Now then," he said, with an almost cheery influence in his voice. "We may be here for some time, so why don't we all get nice and comfortable, eh?"

Steve and Greg looked at each other nervously, then back to the girls. They could tell how terrified the three of them were and it made them both feel totally inadequate that they could not do more to protect them.

"How about," Stud continued, "you all move to the middle of the room and settle down where we can keep an eye on you?" He gestured to the two settees which formed an "L" shape and dominated the centre of the room.

Axe, Skull and Scarface stepped back to form a gauntlet allowing them to pass. Their guns lowered slightly, but still high enough to convey the threat of an assault.

When the group did not immediately respond to Stud's suggestion, he suddenly became less agreeable and more threatening.

"Come on; move," he bellowed. "I won't ask again!"

The sheer malice in his voice jerked the friends into action.

Steve and Greg turned back to let the ladies go first, forming a protective barrier around them with their bodies. Neither of them felt comfortable moving closer to the bikers but their choices, for now at least, seemed negligible.

Scott on the other hand, had other ideas. Instead of complying with Stud's demand, he flipped his keys over his finger and slipped them into his pocket, and then he looked Stud straight in the eyes and said. "Do you know what; I've had enough of this?" He held out his arms as if to show he was not hiding anything. "If you won't let me leave, then I'm not going to sit around here watching you lot get drunk. I'm off upstairs!"

And with that, Scott turned on his heel and before anyone could stop him he began to take the stairs two at a time.

Obviously shocked by Scott's bravado, Stud took a moment to respond. But by that time, Scott was half-way back up the stairs.

"Oi!" Stud yelled, after him. "Get the fuck down 'ere, now!"

"Whatever dude," came back Scott's unconcerned reply, as he continued on up.

Stud began to raise his weapon, and then thought better of it. Scott was already too far away for a clean shot, and besides which Reaper was already pissed off at them for shooting the two people in the bank without good reason, and he had warned them not to fire on the kids unless it was absolutely necessary.

For all his fearsome reputation, Reaper lived by a code of his own and heaven help anyone who crossed it.

In desperation, Stud turned to look at his leader for assistance.

Reaper waved his hand in a non-committal gesture, which Stud understood to mean, 'let him go'.

Stud turned back and looked up the stairs as Scott disappeared with his bags back into his and Jenny's bedroom.

Skull looked at his leader. "Shall I go after 'im?" he asked, moving towards the stairs in anticipation of an affirmative response.

"Na, let 'im go," replied Stud, still not completely happy with Reaper's reaction. "'e won't be goin' anywhere."

"What if 'e 'as a gun or something up there?" asked Axe, feeling uneasy about letting Scott disobey a direct order and it going unpunished.

Stud had not considered that as a possibility.

He turned back to look at Reaper for a reaction, but the big biker was busy trying to turn the television on with the remote control.

Stud decided it was best all around just to comply with Reaper's original order, regardless of what his gut was telling him to do.

"Nah, don't bother, 'e won't try nothing when we've got his mates down 'ere with us."

As they walked towards the sofas, Carey decided to offer some assurance for the benefit of all of them. "We don't have any weapons in the house," she stated, hoping that it would end the debate over what to do about Scott. Even though he had acted like a complete bastard to Jenny, no one wanted to see him being shot for his stupidity.

They all settled down around the television which Reaper finally managed to turn on.

Reaper flicked through the channels until he found a local news report. The story of their raid was naturally the lead feature.

The cameras scanned the area around the bank showing a mass throng of people cordoned off behind police tape, eagerly watching the scene unfold. There were several police cars and a couple of ambulances within the cordon, and from behind the reporter you could just make out the bank staff and customers, each one with a blanket around their shoulders, being led from the building into the waiting ambulances.

The reporter mentioned the fact that of the two individuals who had been shot during the robbery, one had already been pronounced dead, whilst the other was still in a seriously critical condition.

At the mention of the victims, Axe and Scarface leaned in towards each other and clinked their bottles together as if in celebration.

Their gesture caught the eye of Reaper who looked over at them disapprovingly. Both men realised that they had overstepped their boundaries so they looked away in disgrace.

Snake passed out more beers to the gang, leaving the empties discarded wherever they lay.

Sharon had to fight the urge to get up and start clearing away the debris. As much as she hated untidiness she suspected that her gesture may well not be appreciated by those causing the mess, so she managed to stay put and tried to ignore it.

The five friends were all huddled on one of the sofas, squidged up tightly together as it was only designed to seat four people, but none of them wanted to be separated from the group at that moment. Steve and Greg sat on the outside with Jenny in the middle sandwiched between Sharon and Carey. Sharon held Jenny's hand and every so often gave it a gentle squeeze for comfort as her boyfriend had deserted them and was not there do it himself.

While they continued to watch the live coverage of the robbery, they heard the distant roar of an engine growing louder as a vehicle approached from the main road.

Other than Reaper, all the male bikers stood up and moved over to the windows to get a better look.

Soon Tom's 4 x 4 emerged from behind the surrounding trees and pulled up outside the lodge. He tooted his horn twice to announce his arrival, and then the bikers watched as he, Adam and Jan, all climbed out and started to make their way towards the porch.

The others all looked to Stud for instruction. This time he did not need Reaper to advise him. Stud ran over to the sofa where the five friends were seated and ignoring Steve who was the closest to him, he grabbed Sharon by the elbow and wrenched her up to a standing position.

"Owww," she squealed, as her shoulder took the brunt of the force.

"Hey!" Steve shouted angrily, rising to defend his girlfriend.

Still holding Sharon's elbow tightly with one hand, Stud swung his gun around in the other and caught Steve a glancing blow across his chin with the butt of the weapon.

Jenny screamed as Steve fell back against the sofa from the force of the blow, clutching his chin.

Sharon tried in vain to yank her arm free so that she could attend to her boyfriend's injury, but Stud had her in a vice-like grip and was not about to let her go. He pointed his gun down at Steve who in spite of his jaw looked as if he was about to try and stand up to the biker again.

Thankfully, when Steve saw the gun aiming at him, he slumped back down.

"Now fuckin' stay there!" Stud demanded, with an almost demented look in his eyes.

Once he was sure that his instruction was being obeyed, Stud dragged Sharon over to the window so that she could see Tom and the others.

"Who's that?" he demanded.

Sharon was shaking through a combination of fright and anger. As a result, her voice came out in a tiny girl-like squeak.

"That's Tom and his son, and our friend Jan."

"Well get rid of 'em," Stud shoved Sharon towards the front door as he spoke, and then pointed his gun in her direction. "Now!"

Even though there was still vitriol in his tone, Stud kept his voice down as Tom and the others were approaching the door from the other side and he did not want them to hear him.

The other bikers moved back from the window. Protected as they were from the outside by the net curtains, they still did not want to be seen by the new arrivals.

Sharon looked over at her friends, helplessly. She was visibly shaking and there was a faint suggestion of tears starting to form a screen over her eyes. But she realised quickly that it was down to her now to do everything she could to prevent Tom and the others from crossing the threshold.

Sharon did not know what she was going to do, or how she was going to do it, but the fact remained that she possibly only had once chance to keep the others out, and if she did not, then their lives might also be in danger as a result.

With an unsteady hand, Sharon reached for the door handle.

CHAPTER TWENTY EIGHT

Sharon wiped her eyes to clear away any trace of tears and attempted a warm smile as she opened the door. She had hoped to catch the new arrivals before they made it to the porch, but it was already too late. Jan was immediately behind the door when Sharon opened it, with Tom and Adam directly behind her.

Jan, genuinely happy to see her friend, flung her arms around Sharon and gave her a big hug. Still unsure of how she was going to achieve her orders, she reciprocated but held onto Jan far longer than she expected. Jan took it as a sign of how happy Sharon was to see that she was alright after her accident, and she appreciated the sentiment.

When Sharon finally released her hold the others quite naturally expected her to step back to allow them to enter. But instead she stayed where she was, blocking the doorway, and an awkward silence followed as Sharon tried desperately to figure out how she was going to get her friends to leave, without making them suspicious.

Finally, Jan asked, "Well, are you going to let us in or are you guys throwing an orgy, or trying to hide a dead body without us seeing?" Jan spoke in jest and both Adam and Tom started laughing behind her.

Sharon too, attempted a chuckle, but her situation was becoming more desperate with each passing second.

Eventually, an idea struck her.

Sharon moved forward, closer to the three new arrivals, and was about to close the door behind her as if to stop those inside hearing, but then she realised that with Stud and the others just behind the door they would doubtless suspect that she was up to something if they could not hear what she was saying, so Sharon left it ajar.

Barely above a whisper, Sharon said, "Jenny and Scott have had a huge bust-up, and Jenny is very upset at the moment." She waited for some kind of reaction, but all she had in response were concerned looks from everyone.

She realised that her plan was not working.

The excuse she had given-though true in effect-was hardly sufficient to prevent her friends entering the lodge.

"Is she alright?" Jan asked, quizzically, realising that there must be more to the story than what they had just been told.

"Yes," replied Sharon, biting her bottom lip for inspiration. "Scott hit her!"

There, it was out.

Sharon had not intended going so far, but the anxiety of having to keep her friends safe was building up inside her and she was afraid that at any moment she might just scream out for them to run and get away from the lodge, and that she knew might be the end for all of them.

But instead of her revelation having the desired affect, Jan took a step closer. Placing her hand on Sharon's arm for comfort, she asked, "Is she ok, what the hell did he do to her?"

Sharon could see that her plan had backfired.

Adam especially seemed to be growing angrier judging by the look on his face.

Sharon could feel the bikers from behind starting to get agitated at the length of time she was taking to get rid of Jan and the men. She decided to go for broke.

"It's ok, she's just a little bruised, and in shock," she looked nervously from one face to the other as she spoke. "The fact is that Scott has decided to leave, and Carey and I are trying to calm Jenny down, and…I just think it might be easier if you all came back a bit later…when it's all over."

Her suggestion seemed to hit the three of them like a hard slap in the face.

Jan was naturally upset by the fact that Sharon did not seem to want her to comfort their friend as well. Tom owned the lodge and Sharon was not even a tenant under the rental contract, so technically he could enter whenever he chose, without permission. And here was she, effectively asking him not to.

She had definitely put them all in a very awkward position, but she alleviated the guilt by telling herself that it was all for their own good.

The two men seemed readier to accept the situation than Jan. Sharon could tell from the look on her friend's face that she was not happy with the situation. Not that Sharon blamed her; if their roles had been reversed, she too would feel as if she was being excluded from the group for no apparent reason. At least, no feasible one.

Sharon desperately wished that she could think up something a little more believable, but what?

A flu epidemic.

A chemical spill.

The plague!

What possible excuse could she have made up on the spot that would not only sound believable, but would also make Jan and the boys want to leave the lodge?

"Sharon," Jan said, in the calmest voice she could muster under such odd circumstances, "I could really do with a change of clothes right now; these ones are beginning to stink." She held out the top of her shirt for emphasis.

"Please," Sharon pleaded, "can't it wait a bit, you can change when you come back, later." She could feel that her negotiating skills were far below par, and wondered what must be going through Jan, Tom and Adam's thoughts right now.

Jan released a huge sigh, everyone could tell that she was beginning to grow irritated with Sharon's attitude, but she still wanted to maintain her composure. None of this made any sense to her. If Scott and Jenny had had another fight then what possible difference would it make if Jan came in to collect a change of clothes?

Jan was after all, as much Jenny's friend as Sharon and Carey.

Or was Sharon seriously suggesting that Jan's appearance would somehow upset their friend even more?

That idea made Jan even angrier. "Shez, I need to change my clothes now!" Jan was trying hard to keep the edge from her tone, but it was still starting to creep through despite her best efforts.

"We could always drive into town and get a coffee or something, kill some time?" It was Tom making the offer. Like Jan, he too felt that there was more to the situation than Sharon's explanation for why she did not want them to come in. But unlike Jan, he was willing to let it pass for now and leave things until the situation-whatever it was-calmed down.

Jan spun around and shot Tom a hurtful glance. She certainly did not want to come over as vindictive about this, but her wanting to come in for a change of clothes especially after what she had been through over the last few days, did not, to her at least, seem in any way unreasonable.

Jan spun back to face her friend. "Shez, I really do not know what is going on, and to be honest, right now I am beginning to lose interest." There was a defiant undertone in her voice now which conveyed the message to everyone that she was not going to let things drop until she had her way. "I need a change of clothes right now, before I go anywhere, and frankly, I don't know why you are making such a big fuss over everything!"

Just then, the front door swung open and a large hand grabbed hold of Sharon's collar and yanked her roughly back inside.

Before the three outsiders could react, Stud and Axe appeared in the doorway, each brandishing their weapons.

Jan instinctively let out a yelp and took a step back.

Tom grabbed her and pulled her behind him to protect her.

Adam stood his ground, ready to pounce, but his common sense told him he would not be able to rush the gunmen before they would release both barrels at him.

Stud smiled at the three captives. "That cup of coffee was a mighty good idea, you should have gone."

"I take it that it is too late to change our minds?" Tom asked, trying to keep the humour out of his voice.

"You got that right!" Stud replied, moving backwards and signalling with his gun for the three of them to enter.

Adam looked back at his father and winked.

Tom immediately knew the signal. It meant that Adam was going to try and charge the men once he was close enough, to try and grab their weapons from them.

Tom stared back at his son and shook his head.

Adam frowned, but relaxed his stance. Whatever the circumstance he still took his lead from his dad, and if Tom said not to try it then he would stand down.

Adam raised his arms slightly as he walked through the door. When he saw the other bikers standing around and pointing their guns in his direction, he was glad that as usual he had heeded his father's warning.

Otherwise, he might very well be dead by now.

Tom reluctantly brought Jan around in front of him and, keeping his hands on her shoulders, he guided her through the door.

Once they were all inside, Axe slammed the door shut.

Jan snuggled up closer to Tom when she saw the rest of the bikers spread throughout the room.

Having been roughly dragged back into the room and thrown to one side, Sharon was now in Steve's arms, sobbing uncontrollably. As far as she was concerned she had had one chance to keep her friends from any possible danger, and she had blown it.

Realising the position she had unwittingly put her friend in, Jan gently eased away from Tom giving his hand a gentle squeeze, and then manoeuvred her way through the gunmen to where her friends stood.

When she reached Sharon, Jan put out her hand and rubbed it up and down Sharon's arm, comfortingly.

Sharon looked around and broke away from Steve, then hugged Jan tightly, her tears still gushed forth making it impossible for her to speak properly.

"I…I tried…so hard to make…I'm so sorry….."

Jan shushed her quietly, trying to comfort her like a parent with their child after an accident.

"It's ok Shez, it wasn't your fault, it was my pig-headed stubbiness that got us into this." She held her friend away and looked her in the eyes. "You know what I'm like, can't take a hint to save my life."

Sharon managed a laugh through her sobs. Carey came over and offered her a tissue which she accepted, gratefully.

Tom and Adam moved closer together and glanced around the room to take in the full gravity of their situation.

There appeared to be six male bikers, including some pretty mean ugly-looking thugs, all of whom were armed with guns and several assorted bladed weapons.

Of the four girls, the tall blonde one was definitely carrying something inside her jacket, but the three others, the little dark-haired one and the two cute blondes, appeared not to have anything to hand that could be classed as a dangerous weapon, although it was impossible to tell for sure what might be concealed under their leathers.

The two pretty blonde girls caught Tom's eye as he was glancing in their direction, and smiled at him. One of them gave him a knowing wink, and then turned to whisper something to her friend before they both laughed to themselves.

Tom suddenly felt a sharp dig in his lower back.

He turned to see Axe standing directly behind him, holding out his shotgun like a cattle prodder. Tom realised that it was obviously that which had just stabbed him.

"Move!" demanded Axe, pointing over to the sofa next to the one the students were seated on.

Having seen his dad manhandled in such a barbaric way, Adam was ready to throw a punch at Axe, but fortunately Tom reacted faster and guided his son over to the sofa.

As they sat down, Jan came over to join them.

Each sofa was built to sit four individuals comfortably. So when Sharon and the others moved to reclaim their seats it was obvious that five of them was a squeeze.

"Why don't one of you come over here with us?" suggested Jan.

Adam could not help but notice Jenny's face. Though she had tried to hide it with make-up, he could definitely see that she had bruises underneath.

Having realised that Sharon's excuse for not letting them in was a ploy to keep them out, Adam had presumed that her story about Scott hitting Jenny was all part of the fabrication, but now he was not so sure.

It was then that Adam realised that Scott was not in the room.

He wondered for a moment if Scott had become too mouthy with the bikers and ended up on the receiving end of one of their firearms.

No great loss, thought Adam.

But if that no good bastard really had hit Jenny, then boyfriend or not he was going to have a serious one-to-one with him afterwards.

If, that is, they all survived whatever it was the bikers had in store for them.

To Adam's delight it was Jenny who stood up and walked over to their sofa. Naturally, it did make perfect sense seeing as the other four were made up of two couples. Tom sat at the farthest end with Jan next to him and Adam next to her, so Adam shuffled over to leave a space for Jenny between him and Jan.

Jenny smiled at Adam when she took her seat, and he reciprocated, warmly.

All three of the men now had their arms around their respective partners comforting them, including his father with Jan. Jenny was the only one left with no one to cuddle her, and Adam desperately wanted to step up to the plate but he knew that it would be over-stepping the boundary.

If only he knew what had really happened to Scott.

If the bikers had shot him, where was his body?

Adam surmised it could have been dragged outside and dumped in one of the outbuildings, but if that were the case then there should at least be some kind of evidence that a murder had taken place. Some splashes of blood at the very least.

Unless of course he had been shot outside.

Adam decided not to dwell on it anymore.

Just then he noticed that Jenny was starting to cry. He did not know the reason, and to a point, he did not care, because it gave him all the excuse he needed to comfort her.

Adam slid in closer and gently eased his arm around Jenny's shoulders.

To his delight she did not resist, and she leaned her head against his shoulder and snuggled into his chest as if they had been in this position a hundred times before.

Tom looked over Jan's head at his son.

Adam merely smiled back with a look of contentment on his face his father was very glad to see. It was true that the circumstances they were in were far from being ideal, but they were all striving to be relaxed and lost in the moment, unsure of what future they had left to look forward to.

CHAPTER TWENTY NINE

During the course of the afternoon the bikers made themselves completely at home. They switched channels back and forth trying to keep up with the latest news on their triumphant raid earlier in the day, whilst they demolished the various bottles and cans of alcohol they had brought with them.

Once that supply ran out, they started on the students, and then finally on the wine that Tom had stored in the small basement cellar.

Along with the alcohol there were copious amounts of drugs being passed around, mostly in the form of hash and cocaine, though Tom and the others did notice several pills of different colours also being consumed with abandon.

After copious amounts of alcohol and drugs had been consumed, the females in the gang started being passed around the male members like a human version of pass-the-parcel. They took it in turns to pleasure the male bikers' one at a time. All except the tall blonde one the students noticed. She stayed with the gigantic one exclusively.

The students had sussed out earlier on that he must be the overall leader of the gang, even though he seemed to be making the least amount of noise compared to all the whooping and hollering the rest of them were engaged in.

As the afternoon drew on, the light outside began to fade. Tom was ordered to make up a fire and the lights were switched on and dimmed to a soft glow. Under other circumstances the setting would have been quite romantic.

At one point, the bikers ordered Sharon and the girls into the kitchen to prepare food for everybody. Tom, Adam, Steve and Greg were told to remain on the sofas where they could be seen at all times.

None of them had been offered the chance to share in the alcohol being consumed, which in many ways Tom was pleased about for it meant that if it came to a show-down he and the boys would have a much better chance of overpowering the bikers due to their spaced-out condition.

That aside though, Tom could have murdered a coffee, and he knew that Adam would be the same.

As if by some psychic link, Jan and Jenny appeared from the kitchen with steaming mugs of coffee for the boys.

When Jan placed Tom's mug in his hand, he whispered to her. "If this is the last drink I have before I die, I'll go a very happy man."

Jan swatted him playfully on the arm, careful not to make him spill the hot liquid on himself, or her.

"Don't say that," she scolded him, "it's not even remotely funny."

Tom looked suitably admonished as they locked eyes for a moment before Jan returned to the kitchen.

When the food was ready, Stud ordered the girls to serve them all rather than the bikers having to help themselves.

The selection was fairly simple due to limited resources.

Toasted sandwiches, frozen pizza, oven chips and some assorted party platters the students had bought for a quiet night in.

The girls watched in disgust as the bikers grabbed handfuls of food and shovelled it into their mouths without even bothering to take a single bite.

The female gang members were more discreet, especially the two slight blonde girls who nibbled delicately on a couple of pizza slices each.

The students made some soup for themselves and the men, and Jan and Sharon brought it over to them with some sandwiches.

Jenny and Carey were still dishing out the last of the food for the bikers when Scarface suddenly leaped up and grabbed Jenny by the wrist, forcing her to drop the plate she was holding which fell to the ground and smashed, sending oven chips sprawling across the floor.

Jenny screamed out in pain and surprise, but the biker tightened his grasp on her wrist to prevent her from pulling free.

Everyone stopped what they were doing upon hearing Jenny's cry. Adam put his plate on the floor and turned his full attention towards Jenny's direction.

Scarface pulled Jenny closer to him. She was powerless to resist, the biker's grip was much too strong. She tried to pull her face away as his grew closer, but it was no use. Jenny could smell the combination of stale beer and smoke from his fetid breath. That, plus his overpowering body odour, made her want to heave and she had to fight to keep herself from spewing all over him.

Adam, seeing the distress that Jenny was in, started to rise to his feet, but Tom leaned across the sofa and pulled him roughly back. He knew that when it came to the protection of others, especially a damsel in distress, that his son had no regard for his own safety, which meant that he was often too hasty and rushed in without taking a step back and considering an alternative.

Adam shot his father an angry glance, but Tom was relentless and held onto his son's arm until he felt he had calmed down.

By now, Scarface had pulled Jenny so close to him that from across the room it appeared to Adam as if they were about to kiss, though in his heart he knew that that could not be the case.

Jenny could see from the distant, hazy stare in Scarface's eyes that he was well and truly under the influence as a result of his excesses, he was even having trouble focussing on her face even though she was directly in front of him.

"I remember you," the biker slurred his words as he spoke, dribble sliding down from one side of his mouth meandering its path through a mixture of dried on pizza topping and mayonnaise. "You were the bitch 'oo disrupted my pleasure in the alleyway behind the bar, just as Angel was about to finish me off."

The memory of the event of which Scarface spoke flooded back to Jenny. She remembered coming across him and Angel in the alley when she became separated from the rest of the group. It was not a memory she cherished or particularly wanted to have recounted for her.

Jenny felt the biker's grip on her wrist loosen as he swayed back and forth trying to focus on her. She tried to pull herself free, but he was too quick. Scarface grasped her wrist even tighter as he tried to stand up and get his balance.

Leaning back against the wall he forced Jenny's hand against his groin and pushed it down.

"I think you owe me somethin' don't you?" He sneered as he began to gyrate with his hips, pushing his groin against her palm.

The sensation of feeling him grow harder through the leather of his trousers revolted Jenny, especially as she knew that part of the reason was caused by her hand rubbing up against him.

"Let me go, you're hurting me," she screamed, closing her eyes and turning her face away, unable to witness the macabre act she was being forced into complying with.

She could hear raucous laughter and cheers of encouragement coming from the bikers. Their lewd behaviour being spurred on by Scarface's actions and her unwilling participation.

Out of nowhere, Adam was suddenly by her side, his hand clasped firmly around her attacker's neck, squeezing tightly.

Jenny opened her eyes and turned back around to see the biker's face beginning to turn a deep shade of scarlet as his air supply was being restricted by Adam's firm grasp.

"Now let her go!" Adam's voice was strong and forceful and everyone in the room could tell that he meant business.

Jenny could start to feel Scarface's grip on her wrist slacken, so she pulled her arm free and began rubbing her wrist to reduce the soreness from where she had been held.

The veins in Adam's head were starting to stand out with the pressure he was exerting on the biker's throat.

Scarface tried grabbing Adam's wrist with both his hands to pull him off, but this only seemed to incite Adam to put every last ounce of his strength into squeezing tighter.

Jenny could tell that Scarface was beginning to lose consciousness. His eyes bulged out of their sockets and his tongue lolled out of his mouth as he gasped, trying desperately to force air into his lungs.

Everything that happened next did so in such rapid succession that Jenny was not sure as to the exact order of proceedings.

Just as Scarface was about to black out, there came the sound of multiple hammers being cocked back and in a split second the biker's full arsenal of weapons were suddenly trained directly at Adam.

Tom had somehow managed to race to his son's side without Jenny even hearing him take a step from behind. There were screams coming from the sofa as Carey and the rest of the students began calling to Adam to release Scarface, and then Jan, shouting at Tom through wracking sobs, to be careful.

Tom, still standing behind Adam, wrapped his arms around his son and forced him to release Scarface just as the biker finally fell to the floor. Tom spun Adam around so that his own back was in the direct line of fire should the bikers start to unload.

Jenny could see from the strained look on Adam's face that he was livid at having been pulled off her attacker. But she was glad that Tom had intervened, otherwise Adam might have been shot, had he not been made to let go when he was.

Although his aggressive action had initially taken her by surprise, she now realised that he only reacted the way he had to protect her, and for that, she now felt incredibly attracted to him. Not just for his good looks, but also for his kindness and bravery. After all, he had risked being shot multiple times just to save her modesty.

She could see that Tom was still struggling to calm his son down, so she reached out her hand and placed it gently on Adam's cheek. The sentiment of her action was not lost on Adam and he immediately ceased struggling with his father and focused on Jenny.

The bikers still had their weapons trained on Tom's back and he could sense that some of them had very itchy trigger fingers. So as soon as Adam began to relax after Jenny's gesture, Tom released his hold on him and raised his arms above his head.

"It's all ok now," Tom offered, still not turning around to face the firing squad. "Everything is going to be fine, just let us return to our seats. No need for any hysterics."

As Tom, Adam and Jenny began to walk back to the settee the bikers began to lower their weapons.

Just then, there came a shout of anguish and a scrabbling of limbs as some of them tried to help Scarface back into his chair.

But he was having none of it!

Still unable to fully stand unaided, Scarface flailed around wildly, trying to wrestle a gun from one of his fellow gang members as he struggled to maintain his balance.

The others instinctively knew what he was going to do. Having been insulted and made to look a fool in front of his gang, it was understandable that he wanted revenge, and under normal circumstances the others would have stood back and let him get on with it.

But they knew that Reaper had said that this place was only to be used as a hideout until it was safe to move on, and he did not want a bloodbath being left in their wake. He was already mad enough about the two shootings in the bank earlier, so none of the gang wanted to make him any more irritated with them.

Before Scarface had a chance to even level his weapon at Adam, Stud barged through the others and grabbed hold of his gun.

Scarface tried to shake him off, but when he realised it was his leader, he reluctantly let go of his weapon.

Stud put a calming hand on the biker's shoulder.

"Not this time," he chided.

Scarface knew that there was no point trying to argue with Stud. There were certain lines you did not dare to cross. So instead he relinquished his gun and stormed off to the back of the lodge, kicking an occasional table by the main door, sending the empty vase upon it flying until it shattered against the far wall.

With the excitement over, Tom allowed Adam and Jenny to sit down before making his way over to Jan. He could see that she had been sobbing, and tear trails still streaked her flushed cheeks.

Jan half-stood up to meet him as he slumped down beside her. Taking her in his arms he held her closely as a fresh batch of tears started to flood. Tom tried to calm her down as she buried her face into his chest and continued to sob.

Adam looked at Jenny. "Are you alright?" he asked, the concern in his voice evident.

"I am now," Jenny sighed. She turned for a moment and looked at Tom and Jan snuggled together, then she turned back to Adam. "But I could use a hug."

Adam pulled her towards him and held her close.

When they parted, they stared into each other's eyes for a moment, and then they kissed.

"Oi, what's all this going on here then, ay?"

Everyone turned to see Scott making his way down the stairs.

Jenny's immediate reaction at the sight of Scott approaching was to break away from Adam, the feeling of guilt automatically overwhelming her. But to her credit, and much to her own amazement, she stopped herself, and held Adam closer as if for protection.

"What the fuck do you think you're doing with my girlfriend?" demanded Scott, as he reached the bottom of the stairs. His eyes were locked firmly on Adam as if he was oblivious to anyone else being present.

As he started drawing closer to where they were sitting, Adam kissed Jenny gently on the forehead and then eased himself away so that he could stand up to face his opponent. Jenny tried pulling him back down, but she knew that resistance was futile.

Adam moved around the sofa and the two men squared up to each other. Although Adam was tall and broad-shouldered like his father, he could not compete with Scott's overall muscle mass which he exacerbated by pushing out his chest and flexing his arms. Even so, Adam was not in the least bit intimidated. The anger that he had built up inside him as he watched Scarface attack Jenny had started to subside. But upon seeing Scott and remembering how Jenny had ended up with a bruised face, he could feel his fury rising once more.

Anyone who hit a woman was a coward in Adam's book, and he was happy to show them up for what they were.

Tom instinctively rose to his feet. He did not wish to appear like a father running to the rescue of his son, and he knew that Adam was more than capable of holding his own in a fair fight, but under the circumstances he preferred to have Adam unharmed in case the situation changed and they managed to over-power the bikers.

If that happened, they would need everybody on board. Even Scott if he could just stop behaving like a moron.

As Tom started to make his way towards the two men, Jenny shot up and ran around the sofa, beating him to it. She wedged herself between the two men and looked straight up at Scott, but he did not respond, keeping his gaze fixed on Adam, trying to gain a mental advantage.

"Scott, this is none of your business," Jenny cried, trying desperately to keep the trembling out of her voice. The last thing she wanted to see was a full on fight between her ex-boyfriend and Adam, because she knew that she would feel guilty for being the cause, regardless of the outcome.

"Scott," Jenny called again, this time even more in earnest, but he continued to ignore her pleas.

Tom appeared and placed his hands gently on Jenny's shoulders so that he could move her out of the way before she ended up on the receiving end of a mis-timed swing.

At first she was reluctant to move, but then she soon realised that her intervention was not having the desired effect.

Reluctantly Jenny allowed Tom to take her place.

Tom braced himself. Judging by the two men's body language they were just about ready to let rip on one another. They were barely two feet apart, so Tom wedged himself between them before he started speaking.

"Look lads," he began, keeping his voice as low as he could so as to stop the bikers from hearing what he was about to say, whilst making sure that he did not sound at all condescending. "I know you probably have some pent up aggression that you can't wait to unleash, but think about it for a moment, there's only them and us, and we're part of the "us", so we need to pool our resources not divide them, as we may only get one chance to overpower them and then it will be all hands on deck, know what I mean?"

Tom could tell that Adam was taking in everything he said by the way he was visibly relaxing his stance. His son certainly had a temper but he was also more than capable of seeing the bigger picture once it was presented to him.

Scott on the other hand still looked about to launch an attack.

The others on the sofa were close enough to hear what Tom was saying and obviously agreed with him.

"You're out of order Scott," said Carey, barely above a whisper.

"Not now, mate," added Greg, also trying to keep his voice low.

"Stop being such an ass, and sit down!" Sharon demanded.

But it was Skull shouting from across the room that finally brought Scott out of his reverie.

"Shit, it's the old bill!" he yelled, ducking behind the curtain in front of the large bay window.

The other bikers immediately took up defensive positions, hiding behind furniture and ducking into alcoves for protection, their weapons drawn.

Even Reaper threw himself out of his chair for the first time since their arrival, almost sending Deedee flying, as he moved closer to the nearest window to try and take a peek outside.

"Hit the lights," Stud cried out to no one in particular.

There was a general shuffling and scraping of furniture against the floor as the bikers scrambled to find the light switches.

Suddenly, the whole place was plunged into darkness, save for the eerie glow from the fire Tom had made up earlier.

Tom pulled Adam away from Scott and they re-took their seats on the sofa alongside Jan and Jenny. He did not bother to look back to see what Scott had decided to do.

Just then, they all heard the sound of a vehicle making its way slowly up the drive. It came to a halt just outside the porch.

There was no shadowy glow from blue warning lights, which meant that whatever the reason for police showing up, it was not classed as an emergency.

Tom surmised that they might just be visiting all the homes in the area just to warn the occupants to keep an eye out for the gang. But he suddenly had a sinking feeling in his gut that this scenario was not going to end well, whatever happened.

They all heard a car door slam.

"Damn it," whispered Skull. "'e's coming in!"

"Grab one of them girls as 'ostage," demanded Reaper, not directing his order at any particular gang member.

Axe, being the closest, crouched down and scuttled over towards the nearest sofa. Tom and Adam instinctively held their respective partners tightly, neither willing to relinquish their hold no matter what.

There was a knock at the outer door.

Axe reached Jenny first, but he moved past her, possibly because he knew from before that Adam would not let her go without a fight.

Tom tensed, waiting for Axe to confront him to let go of Jan. He lifted his arm from around her shoulders and placed it protectively in front of her like a human seatbelt.

But to his surprise, Axe continued past them and grabbed Sharon, tugging her violently away from Steve.

Steve, initially taken unaware, moved to snatch his girlfriend back. But Axe was ready for him and sent him flying back against the sofa by smacking him on the nose with the butt of his gun.

There was a *squelching* noise as the solid wood of the gun butt made contact, splattering blood and cartilage across Steve's face. Greg and Carey moved in to help their injured friend. Jan reached over and grabbed a handful of tissues from a nearside table and held them over Steve's face to staunch the blood flow, until he managed to take hold of them himself.

They all heard the porch door being swung open, creaking loudly on the hinges which Tom had been meaning to lubricate for ages.

A voice from outside cried out. "Hello, is anybody there?"

Axe yanked Sharon forcibly across the floor, back towards the front door.

Steve, having regained his composure, lurched forward towards them, intent on grabbing Sharon before she became some kind of human shield for the bikers.

Sharon kicked and strained to break free from Axe's grasp. The biker could only afford to hold her with one hand as he held his shotgun in the other and was not prepared to relinquish it, especially with the police outside the lodge.

With a supreme effort, Sharon managed to wrest her arm free just as Steve reached out for her. Steve pulled her behind him and faced Axe as he swung the barrel of his gun up so that Steve was looking directly into it.

There was a knock on the inner door.

Everybody froze for a moment.

The only audible sound came from the wood crackling in the fire.

Steve's eyes were locked on the dark twin tunnels aimed directly at his face. He realised that all it would take was for Axe to jerk or twitch suddenly and both barrels could go off, leaving him without a face.

There was a sound of shuffling near the front door. One of the bikers appeared to be moving into position in case of a break-in, but none of the students could tell which of the gang it was from their position.

There was a second knock on the door, louder than the first.

"Open up, it's the police!"

Suddenly the front door was yanked open from inside and before anyone else could move, Scarface opened fire with both barrels, screaming as he did so.

The uniformed officer outside slumped to the floor of the porch.

CHAPTER THIRTY

Stud could tell without even looking at the expression on his face, that Reaper was not at all happy with the shooting of the officer.

The big man placed his hands against the sides of his head and let out an enormous grunt of anguish and irritation.

Deedee immediately put her arms around his waist from behind to try and calm him down. That usually did the trick.

Stud grabbed hold of Scarface by the collar and heaved him backwards, sending the biker crashing against the nearest wall. Scarface slammed into it headfirst, before slumping down to a sitting position on the floor. He dropped his gun and held his head in his hands. The pain from the impact thundered through his brain and for a moment he felt as if he were about to lose consciousness.

Once the initial bout of throbbing had subsided, Scarface looked up at his leader with a genuine look of hurt and betrayal in his expression.

"What the fuck was that for?" he blurted out, sounding more like an admonished child than a vicious thug who had just shot a complete stranger.

The rest of the bikers all stood around watching Stud as he walked over to where Scarface lay. Bending down to bring him closer to his gang member's level, Stud roared, "Who asked yer to shoot the bastard?"

Scarface opened his mouth to answer, but then thought better of it and shut it again. He realised, even in his half-delirious and drug-addled state, that he did not have an answer worth offering.

Stud waited for a moment and then when he realised that no answer was coming, he raised himself back up and walked over to where the shooting victim lay.

Some of the other bikers crowded around him to bear witness to their colleague's handiwork.

Stud tilted his head to one side as he stared down at the body. The uniform he was wearing did not look like any copper's uniform he had ever seen. Instead of the usual dark navy trousers and jumper, this one was wearing a dark green version.

Stud ordered Axe to switch the lights back on as he squinted in the shadowy darkness to try and fathom what sort of uniform the man had on.

There was an insignia on his jumper's left breast which looked like a tree with some words written below it.

Stud leaned over to take a closer look.

The room was suddenly flooded with light as Axe flipped all the switches together.

Stud focused on the words on the man's jumper.

Forestry Commission.

He lifted himself up and looked back at his gang, and then they all turned towards Scarface who was still on the floor, too groggy from the blow to his head and his over consumption of booze and drugs to notice that he was suddenly the centre of attention.

They all waited for Stud to speak first.

"Forestry commission!" he announced, after a moments hesitation. He did not try to mask the exasperation in his tone. "You shot a fuckin' gamekeeper you twat!"

"Huh," was the only reply Scarface had the capacity to offer under the circumstances.

Upon hearing Stud's words, Tom suddenly had a horrendous thought.

He turned towards Adam and immediately realised that his son too was thinking the same thing.

The pair of them climbed off the sofa and swiftly ran to the front door to inspect the body lying in the porch.

Upon seeing the two men approach at speed, the bikers whirled around and aimed their weapons directly at them.

Tom, in the lead, held up his hands in surrender. "We just want to see if we know him," he said, appealing to Stud to allow them past.

Stud indicated to his men to let Tom and Adam pass.

The second Tom saw the body he recognised his friend, Jed Solomon.

Tom's heart sank. He turned to Adam and could see immediately that he also recognised the Ranger.

Jed was lying on his back with his eyes closed. His uniform jumper was littered with holes from the shotgun discharge. Jed's head was closer to the outer porch door than Tom would have expected it to be as he was knocking on the inner door just prior to being shot. But then he surmised that the force of the gunshot must have been sufficient to catapult him backwards.

A few more inches and his head would have smashed against the outer glass door.

Not that it mattered now, presuming that he was already dead.

While the bikers were mumbling and muttering between themselves, Tom shot past them and knelt down beside his friend.

He placed his fingers against the side of Jed's neck to feel for a pulse. Though he had already convinced himself that his friend was dead, he had to be sure.

Sure enough, there was no beat.

Tom pressed his fingers in a little harder.

"There's someone else in the van!" The shout came from Pete 'the snake'.

Everyone, including Tom, looked out into the dusky twilight to try and make out if Pete was right. Sure enough, though apparently slumped down in their seat, there was definitely someone sitting in the passenger seat of Jed's van.

"Go and get 'em," ordered Stud from behind the door.

Immediately, Pete and Skull barged past Tom, almost tripping over Jed's motionless body, in an effort to make it outside, quickly.

"An' no fuckin' shooting 'em!" Stud screamed after them. Obviously, after what had happened with Jed he felt he had to make his orders crystal clear so that there was no confusion afterwards.

From the back of the room the students began to move forward, curious about who else was about to be dragged into this nightmare.

They inched forward slowly and quietly, not wanting to alert the bikers unnecessarily just in case they suddenly found themselves staring back into the barrel of a gun.

They congregated around the main bay window. With the bikers clustered around the front door they were not in anyone's way, and they still had a good view of Jed's van outside.

They watched as Pete and Skull approached the van. Their weapons were drawn, but pointing slightly skywards, making sure that they heeded Stud's warning. The last thing they probably wanted was another accidental shooting, especially when they saw how Scarface was treated after shooting Jed.

The students watched as the two bikers surrounded the van. Skull bent down and looked in through the passenger window and then jerked up and said something to Pete over the top of the vehicle.

Pete then moved around the van to join his comrade as Skull pulled violently on the passenger door handle to open the vehicle.

The door would not budge.

Whoever was inside must have locked it. Not that anyone could blame whomever it was, seeing two armed thugs approaching them.

Without waiting for further instructions, Skull smashed the passenger window with his gun, and then put his hand inside through the shattered glass and opened the door from inside.

Everyone watched as Skull dragged a woman out of the vehicle, helped by Pete, once he had caught up with him.

The woman struggled and screamed as she was man-handled by the bikers, until finally they grabbed an arm each and literally dragged her kicking and screaming through the snow, towards the lodge.

As they reached the porch entrance, they realised that there was no way of making it into the lodge past Jed's body, whilst supporting Joanne, without walking over him.

Seeing the complication, Stud turned back to the students and yelled at them to help Tom carry the dead Ranger inside.

Adam quickly moved through the bikers and bent down to assist his father.

Greg followed behind, leaving Steve with the girls.

As the three of them lifted Jed off the floor, he suddenly let out a huge gasp followed by a bout of coughing and spluttering.

Shocked by the sudden signs of life from his friend, Tom barked out orders to his helpers to take Jed over to the biggest of the couches and to lay him down, gently.

Although Tom was encouraged by his friend's sudden sign of life, he realised that he was by no means out of the woods.

There was blood seeping through the puncture wounds on Jed's torso and staining his jumper. Tom looked around for a cloth or a towel to help staunch the flow, but he could not see anything to hand.

He called over to Jan who was still standing with the rest of her friends, awaiting the arrival of the new hostage.

Jan ran into the kitchen and searched through the drawers until she found some clean tea towels. She carried them over to Tom who was in the process of slicing through Jed's jersey with his hunting knife.

When the sight of Jed's wounded chest was revealed, Jan took a step back and almost fainted from the sight of all the blood covering his upper body. She managed to right herself and take a few much needed deep breaths, until she began to feel more in control again.

The thickness of the Ranger's outer clothing had made the condition of his wounds quite deceiving.

Tom placed the towels over as many wounds as he could and held them down to soak up the blood, and he hoped, help it to coagulate and prevent any more from gushing out of his friend.

Adam, standing behind his father, asked, "Do you think he's going to be ok?"

Tom did not look back. "I hope so," he sighed, "but we need to get him to a hospital pronto."

Adam spun around and made his way straight over to Reaper. He stood before the big biker who had retaken his seat after Deedee had calmed him down. He was watching the latest arrival being dragged into the lodge with mild fascination.

He did not acknowledge Adam's presence, but Deedee made sure that she could see what he was doing, just in case he tried anything.

"Look, that man over there your mate shot, he's still alive," Adam was still speaking to the side of Reaper's turned head. "We need to get him medical attention fast, or he may die!"

Reaper, still totally uninterested with Adam's pleading, continued to watch Joanne being roughly dragged through the main door by half the gang. As slight as she was, she managed to put up one hell of a fight, and it took four of the bikers to carry her over the threshold, much to the amusement of Reaper and the rest of the bikers.

Finally, Adam had had enough.

"Hey, I'm talking to you!" he screamed, reaching down for Reaper's lapels to force him to pay attention.

Before Adam could gain the biker's full attention, Deedee produced a huge machete from inside her jacket and held the sharp end of the blade against Adam's throat.

Adam instinctively held up his hands in resignation.

He looked back at his assailant. Deedee watched him, intently. Her eyes, unblinking, had a look as cold and as hard as the steel of the knife she wielded.

Finally, Reaper turned around to see what was going on.

When he saw the apprehension in Adam's eyes as the result of the precarious position he was in, a huge smile spread across Reaper's face.

"Fancied yer chances did yer boy?" the big man growled.

Upon hearing his voice, Stud left the rest of the gang to deal with the girl and strode over to his leader's side, his gun raised in anticipation.

Adam, trying to avoid any sudden movements which might give his captors an excuse to begin another assault, looked Reaper directly in the eyes. Trying to keep any trembling out of his voice, he said, "No, I just wanted to ask for your permission to get this man to a hospital." He pointed over his shoulder with his thumb.

Reaper thought for a moment, then replied. "Nah."

Adam could not control the growing rage inside him.

"Nah," he shouted, mimicking the biker. "Is that all you've got to say?"

The smile on Reaper's face was quickly replaced by a scowl.

Unperturbed, Adam continued with his quest. "This man happens to be a friend of ours which your trigger-happy mate shot without any reason whatsoever, now if we do not get him some medical attention soon, he is going to die and that will be murder."

"Not if there aren't any witnesses." The coldness of Reaper's reply stunned Adam. After all, up until now he had been the one demanding from his men, that no one else was to be shot. And he had certainly not been best pleased when Scarface had fired at Jed.

But now his attitude seemed to have changed, and Adam could not help but wonder if it was because he had forced the issue with his threat.

Adam took a deep breath to try and regain his composure. Going in with all guns blazing was apparently the wrong tack with Reaper.

"Look," he sighed, "the poor guy didn't do anything wrong, there was no need to shoot at him."

"Then why did he say 'e was the old bill?" Stud demanded.

"That was just his sense of humour," Adam turned to the second in command, hoping he might be able to gain some ground further down the food chain.

"Huh, well serves 'im right for being such a prat," Stud replied, without any sign of remorse or compassion.

Adam realised that he was not going to get the bikers to see sense, and that the best he could do was help his dad try and keep Jed alive for as long as possible, until they could figure out some way of reaching help.

The other bikers finally managed to carry the new arrival over the threshold and threw her unceremoniously across the floor, towards where Sharon and Carey were standing.

They immediately recognised Joanne from the camping store, and both of them bent down to try and help her.

Joanne had stopped screaming and crying; now that she was safely inside, she knew that there was no imminent means of escape. Not that she would have tried to run away into the hills, knowing what was out there.

She calmed down when she saw the students. Her worst fear up until that point had been worrying what the bikers had in store for her once they managed to haul her inside. At least now she knew that she was not alone, and there was safety in numbers.

Sharon and Carey helped Joanne up to her feet and escorted her over to the other sofa, across from where Tom and Adam were administering to Jed.

They could tell from her condition that not only was she scared out of her wits, but she was also freezing, and shivering inside Jed's uniform fleece.

Without bothering to seek permission from their captives, Sharon made her way back into the kitchen to make Joanne a hot drink to help warm her up.

At that moment, the sound of the Beast's howl echoed around the surrounding area.

****

In the melee that ensued after the shooting of Jed, no one noticed Scott slip quietly away back upstairs.

No one that is, except for Angel.

She had remembered Scott from the first time she saw him in the bar when the students first arrived. She had always liked men with muscles, the bigger the better and he certainly had plenty of them.

When he and Adam had squared off earlier, Angel was hoping that they would start a fight because that would have been a real turn-on for her. Seeing two beefy men beat the crap out of each other had always been one of her secret fantasies. She had witnessed several fights since joining the Warlords, but most of the bikers were out of shape due to overindulgence in alcohol, or else simply too weedy to warrant her attention.

No, Scott was what a man should look like. And from what she could tell, he was finished with that girl, Jenny. Besides, she seemed to have moved on to Adam, so the coast was well and truly clear for Angel to move in.

She followed Scott upstairs and into the bedroom. At first, he did not seem to notice that she was there. When he turned and saw her he barely acknowledged her and slumped down on the bed with his hands behind his head.

Angel knew that most men found her extremely attractive, and she could usually tell when a man was going out of his way to pretend not to be interested.

After a moment, she asked in her coyest voice. "Ok if I come in?"

"If you want." Scott continued to ignore her, keeping his gaze fixed on the ceiling above him.

Angel sauntered in, making her way as far as the foot of the bed.

She leaned against the footrest, making sure that she dipped low enough so that Scott could get a good look at her cleavage if he ever bothered to stop surveying the ceiling tiles.

"It's pretty scary all that commotion downstairs," Angel continued. "Let's hope that poor bloke Scar shot is going to be ok."

Scott finally glanced down in her direction.

Angel could see his gaze hovering over her breasts. She did not bother trying to pretend that she did not notice, and when he raised his eyes to meet hers she smiled at him, knowingly.

"Enjoying the view?" she asked, candidly.

Scott felt his cheeks flush. His embarrassment caused Angel to giggle like a teenager watching her sports hero remove his top on the training field.

Angel sashayed around the bed, making her way towards Scott.

Without bothering to ask permission, she plonked herself down on the bed next to him. Scott watched as Angel stretched out an arm, tentatively hovering for a second over his abdominal region before lowering her hand to cover his stomach.

"Ooohh," she purred, "that's an impressive set of abs. I bet they take some work?"

Angel could feel Scott tremble slightly at her touch.

She glanced down at his track bottoms and noticed the fabric starting to rise just below his waist.

Enjoying the power she exuded, Angel allowed her hand to drift down towards Scott's growing bulge, keeping her eyes fixed firmly on his face.

Scott closed his eyes and moaned softly as Angel's hand gently caressed and stroked him.

As Scott squirmed and jerked at her touch, Angel slipped her hand inside the waist band of his bottoms and curled her fingers gently around his rigid shaft.

As she felt him nearing fulfilment, Angel leaned over the bed and placed her lips over his. Their mouths opened in unison and their tongues danced, darting in and out, feverishly exploring each other.

Angel tightened her grip and moved her hand back and forth more swiftly.

She could tell by the soft whimpering noises that Scott was making that he did not have long to go.

Seconds later, she felt him explode as he cried out in ecstasy.

Angel pumped him a few more times to ensure that he was fully spent, and then she removed her hand and held it up before her. She watched for a moment as the gooey white ejaculate clung to her fingers, turning her hand back and forth so as not to let it drip onto the bed. She then closed her eyes and seductively slipped each finger in turn into her mouth, licking them clean with relish as if she was enjoying some luxuriously rich and creamy dessert.

From below her, Scott watched intently.

He was amazed at how quickly Angel had managed to arouse him considering the problems he had been experiencing lately.

She certainly was adept at her craft.

When Angel was finished, she licked her lips provocatively and made a point of swallowing with a loud gulp. "Mmmnnn, tasty," she whispered breathlessly, her eyes still clamped shut.

When she opened them and looked down at Scott he had beads of perspiration popping on his forehead, and a relaxed smile of satisfaction across his face.

Angel curled up next to him on the bed, draping one leg across him, and wrapping one hand behind his neck to pull him in for another passionate kiss.

When they separated, Angel rested her head on Scott's enormous chest and listened to his heart thumping.

After a while, she asked, "You were ready to leave earlier, what stopped you?"

Scott could feel himself starting to drift off. He rubbed his eyes with the fingers of one hand and shook himself awake. "Your friends and their guns, what else?" he replied.

"Where were you planning to go?"

"Back to London of course, away from this dump and those deadbeats I once called friends."

There was almost a touch of venom in his voice when he mentioned his former friends, and Angel could not help but wonder why he had come up here with them if he felt that way.

Perhaps, she thought, it was loyalty as his ex-girlfriend downstairs was clearly close to the rest of them.

Or maybe, she had laid a guilt trip on him for not coming.

Either way, Angel was confident that Scott was no longer interested in Jenny or any of the others, and that suited her perfectly.

Before the bikers had entered the property that afternoon, Angel and the other girls had been sent on a rekey mission to suss out the lay of the land. It was while she was scouting around at the back of the lodge that Angel had discovered a fire escape with a telescopic ladder.

At the time she had decided to keep this information to herself, although she was not sure why she felt the need for such caution.

Now she was glad that she had.

Angel snuggled up closer to Scott. "If I told you that there was another way out that my lot downstairs don't know about, would you be interested?"

Scott immediately sat up, with Angel still draped across him.

"Where?" he demanded, his interest well and truly piqued.

Angel lifted herself off him and gazed into his eyes. "I can show you, but you must promise to take me with you. I don't want to be around that lot downstairs anymore."

She could tell by his expression that Scott was certainly intrigued by the prospect.

He thought for a moment, then said, "Ok, it's a deal, now show me where."

Just then, they too heard the Beast roar.

CHAPTER THIRTY ONE

"What was that?" shrieked Angel as she grabbed hold of Scott's wrist and gripped it tightly.

"Dunno," replied Scott, listening intently for any further cries.

Then he remembered. "Jenny said that she saw something outside the landing window the other night." He kept his voice low, not wanting to alert those downstairs that they were on the move. "She said that it was a big, hairy monster, like an ape or something, we all thought she was crackers."

"Well whatever it is, it sounds real enough to me," said Angel, tightening her grip.

Scott pulled his hand away, completely unconcerned whether or not Angel took offence. He grabbed his jacket and pulled it on before grabbing hold of his case and making his way to the door.

He looked both ways down the corridor to ensure that they were alone.

Angel appeared at his side and followed his gaze.

They could both hear the ruckus from downstairs and Scott was pleased as the noise would help to cover their tracks. If there was a chance of escape he intended to take every advantage of it, even if it meant having to take Angel with him.

Ideally, after everything that had happened lately, Scott would have preferred to set off alone. But he knew that he needed Angel to show him the escape route, and if he tried to dump her after that, she would probably scream the place down and bring the rest of her gang running up to investigate.

So for now at least, he was stuck with her.

Once he was convinced that the coast was clear, Scott turned to Angel.

"Which way?" he whispered, keeping his voice low so as not to attract attention.

Angel looked back and forth along the corridor a couple of times as she tried to get her bearings. She had only seen the escape ladder from the outside and she needed to calculate where she had been standing at the time.

"Well!" Scott's patience was already wearing thin and their lack of movement was not helping.

Angel held up her hand to quieten him. "Just a sec, I need to figure this out without being rushed."

Scott was furious with Angel's remark and under normal circumstances he would have stormed off on his own to find the way out. But he knew that stealth and silence were key to them making their way out undetected, so for now he elected to bite his tongue and to let Angel do her thing.

After a few seconds, Angel turned to the left and pointed.

They crept along the landing in single file, being especially careful when they passed the top of the stairs just in case someone below saw them move, out of the corner of their eye.

A creaky floorboard almost scuppered their plans, but fortunately Angel's reflexes saved them as she hopped off it before it took the full brunt of her weight.

Scott gave the plank in question a wide berth.

When they reached the end of the corridor, Angel turned to the right. It was a dead end which only stretched a few feet in front of them, but there was a window on the left and next to that was a large sign announcing that it was a fire escape.

Scott opened the window which was one of the old fashioned sash varieties. He eased the main pane up as slowly as he could in an effort to lessen the noise. When he looked out, he could see the fire ladder Angel had mentioned. It was housed inside a large metal frame to protect the climber from falling.

Reaching out, he managed to unhook the brackets which held it in place.

The telescopic side of the ladder immediately began to plummet to the floor, rattling against its casement.

Scott shot his hand forward and managed to grab hold of the top rung just as it was about to disappear into the protective shaft. He held it there for a moment, half expecting the noise from the apparatus to bring everyone outside to see what was causing it.

But fortunately for them, no one appeared.

Scott lowered the ladder gently, one rung at a time, until it was fully extended.

He then climbed out onto the frame and carefully began to make his way down.

Angel waited for him to reach far enough down so that she was confident she would not step on him as she made her descent, then she hoisted herself out onto the ledge and began her climb.

The night air was freezing, and Angel wished that she had taken the time to zip up her leathers before starting down.

The wind whipped through the metallic frame which surrounded them, whistling loudly as if trying to alert the others to their escape.

When Scott reached the bottom, he immediately took off towards where his van was parked, bothering to wait for Angel.

Seeing him disappear, Angel almost called out to him to wait, but she managed to stop herself just in time. If they were caught now, she knew that she would have a hard time explaining away her situation to the rest of the gang. And she had seen before how deserters were treated, and that was definitely not the fate she had in mind for herself.

Luckily for them, Scott's van was parked out of sight from the main living area inside the lodge. Even so, Scott made a point of only opening the back doors far enough to squeeze his bags in, so as to avoid the annoyingly loud creak they made when fully ajar.

As he locked them, Angel appeared at his side.

"Why didn't you wait for me?" she hissed, keeping her voice low.

Scott merely looked down at her. "You're here now aren't yer," he replied, making Angel feel more like an annoying little sister trying to tag along after her big brother when he was sneaking away for a private rendezvous, than a potential girlfriend.

Angel stuck her bottom lip out in a pout as she zippered up her jacket.

Scott pretended not to notice and turned away towards the driver's door.

Though the van was out of sight, the noise from the engine would certainly alert those inside the cabin.

Scott thought for a moment.

He could not run the risk of the bikers hearing their escape. Even though he could not see where they had parked their bikes, he suspected that they would not be too far away, and in these icy conditions he was confident he would not be able to outrun them.

Angel sidled up beside him, shivering.

"What are we waiting for, it's freezing out here?" she whined.

Scott held his finger to his mouth for silence, but he could tell from the frustrated look on Angel's face that she was not going to take the hint.

"I'm thinking," he scowled. "We need to get the van away from here before I turn on the engine. Otherwise it'll alert the others to the fact that we're escaping."

Angel bit her bottom lip in thought.

Then she whispered. "Why don't we push the van down the hill and start her up once we're at the bottom? They won't be able to hear us from there."

Scott considered her suggestion. In truth it was not such a bad idea. He could probably handle pushing the vehicle and she could do the steering until they reach the brow, and then he could take over and guide them down until the van reached the bottom.

By the time anyone realised that they had gone, they would be half-way to London.

"Come on," said Scott, shoving Angel towards the driver's door.

When she climbed in, Angel immediately began sliding across the seat towards the passenger side.

"What are you doing, dozy?" Scott seethed. "You need to steer until I can take over."

Angel suddenly looked horrified. "But I can't drive," she mumbled, looking sheepish.

Scott reached in and grabbed her by her jacket, pulling her roughly back over the gearstick into the driver's seat.

"Hey, ow, that hurts," squealed Angel.

"You don't need to know how to drive," Scott spat through gritted teeth. "You just have to steer the wheel, a fuckin' three-year old could do it!"

"All right, all right, you don't have to be so rough." Angel settled into her new seat. Her feet could not reach the peddles but according to Scott that was not an issue. All she had to do was steer the vehicle until he could jump in and take over. Instinctively, Angel reached over and yanked the seatbelt across her. The metal clamp at the end looked dented and slightly bent and at first it refused to engage in the plastic slot, but after several failed attempts Angel succeeded in locking it in.

Scott slipped the keys in the ignition and turned them over one notch to release the steering lock, checking to ensure that there was full play in the wheel.

"Right," he said, almost barking an order rather than offering an instruction. "Now release the handbrake," he pointed down at the lever, "and keep a tight hold on the wheel."

Scott made his way to the back of the van and braced himself to start pushing.

After a moment, he called out as loud as he dared. "Have you released the brake yet?"

He watched the open driver's door as Angel stuck her head out and signalled for him to come over to her.

Scott made his way back to Angel. "What now?" he roared under his breath.

Angel looked up at him helplessly. "I can't get this stupid thing to release, it's too tight," she whined, pointing at the handbrake.

Scott reached over her and gripped the handle firmly before popping the top with his thumb and setting the stick down.

Without saying a word, Scott pushed himself back up by placing his hand between Angel's legs and shoving at the seat.

Once he was back outside, Scott walked behind the vehicle and, digging his feet firmly in the snow, leaned in against the back of the van and began to heave with all his strength.

The van began to edge forward slowly, but Scott was hampered by his boots constantly sliding out from under him, as he pushed.

Eventually, he managed to start making ground and the van began to roll forward at a more consistent pace.

As they neared the top of the hill, Scott glanced back over his shoulder at the lodge. Fortunately, they were still out of sight from the main entrance, and once they were over the brow there would be no way that anyone from inside could see them.

Scott was glad that he had managed to escape from the rest of the group. God knows how long they were all going to be held prisoner in there by that gang. He considered that once he was at a safe distance, he should contact the police and tell them what was going on. But first he needed to ensure that he was far enough away so that the police did not insist that he return as a witness, to give evidence.

He could always make his statement once he was back in London. Surely any police station would do?

Scott peered around the van to check how close they were getting to the edge.

The wind was really beginning to whip up, and the first flakes of snow were starting to fall.

Scott estimated that after a few more feet he would be ready to take over the controls from Angel. It irked him that he had to take her along, but at this moment he had little choice. He knew full well that if he threw her out she would go running back to the lodge to raise the alarm, and he could do without that sort of hassle.

Besides, she had helped him to escape, so he supposed he did owe her something for that. But if she grew too whiny or irritating on the journey back, Scott decided he would dump her off at the nearest rest stop and leave her to defend for herself.

Scott braced himself for one final push.

As he heaved forward, his foot slipped on the snow, and he lost his traction.

Scott fell forward as the van moved off and he struck his forehead hard against the bumper.

Cursing, Scott scrambled to get back on his feet. His head began to throb from the impact and the wind kept blowing snow into his mouth and eyes. Now he wished that he had retrieved his goggles from his pack before throwing it in the back of the van.

Lurching forward, he managed to reach the back door of the vehicle. He grabbed the handle and used it to boost himself up until he was confident that his legs could support him once again.

Up front, he could hear Angel calling out to him in panic. She had obviously realised what was going on and was naturally concerned that she would be left in charge of the vehicle once it started its descent if Scott could not make it back to her in time.

In his mind Scott was willing her to shut up before she gave away the game, and brought everyone running.

With a supreme effort, Scott raced around the side of the van and grabbed hold of the open driver's door just as the front wheels slipped over the edge of the slope.

Scott reached in and grabbed the steering wheel from Angel's trembling fingers and tried to hoist himself inside, but his foot slipped on the footplate and he lost his balance.

Scott managed to keep hold of the wheel as his legs were dragged along the ground.

As the van started gathering speed, Scott's weight was pulling the steering wheel over to the right, sending them towards the edge of the road and the sheer drop to the valley below.

Angel screamed at him to let go, not realising in her frightened state that if he were to release his hold he would no doubt fall back onto the ground, thus leaving her in total control of the van. A position she did not relish being in under any circumstance.

Angel grabbed the wheel and fought desperately to bring the vehicle back onto a straight path, but she did not have the strength to pull back against Scott's weight.

Scott managed to regain his feet, and for a moment he was running beside the van until he felt confident enough to try once again to mount the runaway vehicle.

Grabbing the door for support, Scott heaved himself inside, landing squarely on Angel who was still secured in position due to the seatbelt.

With Angel in his way, Scott did not have enough room to manoeuvre himself around to face the front. His legs were still dangling out of the open door and each time he tried to slide them in, his knees crashed against the steering wheel, preventing him from going any further.

The van veered precariously from side to side as both Scott and Angel fought for control of the vehicle.

Angel screamed, as a result of Scott's full weight bearing down on her legs and trapping her in her seat, and the fact that she felt that at any minute the van, with both of them in it, would go careering off the end of the path and plummet down the hillside.

Finally, Scott yelled at her. "Move over you stupid bitch, I can't get my legs in."

Angel could feel tears welling in her eyes. Not because of Scott's behaviour, but more to do with the fact that they were about to lose control of the van.

"I can't," she shouted back. "You're crushing me."

Scott, realising that Angel was right, grunted and heaved himself to one side to allow her to slide out from under him.

Angel, relieved at the lack of pressure on her legs, tried to push herself off the seat, but the belt kept her wedged in place.

Letting go of the wheel with one hand, Angel tried unsuccessfully to release the belt. She depressed the catch as far as it would go but the buckle still refused to come out.

Releasing the wheel, Angel turned in her seat and tried to prise the catch open, but it appeared to be stuck fast. She began frantically pulling on the belt in anger and frustration but again, without success.

Unable to support his weight against the wheel anymore, Scott slumped back down onto Angel's legs. She shrieked in pain at the sudden impact. With her body twisted to one side in a futile effort to release her belt, the fabric of the restraint was cutting into her neck, with the angle of Scott's body causing it to tighten against her throat.

Angel struggled to push Scott off her, but her puny effort was no match for his huge bulk.

Angel started to gag.

She tried several times to take in air but each time the belt across her neck seemed to grow tighter and more restrictive.

She could feel her face turning blue from the lack of oxygen.

Angel was no longer able to cry out to Scott, who seemed totally oblivious to her predicament.

Almost hysterical with the thought of losing consciousness, she began a frenzied assault on her captive. Unable to use her legs, she slapped and punched at Scott with what little strength she had left, but her pitiful pounding amounted to a mere irritation to the bodybuilder, as he tried relentlessly to manoeuvre his legs into position to take control of the van, as it continued to gather speed rolling down the hill.

In a last ditch effort to free herself, Angel reached out and grabbed the wheel from Scott, pulling back on it with her full weight.

Scott, still unbalanced in his seat, was taken unaware by Angel's sudden action and the wheel slipped from his grasp.

As the van lurched dangerously close to the rock formation on the side of the slope, Scott reached out and grabbed the wheel again, yanking back on it with all his weight, causing Angel to relinquish her hold altogether.

The movement made the van swerve violently to the right, before Scott had a chance to readjust his position.

Before he could regain control of the wheel, the van's tyres lost their purchase on the frozen ground and the vehicle veered uncontrollably, before listing to one side and hurtling over the edge.

****

When Angel opened her eyes, she was still wedged inside the mangled heap of metal which had once been Scott's van.

Scott was nowhere in sight.

She took a moment to take in her surroundings and to ascertain her condition.

The last thing Angel remembered was the van veering over the edge just as she began to lose consciousness.

Miraculously, she appeared to be in one piece. The seatbelt had kept her cocooned inside the protective shell of the vehicle as it had slipped and bounced down the hillside, finally landing on its side in the snow.

Angel found it quite ironic that the belt which she believed earlier would take her life by strangulation, was now in fact the thing which may have saved her.

Angel looked about the twisted metal of the van. There were several impact dents all around her, from where the vehicle had obviously bounced down the hill. Fortunately for her, none of them were close enough to have caused her any damage.

The front windscreen was missing altogether, and all the other glass panels had been smashed. There were shards of glass littering the inside of the vehicle, some of which were scattered upon her, but luckily none of them had scratched her face or gone into her eyes. Angel surmised that she must have had them shut as she was unconscious during most of the accident.

She tried to move. Her neck was twisted to one side but it did not hurt when she shifted her weight to release it. That was a relief. She had heard tales of accident victims being paralysed after some good Samaritan inadvertently moved their heads in an effort to revive them.

Gradually, Angel ensured that all her limbs were still in working order as she carefully tried to extricate herself from the vehicle.

The seatbelt, which could very well have saved her life, was still locked in place.

Reaching down, Angel popped the plastic tab.

The metal buckle slipped out without any reluctance.

Angel smiled to herself as she contorted her body to allow her to shuffle out through the empty windscreen frame.

Once outside, she stood erect and stretched out her aching limbs.

Again she looked about her for any sign of Scott, but there was none.

Although she had been raised a catholic, Angel had never been religiously minded. However, she offered up a silent prayer of thanks for her survival before deciding what to do next.

She had no idea how long she had been out for. The sun had almost completely disappeared beyond the horizon when they first set off, and now the sky was completely dark, and the temperature was very cold.

The wind howled around her, and the snowfall appeared to be growing heavier.

The question was what to do now?

There was no way Angel would ever make it back into town, and even if she did, what would be her plan of action?

She might be able to hitch a lift from a passing truck driver, or a holiday maker on their way home, but where would she end up?

And, with whom?

On the other hand, if she were to make her way back to the lodge, what possible reason could she give for having left in the first place?

She thought for a moment.

Perhaps she could say that she followed Scott outside in an attempt to convince him not to leave, or even to try and stop him.

No! The gang would never swallow that. After all, if that had have been the case all she would have to have done was call out to them from upstairs and they would have stopped Scott leaving, without her ever having to venture outside.

How about if Scott had kidnapped her?

Yes, that was far more plausible. She would say that he grabbed her and dragged her down the fire escape, with her kicking and screaming all the way, naturally. And then he bundled her into the van and tried to drive off with her.

But then she struggled so much that he eventually lost control of the vehicle and they ended up going over the cliff.

She was lucky to be alive.

In more ways than one!

Naturally, she would lay on a few tears just to ensure that the likes of Reaper believed her, but it was a completely plausible tale so there was no need for her to fear any reprisals.

With her story intact, Angel began the long trek around the hillside and back up to the path which led to the lodge.

She shoved her hands in her pant pockets, for warmth.

Ordinarily, her leathers were more than sufficient for stopping the wind dead when she was on the bike. But even they seemed woefully inadequate against the biting cold which managed to cut through her armoured defence, right to the bone.

Angel put her head down to protect her face from the snow flurries. Her eyes were already starting to sting and with the wind whipping towards her, she knew that it would only get worse the longer she tried to look straight ahead.

As she climbed to the top of the first ridge, Angel's boots seemed to be sinking further and further into fresh snow with every step. This in turn made the going more arduous and by the time she reached the first peak, she was breathing heavily and she could feel the perspiration starting to build up under her outfit.

A long hot bath and an even longer drink was what she needed, and she hoped that when she finally reached the lodge that both could be provided for her.

As much as Angel had been looking forward to her new adventures in London, she was grateful that they had not travelled so far out as to make her return impossible.

The gang still afforded her protection and company, and there was a great deal to be said about a nomadic existence on the open road.

With the snow coming down even harder, and her legs sinking deeper into the snow to hamper her progress, Angel decided to walk around the next ridge instead of wasting more energy by climbing it.

The extra distance was not enough to warrant concern and besides, it would all be on even ground which would make the journey less arduous overall.

As Angel made the bend she lifted her head to get her bearings.

Instead, she came face to face with the Beast!

As her mind reeled to take in the scene before her, Angel was frozen to the spot.

The Beast stood erect, with its massive form blocking out the scenery behind it. The moon overhead, peeking out from behind shifting clouds, cast an eerie shadow around the creature making it appear, to all intents and purposes, as if it were cloaked in a veil of darkness which spread out to encase the surrounding area, and trap anyone who happened to be stranded within its scope.

On the ground directly in front of the Beast, lay the mangled remains of Scott's body!

The snow surrounding his mutilated corpse was drenched in blood, most of which had seeped through the icy ground, leaving behind a faint tinge of bright red.

The thick fur which covered the Beast was also matted with congealed blood from its mouth all the way down its torso and even onto its legs. The creature had evidently held Scott's writhing body up to its mouth while it fed upon his flesh, tearing out huge chunks with its massive jaws, allowing the warm blood to drip and splatter against it while it feasted.

Angel glanced back up at the Beast.

The thing's gigantic chest rose and fell slowly, as it breathed in great lungfuls of the freezing air.

Its mouth was open wide enough for Angel to see the rows of razor sharp, blood splattered teeth, which filled its cavernous maw.

When she reached its eyes, she saw that they held a malevolence she could not have imagined, even on the face of her worst enemy.

There was no escape!

Angel knew that, instinctively.

If she tried to run, the Beast would be upon her in seconds. And if she stayed where she was, the Beast would be upon her even sooner. It was only waiting because there was no reason not to. She could tell from the expression in those hideous eyes that it too knew that Angel had nowhere to hide.

The Beast could do with her whatever it wished.

It could just as easily play with her like a cat torturing a frightened rodent, or swoop down on her from above like a seagull homing in on a tender morsel, regardless of whether or not it was on offer at the time.

Angel knew that she was trapped. But it was not in her nature to give up without a fight.

Without warning, she turned on her heel and ran back in the direction of the van as fast as she was able.

The deep snow hampered her progress and the effort of having to lift each foot out of the deepening snow sapped the strength from her weary body. But still she refused to give up.

Angel could feel the onset of a cramp in her side as a result of her exertion.

She tried to scream as she ran; praying that some armed poacher or game keeper might be in the vicinity and hear her cry. The chance of rescue, no matter how feeble, was enough to give her the hope that she so desperately needed to battle through the pain and keep going.

With her blood thundering in her ears, Angel could not hear the Beast approach from behind.

Nor did she sense the crushing blow which ended her short life!

CHAPTER THIRTY TWO

From the moment that they heard the Beast roar, everyone inside the lodge was on edge.

Joanne especially seemed petrified by the bellow. Upon hearing it, she had shuffled away from everyone else and cowered in a corner of the room, with her legs bent and her arms wrapped around her knees.

Jenny too had something to fear. Having seen the Beast, even though it was only for a fleeting moment, she knew only too well what was out there, and from the glazed look of fright on Joanne's face, Jenny suspected that she too had seen the creature.

Tom and Adam were taking it in turns to try and keep Jed alive. He seemed to have settled somewhat, but there was still an awful lot of blood loss from his chest wound.

Jan was running back and forth from the kitchen with fresh towels, cloths and anything else she could find to help Tom staunch Jed's wound.

The bikers were all on their feet, even Reaper, all of them staring out into the fast-approaching night, searching for any sign of whatever it was that had made that hideous cry.

Steve and Greg were comforting their girlfriends. Both men exchanged a subtle knowing glance, as if conveying to each other a pledge to protect the other's partner should anything happen to them.

Feeling somewhat of a kindred spirit, Jenny made her way over to where Joanne cowered in the corner. As she approached her, Joanne did not turn to face her; instead she kept her eyes fixed firmly on the floor in front of her, with a frozen gaze.

Jenny reached forward and gently placed her hand on Joanne's shoulder.

Joanne immediately pulled away from the girl and began shrieking, as if she were being attacked or molested.

Jenny tried her best to calm her down, but the more she tried, the worse Joanne seemed to get.

Finally, with a yearning look of helplessness, Jenny turned to her friends.

Sharon and Carey both broke away from their partners and moved forward towards the screaming girl. Neither of them had any idea how to handle the situation, as Jenny had not done anything to create such a stir in the first place.

"Keep that bitch quiet, before I come over there and do it for yer!"

The threat came from Stud. There was a distinct edge to his voice which told the girls that he too was more than just a little nervous concerning what might be outside.

Jenny backed away from Joanne and the three girls sat back and tried to calm the screaming girl down with words of comfort, both ensuring that they did not move in too close, just in case it caused her to lose her self-control, completely.

Eventually, Joanne stopped screaming. She continued to rock herself back and forth. Her eyes never left the space before her, as if she were afraid that losing her concentration would somehow cause the Beast to find her, sooner.

"I think perhaps it would be better if we just left her to it," whispered Carey, not wishing to sound unfeeling, but at the same time wishing to avoid another outburst for fear that one of the bikers might make good on Stud's promise.

"Good idea," agreed Sharon, placing her hand on Jenny's arm. "You did your best," she assured her friend, "but maybe for now it's better if we just leave her alone."

Jenny turned to her friend and nodded her agreement.

The three of them retired back to the sofa.

"How's your pal doing?" Carey asked Tom, nodding towards Jed.

Tom sighed. "Not good, if we don't get him some proper medical attention soon I'm not sure he's going to hold out for much longer."

"Here dad, let me take over," offered Adam. Seeing the exhaustion on his father's face made him realise how much the toll of treating Jed was taking out of him.

He knew that Jed and his dad had known each other for quite a while and he appreciated how helpless his father must be feeling at being prevented from giving his friend the best possible chance of survival.

Tom stood up and thanked Adam for his intervention.

Tom staggered wearily over to an armchair and sank into it. He appeared every bit as if he had the world on his shoulders. The truth of the matter was that, not only was he concerned for his friend's life, but he also felt responsible for everyone else in the lodge, that the bikers were holding captive.

After all, this was his place and everyone in it was here at his invitation.

Deep down, Tom knew that there was nothing he could have done to prevent this situation from occurring, but to him, there was little comfort in that fact. The bikers had proved themselves to be a volatile lot, and now that they were armed and tanked up on booze and god knows what drugs, Tom was afraid that anything, no matter how innocent or irrational, might set them off at any minute.

While Tom was lost in thought, Jan slipped onto the arm of his chair and put her arms around his neck. He looked up at her and smiled, and then he pulled her in closer and cradled her for a much needed hug.

They could hear the bikers discussing what they should do regarding the roar they had heard outside.

Some seemed to be in favour of setting off with their guns loaded to try and hunt down whatever it was that had made the noise. Others seemed slightly more reluctant to leave the relative safety of the lodge.

From what Tom could tell, it was the big one with the long greasy hair and the enormous goatee that seemed to be making the final decision, whenever an idea was put forward. Tom gathered that he must be the overall leader of the gang as none of the others seemed to question any of his decisions.

Tom glanced over at Joanne huddled in the corner.

He watched her for a moment, sitting in a ball with her eyes staring straight ahead of her.

"Is she ok?" he whispered to Jan.

Jan looked over his shoulder at the shivering girl. "I hope so," she replied, keeping her voice low enough so that Joanne could not hear her, even though she was not sure whether Joanne was actually able to take in anything that was going on around her, at the moment. "I think the girls tried to help her but that was when she started screaming."

"I'm sure I know her from somewhere."

"We met her the other day; she works in the big camping shop in town."

Tom nodded. "That's where I know her from."

"She seemed really nice," Jan continued. "I wonder what's happened to her."

"Whatever it is," Tom replied, thoughtfully, "I'm sure that Jed was trying to help her, until these idiots decided to get trigger-happy." He indicated towards the bikers with a nod of his head.

Jan put her mouth up against his ear. "Ssshhh," she whispered. "Please don't let them hear you."

Tom knew that Jan was right.

There was no point in getting himself killed for the sake of speaking his mind.

He held Jan a little closer and planted a loving kiss on her forehead.

Just then, from the corner of his eye, Tom saw that Jed was starting to shudder and jerk uncontrollably.

"Dad!" Adam turned to his father, in despair.

Tom eased Jan back onto the floor and raced over to join his son.

Jed's whole body seemed to be going into a spasm of some sort, and although Tom was no medical expert, the signs did not look good.

The towel Adam was holding over the Ranger's chest was drenched in fresh blood, which told Tom that his attempts to staunch the blood flow had not worked.

"Take the towel away, Adam," he said, distractedly.

Adam did as he was asked.

They could both see tiny eruptions of blood bursting from the various holes in Jed's upper body. Every few seconds the man's entire body would jolt and judder as if someone was passing an electrical current through him.

Jan arrived with some fresh towels. They were much smaller than the others which had already been used, but they were all that she could find.

Tom grabbed a couple gratefully, and re-covered his friend's wounds.

Jed continued to twitch, but the spells seemed fewer than just a moment ago, as well as being slightly further apart.

Whether or not this was a good indication of his friend's condition was still a mystery to Tom, but he suspected that it would not turn out to be a positive sign. All he knew for sure was that if he did not get Jed to a hospital soon, his chances of survival would continue to diminish with each passing minute.

Keeping the pressure on the replacement towels covering Jed, Tom turned on his knees and called out to the bikers.

"Please, for the love of god," he pleaded. "Let me get this man some medical attention before it's too late!"

His shouts caught the attention of the gang. They all turned towards him, but none of them came any closer or acknowledged his concerns.

Tom even thought that he caught a few of them laughing at him.

He had to fight an irresistible urge to lunge at them, and lay into as many of them as he could. He knew full well that he would never survive the onslaught, and the chances were that they would do far more damage to him than he ever could do to them. On top of which, if he were to make a stand he knew that Adam would be right behind him, and the consequences of that were not worth taking a chance on.

But he wanted so badly to make them take notice.

Instead, he decided that his only option was to try and appeal to any last shred of humanity any of them still possessed.

"Please, I'm begging you," Tom urged, beseechingly. This time he focused his plea at Reaper. The big man was still turned in his direction and Tom knew that if he could get through to him then the others would have to comply.

But his hopes were in vain.

Reaper turned to Stud and said something which Tom could not hear. But he soon realised what it must have been when Stud walked half-way between where the other bikers stood and Tom and bellowed down in his direction. "No one goes nowhere until after we're gone, alright?"

Just then, the lights went out!

There were a few screams from some of the girls, including Kim and Stacy who had been sitting together ever since Jed made his entrance, huddled in a far corner behind the main group of bikers, sharing what was left of a bottle of red.

"What the fuck's goin' on?"

From the depth and the gruffness of the voice, Tom surmised that the question probably came from Reaper.

In the eerie glow given off by the flickering from the open fire, the group could see the bikers shoving and pushing each other as they tried to distance themselves from the front door.

In the bamboozled shuffling that followed, one of them crashed against Reaper, then backed off immediately, apologising to the huge man as he subsequently backed into one of the other gang members, who in turn did likewise to someone else.

In the confusion there was the sound of metal clanging against stone, as one of the bikers dropped their gun.

The blast that followed as the gun erupted; sent shot pellets ricocheting off the mantelpiece behind the couch, which was where some of the students were seated.

They all dived for cover.

Fortunately, the blast had been too high to reach any of them as they were all sitting down. However, they all instantly recognised the possible consequence, had any of them been standing at the time.

The gunfire was followed by more shouting from the bikers as they accused each other of causing the accident, until finally Reaper's bellowing voice cut through the argument and everyone went quiet.

After a couple of seconds, Adam felt that it was a good time to answer Reaper's original question.

"It's the generator, it must have packed up, that's why the lights have all gone out."

Tom shot his hand out to stop Adam saying any more. Tempers were already running high and the last thing he wanted was for his son to antagonise the big man and end up on the receiving end of his wrath.

A long silence hung in the air.

No one else wanted to speak whilst Reaper considered Adam's explanation.

Finally, Reaper took Stud over to one corner and the two of them began talking in hushed tones.

Once they were done, Stud walked across the room and spoke directly to Adam. "Can you fix this thing?" he asked, his tone making it sound more like an instruction, than a question.

Adam looked down at his father before answering.

Tom, aware that Stud was close enough to see what he was doing, shook his head slightly from side to side. The last thing he wanted was his son going outside alone, especially with whatever it was that made that howl possibly lurking in the shadows.

Adam sighed. Ordinarily, he would never go against his father's wishes, but he knew that everyone, and especially Jenny and her friends, would feel a whole lot safer with the lights back on.

Adam winked at his father, and then turned to face Stud. "Yeah, I can do it."

"Right then," said Stud. "Where is it?"

"Outside in the shed at the end of the yard," replied Adam, pointing outside the window into the darkness.

Stud looked back over at Reaper.

Reaper nodded.

"Wait a moment," Tom broke in. "He's not going out there alone, I'm going with him." He looked over to where Greg and Steve were standing and gestured for one of them to take over from him, to help with Jed.

Jed's convulsions had calmed down, and now they were no more than minor tremors. Tom hoped that that was a positive sign, but deep down he still had doubts.

Either way, he had not given up on his friend yet, and he refused to do so until the end.

Greg looked at Steve and pulled a face. Steve remembered how squeamish his mate had always been when it came to blood, so he knelt down and took over from Tom.

As Tom started to stand up to join Adam, Stud held up his hand to stop him.

"You 'aint goin' nowhere," said the biker, fixing his eyes on Tom. "Now sit back down before yer get hurt."

In defiance of the biker, Tom raised himself to his full height so that now it was Stud who had to look up to him.

Tom pointed at Adam. "My son is not going out there alone." He managed to keep his voice steady and calm, although inside he was raging. "Now either I go out there with him, or we stay here in darkness, your decision."

Stud puffed out his chest and tried to broaden his shoulders as he faced Tom.

He could not believe the man's defiance.

Did he not realise that Stud could have him shot on the spot for his lack of obedience? Stud was a man who was used to people doing as he commanded. His arrogance made him want to make an example of Tom.

But first, he knew that he needed Reaper's permission.

Stud turned to his leader for approval.

Reaper, reading Stud's thoughts, shook his head. He was not at all happy with the way things had been going this afternoon and he had decided that he needed to keep some order.

Not to mention the fact that if they shot another victim, the overpowering stench of blood from the two of them might just incite whatever was outside to come in, and search for the source.

And Reaper for one, did not relish the thought of meeting whatever it was, face to face.

Finally, the big man said to Stud. "No one goes out alone, send one of your men with him, make sure he doesn't get any smart ideas like trying to take off once he's outside."

Neither Tom nor Stud was overjoyed by Reaper's announcement, but they both knew that his word was final.

For Tom's part, having one of the bikers with him was better than sending Adam out alone. After all, there was a certain amount of safety in numbers.

Stud on the other hand would have preferred to send Adam out alone. After all, they could always hold his father and his girlfriend as hostages to ensure that he came back.

If he was in charge, things would have been different.

Someone else not overjoyed at the prospect of Adam going outside, was Jenny. Unlike the others who had only heard the Beast, she had actually witnessed it close up, and she could not bear the idea of Adam coming face to face with the creature outside, and unarmed.

Judging by the behaviour of the bikers so far, she was not at all inspired by the prospect of one of them possibly being Adam's best chance of survival if they were attacked.

In fact, she was convinced that whichever biker they sent out would be more likely to shoot Adam and leave him as bait to make good his own escape, rather than protect him should the Beast attack.

Jenny was not sure if it was as a direct result of having been treated so badly by Scott, or just the fact that Adam made her feel so special by acting so protectively towards her, but either way she had to fight the urge to wrap her arms around him in front of everyone, and beg him not to go outside.

If they were in a relationship, she would not have thought twice about doing it. But as it was, she was more afraid of scaring him off if she was that over-affectionate, at this stage.

To her surprise, almost as if he had read her mind, Adam walked over to her and gave her a huge hug, and whispered in her ear. "Don't worry, I'll be back soon."

Jenny squeezed him tightly. "I don't want you to go," she pleaded, her voice tiny and beseeching, like a child not wanting to see a parent leave them behind.

Adam held her more firmly. "Don't worry, I promise I'll be back in one piece."

They continued to hold each other until they heard Stud's voice booming out from behind them.

"Scar, you go with him, make sure he doesn't try anythin' funny."

Adam gave Jenny a final cuddle, and then he turned to see who had been chosen to be his partner in crime.

To his dismay, Scarface, the one Adam had had a run in with earlier over Jenny, and the same trigger-happy moron who had gunned down Jed, moved forward.

When he saw Adam looking at him, a wide grin spread across his face.

"Terrific," said Adam, under his breath.

CHAPTER THIRTY THREE

Adam shrugged himself into his winter coat, pulling the hood over his head.

At the front door, he looked down at the shotgun Scarface was tilting up in his direction, and then back up to the face of the owner. Scarface still had a huge smirk on his face, and Adam began to suspect he knew why.

"There's really no need for that," Adam said, indicating to the gun. "I'm hardly going to make a run for it and leave my dad and girlfriend behind, am I?"

Across the room, through her tears and fear for his safety, Jenny felt a warm glow when she heard Adam call her his girlfriend, out loud.

Now she wished more than ever that he did not have to go out.

She struggled to fight the urge to run over to him and hold him, possibly for the last time. The mere thought of it brought a fresh batch of tears brimming over.

At the door, Scarface laughed at Adam's suggestion.

"Well this is just a little bit of insurance for my piece of mind, innit," he sneered, before shoving the barrels of the gun against Adam's back, pushing him outside the door.

Once the two of them were outside, the rest of the gang crowded around the front door to watch their colleague take his charge to the generator shed.

The night was turning bitterly cold and the snowfall was growing heavier by the minute.

The moon hid behind a curtain of thick cloud, unable to penetrate the darkness sufficiently to afford them any kind of useful illumination.

Fortunately for them, the shed was no more than fifty feet away, and even from here they could make out its rough silhouette in the distance. But nevertheless, with the sheer lack of any source of purposeful light, the entire area took on an eerie spectral glow, which in turn made the short journey seem like an eternal one.

Adam fumbled in his pockets for a torch. He could not remember if he had left one in this coat, but under the circumstances he decided it was worth a try, especially as once they reached the shed-if they did-it would be even darker in there and he would have to try and gauge where the levers and buttons were, by feel.

The butt of Scarface's gun smacked Adam firmly in the middle of his shoulders. The force of the blow, and the fact that it took him by surprise, sent him sprawling in the snow, face first.

Adam pushed himself up out of the snow. He coughed and spluttered to clear the ice from his nose and mouth. He made it up as far as his knees, but before he had a chance to try and stand, he felt the twin barrel pressing against the back of his neck.

Adam slowly raised his arms as if to prove to Scarface that he was not concealing any hidden weapon.

"That's more like it," scowled the biker. "I told you no funny business."

"I was looking for a torch," Adam replied, unable to keep the exasperation out of his voice. "In case you hadn't noticed it's dark out here, and it's going to be even darker inside the generator shed."

Scarface rubbed his stubble with the back of his hand. His other hand gripped the trigger casing of the gun.

Finally, he said. "Well don't make any more sudden movements, or next time I won't bother givin' yer the butt end, understand?"

Adam nodded. "May I please get up now?"

He felt the barrels being moved away from his neck. The jagged sawn-off end scraped him just below the hairline.

Adam rose slowly to his feet. As he did so he lowered his arms, but did not bother looking back at his captor.

"Keep movin," Scarface instructed.

They walked towards the dim outline of the hut. Their boots made loud crunching sounds on the fresh snow, but it was barely audible above the howling wind which whipped the flurries directly at them, as if purposely trying to hamper their progress.

Most of all, Adam kept his ears open for the Beast.

He remembered the bloody remains of the leather jacket that he and his father had found near the lodge the day the students arrived. He now wondered if it had been discarded by one of their captors. But then that would not explain the blood. Whoever had lost that jacket had also lost a fair amount of it, and there were no obvious signs on any of the bikers that they had recently suffered such an injury.

All of which led Adam to the possibility, that whatever had made that noise might also have been responsible for what was left of that jacket.

Not to mention, the owner.

When they finally reached the hut, Scarface ordered Adam to go inside and deal with the generator, whilst he remained outside in the relative safety of the open air.

The hut was easily big enough for both men to go in, but Adam assumed that Scarface felt safer outside where he could see an approaching assailant.

Adam propped the door open as wide as it would go, to allow in as much light as possible. Though in truth, what was available was woefully inadequate for the job at hand.

Adam fumbled around in the darkness trying to locate the fuel gauge. When he felt the round glass-covered dial he rubbed it clean with the back of his glove, but he was still unable to see how much fuel was indicated by the needle.

Hoping that there was still an adequate amount to be going on with, Adam felt his way along the apparatus until he felt the power switch.

Sure enough, it was in the off position.

Keeping one hand on that, he reached across until he managed to find the lever on the pump.

Stretching across as far as his stride would allow, Adam began to pump the handle back and forth until he could hear the motor starting to churn.

Once he was sure that it was ready to catch, he flicked the generator switch on.

Nothing happened.

Cursing to himself he repeated the process again, this time leaving the switch until he had thrust the handle to exhaustion.

There was still no response.

He decided he would have to attempt to add more petrol to the cylinder, without spilling any on the machinery or on himself in the darkness, during the process.

"What the hell is takin' you so long?" Scarface called, from outside.

Adam turned around. The biker's body was blocking the doorway of the hut, masking what little light was filtering in from the moon outside.

"I need to fill the tank, I think it's empty," replied Adam, keeping his voice calm.

"Get a fuckin' move on will yer, I don't wanna be out 'ere all night."

"Well if you step back a little and stop blocking the light, then maybe I could find the canister a little sooner," Adam snapped back, tired of the man's stupidity.

"Oh yeah," taunted Scarface. "Move out of sight so that you can go for that meat cleaver, or revolver, or whatever it is you've got hidden in there." He sounded very pleased with himself for sussing out Adam's ulterior motive. "Do you think I'm fuckin' stupid or summink?"

You don't seriously want me to answer that do you? Adam thought to himself.

Deciding that there was no point in antagonising the biker any further, Adam turned back to face the darkened cavern of the hut and proceeded to try and locate the canister.

"I asked you a fuckin' question dickhead!"

It appeared that the biker was not willing to accept Adam's silence as an answer.

Adam turned back to face his watchdog.

Scarface had his gun aimed directly at Adam's chest, and at this distance Adam realised the biker could hardly miss.

"What kind of answer do you expect me to give to such a question?" Adam asked, holding his arms out at his sides to show that he had no intention of trying to provoke the biker.

But his lack of goading seemed to have the opposite effect.

Scarface moved in closer, the barrels of the shotgun now only inches away from Adam's chest.

Even in the dim light, Adam could see the look of sheer loathing on the biker's face.

"You think you're so fuckin' clever don't yer?" Scarface spat through clenched teeth. "First you make a fool of me over that bitch, an' now you talk down to me 'cos you think I'm thick."

"Now hold on just a minute," replied Adam, keeping his tone level so as not to give Scarface an excuse to shoot. "I am not talking down to you, and you attacked my girlfriend remember? Did you expect me to just sit there and do nothing?"

Adam heard the loud click of the hammers being pulled back on the shotgun. The noise reverberated throughout the hut.

At such close quarters Adam knew that even if he tried to rush Scarface the end result would be a face full of shot.

He had nowhere to run to, and nowhere to take cover.

The biker seemed intent on shooting him regardless.

Scarface increased the pressure on the first trigger. Though slight, the action was not lost on Adam.

Adam tensed himself, awaiting the first impact.

Scarface took a step backwards so that he was back outside in the open, but he kept the gun trained on his captive.

"Now this is what's goin' to 'appen," he sneered. "First, you're goin' to try and make a run for it, an' then, I'm gonna shoot you down."

"I'm not going to run anywhere," Adam assured him.

Scarface laughed. "No matter, that's what I'm gonna tell 'em."

"But if you shoot me in the front," Adam offered, trying desperately to think of some way to reason with the man, "how can you say I was trying to run away?"

Scarface thought for a moment, and then said. "No matter, they won't be coming out 'ere to find you till we're long gone, we won't let 'em."

Adam knew that he was right. The man might be insane but he had obviously given the matter some thought which somehow made the scenario even worse.

Scarface raised the gun so that his eye was level with the sight. "Now get this fuckin' thing up 'n' runnin', 'cos when you're done an' I've wasted you, I'm going back to that shack to have some real good fun with that bitch o' yours."

The biker's words caused Adam's blood to boil. He was ready to take his chances and charge the man regardless of the consequences, for he knew that if Scarface did kill him, which he clearly intended, then when the biker went back to the lodge not only would he rape and possibly kill Jenny, but he surmised that his father would also be killed when he found out that his son was dead.

Adam knew his dad, and he was sure that he would attack Scarface, without any concern for his own safety.

There was no point in arguing anymore.

Adam knew that the biker had made up his mind, and it was clear now what his incentive was, Jenny!

Adam realised that he had limited time to think and act.

Once the generator was refilled and working, his time was up!

Adam slowly turned away from Scarface and began feeling his way around the hut, trying to locate one of the spare petrol cans.

He managed to find one, but when he shook it it turned out to be empty.

He continued with his quest. All the time Adam was trying to figure out some way of either getting the gun away from his captor, or of somehow managing to come up with a reasoned argument which would cause Scarface to reconsider his course of action.

Neither option seemed viable at the moment, but he knew that he could not afford to give up hope.

Suddenly, he heard a scream from behind.

Adam swung back around.

Scarface was gone from the entrance!

Adam waited for a moment. He held his breath, to allow him to hear more clearly.

There then followed another scream, this one muffled and sounding further away than the first.

After that, there was silence.

Frantically, Adam felt about in the shed trying to find something which he could use as a weapon. Something had managed to overpower and grab Scarface, a madman with a gun, who did not even get a shot off before being captured.

Finally, Adam located what felt like a crowbar. It was not much but it was better than nothing. At least he might be able to get a few good whacks in, before he was overpowered.

Adam's heart raced as he faced the open doorway.

It was then that he realised that he had been holding his breath since he first heard Scarface scream. He let it out, and then slowly took in a deep lungful, trying his best to keep the noise down. The air was cold and harsh on his throat, but he managed to keep himself from coughing.

The last thing he needed was to draw attention to himself.

Once his breathing had evened out, Adam edged his way towards the door.

Outside, the force of the wind whistling through the trees and around the outbuildings, was deafening.

Adam strained to hear anything which might indicate the presence of the biker's assailant. In his mind he could picture himself emerging from the hut and being hoisted into the air by whatever it was, and being carried off into the night, never to see hearth or home again.

However, the alternative was just as unappealing. To wait where he was, until the thing came back for him.

He had to take a chance and make for the lodge.

Scarface was obviously taken unawares, whereas, he was at least prepared.

Adam could feel the precious seconds ticking by.

The longer he left it before deciding to move, the more time that the Beast would have to dispose of Scarface, and return for him.

But what if it is already waiting outside for me?

Adam gripped the crowbar tightly in one hand and counted to three in his head before leaping through the open doorway.

He landed firmly on his feet. The soft newly-fallen snow came up past his ankles, from the impact of his landing.

Adam spun around in the direction he imagined Scarface had been taken.

There was no sign of anyone, or anything.

He was about to turn back for the lodge, when he noticed something half-buried in the snow.

It was the biker's shotgun.

Adam thought about leaving it where it was and just running back to safety, but then he reconsidered his option. The gun was only a couple of feet away and was another weapon they could use against whatever was out there, should it decide to attack the lodge.

Checking the area around him once more, Adam trudged over to the gun and picked it up. The hammers were still drawn back ready to fire, so he released them, not wanting to risk the weapon discharging in case he should trip or fall on his way to the lodge.

Adam started back. Each step seemed to take an eternity as he sunk further and further into the snow, the soft surface impeding his efforts to increase his speed.

He tried to look back over his shoulder a couple of times to check that the coast was clear, but on each occasion he almost lost his balance, so he decided it was not worth the risk to try again.

When he finally reached the porch steps, Adam threw himself forward and had to grab the door handle for support. He yanked the door open and pulled it closed behind him. Although it offered no real protection due to its flimsy construction, psychologically, it made him feel protected.

The front door had been locked, so Adam pounded on it with his gloved fist until someone opened it.

Without speaking, Adam barged past the bikers loitering in the entrance and flung himself inside.

CHAPTER THIRTY FOUR

Upon seeing his son return, Tom rushed over as Adam slumped to the floor, exhausted from his exertions, and grateful to have made it back in one piece.

Tom knelt down beside him. "Are you alright son?" he asked, concerned at Adam's condition.

Adam pulled back his hood. His face was red with beads of perspiration streaming down from his forehead. His breathing was still coming in huge gasps.

He looked up at his father and held up the 'ok' sign with one hand.

"Come on, let's get you up," Tom grabbed Adam's left arm to give him some support.

Adam was still holding Scarface's shotgun in his left hand.

Seeing the other bikers with their backs to him still facing outside, he glanced at his father and indicated to the gun. In his present state he was not sure if he could trust himself to decide whether or not it was worth trying to turn the tables on the bikers, and give them a taste of their own medicine.

Tom immediately understood his son's intimation.

Had it have just been the two of them, he might have thought the situation warranted the risk. But as there were all the others to consider, Tom was not prepared to do anything irrational or dangerous on the spur of the moment.

Tom shook his head, and Adam released his hold on the gun as he stood up, leaving it on the floor.

As the two men turned to make it back to the rest of their group, Stud's words stopped them in their tracks.

"Oi, where the fuck is Scar?"

Adam stopped and patted his dad on the back before turning back to face the bikers.

The five remaining male bikers were all standing in a row with their guns levelled towards Adam, making him feel like a condemned man facing a firing squad.

He had a horrible feeling he had just escaped the frying pan and landed squarely back in the fire.

"Well," demanded Stud. "I asked you a fuckin' question!"

Having regained his composure, Adam took a deep breath before trying to explain. He knew full well that no matter what he said, there was a good chance he would not be believed.

"I'm afraid whatever made that cry we all heard earlier must have taken your mate, to be honest, I was in the hut and didn't see it. But one minute he was there and the next he was gone, sorry."

Stud walked slowly towards Adam, his gun raised to chest level.

This was sadly a very familiar scenario for Adam, and for the second time within a few minutes he began to wonder if his time were up.

Stud stopped when his gun barrel was pressed up against Adam's chest.

"Now wait just a minute," Tom broke in, stepping forward and holding out his hand towards Stud.

Stud swirled around so that his gun was now facing Tom. "Shut up an' sit down," he snarled.

Tom held up his hands in surrender but refused to back off.

Stud, infuriated by Tom's disobedience, raised his gun to Tom's eye level.

As he appeared as if he were about to let loose with both barrels, Tom heard Jan scream from behind. "Tom. No!"

Adam swiftly moved between his father and the gun. "It's ok dad," he said, looking directly down the twin tunnels of Stud's gun. "Just go and sit down, I'll sort it."

Reluctantly Tom edged backwards; his eyes were fixed on Stud's, conveying a message of warning without words.

Stud waited until Tom had moved clear away, before he returned his attention to Adam. "Well?" he repeated.

Adam gulped. "I told you, I was in the generator hut trying to get the lights back on, your mate was outside. The next thing I heard a scream, I turned around but he was nowhere to be seen."

"And how did you manage to get his gun away from him?"

"I didn't." Adam knew that the biker was trying to trip him up, so he chose his words carefully. "When I heard him scream I turned around and came outside, but like I said, he was gone, there was no sign of what took him and his gun was lying on the floor, so I picked it up for protection in case the thing came after me."

"Did you go looking for him?" This came from Skull, back at the door.

Adam looked over. "No, to be honest I was crapping myself so I just came back here."

Stud considered his response.

It sounded plausible, even if was not what Stud wanted to hear.

After a moment, he turned around to face Reaper, keeping his gun trained on Adam.

In the dim light from the fire's glow Stud could tell that Reaper too believed him.

Stud began to lower his weapon.

"What if 'e's lyin'?" This time it was Axe who spoke up. "What if he shot Scar and left him out there bleedin' to death?"

Stud raised his weapon once more.

He stared at Adam as if Axe's supposition had changed his decision about whether or not to believe Adam's version of events.

In his defence, Adam pointed to the shotgun he had left lying on the floor when Tom helped him up. "Look, if you don't believe me then check the gun, you can tell it hasn't been fired recently."

As he spoke he realised that it was not that long since Scarface had shot Jed, so perhaps his argument was not the best one to offer.

His only hope, if they did decide to check it, was that the biker re-loaded before they went out, so there should still be a full shot in each chamber.

As it was, Axe had another alternative up his sleeve.

"Maybe 'e didn't shoot 'im, maybe 'e bludgeoned him to death with something from the hut, so we wouldn't get suspicious when 'e brought the gun back."

"Yeah," agreed Skull. "I bet if we go out there now we'll find Scar beaten to death, wiv the weapon lyin' near 'im covered in blood."

Adam released a big sigh. "You know what lads," he directed his statement towards Skull and Axe, "please go outside and be my guest, I'm obviously not going anywhere so if you find your mate bludgeoned to death, you can come back here and take your revenge on me, how about it?"

Adam's suggestion had obviously hit a raw nerve as both bikers advanced towards him, shuffling their weapons as they moved.

Fortunately for Adam, Reaper held up his hand to staunch their assault.

The big man turned to the two bikers. "Go outside and see if you can find Scar," he pointed towards Adam. "'e's right, if 'e 'as killed 'im, it'll be 'is turn next!"

Skull and Axe exchanged a worried look. As much as they both relished the opportunity to take their revenge out on Adam for their friend's death, neither one of them seemed overly keen to go outside, and possibly end up face-to-face with whatever it was that had taken their colleague.

The pair of them turned to their leader, Stud. It was almost as if they hoped he might intervene and suggest an alternative solution.

But Stud knew better than to question Reaper.

He nodded his head to the two men, and reluctantly, they prepared themselves for their venture.

Stud ordered Pete the snake to retrieve the gun Adam had dropped, and to bring it to him.

Eyeing Adam, Stud checked the chambers. He was satisfied at least that they were both still loaded. He handed the gun back to Pete and ordered him to keep watch over the students.

Adam finally managed to join the others.

Jenny threw her arms around him, tears streaming down her cheeks. She had been convinced moments ago that Adam was going to be shot, but at least for now she felt safe again in his embrace.

Jan too was relieved that Tom had made it back to her, in one piece. She looked up from tending to Jed and gave him a relieved smile.

Everyone else seemed a little more relaxed, now that the latest tension had been broken.

Steve and Greg attended to the fire which had started to burn down. It was not just the heat it gave off, which was much needed, but it was also their only source of light for now.

Only Joanne still sat away from the main group.

After their initial attempt to bring her into their circle, the girls had decided that she needed time and space to herself. They hoped that she would come around soon though. Sharon especially found it hard to believe that the girl curled up on the floor with the frozen stare and ghostly pallor, was the same one they had met in the camping shop on their first trip into town.

Pete took up his position, as Stud waited by the front door to see Axe and Skull out.

Deedee had taken up a lookout post near the main window, in case the Beast should suddenly appear, unannounced.

Stacy and Kim were clearly not enjoying the proceedings one bit, and were still huddled together in the far corner of the room, looking even more scared and frightened than Joanne.

Axe and Skull checked that their weapons were loaded. Each held a shotgun and had a handgun tucked into their belts. Axe also had what looked to the students like a meat cleaver, sticking out of his back pocket.

Both men looked like they wished that they were somewhere else, right at that moment.

"Keep yer eyes peeled," advised Stud. He felt obliged to offer them some sort of pep talk under the circumstances. "An' if yer see anything, make sure you blast it to kingdom come, right!"

The two bikers nodded their response.

Once outside, both men looked at each other resignedly, before beginning their search.

The snow was still coming down heavily, and with the wind pounding their ears and driving the snow directly at them, they both felt as if they were caught in a blizzard.

Once they were about twenty feet from the lodge, they stopped and surveyed the surrounding area. Their feeling of exposure was overwhelming, and both men continually spun around on the spot to make sure that no one *and nothing* had a chance of creeping up on them, and taking them unawares.

The wind made the branches of the trees which circled the end of the compound, move violently back and forth, making it virtually impossible for either of the bikers to discern if something was using them for camouflage, waiting to pounce when the opportunity presented itself.

At one point or another, both men had to reluctantly let go of their weapons with one hand to shield their eyes from the drifting snow, in an effort to prevent it seeping behind their lids and causing a burning sensation, which would make seeing anything almost impossible.

After they were sure that there was nothing in the immediate vicinity, Axe turned to his colleague. "Should we check out those sheds first?" he half-shouted, using the nose of his gun to point toward the outbuildings.

Skull nodded. "I suppose we'd better, just in case that bastard has buried Scar's body in one of 'em."

Axe turned towards his friend. "You don't really think 'e killed 'im d'yer?" he asked, anxiously.

Skull shrugged his response.

They entered the first shed, which was really no more than a lean-to being held together with string and gum. It appeared to be a storage area for rusty pieces of old equipment, and discarded machinery.

It did not look as if anything in the shed had been moved in years, and some of the equipment was actually rusted together, so there did not appear to be anywhere that Adam could have hidden Scarface in there.

The next outbuilding housed the generator and spare wood for the fireplace. The two bikers rummaged around, but once again there was no evidence of anywhere to secrete their friend.

As they emerged from the generator shed and started to make their way towards the last one on the property, Skull suddenly grabbed his friend by the arm, and stopped him in his tracks.

Axe shrieked out loud, before he could stop himself.

"What!" he yelled, still trying to take control of his vocal chords.

Skull pointed down towards the ground in front of them.

When Axe looked, he saw some dark patches which seemed to be coming up through the snow. They looked like oil spills from a cars leaking radiator, but in the dim light it was impossible to tell what exactly had caused them.

Skull bent down for a closer look, while Axe stood guard.

After a moment, Skull rose back to his feet, scratching the back of his head.

"What do you reckon?" Axe asked, managing to keep his pitch down.

"Dunno, could be oil, might be blood," Skull answered, still looking down at the splattered mess.

Just then, the Beast howled!

The sound of its cry reverberated around the cloistered area where the bikers stood, making it impossible for them to discern where exactly the noise emanated from.

Axe and Skull both spun around back and forth, guns raised, hammers cocked, expecting an attack from all angles.

A huge gust of wind shook the trees before them.

Axe, not being able to contain his panic let off both barrels. The sound of his gun echoed around them, momentarily drowning out all other sounds.

When the ringing in their ears subsided, there was nothing left to hear except the wind.

Axe dropped his weapon on the floor and retrieved his handgun from his belt, and his cleaver. Forgetting for a moment that he had tucked the end of the cleaver into his pocket, he ripped the fabric as he wrenched it out.

Axe cursed his own forgetfulness, and then he turned his concentration back to the matter at hand. Being right-handed, whichever weapon he placed in his left felt awkward and unwieldy, but he still felt better having some sort of back-up.

Skull began to move forward, cautiously.

"Where're yer goin'?" Axe yelled, anxiously scouring the area for any movement which did not appear to be from nature.

Skull stopped. "Where d'yer think, to look fer it?" he called back.

"What!" Axe replied, not trying to mask his surprise at his mate's suggestion. "We came out 'ere to look for Scar, not the abominable fuckin' snowman!"

Skull turned back to stare at his comrade. "You 'eard what Stud said, when we see it, blast it?"

"'e said 'if', not when!" Axe was starting to feel his legs go from under him with fright. He for one did not need to see the Beast up close, to appreciate how dangerous it was. Hearing it roar from this distance was more than enough for him.

"Well I ain't goin' back in there to tell Stud and Reaper that we 'eard the Beast an' were too shit scared to find it an' kill it, so come on."

Skull turned around and began moving forward once again, not bothering to wait for Axe. He knew full well that Axe would not have the guts to return without him, because if he did, then Reaper would more than likely just throw him back out in the snow, possibly unarmed this time.

After a few seconds he heard the sound of his fellow biker crunching after him.

They checked out the last hut.

This one was full of garden furniture. Tables, chairs, recliners, barbeque equipment including firelighters, several sacks of coal, and a couple of stand alone barbeque units.

But still there was nowhere to conceal a body.

Skull turned to Axe. "I reckon that bloke was tellin' the truth about what 'appened to Scar."

Axe's complexion had lost its red hue, which had been created by a combination of the alcohol he had consumed during the day, and the cold. His face now had a ghastly white pallor as he stood shivering just inside the doorway of the hut.

Skull smirked to himself. "Guess we'll jus' 'ave to go out an' kill it ourselves," he chuckled, amused by the ever-increasing look of terror on Axe's face.

Skull pushed past his partner and headed for the door.

Axe grabbed him by the elbow as he passed.

"Oi, what're yer doin'?" demanded Skull.

Axe was visibly shaking, more from fear than the cold, and they both knew it.

"Look," he said, beseechingly. "Why don't we jus' go back an' say we couldn't find it? No one needs to know, we'll be gone from 'ere soon enough."

Skull considered the offer for a moment before brushing his mate's arm off him, and striding proudly towards the door. "You do what yer want; I'm for killin' that thing an' 'anging its 'ed off me 'andlebars."

Axe knew any further argument was futile.

He also knew that he could not return without Skull.

Unless of course he killed him and then reported back that the creature had done it, and then he could say that he had killed the thing himself.

He would be the hero.

But then he would have to show them the proof.

And besides, he really did not have the stomach for killing his friend. Shooting someone who got in the way during a hold-up was one thing, but killing one of your own was a death sentence, if you were caught.

Axe decided he had no choice but to follow Skull into battle.

Skull was already at the door. "You comin'?" he called.

Before Axe had a chance to answer, the Beast's huge arm swung inside the hut and grabbed Skull from behind by the neck, yanking him outside before he had a chance to defend himself.

Axe heard his friend call out, as he disappeared from view.

For a moment, Axe was frozen to the spot. He clutched his revolver and cleaver tightly until he could feel his knuckles starting to crack.

From outside he could hear the Beast roaring and Skull screaming, but still he felt unable to respond.

Such was his fear that he actually felt unable to do anything, including running back to the lodge for safety, whilst the Beast was pre-occupied with the other biker.

The seconds passed like hours, and all the while Skull's cries grew louder and more desperate.

Until finally, they stopped altogether.

Axe was trapped.

With the Beast outside, probably just out of view from where Axe stood, glued to the spot, the biker was convinced that it was waiting for him to emerge into the night, so that it could dish out the same fate to him that it had to his friend.

Axe screamed out Skull's name.

He was not expecting a response, and none came.

Even the roar of the Beast had stopped, although Axe convinced himself that if he listened carefully he could still hear the thing breathing just outside the open doorway.

Possibly even with its mighty head pressed against the wood of the hut, listening for Axe to take his first *and possibly last* steps, moving outside towards his doom.

But Axe was too smart for that!

No way was he going to present himself as a tasty morsel for whatever had just torn his friend apart.

In his mind he could see the Beast through the wooden surround of the shed.

He imagined that it was standing just outside with nothing separating them other than a thin panel of wood.

There was no way he was going to be outsmarted by a knuckle-dragging throwback.

It can wait outside for him all it wants, but he was the smarter of the two.

"This is for Skull and Scar you miserable little bastard!" Axe raised his revolver and fired at the wooden panel before him, until the gun just clicked on an empty chamber.

He had half expected to hear the creature cry out in pain when it was hit, but he reasoned he may have caught it so far off guard, that it was dead before it even realised what was happening.

Axe surmised that, as big as it was, the snow would have cushioned the sound of the Beast falling down, dead.

He waited for a moment, trying to lower his breathing so that he could hear more clearly.

The wind from outside the hut gushed violently, and slammed the hut door back into its frame.

For a moment, Axe stood petrified in the darkness.

Outside, the wind continued to pick up speed.

The moon, suddenly clear of shifting clouds, shone tiny shafts of light through the bullet holes in the shed wall, which Axe had just created with his gun.

Knowing that the gun was empty, Axe still aimed it at the damaged wall and clicked off several rounds from the empty chambers.

Dropping the gun, he gripped the cleaver with both hands tightly wrapped around the wooden handle.

"You bastard!" he screamed out, listening to his own voice echo around him.

Fuck this! He thought. There was no way he was going to end up like the others. He no longer cared what anyone else thought about him, once he was outside he was going to make a break for the lodge. He did not even want to turn back to see if he had managed to kill the Beast, or not.

Rocking back and forth on his heels, Axe took a deep breath before charging the unlocked door.

The force with which he hit the door was far more than was necessary to open it, and Axe lost his footing trying to slow down his momentum, and landed face first in the snow.

Without pausing to catch his breath, Axe scrabbled in the snow, desperately trying to regain his composure.

The cleaver was still firmly clasped in his right hand, so he clenched his fist, and pushed with his knuckles to help boost him back up.

Suddenly, he could hear the guttural breathing which signalled the approach of the Beast from behind him.

He did not dare to look back, instead he concentrated on making it back to his feet and then back to the lodge. But the compact snow and ice beneath him would not allow his feet to make traction, and again he slipped forward in his haste to stand up.

Out of sheer desperation, Axe released his hold on the cleaver so that he could use both hands to push himself off the ground.

He managed it on his second attempt, and considered retrieving the cleaver before heading for the lodge, but at the last second he changed his mind and turned to run, just as the Beast slammed one of its gigantic paws into the back of his head and sent him sprawling back into the snow.

The force of the blow caused Axe to see stars.

He fumbled in the snow for his cleaver, deciding that he needed some sort of defence against the creature, now that he had no alternative but to fight it off.

As he located the wooden handle and grabbed it, he was suddenly hoisted up off the floor, and then slammed back down face first, onto the frozen ground.

As he hit the floor the square edge of the cleaver sliced through his outer clothing, and rammed into his stomach.

Axe cried out in agony, but his screams were masked by the Beast roaring its triumph, as it towered over the stricken biker.

Axe tried to roll off the cleaver in an attempt to try and alleviate the pressure that was quickly building up around his wound, but before he had a chance to move, the Beast grabbed him from behind by his long greasy hair and lifted him off the ground, until his feet dangled six inches above it.

The more he struggled, the more Axe could feel his hair being ripped out by the roots as the Beast held him suspended, but that pain did not compare to the burning in his stomach made by the protruding cleaver.

With its other hand the Beast wrenched the cleaver from the biker's body, giving Axe cause to scream even louder than before.

With tears flooding down his cheeks and blurring his vision, Axe did not see the Beast swing the cleaver towards him, severing his head from the rest of his body with one blow.

As Axe's headless corpse slumped to the ground the Beast held up the biker's head by the hair, allowing it to dangle from its mighty paw like a macabre trophy, as it let forth another huge roar of triumph.

CHAPTER THIRTY FIVE

From inside the lodge, Stud and Reaper could barely make out the Beast's silhouette through the falling snow. They had both moved away from the door and were now perched at the far end of the living area so that they could at least see something of what was happening outside.

They had witnessed Axe's beheading, but from this distance, and under these conditions, they were still not a hundred percent sure that what they had seen actually took place.

As the clouds overhead parted momentarily, they both had a clear view of the Beast, rising up out of the snow at the far end of the courtyard, the meat clever in one hand and Axe's severed head dangling in the other.

When the Beast roared, the entire lodge seemed to shake.

The students were all hovered around the sofas at the back of the room, so they were unable to see what the bikers were looking at.

Likewise, Tom and Adam were attending to Jed. His repeated bouts of laboured breathing were a definite cause for concern, but at least now they seemed to have staunched his bleeding.

Jenny played her part by sourcing whatever she could find from the kitchen to help with the operation.

Steve and Greg were busy attending to the fire. A vital commodity as it was still their only source of heat and, more importantly right now, light.

Joanne was still huddled in the corner next to where Reaper and Stud were now standing. Their presence had not inspired her to move closer to her friends, as she continued to stare ahead with a fixed gaze whilst rocking back and forth with her arms around her bent knees.

But when the Beast roared, she definitely heard it!

Pressing her hands tightly against her ears, Joanne began moaning loudly as her rocking became more frenzied.

As Reaper watched through the frosted glass, the Beast finally turned in its tracks and lurched out of sight, still clutching its trophies.

Stud turned towards the students. His stance cast an eerie shadow over the room from the glow of the log fire. "For fuck's sake, someone shut 'er up!" he bellowed.

The three girls all looked at each other.

As much as they feared another outburst from the petrified Joanne if they tried to comfort her again, they could not leave her like this, especially with the two bikers standing over her and obviously growing less tolerant with the situation.

Finally, Jan walked over to the stricken girl and squatted down next to her.

Placing her hand over Joanne's, with a gentle pull she managed to open a space so that she could slip her fingers inside the girl's, and hold her hand.

Joanne seemed to take comfort in the action, and squeezed Jan's hand back in response. It also had the effect of quietening her down somewhat, and her shrieks grew less and less frequent, and eventually came out as quiet whimpers.

Jan turned back to the others as if to say *what now?*

Tom offered her a comforting smile and a reassuring wink, but for the moment his priority had to be Jed, and besides, he knew that Jan had the situation well in hand.

In unison, Sharon and Carey stood up and slowly approached their friend.

Neither of them wanted to be the one responsible for breaking the calming influence Jan obviously had on Joanne, but both could see that their friend would welcome some assistance.

They both decided to stop a few feet away from Joanne, so as not to spook her.

"Do you think we should try and move her over to the settee?" Sharon asked.

Jan looked up at her friends. "It might be an idea; she must be getting awfully uncomfortable down here."

Jan felt bad that they were talking about Joanne as if she was not there in front of them, but under the circumstances she wondered how much of their conversation the girl could actually understand.

The unnerving stare on Joanne's face, made Jan wonder if the poor girl had been irrevocably affected by whatever she had witnessed or experienced before being brought to them by Jed.

At least for the moment she was safe with them, as well as being inside, warm and dry.

As Joanne was still clutching her hand, Jan tried to speak to her directly.

"Joanne," she said, softly. "How would you like to come with us and sit somewhere more comfortable?"

Much to everyone's surprise, Joanne nodded her head. It was only a slight movement, but enough to confirm her acquiescence.

Sharon and Carey both leaned down to help Jan.

Then they heard the Beast roar once more!

And this time, it sounded even closer than before!

Immediately upon hearing the Beast, Joanne slumped back to the floor and began screaming again. She released her grip on Jan's hand and instead wrapped her arms around her, holding her tightly in a desperate embrace.

Jan tried to calm her down as best she could.

Joanne's screaming was so loud it penetrated Jan's eardrums, until she felt like they might pop.

Jan rocked the girl back and forth, like a kindergarten teacher comforting a child who had fallen over and grazed their knees.

Meanwhile Stud and Reaper moved away from the pair of them and stood closer to the front door, checking the outside through the pane in the panelling for a better view.

Joanne was not the only one visibly shaken by the approaching sound of the Beast. Kim and Stacy too were sitting hunched up on an armchair, holding each other and crying quietly.

Deedee moved away from the sobbing girls and went to join her boyfriend and Stud.

Pete, obviously feeling left out, did likewise, but he kept his gun trained in the direction of the students, as per his initial instructions

The four of them stood around talking in hushed tones, while Jan finally managed to get Joanne back under control.

This time, however, when she tried to help the girl to her feet to move somewhere more comfortable, Joanne was having none of it. She purposely made herself into a dead weight, making it impossible for Jan to budge her.

Seeing their friend's predicament, Sharon and Carey moved in to help, but Jan shook her head as if to ward them off. Joanne had clearly changed her mind and Jan did not think that it was in anybody's best interest to have her start screaming the place down again.

As the two students re-took their seats on the sofa, the four bikers broke off their meeting.

Stud walked away from the others and came and stood near to where Joanne and Jan were squatting, but he aimed his announcement in the direction of Tom and Adam.

"Right, listen here," he announced. "Me, Reaper an' Pete are goin' out to see to that thing, but in case you get any funny ideas, Deedee is going to keep you covered, an' she ain't afraid to shoot anyone who tries anythin', understand?"

Some of the group looked over to where the tall blond was standing.

She held a shotgun under her arm, and looked to all intents and purposes as if she really did know how to use it.

When Adam caught her eye, he saw a cruel twist of a smile begin to creep across her face.

"Oh, an' another thing," continued Stud, almost as an afterthought. "We need someone to act as bait." He looked down at Joanne. "She'll do."

There was a general gasp of shock and several objections from the group, mortified that the biker would even consider such an idea, let alone want to use an innocent girl in their warped plan.

Stud aimed his gun in the direction of the group, sweeping it back and forth as he yelled. "SHUT IT!"

The group backed down.

Though none of them was prepared to let Joanne be taken without offering some sort of resistance, they were in no doubt that Stud would use his weapon if riled.

Finally, Tom left Adam with Jed and slowly rose to his feet.

He held his hands out before him, in order to show Stud and the other bikers that he was not planning on being confrontational, but he was not prepared to allow the biker's plan to be put into operation.

"Alright look," he said, calmly. "You need a victim to use as bait, use me."

There were immediate objections from Adam and Jan, but Tom raised his hand to quell them. He realised that the bikers were in charge and the last thing he wanted was for them to start shooting people, because they objected to their plans.

Likewise, he could not stand by and watch as one of the others was taken outside and tied to a stake, or whatever the biker's plans were.

And besides, he could take care of himself, and he was not afraid to hold his own if the situation called for it.

Stud turned his head and looked at Reaper.

The big man shook his head without even considering the option.

Stud turned back to Tom. "Forget it," he said, raising his weapon in anticipation of Tom's reluctance to accept the decision.

Tom held his ground, but was careful not to appear aggressive.

"Come on," he replied, looking past Stud toward his leader. "The benefit of having me as your hostage is that I will come quietly and not give you any trouble."

He turned around and indicated to Joanne sitting scrunched up in a ball on the floor. He wondered if she even knew what was being discussed around her.

"Look at the state she's in," he continued. "You'll have a devil of a job dragging her outside, and one of you will have to keep her upright, instead of helping the other two kill the Beast."

Stud knew that there was more than just a modicum of truth in Tom's words. But he also knew that Reaper would not want to risk someone as big and as strong as Tom turning on them, once they went outside.

No. It had to be one of the girls, someone who appeared weak and vulnerable.

Just then Jan removed her hand from Joanne's and stood next to Tom, holding his hand and squeezing it.

As much as she hated the idea, she knew that there would be no point in arguing with him. He had made up his mind to sacrifice himself to save them, and as much as she loved and admired him for it, deep down she wished there was another way.

Tom bent down and wrapped his arms around her.

Jan hugged him back with tears brimming over her lids, as she realised this might be their last embrace, ever.

As they released their clinch, Stud leaned over and grabbed Jan roughly by the wrist, yanking her behind him towards his remaining gang members.

Jan stumbled and almost lost her footing from the force of the action, but Pete managed to catch her, and stopped her from falling.

Before Tom had a chance to react, Stud rammed the barrels of his gun into Tom's chest and pulled back the hammers.

"Dad!" Adam called out from behind; there was genuine fear in his voice.

Tom froze.

He knew instantly that if he moved, his days would be numbered. From the look in Stud's eyes, the biker was almost willing Tom to give him just the slightest excuse to pull the trigger.

But Tom held his composure, breathing slowly, as he looked past his assailant to see that Jan was alright.

There was no way, regardless of the circumstances, that he was going to give the biker an excuse to shoot him. At least if he remained alive there was a chance he could save Jan from whatever fate they had planned for her.

Jan caught Tom's gaze.

Silently she pleaded with her eyes, telling him not to make any sudden movements.

Tom looked back down at Stud.

The leering grin on the biker's face, told him that there was no use asking again to take Jan's place, but he could not help himself.

Holding back the tears, Tom mouthed the words. "Please, no."

But Stud merely laughed in his face, and shoved him backwards with the gun.

"Sit down," he barked, keeping his sights trained on Tom.

But Tom still stood his ground, unwilling to move as if to do so would signify his acceptance of leaving Jan to their mercy.

Stud's face grew darker, at Tom's reluctance to obey him.

He advanced, his gun held high, aimed at Tom's face.

From behind Stud, Jan screamed. "No!"

Adam sprang to his feet and grabbed his father by the shoulders. He placed himself between Tom and Stud's shotgun and slowly eased Tom back towards the sofas.

Reluctantly, Stud locked the hammers on his gun back into place, and gave Tom one last look of triumph as he returned to his fellow bikers and their new bait.

CHAPTER THIRTY SIX

Once Jan had bundled up-a courtesy the bikers, surprisingly, allowed her-she was shoved out into the night in front of Pete. Stud and Reaper followed behind, all of them armed to the teeth.

Inside the lodge, Deedee stood at the open doorway watching her man go into battle, whilst ensuring that her weapon was trained on the group inside.

Tom moved away from the rest of them, and went over to the large bay window to look outside.

Deedee watched him closely, her body tensed against the butt of the gun. But when she saw what he was doing she relaxed a little and continued watching the scene outside.

Reaper and the other two bikers stopped short once they reached twenty feet from the lodge. Stud ordered Jan to carry on walking until he gave her the order to stop.

Jan complied without resistance.

In her mind she spoke a silent prayer, not just for her safety, but for that of all her friends, and especially Tom.

The snowfall had started to abate and the full moon shone brightly through thin wispy clouds as they drifted past, illuminating the heavens and reflecting off the freshly fallen snow, making the outside clearer and brighter than the glow from the fire inside the lodge.

Jan walked on slowly, unconsciously taking smaller steps as she left the others further behind her.

The wind was still whistling loudly through the trees, and with her hood covering her ears she was afraid that she might not hear Stud when he called for her to stop.

The last thing she needed was for him to think she was disobeying his orders.

He might go back and take it out on Tom!

Or, drag one of the other girls out to use as bait, as well as her!

Jan began to take a momentary break in between steps to listen out for the biker's voice.

She was now only thirty or so feet from the tree-line, and she could not think of a reason why the biker would want her to reach that far, and end up out of sight.

Finally, she heard him bellow.

Jan stopped dead in her tracks and waited.

Her peripheral vision was hemmed in by her parka hood, and with the wind reducing her capacity to hear, Jan felt very alone and isolated where she stood.

In her mind she drifted back to earlier that morning, waking up in the warmth and comfort of Tom's embrace, feeling so utterly safe and above all else, protected.

What she would not give for another cuddle from him, right now.

But then she realised that she might have already had the last one she was ever going to experience from him, or anybody else for that matter.

Hot tears began to well up in her eyes again, and she left them to fall without bothering to wipe any away. They streaked their way down her cheeks and dripped off her chin, before being soaked up by the padding of her jacket.

The wait was becoming eternal.

Each second that passed felt like an eternity to her.

She studied the waving trees in front of her and watched for any sign of movement, other than that caused by the wind.

She could hear the bikers shouting to each other from behind, their voices carried on the wind, too far away for her to make any sense of what was being said.

Suddenly, the night was filled with screaming!

Jan turned around just in time to see Pete being hauled up off the ground and held aloft by the Beast.

Jan stuck her gloved hands over her face, not wanting to see what would doubtless happen next.

Before either Stud or Reaper could react, the Beast drove Pete's body down onto its knee at speed, breaking his spine.

When the Beast let go of him, Pete's lifeless form flopped onto the snow.

The deed spurred the other two bikers into action.

Stud began to scream out loud, as he aimed and let loose with both barrels, his target increasing in size as it ran closer towards him.

Stud felt sure that he must have hit the Beast several times, but it continued towards him gaining speed until, before he had a chance to turn and run, it swiped him with one of its monstrous arms, and sent Stud flying off into the air.

The Beast turned its attention towards Reaper.

The big man was almost as tall as the Beast itself, but even from this distance he could see its elongated bloody claws, not to mention its razor sharp teeth when it opened its mouth to growl, and he wondered just how effective his weapons were going to be against it.

There was no man alive on earth that Reaper was scared of.

No man from whom he would run away and refuse to fight.

But this thing was no man!

The Beast had its back to the lodge and was cutting off any chance of Reaper retreating there.

Reaper took in a large breath, as he noticed the Beast starting to approach him.

From behind the Beast, he could not see Deedee starting to walk out onto the lodge's porch. Her gun was raised, trying to hone in on a decent shot.

Deedee squinted through the sights, lining them up with the back of the Beast's massive head, but she was still too anxious to shoot, for fear the shots might fly astray and hit Reaper.

Her only hope was to move closer in on her target.

She moved forward, allowing the porch door to swing back on itself.

She did not hear the wood slam into the frame, as all her attention was on the scene before her.

Deedee reached the edge of the porch and was about to start her descent, when she was hit from the back by Tom's charging body, which sent her sprawling forward down the stairs, and into the snow.

Her gun flew from her grasp, and landed a few feet away with a soft thud.

By the time she had regained her feet, she could see her assailant edging his way around the outskirts of the clearing, carefully making his way towards the stricken Jan.

Deedee scrabbled around in the snow for her gun.

The Beast, seemingly unaware of her presence, continued its advance on Reaper, who had still not raised his weapon in defence.

The Beast drew closer.

Barely ten feet separated the two of them now, and for the first time in his life Reaper knew the meaning of the word fear.

The Beast was taking its time.

Stalking its prey!

A sudden blast from behind took the Beast by surprise.

It turned on the spot and glared back at Deedee, as she fumbled in her pocket for some fresh cartridges.

The Beast growled at her, baring its yellowed fangs in anger.

At that moment, Reaper saw his chance.

He raised his own weapon so that the end of the barrel was only a couple of feet from the Beast's head.

He pulled the trigger.

Nothing happened. His weapon had jammed.

Reaper shuffled the weapon from hand to hand, frantically trying to find some way to release the shells inside.

Eventually, he dropped the shotgun and reached inside his belt to withdraw his magnum.

The creature turned as the gun came into sight, but before Reaper had a chance to squeeze off a round, the Beast slapped the gun out of the biker's grasp.

Reaper made an attempt to turn to locate his prize possession, but it was lost in the deep snow.

As he turned back, the Beast was upon him.

It grabbed hold of his long goatee and jerked his head up, before sinking its fangs into the soft flesh of his neck.

Reaper, standing at nearly seven feet, with shoulders as broad as he was tall, a man who had never shied away from a battle in his life, the most feared and hated biker in the country…wet himself!

The feeling of the warm urine trickling down his legs was only momentary, before the blood pumping from his neck wound ended his life.

The Beast still supported the biker's body as it drank deeply from the wound, savouring each mouthful.

It only stopped when it heard a war cry from behind and turned just in time to see Deedee launch herself at it, with her teeth bared, and a wide-eyed maniacal expression on her face.

Although she was very slender, Deedee was also wiry and she too knew little of fear.

She leapt into the air and flung her arms around the Beast's neck, squeezing hard, and trying to bite through its thick matted fur to give it a taste of its own medicine.

For a moment the Beast was stunned, but quickly regained its composure.

Most humans it had encountered did not charge at it, it charged at them.

The Beast allowed Reaper's body to fall to the ground before it flung its mighty arms around Deedee's waist, and with a single squeeze, it broke her spine, too.

The Beast held Deedee's limp body under one arm as it raised its head and howled at the moon in victory.

****

From thirty feet away, Stud looked up from the snow.

He had come to a few minutes earlier, and had watched the battle ensue between the Beast and the other two bikers.

He knew now that there was no glory to be had in facing the Beast again, especially as the conclusion was obvious to him.

He wondered if he could play dead long enough for the Beast to leave.

But then, would it leave, or would it stay and feast on its kills, including him?

There was always a chance that the Beast might concentrate on those hiding in the lodge, which might give him ample time to escape undeterred.

But how big a risk was he willing to take?

If the Beast did decide to concentrate on the bodies out here, it would be too late for him to make a break for it, by then.

Stud looked up and studied the compound.

He was possibly no more than twenty or so feet from the lodge, and at least once he was inside, there were more weapons and more hostages to send out if need be.

Even if he had to sacrifice Stacy and Kim, who would care?

They came with Reaper, and there would be no one left to tell the tale anyway.

Stud watched as the Beast bent down, and picked up the prone body of Reaper by the front of his jacket. It still held Deedee firmly under its other arm, and Stud wondered if it was planning to store them for hibernation.

The main point was that the Beast's attention was elsewhere.

Stud cautiously began to crawl in the direction of the lodge.

He kept an eye open to spy on the Beast as he made his progress, he knew how quickly and quietly the Beast was able to move in the thick snow, and the last thing he needed was the creature to grab him from nowhere just as he was about to make it to sanctuary.

The Beast was obviously otherwise detained.

Stud moved a little faster now, slithering through the snow like a lizard, propelling himself forward using both his legs and arms.

Closer now, only ten feet to go.

After one last glance behind, Stud sprung forward and ran for the porch steps.

He could hear the Beast roar its displeasure from behind, but he kept his head down and ran for all he was worth.

Stud ripped open the porch swing door and plunged through the main entrance, running straight into Adam's fist shooting out from behind the jamb.

The blow was enough to stagger Stud but not enough to knock him out.

That came with the second punch Adam threw, once he had recovered from letting fly with the first one.

****

Tom and Jan huddled together in the undergrowth protected by the thick mass of trees which surrounded them.

Jan buried her face in Tom's chest, as the Beast set about defeating the bikers, one by one.

He watched as Stud tried to sneak back into the lodge, and from this distance he could just about make out his son, knocking the biker out cold.

Once the carnage was over, they watched together while the creature stood its ground and studied the lodge.

Tom prayed that the Beast would not attempt to gain entry as he knew that the wooden structure would not be able to withstand an attack from such a mighty foe.

In truth, he knew that if the Beast did launch an attack, he would have to leave Jan in the relative security of her woodland protection, and go and help defend Adam and the others from attack.

It made him realise just how fragile life can be, and why happiness was so important.

He gazed down at Jan and kissed the top of her head.

She turned and looked up at him, and their eyes passed a secret message between them.

As their lips met, they both heard a sound in the distance which gave them hope.

The sirens sounded far away to begin with, but with each passing second they grew louder as the police vehicles came closer.

Jan and Tom looked at each other and smiled, and then they hugged and held each other closely, as they finally heard the sound of rubber wheels crunching the snow on their way up the hill.

When the first patrol car came into sight, Tom stood up and began waving frantically to draw their attention.

The first officer to exit a vehicle was Stan Reynolds, and he recognised Tom immediately.

As the other cars pulled in around them, Tom walked over to Stan with Jan snuggled up next to him.

As they reached the patrol car, Tom looked back.

The Beast was nowhere to be seen.

"Hi Tom," said Stan, cheerily. "We've had a lead that there are some bikers in the area who may have been involved in a bank raid earlier today."

Tom looked at Jan, and smiled. "Really."

"You wouldn't happen to know anything about it, would you?"

SNOW BEAST – EPILOGUE

The Snow Beast travelled further and further away from the area surrounding the lodge, and the melee it had left behind.

To begin with, it hid out in some of the many sheltered havens it had found over time, which were still in the vicinity of the place it had come to think of as home.

But soon it sensed the approach of men.

Fierce men, who carried their weapons of death.

The Beast knew instinctively that they were hunting for it.

Although it was perfectly adept at camouflaging itself amongst the snowy hills and mountains, with their numerous outcroppings and secreted caverns, there was something different about this group of men which it had not felt from any other such pack before.

Whereas others had been hunting whatever they could find to kill, the Beast knew that this particular group were only looking exclusively for it!

The Beast roamed far outside its own territory, the scent of its hunters still evident whenever it stopped to rest.

On a few occasions the Beast even crept out at night, and spied on their camp.

There were several of them, far more than the Beast had ever seen in one group before.

But still part of it wanted to rush down and tear into them, causing as much havoc as it could before finally being taken down, and its long journey ending.

Each time it felt ready to give up and go into battle for the last time, something called it back.

Nothing it could see or hear, just a feeling.

And so on it went, further and further away from any familiar scents or smells, into unknown territory, having to seek out new places to hide and rest, and feed when it could.

Finally, the scent of the men dissipated.

The Beast continued on its journey, not wanting to settle too close to where it had last sensed danger.

Eventually, it found a valley that was deeper than any it had stumbled on before.

The air was cool and crisp, and there was absolutely no scent of man anywhere on the wind.

The Beast found itself a deep cavern with a secreted entrance, and finally it lay down to rest.

****

It was shaken from its slumber by the sound of something approaching from within the depths of the cavern.

The Beast leapt up, ready to pounce and do battle with whatever came at it.

It sniffed the air.

There was a definite scent, an unfamiliar one, but not of man.

The Beast heard the scrabbling just around the next bend.

It considered flight, but instinct held it back.

For the first time ever, the Beast sensed that whatever it was that was drawing closer to it, it did not pose any threat whatsoever.

The Beast waited.

A moment later a small furry head peeked around the corner and looked straight at the Beast.

In the dim light of the cavern, its two black eyes surveyed the enormous size of the creature before it, but the Beast could tell that those eyes held no fear, no hatred, nothing in fact, but curiosity.

The Beast relaxed its posture. It instinctively knew that there was no threat from this latest arrival.

The small creature moved itself into full view, and began to sniff the air.

It moved closer to the Beast, but stopped short when it was about ten feet away.

It continued to sniff the air, and then it let out a tiny cry.

Intrigued by what was happening, the Snow Beast slumped back down on the solid rock floor and watched, as two more little Beasts emerged from behind the same corner the first one had come from.

They tentatively joined their little friend and then the three of them, in unison, shuffled over to the Beast and began to snuggle themselves against its fur, as if they were looking for somewhere safe and warm, to sleep.

The Beast was overwhelmed, and felt a stab in its heart it had never known.

It did not know how to deal with this feeling, but something deep inside told it that it was good.

As the three cubs snuggled down, the Beast looked back over to where they had appeared from, and there staring back at it was the face of another, like itself.

Again there was no fear of danger or trepidation with this new member, only a mixture of curiosity, warmth, and something else that the Beast had known itself for most of its life…longing.

The Beast suddenly realised something it had never even considered before.

It was not an *"it"*, it was a male.

A male of a species that he had always believed that he was the only one of. But no more!

The Snow Beast called to the female to come closer and to join him, and her cubs.

She edged her way forward and after the two of them grew accustomed to each other's scent, she snuggled down against the Beast along with her cubs, and together they slept.

Winter would soon be over!

SEVERED**PRESS**

 facebook.com/severedpress
 twitter.com/severedpress

CHECK OUT OTHER GREAT
HORROR NOVELS

DEATH CRAWLERS
by Gerry Griffiths

Worldwide, there are thought to be 8,000 species of centipede, of which, only 3,000 have been scientifically recorded. The venom of Scolopendra gigantea—the largest of the arthropod genus found in the Amazon rainforest—is so potent that it is fatal to small animals and toxic to humans. But when a cargo plane departs the Amazon region and crashes inside a national park in the United States, much larger and deadlier creatures escape the wreckage to roam wild, reproducing at an astounding rate. Entomologist, Frank Travis solicits small town sheriff Wanda Rafferty's help and together they investigate the crash site. But as a rash of gruesome deaths befalls the townsfolk of Prospect, Frank and Wanda will soon discover how vicious and cunning these new breed of predators can be. Meanwhile, Jake and Nora Carver, and another backpacking couple, are venturing up into the mountainous terrain of the park. If only they knew their fun-filled weekend is about to become a living nightmare.

THE PULLER
by Michael Hodges

Matt Kearns has two choices: fight or hide. The creature in the orchard took the rest. Three days ago, he arrived at his favorite place in the world, a remote shack in Michigan's Upper Peninsula. The plan was to mourn his father's death and figure out his life. Now he's fighting for it. An invisible creature has him trapped. Every time Matt tries to flee, he's dragged backwards by an unseen force. Alone and with no hope of rescue, Matt must escape the Puller's reach. But how do you free yourself from something you cannot see?

CHECK OUT OTHER GREAT
HORROR NOVELS

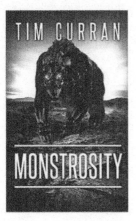

MONSTROSITY
by Tim Curran

The Food. It seeped from the ground, a living, gushing, teratogenic nightmare. It contaminated anything that ate it, causing nature to run wild with horrible mutations, creating massive monstrosities that roam the land destroying towns and cities, feeding on livestock and human beings and one another. Now Frank Bowman, an ordinary farmer with no military skills, must get his children to safety. And that will mean a trip through the contaminated zone of monsters, madmen, and The Food itself. Only a fool would attempt it. Or a man with a mission.

THE SQUIRMING
by Jack Hamlyn

You are their hosts.

You are their food.

The parasites came out of nowhere, squirming horrors that enslaved the human race. They turned the population into mindless pack animals, psychotic cannibalistic hordes whose only purpose was to feed them.

Now with the human race teetering at the edge of extinction, extermination teams are fighting back, killing off the parasites and their voracious hosts. Taking them out one by one in violent, bloody encounters.

The future of mankind is at stake.

And time is running out.

CHECK OUT OTHER GREAT HORROR NOVELS

BLACK FRIDAY
by Michael Hodges

Jared the kleptomaniac, Chike the unemployed IT guy, Patricia the shopaholic, and Jeff the meth dealer are trapped inside a Chicago supermall on Black Friday. Bridgefield Mall empties during a fire alarm, and most of the shoppers drive off into a strange mist surrounding the mall parking lot. They never return. Chike and his group try calling friends and family, but their smart phones won't work, not even Twitter. As the mist creeps closer, the mall lights flicker and surge. Bulbs shatter and spray glass into the air. Unsettling noises are heard from within the mist, as the meth dealer becomes unhinged and hunts the group within the mall. Cornered by the mist, and hunted from within, Chike and the survivors must fight for their lives while solving the mystery of what happened to Bridgefield Mall. Sometimes, a good sale just isn't worth it.

GRIMWEAVE
by Tim Curran

In the deepest, darkest jungles of Indochina, an ancient evil is waiting in a forgotten, primeval valley. It is patient, monstrous, and bloodthirsty. Perfectly adapted to its hot, steaming environment, it strikes silent and stealthy. it chosen prey: human. Now Michael Spiers, a Marine sniper, the only survivor of a previous encounter with the beast, is going after it again. Against his better judgement, he is made part of a Marine Force Recon team that will hunt it down and destroy it.

The hunters are about to become the hunted.

Printed in Great Britain
by Amazon

79434562R00153